Blink

...and you die

By Ken Little

Cover design by:

Joshua Lee Sondelski (http://joshualeecreative.com/)

ISBN-13: 978-0692305874 (Ken Little)

ISBN-10: 0692305874 (Ken Little)

Table of Contents

Dedication

To the other writers in my house: My beautiful wife Cyndy and my daughter Emma.

And to my faithful writing buddy, Bailey.

Preface

"Life is what happens to you while you're busy making other plans." – John Lennon

Jim Jackson thought his life was on the perfect path – responsible job, beautiful wife, good health.

He was dead wrong.

Chapter 1 – Monday – Russell

It was mid-afternoon and even with a light rain and a chilly wind off the lake the sidewalks were crowded.

Russell Jameson walked with a purpose; head down and hat pulled low. In his grey overcoat and modestly priced suit, he was almost invisible in the crowd. And that's just the way he wanted it.

Impersonal fit him just fine. Nothing stood out in any way. He could walk past you 10 times and you still couldn't come up with a description that didn't fit almost every man on the downtown sidewalk.

Everything about him was just what he wanted you to see. Today he was Russell Jameson. Tomorrow, he could be someone else if it suited his needs. He had many identities and had no problem remembering who he was at any given moment. He would not respond to his real name – it had been a long time since he was that person and he was too well trained for that simple trick.

Each one of his identities was a stone-cold killer, as they say in the movies. This made him smile every time a movie character used that cliché. In his case, it was literally true. He was lucky; most people never really discover who they were meant to be. He found out early in life and lived his purpose to the fullest.

He walked among them, worked among them, chatted with them, but he wasn't like them. He had no remorse, no empathy, no connection to the rest of the human race. He killed for money, but mostly he killed for pleasure.

Thanks to the United States Government, he was an efficient killer.

Today, he had a task to complete and he stayed focused on that task, not thinking about the past or the future. The task was part of a larger mission. Successful missions were broken down into individual steps or tasks. Each step or task must be completed in the correct order and without mistakes. When he did this, the mission was always a success. Sometimes the unexpected forced a change of plans, but he was smart and could make changes on the fly without jeopardizing the mission.

When this mission was complete a man Russell barely knew would be dead. He didn't like or dislike the man, that wasn't relevant. The mission was for money, but truth be told, he would do it for nothing if asked. He didn't need the money. His day job paid well and there was plenty of work. He had no dependents, no pets, and no attachments of any kind. His financial needs were modest, but people don't respect your work if you give it away. His usual fee of $10,000 had already been deposited – split among three different accounts at different banks and under different names. He had accounts at 12 banks all under different names. He could tell you the name and address of each account holder, the account number and current balance of all 12 accounts.

All of his paid work came from one source. The man had similar training thanks to the government. However, he almost never met him in person. They communicated over a secure network he created using prepaid phones. Most instructions were passed via text messages. A few times they talked, but always in code. The man had a protocol that called for switching to new phones every 24 hours during a mission to avoid government snooping. They had a complicated system for changing phones, passwords to the network, and contacting one another that Russell memorized without any written instructions. After a mission, the phones were destroyed, passwords changed, and there was no contact until the next mission.

His frequent employer was cautious and with good reason. He and Russell both knew how vulnerable electronic communications were. The two made good use of these vulnerabilities.

Today, Russell was on his way to a bank where he kept a safe deposit box, one of several at different banks – all with identical contents. Retrieving the contents was a simple, but necessary task that was part of the current mission. Surprisingly, it didn't go as planned and Russell had to make adjustments.

His "adjustment" would have unexpected consequences that changed the lives of dozens of people forever.

Chapter 2 – Monday – Jim

"Justice is Blind," the ancient concept that justice must be dispensed impartially is a cruel joke for people like Jim Jackson.

Eight months ago, he was on top of the world and then in the blink of an eye his world was gone. He thought his life couldn't get any worse, but he was wrong.

"It makes me sick. That's how it feels. Eight months later and I still feel like I've been hit in the stomach every time someone knocks on a door," Jim said.

"Go on," Judy, the grief support group facilitator said.

"What do you want me to say? The second hardest thing I've had to deal with is all the 'helpful' people in my life who want to know how I feel. How do you think I feel?" Jim said aware that his voice was rising.

The meeting room in the church basement was silent for a moment except for muted street sounds. This part of the northern end of downtown emptied by 6:00 p.m. on weekdays. The room had a sofa, a loveseat, and several over-stuffed chairs roughly organized in a circle. There were several end tables with lamps providing the lighting.

Judy and the five other people in the support group were watching him, except for the only other male in the group who was staring at his feet.

"How am I supposed to feel? Nobody ever told me what this is like. I grieved when my parents died, but they were old and had good, full lives. I didn't want them to die of course, but I have a lifetime of memories with them.

"But Sally," he began to choke on the knot in his throat he couldn't swallow or spit out.

"We were married just 18 months. We both established our careers before considering a commitment like marriage. We're in our 30's and solid, but when we met, it was like we were kids again. I knew I'd marry her and that we would have a great life and grow old with our memories together."

The knot caught in his throat again and his face felt hot.

Again, the room was silent.

"Please go on," Judy urged softly.

"What for? Nothing that happened before that day matters anymore. We dated for a short time, we married, and I felt better and stronger and more confident than I ever had. I know we did wonderful things and took trips and read books, but, don't you see, none of that matters anymore," Jim said.

"Why not?" asked Mona, one of the other group members.

"Because the knock on the door took it all away. It changed everything. Nothing will ever be right again and just when I think I may be able to go on, someone knocks on the fucking door," Jim snarled.

Mona sank back into the sofa as if Jim had just slapped her for being a stupid little girl.

"I'm sorry," Jim said. "I didn't mean to yell at you."

"Jim, it's okay to yell here. We all know what you're going through, because we have all been there and some of us are still there. What's important is that you're honest with your feelings," Judy said.

Jim was sure he was going to hate her before this was all over. He was here because the company's benefit plan paid for counseling services and the vice president of human resources had insisted on it.

If someone had told him a year ago that he would be sitting in the basement of a downtown church blurting out his feelings like this, he would have thought them crazy. He didn't enjoy being the center of attention even under happy circumstances, but this was almost unbearable.

It didn't take but this brief moment for these emotions to pass and he was back in control. Before this session was over, he would know the psychobabble for this was being "in your head."

"Why don't you continue, Jim?" Judy asked.

"Continue what? I've told you how I feel – what else is there to say?

"She went out for some beer, because the game was starting and she knew I had looked forward to watching it all week. I offered to go, but she just laughed and grabbed her purse and left. It should have been a 20-minute trip, but after about 40 minutes, I began to wonder where she was. I guess I figured that she'd decided to pick up a few more things while she was there. The game I had waited for all week put me to sleep. I woke up, went to the bathroom, and washed my face. I went back to the living room and sat on the sofa. The game wasn't on anymore and it was slowly dawning on me that I had been asleep for almost two hours.

"Then came the knock on the door and my heart stopped beating. For some reason, I knew something awful had happened. I opened the door and a policeman asked me if I was Jim Jackson and did I own a 2003 Ford Escort. Who would have been driving the car this afternoon he asked – and I knew she was dead," Jim said.

"What happened," Mona blurted out, then shrunk back as if she was avoiding a punch.

"Jim, you don't have to give us details if you don't want to right now. Maybe after you have met with us for awhile it'll be easier," Judy interjected.

"No, there is not much to tell. Sally was going to the grocery store and a drunk ran a red light and smashed into the driver's side. The car rolled over twice and burst into flames. Witnesses said they could hear her screaming for a moment, then nothing. There was not even anything left I could identify. They had to get her dental records for a positive ID.

"She was three months pregnant and I didn't even know it," Jim said.

"You act like this happens every day," said Carolyn, one of the other participants. Like the other women, tears were running down her fleshy cheeks.

"Actually, it does," said Vic, the other man in the group.

"He's right, I work for a large insurance company and we see this every day."

"How can you be so clinical about this?" Mona asked, embolden by Carolyn's participation.

"What happened to the guy that killed her?" Vic asked.

"A broken nose from the airbag and that's it," Jim said.

"Was he charged with a crime?" Vic asked.

"Yeah, but he walked after a high-priced lawyer shot holes in the police report. And you know what really pisses me off? My company insures the guy. I would love to see that bastard burn in hell. I'm not supposed to, but I got a look at his file. He'd been charged with DWI three times before and has beaten every one of them. We tried to drop him, but his lawyer apparently scared our legal department into taking a cautious approach," Jim said.

Jim felt an instant connection with Vic, as if they were speaking the same thoughts even though this was the sum of their conversations. Jim did know from the introductions at the start of the session that Vic's wife and children had died suddenly. Now that he thought about it, Vic had seemed guarded about talking at all.

"I don't understand about the knock on the door and why that is so hard?" asked another of the participants named Helen. She was in her 60s and looked confused most of the time.

"That's the crazy part," Jim said. "I didn't understand it either. I couldn't get the sound of that knock out of my head. It made me so crazy that two months after it happened, I found the cop who came to my door. I asked him why he knocked, when there was a doorbell in plain view.

"You know what he said? He said that he'd told people twice before that a loved one died and he didn't want to do it again. He thought that if he knocked, maybe I wouldn't hear it and he could tell his sergeant that he tried but no one was home. He was near the end of his shift and some other cop would have had to contact me or the medical examiner or anyone but him. He said he was sorry. Knowing why he knocked instead of ringing the bell didn't make any difference. I still can't stand that sound."

"That kind of reaction is perfectly normal, Jim. A sound, a smell, a room, almost anything can trigger a strong emotion associated with the sudden passing of a loved one," Judy said in her best clinical voice.

"Everyone here has probably experienced something like that," she said to general nodding by the group – by everyone except Vic who hadn't taken his eyes off Jim since their earlier exchange. Carolyn, would you share with Jim and the group again the story of your loss. I think it's time to give Jim a rest and let him get to know others in the group."

"Sure. My father died during a robbery of his convenience store two years ago. The guy just walked in a shot him. No warning. No chance to give him the money. He just shot my dad like he didn't matter at all. It was months before I could go back to the store. I had some people come in and clear the inventory a couple of weeks after the shooting, but I couldn't set foot in the store myself for months. Even then, I only went in once and saw the blood stain on the floor. I sold the store the next week for nothing and was glad to get rid of it. My parents owned the store for 30 years and my dad kept it going after mother died five years ago. Maybe in their honor I should have kept it open, but I wanted nothing to do with it.

"Like your 'knock on the door' I can't go into a convenience store anymore without thinking about my father lying on the floor bleeding to death while some junky grabbed the couple of hundred dollars in the cash register," she said.

"Thank you Carolyn. I see we are about out of time for this week. I hope to see you all next week," Judy said.

Jim wanted to talk to Vic after the meeting, but two other participants blocked his way with a barrage of condolences and 'we know how you feel.' By the time he could politely extricate himself, barely avoiding a group hug, Vic was gone.

As he put on his jacket, Carolyn who had been talking to Judy came over for her coat.

"By the way, did the police catch the guy who murdered your father?" he asked.

"Oh, they knew who did it, but were having a hard time getting enough evidence to arrest the punk. Six months after he killed my father, they found him murdered in an alley. One shot to the back of the head. I guess he got the execution he deserved and saved the taxpayers a lot of money. Before this happened, I was opposed to the death penalty. I still think it's probably applied unequally to the poor, but in this case, someone did us all a favor by blowing this guy's brains out," she said as she walked out the door.

Jim was somewhat taken aback by the vengeful tone of her voice in contrast to her "soccer mom" image.

He reached his car in the well-lit parking lot and had the key in the lock when he became aware of someone approaching with his head down. Jim was mildly concerned, but as the man approached, he raised his head and Jim recognized Vic from the support group.

"Oh, it's you," he said.

"I'm sorry, did I frighten you?" Vic asked.

"No, just startled. You never know these days," Jim said.

Jim extended his hand. "Are we supposed to see group members outside of the meeting?" he asked.

Vic shook his hand and said, "Oh, I think it's all right if both parties agree. After all, this is a support group, not a therapy group."

"You seemed to know about this stuff," Jim observed.

"I guess I've been at this longer than you," Vic said.

"Would you like to get a cup of coffee?" Jim asked.

"Sounds great, but I've a big presentation in the morning and I could use some rehearsal time tonight," Vic responded.

"Really? What do you do?" Jim asked.

"I'm a computer geek," Vic responded. "I specialize in database work. In fact, I've worked for your company, Aargon Insurance."

"How did you know I worked for them," Jim asked.

"Just an educated guess," Vic said. "They are the only large insurance company headquartered here and you impressed me as the type who worked in the headquarters."

"I'm not sure how to take that, but you're right. I'm an Assistant Vice President of Marketing," Jim said. "That used to mean something to me, but now it's hard to find anything worth getting excited about."

"Well, I can honestly say, unlike some of the other busy bodies in your life, that I understand how you feel," Vic said. "The thing is you need some time and to focus on something positive you can do about your situation."

"I'll have take your word for it. Right now it's hard enough getting through one day at a time," Jim said.

"And that's how you do it – one day at a time," Vic said.

"I'm interested in your story. I didn't want to believe it, but hearing Carolyn talk about herself was helpful," Jim said.

"My story is not much different from everyone else in the group. Did you know that everyone in the group suffered their loss through some sudden, violent circumstance?" Vic asked.

"No. I guess I hadn't thought about it. Judy just said the group would be able to relate to my story," Jim said. "I would really like to hear your story."

"Maybe another time," Vic said looking at his watch. "I really need to get some work done tonight."

"Oh. Right. Your presentation tomorrow. Sorry, I've just been babbling here," Jim said.

"I've enjoyed our conversation. I hope we can get together sometime soon," Vic said as he extended his hand. His grip this time was like a vise.

"Let me leave you with this thought though. Conversation is a weak salve for what hurts us. There are other ways men like us can find some comfort without spending the rest of our lives talking about our feelings. We can find justice for our loved ones and peace for our souls if we have the courage. Good night."

Jim watched as Vic disappeared around the corner. His right hand throbbed from Vic's grip and he wondered what justice could bring him peace.

Chapter 3 – Monday – Washington & Russell

"Good afternoon, Mr. Jameson."

Most people would be flattered that a bank guard remembered or even knew their name – but not Jameson and not now; especially not now.

Jameson reacted in a completely normal fashion. He leaned slightly forward and tilted his head backward slightly so as to get the guard's nametag in focus through his bifocals. The glasses he wore were just that – a lens with no prescription. His vision was off the charts good.

"Thank you, uh Mr. Washington," Jameson said.

The guard's nametag read "A. Washington." The twenty something black man was about six feet tall and thin, but his uniform white shirt was starched and looked like it just came back from the laundry, even though it was almost four in the afternoon and mildly stuffy in the entrance to the safe deposit vault.

"It's been awhile since you visited us," the guard said.

That was true. It was exactly 32 days since Jameson had been here.

"I'm flattered that you remember me," Jameson said, which was a lie. He did everything he could to make sure nobody remembered him, but when confronted Jameson knew the sometimes the best lie was the truth. It would be stupid to deny the guard's identification. At that point anything but the truth would draw even more attention.

"Remembering your customers is the key to customer service according to my supervisor. He says that if I want a career in banking, I need to develop the ability to remember my customers," Washington said.

"So, you want a career in banking?" Jameson asked. He was stalling for time to figure out what to make of this surprise.

"Yes sir. I'm in a management-training program here at the bank. They rotate me through all areas of the bank, so I can get a feel for the big picture. When I finish my degree in a year or so, I'll have a shot at a great job here. I hope," the guard said with a smile.

"When do you find time to go to college?" Jameson asked.

"I go to City College at night. Working all day and going to school at night keeps me pretty busy," Washington said.

Jameson had all the information he needed.

"Well, if you're as good at your studies as you are in remembering customers, you'll probably be running the whole show here pretty soon," Jameson said with a chuckle.

"That's very kind of you, Mr. Jameson," Washington said.

Jameson began to move past the guard station in anticipation that Washington would follow him in and help him retrieve his safety deposit box.

But Washington made no move and got an uncomfortable look on his face.

"Mr. Jameson, I'm sorry, even though I remember you, bank regulations still require me to see some identification," Washington said with a note of embarrassment.

"Oh, of course. I'm sorry, I forgot the sign-in procedure," Jameson said. "And don't apologize. After all these security procedures are to protect my valuables, too."

Jameson put down the black briefcase he was holding and pulled his wallet from his coat pocket. He produced his driver's license and signed the entry log.

"Thank you, Mr. Jameson," the guard said and returned the driver's license after noting the picture matched the one in the database displayed on a screen discretely built into the guard station.

He quickly typed in the time and verified all security procedures had been followed.

"This way, please."

Jameson followed the guard into the vault area and to the wall containing his box. He produced his key and handed it to the guard.

The guard used his security key and Jameson's key to open the door and pulled out the safe deposit box.

The gray metal box was four inches tall by ten inches wide and fifteen inches deep.

Washington carried the box back to a viewing room and put it on the table.

"Here you go, Mr. Jameson. When you're finished, just push the button under the light switch and I'll come retrieve the box. Is there anything else I can get for you?" the young man asked.

"Oh, no. Thank you for being so attentive," Jameson said.

The small room had a table with four chairs around it. In one corner of the room was a smaller table with a telephone on it and a pad of paper and pen.

Jameson sat in a particular chair; he knew exactly where the security camera was. He put his briefcase on the table and opened it. Like most things about him, the old style black, solid-wall briefcase seemed out of place in a world of laptop computers and smart phones, but totally in keeping with his image. He then pulled the safe deposit box over next to the briefcase and used his key to open it.

This maneuver put the two containers side by side with their tops up. He took a brown collapsible file folder like attorneys use to store papers out of the safe deposit box and switched it with an identical file folder in his briefcase. The folders were about three inches thick and sized to hold legal documents.

He took a file folder out of his briefcase, then closed the briefcase and opened the file folder that came from his briefcase and began shuffling through the papers, pausing periodically to read one of them.

Anyone viewing the security tape from the camera in the room would only see Jameson reviewing papers from his safe deposit box. Just what Jameson wanted them to see.

As Jameson pretended to read the papers and make notes on a legal pad, he thought about this surprise. It was annoying, but not that unusual. Operations of this type are highly fluid and often require adjustments on short notice.

After about twenty minutes, Jameson replaced the folder in the security box and closed the lid. He pushed the button calling the guard.

Another guard, not Washington, gently knocked on the door and opened it. Without a word the guard took the security box. He and Jameson walked back to the slot where the box was replaced.

Jameson noticed Washington was with another customer. He would be happy to leave without another encounter with the "future bank president." As he walked away from the vault area, he heard his name called and knew it was Washington.

Without turning around he waved his hand in a goodbye gesture and kept going.

The late afternoon air was chilly and held a promise of another cold fall evening. Jameson blended into the crowd perfectly. No security camera would ever get a good look at his face and no witness would ever remember much about him.

At exactly 4:30 pm, his cell phone rang.

"Did you get the package?" the voice on the other end asked before Jameson could even say hello.

"We never talk anymore," Jameson said.

"Did you get the damn package or not?" the voice said with measured slowness.

"Of course, I got it. You act like I've never done this before," Jameson said in a mock hurt voice.

"Fine," the voice said.

"There was a small problem though," he said.

"What problem?"

"Don't worry, it's nothing I can't handle," Jameson said.

"What do you mean, handle? Handle what? What happened?" the voice sputtered.

"You worry too much," Jameson said. "I'll fill you in later."

He closed the cell phone without waiting for a reply. If he could do this by himself, he would.

On the way back to the apartment, Jameson stopped for some takeout Chinese food at a place around the corner. As he left the small restaurant, he realized this was the second time in a month he had stopped here and made a mental note to never go back. Maybe the elderly Asian man behind the cash register practiced the same memory disciplines as the young bank guard.

The nondescript apartment building had an electronic entry system instead of a doorman, which is what Jameson wanted. As he opened the entry door, he automatically lowered his head when he came into the view of the security camera that monitored the small foyer. A nondescript man going into a nondescript apartment.

His sparsely furnished apartment looked like what you might expect of a single, nearing middle-aged man. The walls were bare, which actually made the one-bedroom apartment look bigger than it was. Adding to the appearance of space was the absence of furniture. The kitchen was separated from the living area by a breakfast bar. There was a small table with one chair where most people would eat their meals. The "living" area consisted of a recliner facing down the long wall and placed next to some built in bookshelves. A television sat on a small table in front of the recliner. Against the wall opposite the bookshelves was a folding table like you might find in a school or church fellowship hall. On the table were a laptop computer, a printer, and a telephone along with a few computer books and other papers. Beside the table, on the floor, was another black briefcase. There was no other furniture. The bedroom was just that – a double bed. There was a small walk-in closet. The bathroom was off the bedroom.

He shut the door behind him and locked the three locks on the door. He went directly into the bathroom and climbed on the toilet after putting a towel down to stand on. He lifted the suspended ceiling tile directly above the toilet, slid the black briefcase into the hole, and replaced the tile. The ruse wouldn't foil a professional search, but it was unlikely a common burglar would find the briefcase.

A supper of an inexpensive merlot and, by now, cold Chinese food eaten while standing in the apartment's tiny kitchen had become a habit for Jameson, a man who carefully avoided habits.

He filled his glass again and went to the table with the computer. As the computer was booting up he opened the black briefcase and took out a spiral bound report about one-half inch thick and began looking through the pages. There were three other identical reports in the briefcase. His work as a database consultant was easy and lucrative. Part of his arrangement with Vic was leaving a "backdoor" open in databases he built. This allowed Vic to easily hack his way into the company's network. In turn, Vic referred business to Russell. It was a mutually beneficial way to make a lot of money.

Jameson logged on to his e-mail and found 18 new messages awaiting him. Most were from clients with questions about databases he had built. He spent an hour or so responding to the various problems, none of which were really difficult.

Another 20 minutes looking through several local and national databases gave him the information needed to solve his problem. He glanced at his watch and thought, 'no time like the present.'

Jameson went to the bathroom and retrieved the black briefcase he hid earlier. He opened the brown collapsible file folder and took out a German-made target pistol. The pistol fit diagonally into the folder so it took advantage of the long side of the safe deposit box. The gun fit into a space he hollowed out of a stack of random paper. From any side, it appeared to be a folder of legal papers.

The weapon was about 16 inches long with target sights and a molded wooden handle. The dark wood and cold blackish-gray barrel were pleasing to Jameson's eye and touch; however what he really liked about the single shot weapon was its internal firing mechanism.

Revolvers made noise when fired as the cylinder rotated and the hammer struck the firing pin, which then struck the bullet. Semi-automatic pistols made noise when the recoil from the bullet firing pushed back the loading mechanism and another shell was forced into the chamber.

This pistol was different. It was designed strictly for competitive target shooting. When you pulled the trigger, nothing moved except the internal firing pin, so there was no noise except the sound of the bullet exploding.

You had to manually eject the spent shell and replace it with a live round. Very inefficient if you're in a gunfight, but perfectly acceptable for target shooting or assassinations.

The maker of the small caliber gun, which was quite expensive, put its money and research into the rifling of the barrel and the sights. The tiny grooves in the barrel's interior served to spin the bullet as it was fired in a manner that made the weapon incredibly accurate up to 15 meters. The sights were carefully calibrated for predictable accuracy. Jameson could set the sights at five meters and be very accurate every time. However, thanks to the U.S.

Government, there were even more "enhancements." The pistol had a highly modified barrel that muffled the sound even more. Jameson had used it many times to assassinate a "target" when close range was the only option.

An easy hack into a database let him change the inventory of pistols from the arsenal records of his previous employer. He took several of the pistols and a sniper rifle with him when he left the government's employ as a severance package – not authorized, of course. He had the pistols stashed in different safe deposit boxes at different banks. The sniper rifle and other gear were in a rented storage facility. The small room he rented was climate controlled so ammunition stayed fresh longer and the rifle avoided the heat extremes of summer and winter. He moved to another storage unit in a different location every few months, always under a different name.

Jameson checked the time – 8:35 pm – and put on his overcoat and hat. He opened the pistol's chamber to verify it was loaded and put an extra bullet in his pocket. The gun fit into a sling he had sewn into the interior of his coat. If ever asked about it, the sling also supported his camera and telephoto lens.

A bus ride with two transfers got him to his destination in 55 minutes. Jameson's earlier research suggested the shortest route for his subject was through the park, so he positioned himself at a bus stop with the best view of the park entrance. If this didn't work out, at least he would gain more information for another try later.

It wasn't long before his patience and preparation paid off. He spotted the subject talking with three other people. The subject broke from the group and crossed the street and entered the park. Jameson followed ten paces behind him.

As soon as they were on the walkway inside the park, he picked up his pace and passed the subject with his head down and face hidden by his hat. Jameson hurried ahead until he found the spot he was looking for deep in the park.

There was a park bench with a small light nearby. The walkway was fairly straight past the bench before curving again about 15 paces past the bench. Jameson quickly looked around for witnesses and stepped off the walkway into the shadows and bushes.

He focused on calming his breathing and heart rate and waited. In less than a minute the subject appeared. The young man passed his position. Jameson pulled the pistol from inside his coat and took aim. Just before the subject reached the limits of the park light, Jameson held his breath and pulled the trigger.

The gun made a small pop and was silent. The subject crumpled to the ground like all of his bones suddenly went limp. Jameson looked around for witnesses again. He knew he didn't need a second shot – he never did.

He ejected the spent shell and put it in his pocket and replaced it with the extra bullet he bought. He liked to be prepared. If confronted, he would not admit anything, but he also had no interest in shooting it out with the police. The live round was his.

He put on his gloves and hurried over to the body. He took out the billfold and removed all the cash, then threw the billfold into the bushes. He went through the bag the subject had been carrying and scattered the contents. This all took less than 30 seconds. He stood for a second over the body.

"Sorry about that Mr. Future Bank President," Jameson said in a quiet voice and walked away.

Chapter 4 – Tuesday – Jim & Vic

The doorbell startled Jim from a now too common mid-evening nap in front of his laptop. Work seemed a safe way to get through the lonely nights, but it just wasn't fun anymore.

The house he and Sally bought just months before her death was still not completely decorated. That was her thing and you could tell at a glance where she had spent any time. There were pictures on the walls and dried flower arrangements and throw pillows and all those little things women stick on end tables and mantles and other flat surfaces.

However, two of the three bedrooms were completely bare of any such touches. The den/TV room where Jim spent most of his time had only one wall decorated and the built-in bookshelves were only half full from the bottom up. It had been Jim's responsibility to reach the taller shelves – a job he had successfully avoided to the point it became a running joke between them. Now, it didn't seem important.

The garage was full of boxes of his stuff and her stuff that had not made it to any permanent place in the house. They both had apartments before they married, so it took some time to sort out what to keep and what to get rid of and what they needed to buy. He couldn't bring himself to go through her stuff. In fact, her clothes were still in the drawers in the bedroom and hanging in the walk-in closet.

He stretched and yawned and shook his head to get the cobwebs loose. When he opened the door, it took a second to put the face with a name.

"Hey, Jim. I'm sorry to drop in on you like this. It's very rude, but I was in the neighborhood and, well, here I am," Vic said.

"Vic," Jim said when the light bulb of recognition finally came on. "Of course, come in."

Vic stepped into the entry way and they shook hands. Jim directed Vic to the family room and hastily grabbed some newspapers from the end of the couch. He motioned Vic to sit down. Vic looked to be in is early 50s with close-cut graying hair. He was wearing khaki pants and a blue shirt under a light coat.

"What a lovely home," Vic said. "This is a great part of town."

"Thanks. Do you live around here?" Jim asked.

"No. I live in an apartment just north of downtown. "Do you often bring work home?" Vic said as he motioned to the laptop sitting on the coffee table.

"Yeah. Your assessment of me as a 'corporate man' at the group meeting the other night was right on. I've always taken work home. When Sally and I were married, I promised that one night during the week I would leave the laptop unplugged and we would spend time together," Jim said. "I tried to keep that promise even after she was gone, but it is hard to carry on a tradition that means nothing without her," Jim said.

Vic didn't say anything, but just watched Jim talk.

"Would you like something to drink?" Jim asked. "I've some wine and beer or I could make some coffee."

"A cup of coffee would be great, if it is not too much trouble," Vic said.

The kitchen was just off the family room, but a swinging door kept the two rooms separate. Jim went about grinding some beans and getting the coffee maker ready. As soon as the coffee pot was on, he returned to the family room.

Vic was sitting closer to the laptop, but reading a magazine Jim had left on the table.

"I hope you don't mind, I took a look at your laptop," Vic said.

"Oh, sure. You work with computers, don't you," Jim said.

"I design and trouble shoot large databases," Vic said. "These things have really changed the way I work. It used to be you had to be on site and work on the corporate system. But now, I just connect from my apartment and it's just like I'm there."

"That's what I do," Jim said. "I can do just about anything from here that I can do from the office. They don't give me access to the secure areas, like the personal information of our customers, but I don't have that at work either."

Jim got the coffee from the kitchen and sat back down in his chair facing the sofa. Neither one said anything for a while.

"You're probably wondering why I just showed up on your doorstep," Vic said.

"Yeah. I guess I am," Jim said, but hastily added, "I'm glad to see you though."

"It's just that I've been dealing with this longer than you and thought you might need someone to talk to that wasn't going to end the conversation wanting a hug," Vic said.

Jim laughed. "I guess that's something important to women, but after a while I get tired of women I barely know asking me if I'm all right, whatever that means, then throwing their arms around me before I can even answer the question."

"I know they mean well," said Vic. "But there is a truth about this whole process of grieving, whether you're at work or with friends or in the group session, and that truth is that women want men to be like women."

"I'm not sure I follow," Jim said.

"Women have their own way of dealing with strong emotions that involves a lot of talking about how they feel with other women. This apparently helps them move through the process, but it takes a long time and involves a lot of talking, crying and looking for support," Vic said. "I'm not saying they're wrong. It seems to work for most of them, although it does appear that some women find a degree of security in being a victim and that's where they stay. They let the tragedy, whether it was the loss of a loved one or divorce or abuse, or whatever, come to define them. They really don't want to move on because little is expected of them as long as they are victims."

"You sound cynical," Jim said.

"I suppose you're right about that and I don't mean to suggest that all women or even most women fall into this trap, however a fair number do. The point I'm getting to is that women expect men to react the same way they do to extreme emotions. When men don't, they seem to shift into one of two modes. They either want to smother you with support in the hope you'll respond the way they would or they accuse you of bottling up your emotions and being cold and unfeeling."

"That's what they mean when they say you're 'in your head,'" Jim said. "But I can see some value in talking about your feelings. The brief time I did it at the group meeting actually felt pretty good afterwards."

"I don't disagree with that. It's just that women tend to keep going on and on and on without any steps to resolve the situation," Vic said. "And, sometimes there is no real resolution. Your mother dies of breast cancer – what can you do about it? Nothing will bring her back. However, some people find that seeking some resolution is the only way out for them. For example, a person who lost a loved one to cancer could volunteer with cancer patients or at a hospital or raise money for research. That's where they can take some meaning from a meaningless tragedy."

"What about me? My wife and unborn baby are dead and the bastard who did it is probably sipping Scotch at his country club right now," Jim said. "My understanding was that everyone in the group including Judy lost someone due to violence. Where do we find resolution or is the proper word 'closure?'"

"I hate that word closure," Vic said. "It's a perfect example of psychobabble and women have been led to believe it is some kind of Nirvana. Once you achieve closure, then you can move on with your life and leave all of this behind you. The truth is it never leaves you – it never goes away – and I personally don't want it to."

"Now you're starting to sound like a professional victim," Jim said.

"No that's not right. The difference is I honor my loved ones by keeping their memory alive and I do that by spending time with people like you who are just beginning the process," Vic said.

"I'd like to hear your story, if you're up to it," Jim said.

"Oh, it's not much different than yours. A drunk driver ran off the road and my wife and two children were killed," Vic said.

"I'm sorry, as you said, I know how you feel," Jim said. "When did it happen, was it recently?"

"No. It will be ten years next April the 25th," Vic said.

"And you're still in the support group?" Jim asked. "I'm sorry, that was unkind of me."

"It's a legitimate question. Like I said, one way I'm resolving the conflict is by attending groups like ours. I go to help people like yourself get moving again," Vic said. "Judy and the other grief counselors at the clinic know me and are glad to include me in the sessions. I don't contradict their advice, but sometimes men respond better to other men.

"Men – men like us – are used to attacking a problem or situation and pursuing it to resolution. That's how we conduct our professional lives. That is one of the reasons you have been successful. But, when we hit a problem like how do you fill this emptiness in your life, it is hard to know what to do. Some men drown their sorrow in work or booze or they chase every woman they see. Some men just close up and make sure nothing will ever hurt them again. Others find a way to deal with the hurt that never ends. I do it by helping other men see the possibilities. How are you going to do it?"

"Emptiness. That's a good word for it. It is like part of me was just ripped away in a single instant. I guess one of the things that bothers me the most is how nothing will ever be the same. I want to feel the way I did before Sally died. I want to laugh without feeling guilty. I want to enjoy my work. I want to look forward to something," Jim said. Every good thing in my life involved her in some way or the other. She understood my work. She would watch football with me and even enjoy it, although I know she had zero interest. And when she wanted to go shopping for stuff for the house, I would go with her and enjoy it even though I could care less whether the towels matched the wallpaper in the bathroom," Jim said.

"The time we spent together, even doing the most routine of household chores, was the best time of my life and it's all gone."

"At the risk of sounding like a psychoanalyst, how does that make you feel?" Vic asked.

"It makes me sick to my stomach and it makes me angry," Jim said.

"Angry at who?"

"The prick who killed her of course and sometimes I'm mad at her," Jim said.

"You're mad at your wife for being killed by a drunk driver?" Vic probed.

"I'm mad at her for leaving me alone. Sometimes, I just want to scream, 'Why did you do this to me?'" Jim said. "That's pathetic, isn't it?"

Vic was silent for a moment. "No, I don't think it's pathetic. This is the conflict men face. Anger is a powerful emotion and there is no acceptable way for us to express it. I'll bet I'm the first person you've said that to."

"You're right. I haven't said it to anyone. How could I? I'm alive and she's dead. How can I just think about me?" Jim asked.

"Because 'me' is all you have left," Vic said. "In a split second, you went from being a happy, successful man full of life and looking forward to a wonderful future with the woman you loved to a man alone, uncertain of his future except that it will never be what it should have been. You have every right to be angry. In many ways survivors are more victimized than the ones we lost. Your wife, and my family are dead. They can't be hurt anymore. Sorry if that sounds harsh, but the truth is that you and I and all those like us, men and women, have to live with the truth that one moment life was a certain way and the next it changed and will never be what it should have been. We've had our future stolen from us," Vic said.

Jim began to feel slightly uncomfortable. Vic's voice and body language changed and there was a cold fierceness about him.

"Sounds like I'm not the only one who's mad," Jim said.

Vic's body relaxed and the softness returned to his voice. "Sorry. No, I'm still angry and will go to my grave angry. I came over here to see if you would let me help you and I'm not helping matters much."

"Well, at least I know I'm not completely weird about this," Jim said.

"No, and maybe I need to keep talking to people like us to remind myself that I'm not weird either," Vic said. "But, as you've probably observed for yourself, unless we pretend to be okay, people are going to think us weird."

"I know what you mean. Right after my wife died, everyone was genuinely supportive. The company was very generous with time off and friends were there. But as time went by, I sensed a growing irritation that I wasn't okay, like they're afraid my sadness is contagious," Jim said.

"It's like if you don't get over it, then they can't get back to life like it was before the tragedy. That's the problem though, isn't it?" said Vic. "They can go back to their life, but we've lost ours forever."

"And that makes me angry at them, sometimes," Jim said. "The truth though is I don't know what I expect them to do. It's not right to expect them to feel the way I do. It's not their fault the life I had is gone."

They sat in silence for a few minutes.

"So, what do we do with all this anger?" Vic asked.

Chapter 5 – Tuesday – Shannon & Ling

"Oh, crap!"

The phone on her nightstand was ringing and she couldn't believe it. Homicide detective Shannon O'Brien had just fallen asleep. The alarm clock said 1:35 a.m.

"This better be George Clooney begging for my body," she growled into the phone.

"Well, you're half right," said the familiar voice of Henry the third shift desk sergeant. "It's been a busy night and you're up."

"Wonderful. What's the story," she said wondering where her panties ended up when she undressed.

"Two separate shootings on the west side has the on-duty teams tied up and a citizen just found a body in Baker's Park with a bullet in the back of his head," Henry said.

"Gangbanger?" she asked.

"Don't know, but Baker's Park is near some past turf wars. When can I tell the uniforms you'll be there?" Henry asked.

"I've got to take a quick shower to wake up. Tell them to call the ME, but don't move the body until I get there. And send a patrol car to pick me up," she said.

"How come you don't have a car? When you're on call, you're supposed to take a car home," Henry said in his best 'irritated father' voice.

"Well, I didn't. So if you want me to get there before dawn, send a damn car and tell them to wait out front," she said and hung up. She had the attitude down pretty good, but inside she stung at Henry's rebuke – it sounded just like what her father would have said. The only thing missing was the 'little girl' her father would have added on the end of his rebuke. The difference, of course, is she could give Henry attitude.

She stood in front of the full-length mirror in the bathroom and surveyed her naked body. She had to admit it's not what it used to be when she was in peak shape, but it wasn't bad either. Four workouts a week, five when she could find time, kept her body taut and the competitive kick boxing matches kept her reflexes sharp. Even with the bruises around the rib cage from missed blocks, she still looked good, she thought and nobody would ever mistake her for a man.

Fifteen minutes later, she walked out the front door of her building and climbed into the backseat of the waiting patrol car.

"You O'Brien?" the uniformed officer asked with undisguised surprise that the homicide detective was a woman.

"No, I'm the Easter Bunny – now get moving," she said in no mood for this macho bullshit.

"Hey, I didn't spend the last seven years on the force to be no cabby," he said.

"If you don't put your lights on and get me to the murder scene in the next 10 minutes, you'll spend the next seven years patrolling the garbage dump," she said.

When they arrived at the scene, Shannon saw two patrol cars and the medical examiner's vehicle.

"Thanks," she said to the patrolman, who took off the minute the car door closed squeaking the tires as he went.

"I see your winning personality has made you another friend," said Ling Ya, one of the junior doctors in the ME's office.

When Shannon didn't respond, Ling started walking up the park's path. "The body is about 300 yards into the park," she said.

"So, how's your love life?" Ling asked after a moment of silence.

"What? When did you become concerned about my love life?" Shannon asked.

"Come on. You probably got men all over you," she laughed.

"Yeah! Right! Nothing more attractive than a six foot two broad packing a pistol," Shannon said. "Men think I'm an Amazon dyke or a blonde bimbo."

"Ouch! Reality check time. You're a very attractive woman, but I understand what you're saying. When they find out I'm a doctor they get real excited until they discover I don't have some $300,000 eastside practice, but spend my time cutting up dead people," Ling said. "Of course, nobody is going to mistake me for an Amazon."

"What about the dyke part?" Shannon said half jokingly.

"That's not the term I'd prefer," Ling said.

"I'm sorry. I didn't mean…" Shannon stammered.

"It's all right. I'm not offended. Does it bother you?" Ling asked.

"No. It's not my thing, but it's not something I think about," Shannon said.

"If you ever want to think about it – give me a call," Ling said with a smile.

A patrolman approached that Shannon recognized as she took in the full meaning of Ling's invitation. He had gone through the academy with her, but never wanted to be anything more than a beat officer.

"Hey O'Brien," he said. "How's it going?"

"Great Jesse. Family doing all right?" she asked.

"Yeah. Wife's not excited about me on this shift, but what else is new," he said. "The body was found about 40 minutes ago by a 17 year-old girl who was walking home. She called 911 on her cell.

"What's a 17 year-old doing in this park late at night by herself?" Shannon asked.

"That's probably what her mother is asking her right now. She called home right after she called it in. That's them sitting on the bench," he said. "The girl's name is Alexandra Moore."

"Thanks. I'll talk to them," Shannon said.

The mother was wearing mismatched sweats and sitting next to the girl who was staring at her feet. The girl's long straight hair was not colored or tinted. Her clothes were typical of a teen, but not extreme. They weren't talking.

"Good evening or should I say good morning. I'm Detective O'Brien. And you must be Alexandra," Shannon said.

The girl raised her head and glanced sideways at her mother. "Am I in trouble?" she asked.

"Not with me," Shannon said.

"Mrs. Moore?" she asked and extended her hand.

"Yes. Alexandra is usually a good girl. I don't know how this happened?" Mrs. Moore said.

"I'm afraid I'm going to have to ask you to wait just a few more minutes, but I promise I'll let you go home as soon as I can," Shannon said. "I'll be right back."

Shannon walked on down the path about 10 yards to where several uniform officers, the evidence unit, and Dr. Ya and her crew were waiting. On the ground was a body covered by a yellow tarp.

Shannon pulled back the tarp and automatically braced herself for what was underneath. Three years in homicide had not fully conditioned her for the damage one human was capable of doing to another.

However, in this case, the scene wasn't as grim as she expected. The young black man was lying face down in a small pool of blood. The back of his head was matted with blood, but his face was intact.

Shannon had expected something much worse. When she heard that the victim had one shot to the head, it usually meant either a suicide or an execution. In either case the gun was usually very close to the victim's head, which meant brains and other matter were splattered all over the place.

This murder was almost neat. That it was a murder was apparent by the entry wound at the base of the skull. Not a likely place for a suicide victim to choose.

She pulled the tarp back farther. The young man was dressed in dark slacks and wearing sneakers, but not the expensive type favored by the gang members. He was wearing a heavy shirt, apparently unbuttoned, and an undershirt. His backpack was opened and there were two books and some papers scattered near the body.

"He's Abraham Washington. Age 24. An employee of Union Bank and Trust and a student at Central College," Jesse, the patrolman said.

"Very good, Jesse," Shannon said with mock admiration.

"I could've been a great detective," Jesse said.

"So could Mickey Mouse, if he'd found the guy's wallet," Shannon said.

"It was over in the bushes," Jesse said holding up a plastic bag containing the wallet. "No cash, but the credit cards are still here."

Shannon put on her gloves and took the wallet out of the bag. His ID was still there, but no pictures or any indication of relatives.

"What about next of kin?" she asked.

"We sent a unit over to his apartment. It's about 10 blocks from the other side of the park. There was no answer, but the manager lives on the same floor and let the officer in. She said as far as she knew the guy lived alone," Jesse said.

"How long has he been dead?" Shannon asked the doctor.

"Looks like about three hours or so," Ling said. "I can give you a better time when I do the full autopsy. Obviously, death was by a single gunshot to the back of the head," she said.

Shannon turned back to Jesse. "Gang related?"

"I don't know about that. We haven't had any problems over here for three months or so, ever since the mayor made this park a re-election issue. The action has moved about five blocks south," Jesse said.

"That makes sense," Shannon said. "This kid was not involved with any gang. It must be a robbery-homicide."

"Maybe so," said Ling. "But look at the wound more closely. She shined a small flashlight on the back of the young man's head. "There are no powder burns and I'm pretty sure this guy was standing up when he was shot. That's not a gang MO and whoever shot him did it from a distance."

"So, we have a robber who is either a great shot or incredibly lucky, and who ambushes the victim, then takes only the cash and leaves the credit cards," Shannon mused out loud. "Pretty cold blooded for your garden variety robber."

"We found some more books and other items from the backpack scattered around, but it didn't look like they found anything," Jesse said.

"That's because Mr. err Washington didn't have anything they considered valuable," Shannon said referring to her notes.

She walked around the crime scene trying to get a sense of where the killer might have stood. "Did you find any shell casings?" she asked.

"No," said Jesse.

She walked back to where Alexandra and her mother were waiting. "I'm sorry this is taking so long, but I need to ask Alexandra some questions," she said.

"I pray my daughter is not mixed up with some gang," Mrs. Moore blurted out.

"Mother!" the young girl said between clinched teeth. "I've told you I'm not into that kinda of stuff."

"Tell me what happened, Alexandra, beginning with why you were in the park so late," Shannon asked.

"I was at my friend's house. We were supposed to be studying for a test, but Alicia, that's my friend, really wanted to go see her boyfriend," Alexandra said carefully avoiding looking at her mother.

"The plan was that I would call my mom and tell her we were going to study late so I would just spend the night," she continued.

"After I called mother and told her we were going to study late, Alicia and I went over to her boyfriend's house. His parents weren't there. Her boyfriend had a friend staying with him – he was supposed to be my date – so we put on some music and were dancing," she said.

"The next thing I know the guys are getting out some crack and their pipes. That's when I left," she said. "I thought I could cut through the park and save some time, but it was really creepy, so I ran. That's when I found him just lying there," she said. "I called 911 and went back to the entrance to wait for the police. And I called my mom."

"Did you see anyone in the area of the body or anywhere in the park?" Shannon asked.

"No, ma'am. I didn't see anyone until the police got here, which wasn't long after I called," the girl said.

"Okay. Thank you Alexandra," Shannon said.

"Is my girl in trouble?" Mrs. Moore asked in a trembling voice.

"No. I don't believe so. I think she is telling the truth. Because this is a murder investigation, we'll follow up with her friend and the others involved, but that's just routine," Shannon said.

"Oh, thank God," Mrs. Moore said. "You're grounded for life young lady."

"Mrs. Moore," Shannon said. "It's none of my business, but it seems to me Alexandra realized that she had made a mistake and was trying to fix it. She just made another mistake by going through this park at night. That was dangerous. The fact that a murder was committed here is proof enough of that. Alexandra, you did the right thing to call 911 and your mother. Maybe next time you won't try to run one by your mother like that," Shannon said.

"No, I won't," she said. "I just want to go home."

"Do you have a car here, Mrs. Moore?" Shannon asked.

"No, a neighbor ran me over, but she had to get back because she has kids of her own," the woman said.

"Jesse," Shannon called to the patrolman. "Alexandra is going to give you the name and address of her friend and her friend's boyfriend. Would you mind running them home? They've had a long night."

"Shannon," said Ling. "I'm done here. Can we take the body now?"

"Yeah, I'm done. Did you say time of death was around 10 or 11?" Shannon asked.

"That's what the preliminary look indicates," Ling said.

"I wonder why no one reported the body until the girl found it at 1:30. That could be over three hours it was lying here in plain view," Shannon wondered.

"Jesse, before you go, do you have any idea why no one reported this body on the path for three plus hours before the girl came by at 1:30?" she asked.

"No. Not really. This park has had its problems in the past, but we've been patrolling around here fairly regularly and there have been no serious incidents recently," Jesse said.

"Thanks," Shannon said.

"There is no way he could've been murdered somewhere else and brought here, is there?" she asked out loud.

"No. I don't think so. The blood is pooled around him in such a way that it would've been smeared around if the body was positioned after death. Besides, the amount of blood is consistent with this type of wound," Ling said.

"Any idea about the caliber?" Shannon asked.

"Other than it was fairly small, obviously," Ling said. "The entry wound is not very clean, so I'm guessing the bullet was a small caliber, hollow point that exploded on impact with the back of his head.

"Some of the wound indicated an outward force after entry, which makes me think it was a hollow point and, if it was, I doubt I'll find much in the way of fragments to test," she said.

"This is starting to smell like a professional job," Shannon said.

"Well, that's your call, but wouldn't a professional use a larger caliber gun at closer range to make sure the job was completed?" Ling asked.

"A small caliber gun doesn't make much noise, and if the park was fairly empty, it's possible no one heard it. How far away do you think the shooter was?" Shannon asked.

"I might have a guess after I get this guy on the table, but before then, I would say the shooter was at least 10 feet away, but that is just a guess," Ling said.

"Not the typical distance junkies shoot from or for that matter, most junkies don't shoot at all. They want your cash and their next fix. Maybe this one got nervous and the gun went off and accidentally hit the victim," Shannon mused. "Great. Now I've talked myself into a suspect list that starts with a clumsy junky and ends with a professional killer."

"Excuse me, officer," Shannon called to one of the remaining policemen. "Did you canvas the area for witnesses?"

"Jesse and his partner got here first. We were about two minutes behind them. We secured the crime scene and Jesse and his partner did a sweep. But they didn't find anyone. No one on the street and no one in the park," the officer said.

"Great. A suspect list that includes practically everyone in town and no witnesses," Shannon said.

"I'm headed back downtown. Do you want a ride?" Ling asked.

"Sure. Just let me check with the evidence unit," Shannon said.

After satisfying herself the evidence unit had completed their work, Shannon and Ling got into her car for the trip downtown. The coroner's ambulance took the body to the morgue.

"By the way, where is your partner, what's his name, Koslowski?" Ling asked.

"He started vacation yesterday. I'm flying solo with help from the other teams if I need to interview potential suspects," Shannon said.

"How does that work? Aren't you supposed to work in pairs?" Ling asked.

"Yeah. That's by the book. But with the budget cuts the department is trying to avoid overtime. Usually they hook you up with another detective that is solo also because of vacations or court appearances. No one else is single right now. So, if I need to pickup a suspect, I grab another detective in the office or a uniform to go with me," Shannon said.

They drove in silence for a while and Shannon started to feel slightly uncomfortable. She had never really noticed Ling's delicate features before and found herself staring at the young doctor. Ling turned to look at her and saw something in Shannon's face that made her smile. Shannon felt her face becoming flush and quickly shifted her weight in the seat and turned her head.

Shannon was used to being in control, which might explain her dismal luck with men, she thought. Police work was not for the shy. She had faced down thugs and murderers before with no problem, but this made her nervous. Would Ling think she was a homophobe? Or, even more frightening; be interested in her.

She made a throat clearing sound as she shook her head to get focused on the case at hand. It was going to be tough enough without playing mind games about her sexuality.

"Why him?" she asked out loud.

"Him who?" Ling asked as if her thoughts had also taken a hard right and she was lost before the conversation started.

"The kid back in the park. My money says he was a straight arrow. Nicely dressed, no visible tattoos. Holding a job and going to college. He was probably just in the wrong place at the wrong time," Shannon said.

"What about his job at the bank? Maybe he was involved in something bad associated with the bank," Ling said.

"That's a possibility, but what are the odds a young black man has any kind of job that would give him access to areas where he could embezzle."

"I never would have guessed you felt that way," Ling.

"I don't feel THAT way," Shannon said. "But the reality is a young black man with no college degree is not likely to get high security position in a bank."

By the time they reached downtown, it was close to 4:00 am. "Do you want to get some breakfast?" Shannon asked.

"Sure," replied Ling a little too quickly for Shannon's comfort level.

She wondered why she asked the petite young doctor to join her for breakfast, especially when she wasn't really hungry. She had known Ling for a couple of years and they had worked a half-a-dozen cases together. Ling was pleasant enough and part of the system so she didn't have much interest in the mostly stupid details Shannon's few dates always fixated on.

"Why don't we hit that diner across the street from the courthouse. It is open all night and the food probably won't kill us," Shannon said.

"Sounds fine," Ling said.

'Am I so lonely, I'm going to become a lesbian just to have someone to talk to,' Shannon thought to herself.

They parked in the lot behind the diner and started inside. Out of the shadows stepped a man about six feet tall and dressed like a street dweller.

"Hey ladies, how 'bout a few dollars for a war veteran," he said.

"No," said Shannon and they kept walking.

"What's a matter? You don't respect no veterans?" he said.

They just kept walking, but he stepped in front of them.

"Hey you bitch. How bout I give you something," he growled and grabbed his crotch.

Shannon moved to walk around him, making sure she was between the drunk and Ling, but he reached out with his right hand to stop her.

Shannon stopped and looked down at the man's hand on her shoulder. She reached up with her right hand and grabbed his hand over the top and rotated his arm and pushed down.

The man screamed in pain as she applied pressure with her left hand to his elbow. In a manner of seconds, the man was on his knees.

Shannon pulled out her badge and shoved it in his face.

"My friend and I are going in to have some breakfast now. If you're here when we get back, I'm going to bust you," she said.

"Okay. Okay," he said.

She let him go and he grabbed his arm and pulled it close to his side.

Shannon reached in her pocket and gave the man a five. He looked at her like she was from outer space.

"Be gone when we come out," she repeated.

Ling watched the episode with her mouth open.

Once they were seated inside, she smiled at Shannon.

"What?" Shannon asked.

"I can't believe you. First you try to avoid the guy, then when he pushes it, I'm wondering if I'm going to have to sew his arm back on. Then you give him some money."

"My dad was a veteran," she said.

"You don't know if he is a veteran or just using that as a scam for wine money," Ling said.

"What looks good to you," Shannon said studying the menu.

When the waitress came, Shannon ordered a glass of orange juice, some toast, and coffee. Ling ordered three eggs over-easy, bacon, hash browns, and coffee.

It was Shannon's turn to be surprised. "Where are you planning to put all that food?" she asked in mock amazement.

"You know what they say, 'breakfast is the most important meal,'" she said with a slight blush.

"Yeah, but how can you eat that much and not be the size of a barn. And, besides, you're a doctor. How many dead people have you cut up that were killed by fried eggs and bacon?" Shannon asked and they both laughed.

"If the other doctors in the ME office saw me eat like this, they would never let it go," Ling said. "I get teased a lot about being small. Most of it is good-natured, but you can tell there is some underlying resentment from some of the male doctors and staff. I guess it is a boy/girl thing. Maybe they don't like Chinese-Americans. I know it gets old after awhile. I can't have a conversation with them unless it is about being a woman doctor or being Chinese. They don't seem to understand that I'm a person too," Ling said.

"And in social occasions, it is always 'Dr. Ya' that people want to talk to. ' It hurts when I do this – do I have cancer?' 'What's it like to cut up dead people – do they smell?' I wish I could just be Ling sometimes. A person who likes country music and would love to learn how to ride a motorcycle," Ling said.

"You like country music?" Shannon said with feigned disgust.

"Yeah. What's it to you?" Ling shot back trying to sound tough.

"Oh, nothing. Nothing at all," Shannon said rolling her eyes.

"If you're serious about the motorcycle part, I'd be glad to take you for a ride on mine," Shannon said.

"Get outta here. You have a motorcycle?"

"A twenty-year-old soft-tail Harley."

"I have no idea what you just said."

"Well, let's get together sometime when we both have a day off and I'll show you."

"You're serious? You would really take me for a ride?"

"Why not?" Shannon asked.

"No reason. I just was afraid my acting out in the park earlier might have frightened you off."

"I'll admit I was a little thrown by your invitation."

"I'm so sorry. That was not only rude of me, but very unprofessional. I hope you can forgive me."

"Of course I forgive you. I guess I'm a little confused about how I feel right now. On one hand, I feel more comfortable and at ease with you than I can remember feeling about any man in the past five years. I find you interesting and attractive and I would like to spend more time with you," Shannon said.

"But…" Ling said.

"But, I don't know. Can we just leave it at that for right now?"

"I would really like that and I promise I won't push anything. We'll just spend some time together."

"I'd like that. I'd like that a lot."

Chapter 6 – Tuesday – Russell

Even though he violated his own rules of engagement, the business had gone well, even better than expected. His system was precise and followed a strict protocol, and yet it was flexible enough to handle this problem extemporaneously with relative ease.

In all honesty, Russell had to admit to himself that he had been lucky. Luck was not something one should count on, so it never figured into his equations. Luck is something anyone can have, but you never know when. Luck is the sucker mentality that makes the lottery a multi-billion dollar industry and keeps the lights on in casinos everywhere. It also made cab drivers millionaires, but more often, made millionaires cab drivers when it deserted them.

His luck was not in the execution of his plan, but in the circumstances that made this job possible without the usual extensive preparation. His system was tested and revised and tested and revised again and again. No luck involved there. Part of his system, indeed one of the most important components, was preparation. This involved determining exactly when and where things would come together. In this case, the perfect circumstances were already in place and all he had to do was recognize them.

This problem wasn't the first by any means, but he must acknowledge that it was handled flawlessly, unlike some early situations that had turned out all right, but were sloppy in execution and could have created much more serious problems. He never gave a thought to the young black man he left dead in the park. His only crime was a good memory.

His next mission was tonight, so there was not much time to savor the moment. However, in his usual over-prepared way, he was ahead of schedule. This would normally be the time in the schedule he spent mentally rehearsing the plan, going over contingencies and visualizing the whole process. He had a counter for every possibility and they were so much a part of who he was at that moment he could execute any one of them almost automatically. Should something come up he didn't foresee, he could improvise just like he did at the bank.

The trick with this deal was that he had to go to residential area to make it happen. He hated residential areas. They were so open for one thing. He had to fight a bad case of agoraphobia. In the city, he could walk the streets with complete anonymity. Walk the streets in a residential area without a dog and you stand out. People watch you and remember you.

This was one of those neighborhoods where the old money used to live and had moved on or lost their homes in the Depression. Many of the old houses were cut up into apartments and had fallen into disrepair.

Then the yuppies discovered them and began restoring the old houses to better than new condition. Now, the neighborhood was populated with doctors, lawyers, and business owners. Parts of the area were gated, while others were not, but all of the houses had alarm systems.

People with money spent a lot of time and effort protecting their possessions with alarm systems, security patrols, and gated neighborhoods. Moneyed people put too much trust in these systems, which any second-rate burglar will tell you are jokes and actually help setup people to be robbed by giving them a false sense of security.

His target was no different. A wildly successful real estate developer as a young man, he had been coasting ever since. He still commanded attention because of the properties he owned, but he hadn't built anything new in years. Money to politicians assured him that his properties would not be hurt by any ill-conceived city ordinances.

Russell had rented a car to drive through the neighborhood on a reconnaissance mission. He hated to drive, but there was no other way to see how he would get to the target and how he would exit when finished. Fortunately, rich people like privacy as much as they like security, although this neighborhood left its gate open during the day so domestic help and others could enter. Most of the lawns were well landscaped with mature plantings. The target's home was no exception. The winding driveway led to a three-car garage on one end of the house. Large shrubs on both sides of the driveway virtually blocked any view of the garage from the street. Two passes by the house confirmed either shrub would make a perfect spot to wait.

The target usually went to his country club on Tuesday for a high-stakes poker game after dinner and didn't return until midnight or so. Amazingly, he had discovered this in a newspaper gossip column after a computer search. People had no idea how easy it was to learn everything about them.

The target's wife had been "sent to the farm" to dry out on three different occasions, he found out after a look at the target's electronic bank statements. She would probably be drunk the nights he left her home while he played poker with his buddies.

Russell knew private security cops patrolled the neighborhood and he also knew they probably did half the patrols they were being paid to do. The large shrubs effectively hid most of the driveway from the street, so even if they did come by, the odds of the rent-a-cops seeing anything were small.

He considered several ways of getting in and out of the neighborhood without drawing attention to himself. First rule: don't use a rental car. Cars stand out and have license plates and rental records. Too many ways to trace it back to him.

The simplest plan is almost always the best, he reminded himself. Look how well the action in the park had gone and it was the simplest action to date. He still felt out of his element in this neighborhood, but with his impeccable sense of timing, this action should pose no greater risks than others, he concluded.

He left his apartment around 10:00 pm and took a cross-town bus. He transferred to the bus that the maids and gardeners took and got off several blocks before the main entrance to the neighborhood. The main entrance was not gated, but it was brightly lit and he would be exposed for a longer time than was acceptable under most circumstances.

This would be the most dangerous part of the operation – getting in and out of the neighborhood without attracting attention. However, he had an edge. Thanks to the computer files of the security company that patrolled the neighborhood, he knew when the cars would drive by the target's house and that they would be four blocks away when he entered.

He walked through the entrance under the streetlights without incident at a pace the neither suggested urgency or loitering. He visualized how he would appear to someone driving by or walking by and used his self-control to find the right pace.

Inside the neighborhood, the usual streetlights gave way to more decorative and dimmer fixtures, which were fashioned to look like turn of the century pieces. They gave off a warm light with a slightly yellowish tint designed for form, not function. The resulting glow reminded him of warm summer nights when the moon was full and the small town he grew up in took on a mysterious shimmer. The full moon was bright enough to read by when under its light, but step into a shadow and you disappeared.

As he made his way along the narrow sidewalk, and occasionally a dog would bark as he entered their territory. He felt more at ease than he anticipated. The night was cool and clear. No clouds meant the temperature was likely to continue falling most of the night.

The target's house was coming up on the right. A quick glance around and he ducked under the low hanging branches of the shrub. He settled on the ground, thankful for his waterproof black overcoat. He pulled a black ski mask out of his pocket and tugged it over his head. With black gloves, overcoat, and mask, Russell was invisible to the street. Now he waited.

Several cars passed by without stopping. Russell didn't turn his head until they passed. The second one was the security patrol. He checked his watch: it was 11:30.

A person, walking a dog passed. Russell didn't look up. The dog began sniffing and started yapping. From the high-pitched noise, he guessed it was some little breed, a toy poodle maybe. The woman walking the noisy animal pulled it away with a grunt and continued her walk. The dog barked all the way down the block before giving up. Good thing the lady wasn't walking a German Shepard, he thought.

Another set of car lights headed this way. The time was right for his target, so he reached into an inner pocket and pulled out a small box with a dial on the top. He turned the dial all the way to the right. This little gem jammed the radio signal that operated the garage door opener. Not a big deal at all, but Russell was rather proud of it.

He reached in his coat and pulled out the pistol and checked the safety with his thumb. He knew it was loaded and felt his pants pocket for the extra round. The trick was to wait until the target pulled into the driveway passed him so he could get to a squatting position. He had been sitting so long in the cold that his knees and leg muscles rebelled at standing up. He needed to be on his feet and steady to make this work. He counted on the target being frustrated with the garage door not opening to give him a few seconds to get into position. He was able to stand part of the way up and steady his feet.

There was a small hole in the leaves that gave him a clear line of sight to where the target had stopped – about 20 feet away. The bright red brake lights bothered Russell's eyes while he waited. The target's car was a low sports model – Russell knew this before he came, that's why he could chose the shrub on the left side of the driveway. The light fixture next to the garage door provided a backlight that silhouetted the target. When the target got out of the car he had a clear view over the top of the car. Russell breathed deeply and focused his attention on the car.

The dome light of the car came on and he could see the target getting out of the car muttering about the "Goddamn garage door opener."

Russell briefly closed his eyes, then opened them and fired. The target lurched forward, then backward against the car, and then fell face down on to the driveway.

'Ouch,' Russell thought. 'That must have hurt.'

He immediately shrank back into the shrub to see if anyone reacted to the noise. The next-door neighbor's house was not far, but no lights or sounds came from the house. There was no activity in the target's house either, although he didn't expect there would be.

Now he had a quick decision to make. He could leave immediately or take a chance and close the car door which would extinguish the interior lights and disable the garage door light and might allow the scene to go undetected longer. He decided it was worth the risk. He quickly moved out of the shrub to the light fixture and quickly put his gloved hand up into the fixture and twisted the bulb until it went off. He then went to the car and gently closed the door enough to cut off the interior lights.

He glanced down at the target and saw a stream of blood running down the driveway toward the lawn. Suddenly, he remembered one of the cheers from high school pep rallies: "Blood makes the grass grow – blood makes the grass grow!"

'I'll bet you were a football player,' he thought as he stepped over the body.

He took off the ski mask and put his little jamming device away. One of the side effects of jamming the garage door opener was that its code was erased and the door would never open again until it was re-programmed.

He put on a baseball cap and began walking toward the entrance. Halfway there he saw a woman walking her dog on the other side of the street – probably the same one that barked at him earlier. Russell didn't look her way, but even if she had seen him all she could see was the dark silhouette of a man wearing a hat.

Just before he got to the entrance, he took off his hat and stuffed it in a coat pocket. He walked four blocks north and six blocks east and he caught an inbound bus after waiting 20 minutes. He listened carefully for sirens while he was waiting, but the only one he heard was going the wrong direction. No one had discovered the scene yet.

Sometimes he wanted to watch the police examine his work. He was sure they appreciated the clean, precise craftsmanship.

Chapter 7 – Wednesday – Jim & Sam

"Mr. Jackson?" his secretary said over the intercom line.

"Yes, Samantha. What is it? I told you I didn't want to be disturbed," Jim said. He had to present a marketing plan for a new boat-owners policy in two days and he was way behind schedule.

"Mr. Jackson. There are two police detectives here to see you," Samantha said.

"Really? Send them in," he said. He came out from behind his desk and met the two detectives as Samantha opened the door for them.

He almost laughed at the two as they walked in the door. Both were wearing overcoats and looked like they came from central casting. However, their faces looked all business.

"Mr. Jackson, I'm Detective Barnes and this is my partner Detective Appleton," the taller one said.

Jim motioned to the chairs around a small conference table in his office.

"What's this about," Jim asked. He could think of no reason the police were there to see him, but he couldn't escape that feeling in his stomach he used to get when called to the principal's office as a kid. He got one of those summons in the seventh grade. When he walked into the principal's office, his father was there to tell him his mother had died. And the last time he talked to a cop, it was the worse day of his life.

"Does the name Robert Bonnelli mean anything to you?" Detective Barnes asked.

Without even thinking, Jim blurted out, "Of course it does. He's the bastard that killed my wife. What's the matter? Did he kill some other innocent person?"

"You sound like you hated him," Det. Appleton said.

"Wouldn't you? That piece of shit killed my wife and walked away from it a free man," Jim said.

"No justice," said Det. Barnes.

"Justice! Don't even use that word in my presence. There is no justice. My wife is dead. My life is totally fucked and he walks.

What do you expect from me?" Jim said in a voice so filled with rage it surprised him.

The detectives exchanged glances. "Where were you last night between 10 and midnight?" Barnes asked.

"What's going on?" Jim asked, the implication of their questions now sinking in.

"Mr. Bonnelli was found dead early this morning in his driveway," Appleton said. "He was murdered."

"And you think I did it?" Jim said.

"Well, you don't sound like someone who would miss Mr. Bonnelli very much," Barnes said.

"Yeah, but murder?" Jim said. "I couldn't do anything like that."

"We still have to ask you where you were last night between 10 and midnight," Appleton said.

"I was home working. I've a big presentation in a couple of days and I've put a lot of hours into it," Jim said.

"So, were you alone?" Appleton asked.

"Yeah. I got home from work about 6:30, made some dinner and worked until 2:00 am this morning," Jim said.

"Did you talk to anyone over the phone or e-mail or anything that could establish where you were during that time frame," Barnes asked.

"No," Jim said. "Wait, I did talk briefly to a friend around 8:00 pm."

"Who was that?" Barnes asked.

"Vic. A guy I met at a grief support group meeting last week," Jim said. "We talked for about 10 minutes, but he was the only person I talked to the rest of the night."

"What's this Vic's last name?" Appleton asked.

"You know, I don't know what it is. These support groups are first name basis," Jim said. In the back of his mind, Jim briefly wondered how Vic had found his house if they weren't supposed to know last names.

"Well, it's not really important if he can't verify where you were between 10 and midnight," Barnes said.

"Are you telling me I'm a suspect?" Jim asked.

"Right now, we're just trying to get a picture of what happened and who may or may not have been involved," Appleton said.

"When is the last time you had contact with Mr. Bonnelli?" Appleton asked.

"I've never had contact with him," protested Jim. "The last time I saw him was in court. After dragging the case out for months, his lawyers finally got the charges dropped to a traffic violation. He paid a $500 fine and that was it."

"Okay. I guess that's all for now. Here's my card, if you think of anything else, give me a call. We may have more questions for you later. Thanks for your cooperation," Barnes said.

Although he knew he should just keep his mouth shut, Jim asked, "How did he die, anyway?"

Appleton stared at him for a moment and said, "One shot to the back of the head."

Jim just nodded and the detectives left.

He suddenly felt light-headed and sat down heavily in his chair. He never thought of himself as a violent person, but there was this tiny piece that was glad Bonnelli was dead.

Samantha stuck her head in the door, "Is everything alright?"

"What? Oh yes, that was about my wife's death," he said not quite sure why he hadn't told her the complete truth. Samantha had been his secretary for four years and had never gossiped about him as far as he knew.

Chapter 8 – Wednesday – Sam

Samantha Weatherby was very worried about her boss. She worried about him a lot, which was not unusual considering she was madly in love with him and had been for several years.

Up until a few years ago, Sam – to her friends – spent most of her time caring for a younger sister and an aging mother. She had been doing this since she was 15 and her father dropped dead of a heart attack at work. Her mother, who was not a strong woman to begin with, fell apart and Sam picked up the pieces. Her mother was able to work as a clerk in a woman's clothing store, but made very little money. There was some life insurance money, but not much.

Sam's younger sister Margaret had Down Syndrome and needed help with many basic living activities. Although she was classified as "high functioning," Margaret still needed help and guidance. She was devoted to Sam and Sam loved her dearly.

Her mom was barely able to do anything around the house. It fell to Sam to do shopping, cleaning, and paying the bills. Keeping up with everything was exhausting. In addition to high school, Sam worked part-time on weekends to help make ends meet. As she approached graduation, it was clear college was out of the question. Even if they could afford the tuition, which they couldn't, Sam couldn't be away from home and going to one of the colleges located in town didn't make sense either. She had no time and no money for college. She had no time for herself.

Sam got Margaret into a program that found her a job at one of the businesses operated by a non-profit to provide people with disabilities the opportunity to do something meaningful. The job gave Margaret a great sense of pride. It also let Sam take a fulltime job at Aargon Insurance.

Sam began as an entry-level clerk. She was smart and a quick learner. Thanks to a couple of good managers, she had the opportunity to take advantage of in-house training programs and was given more responsibilities. She moved up quickly and in five years became the secretary to the Assistant Vice President for Marketing. It was not a good match.

Sam was honest and not shy about expressing her opinion. Her boss was from the "Me Tarzan, You Jane" school of management. He resented her opinions, especially when they conflicted with his. To her credit, Sam never disagreed with her boss in front of others. Still, she found herself becoming isolated from what was happening in the department.

Margaret had become even more self-sufficient and Sam began attending night classes. Like everything Sam did, she became deeply involved in her classes. She decided to major in psychology with a minor in marketing. Her hope was to combine the two in a Master's Degree program when she finished her undergraduate degree.

With her work ethic and natural intelligence, Sam got her degree in three and one-half years. Her plan was to continue on the graduate school, however Margaret was diagnosed with ovarian cancer, and her mother began slipping into dementia. She used all her vacation time taking either her sister or mother to doctor's appointments. Her mother was slipping fast and Sam had to find a nursing home sooner than she anticipated.

Sam sold the family home and bought a duplex. She rented out one half and moved in to the two-bedroom other half. She fixed up the other bedroom, which had its own bathroom, for Margaret.

Margaret responded well to the initial treatments, although it meant giving up her job. Unfortunately, she had a very aggressive form of the disease and she died less than three years after her diagnosis. Her death was devastating to Sam.

Her career at Aargon Insurance was not going anywhere and she began looking at Masters level programs. About that time, the Assistant Vice President for Marketing left the company for another position. Soon after his departure, Jim Jackson was named as his replacement.

Sam liked him immediately. There was no pretense or posturing. He frequently ate with the staff in the company cafeteria. At first this put some of the Marketing staff off, but it wasn't long before everyone realized he was the real deal. He was a great listener and eager to here everyone's ideas, including Sam's.

He gave her more and more responsibility and she loved it. Very soon Sam realized that she was in love with Jim. It wasn't that he treated her and all of the employees as people with gifts and talents to contribute to the department. She was in love with the person behind the title. A man she believed to be honest and true. Her love put her in an awkward position. The company had strict policies against employees and supervisors in emotional relationships.

Then Jim began dating Sally and they soon married. He was very happy and she could see that the relationship was good for him, so she kept her feelings in check – he never knew how she felt. When Sally was killed, Sam rushed to his house and helped him get through the initial shock and pain.

As events unfolded, that was only the beginning of his pain. However, it also presented an opportunity – at the appropriate time many months or years away – for her to tell him how she felt. Until then, she kept her mouth shut and tried to be the best secretary and friend she could be.

And she waited.

Chapter 9 – Wednesday – Jim

The two detectives reached their car, which was parked across the street from the insurance company building.

Appleton was in the driver's seat, but he just sat there for a moment staring at the building.

"Problem?" Barnes asked. They had been partners for 12 years and he knew when Appleton was chewing on something.

"What do you think of that guy?" Appleton asked.

"Well, he doesn't seem like the assassin type, but we've been on homicide long enough to know they come in all shapes, sizes, and styles," Barnes said.

"So far, he's the only one with a motive and opportunity," Appleton said.

"Well, it's still early. You know how often we find victims that don't seem to have an enemy in the world until you start digging, then there's a line of people that want'em dead," Barnes said.

"Yeah. But I got a feeling about this guy. He has motive and no alibi for opportunity. What's say we see if he had a means?" Appleton said.

When they got back to the station there was a note from Lieutenant Chumsky to see him.

"What have you got on the Bonnelli murder?" Lt. Chumsky asked.

"Not a whole lot," Barnes said. "A rent-a-cop found the body about 4:00 this morning. He works for the neighborhood association and was on patrol when he spotted the victim's car in the driveway with the driver's door partially open. The victim was in the driveway. He called it in and waited for the uniforms. They pounded on the door for ten minutes before the wife woke up and came down."

"There were no witnesses and none of the neighbors heard anything, but the houses are on fairly big lots. His wife doesn't remember hearing anything either, however I've an idea she loads up just about every night. We have one neighbor, who was walking her dog, in the next block that saw a man walking down the other side of the street in her block about 11:30 or so. But, all she could say about him was that he was wearing an overcoat and a hat. The ME said he died between 10 and midnight from a single gunshot to the back of the head. It appeared to be a small caliber and possibly a hollow point shell. The assailant was not very close to the victim. There were no powder burns, so this doesn't look like a normal professional hit. Could have been from a small caliber rifle," Appleton said.

"What about the wife?" Chumsky asked.

"Well, we can't rule her out completely, but she didn't look like she could hold a shot glass still much less a gun. She could've hired it done I suppose. We'll keep looking," Barnes said.

"Any idea why it took so long for someone to spot the body," Lt. Chumsky asked.

"This is a gated neighborhood, so there's not much traffic and the house in on the end of a cul-de-sac. There're plenty of bushes in the front. It would be easy to drive by and not see anything. The rent-a-cop is paid to look and he had been by the house once before and didn't see anything," Appleton said.

"This guy Bonnelli was a real sweetie. Three busts for DWI, but no convictions. The last one involved an accident where a woman was killed. We just came back from interviewing the husband. He appears to be an upright citizen – good job and lives in a good neighborhood. He was obviously angry at the victim for what happened to his wife and he has no alibi for last night other than he was at home alone, working," Barnes reported. "My partner thinks there may be more to it than that."

"We've seen people killed for a lot less," Appleton said.

"This guy was a big real estate developer and a big political supporter of the mayor. So you can imagine the phone calls I've been getting all day. When are you going to have something for me? Is the husband a suspect?" Lt. Chumsky asked.

"We're on our way to run the husband through the system so see if anything pops up, but without something else, we have nothing on him," Appleton said.

"We'll also start poking around in the victim's life to see if he had any enemies or nasty little secrets," Barnes said.

"Okay, just be discrete. I don't need the mayor and police commissioner on my case because you guys are harassing the political elite," Lt. Chumsky said.

An hour later a clerk brought the detectives a printout on James Allen Jackson.

"Nothing shows up here," Barnes said as he scanned the report. "He was busted in college for marijuana possession, but the charges were dropped. Not even a parking ticket since then. Hold on, what's this?"

"Let me guess," Appleton said. "He owns a small caliber gun."

"Bingo,'" Barnes said. "A .25 caliber Smith & Wesson."

"I think we better talk to the lieutenant," Appleton said.

An hour later and a talk with an assistant district attorney yielded a plan to search Jackson's home for the gun. The DA was running down a judge to issue the search warrant while the two detectives went to Jackson's house. They were afraid he had spooked and gotten rid of the weapon already.

If he hadn't they would make their presence known at the house and hopefully prevent him from disposing of the weapon before they could get the search warrant.

They rang his doorbell and knocked for several minutes with no answer. Appleton looked at his watch. It was 5:39. "Maybe he's not home yet."

"Or maybe he's been here and taken off already. Let's peek around back," Barnes said.

"We don't have the warrant yet," Appleton said.

"I know. Let's just see if his car is in the garage," Barnes said.

They walked around to the side of the house and looked over the back fence. Appleton opened the gate and walked around the corner, then came right back and closed the gate.

"There's no car in the garage. It's full of moving boxes," he said. "Let's go wait in the car."

As they walked down the driveway, a patrol car with its light flashing pulled up and blocked the driveway. A young patrolman jumped out of the car with his hand on his pistol. "Hold it right there," he shouted.

Appleton and Barnes looked at each other and tried very hard not to laugh. "Take it easy son," Appleton said. "We're on the same team."

He reached for his inside coat pocket where he kept his shield and the patrolman shouted, "Keep your hands where I can see them."

All of a sudden, it wasn't funny anymore. "Whoa," shouted Barnes. "We're cops and if you will let me reach into my coat and get my shield, I'll prove it."

"Very slowly and very carefully," the patrolman said as he eased his pistol out of it holster.

"Okay. Okay," Barnes said and he slowly pulled out his shield. The patrolman took several steps forward and examined the badge.

"Sorry," he said, sheepishly. "I was responding to a burglar call at this address."

"No problem," Appleton said. "Call it in and get the name and address of the person who phoned 911."

"Sure thing," the patrolman said and walked back to his car talking into his radio.

"What's that about," Barnes asked.

"If there is a neighborhood busy-body maybe they know something about our boy," Appleton said.

The patrolman return and handed Barnes the information on a sheet of paper. "I'm sorry. I hope I didn't screw up anything."

"No, but it would help if you left. A patrol car with flashing lights might tip off our suspect," Barnes said with a straight face.

"Oh. Right," the patrolman jumped back in his car and took off.

The address was directly across the street from Jackson's house. The two detectives crossed the street and knocked on the door. There was no answer.

"Mrs. Greene? Open the door please. We are the police," Barnes said.

Finally the door opened a crack. "You aren't going to arrest me are you? I thought you were burglars," Mrs. Greene said.

"No. No. But we would like to talk to you. Can we come in?" Appleton asked.

Mrs. Greene's story was pretty obvious to the detectives before she even began telling it. The rocking chair strategically placed before a front window suggested she spent a great deal of time keeping an eye on things.

"Oh. How tragic and sad," she said when they asked about Jackson. "What a lovely young couple. You could just see how much they loved each other. Always holding hands and laughing and carrying on."

"Mr. Jackson and his wife were very nice to me. He came over and fixed a leaky faucet once and she was always stopping to talk when I was working in the yard. Then just like that, she's gone.

"I lost my Fred, my husband, five years ago, but we had been married 43 years. I still miss him every day, but I've all those memories to keep me company. How hard it must be for young Mr. Jackson, to have his bride snatched away like that," she said.

"Is there anything unusual you can tell us about him?" Appleton asked.

"Oh, dear. Is he in trouble," she asked.

"Just routine, ma'am," Appleton said, although he never knew why so many people accepted that non-answer.

"No. I think he works at an insurance company and I was never sure if she worked or not. She was here a lot during the day," Mrs. Greene said.

"Any unusual comings or goings – late hours and such," Appleton said.

"No. Not really. And since the tragic accident, Mr. Jackson stays pretty much to himself," she said.

"What about last night," Barnes asked. "Did you hear him go out late in the evening?"

"I'm sorry. I went to bed about 9:30 and slept like a baby until 6:30 this morning," she said.

"Well, thank you for your help," Barnes said and gave her his card. "If you think of anything out of the ordinary, please give me a call."

As they were leaving, Appleton's cell phone rang. He hung up and motioned Barnes toward the car. "Judge has signed the warrant.

The lieutenant is sending it over with the evidence unit, but we can enter the premises."

"Let's wait a little while. I'm not in the mood for kicking in a door and I think we may learn more if Jackson is here when we execute the warrant," Barnes said.

They radioed the evidence unit and asked them to wait several blocks away so as not to alert Jackson. An hour and fifteen minutes later, Jackson pulled into his driveway. It was dark, but an outside light tied to a timer had already come on and they could see Jackson clearly.

He got out of his car struggling with a large briefcase and a sack of what appeared to be fast food. He was fumbling with his keys when the detectives walked up behind him.

"Working late?" Barnes asked.

Jackson seemed surprised to see them. "I thought we finished this morning," he said.

"As we say in the business, there have been some new developments," Barnes said. "Can we come in?"

"Is this going to take long? Your visit this morning screwed up my whole day and I haven't had supper yet," Jackson said.

The evidence unit had pulled up and an officer approached Barnes with the warrant. Barnes took the warrant and stuck it in Jackson's coat pocket.

"That's a warrant to search your house and premises," he said.

"What?" Jackson said. "What could you possibly be looking for?"

"For starters, the Smith & Wesson you bought before Mr. Bonnelli beat the rap for killing your wife," Barnes said. "You can save us some time by just handing it over."

"You think I killed him? That's impossible. I won't make any pretense that I'm sorry he's dead, but I'm not a murderer. How could you even think that?" Jackson said.

"You had motive, you had opportunity, and you had the means. In detective school, they call that a suspect," Appleton said. "Now, things will go a lot better for you if you just show us where the gun is or did you toss it already?"

"No, I didn't toss it, but I'm not sure where it is. My wife and I both had separate places before we married and combined our stuff. The garage and half the house are full of unpacked boxes. We took our time unpacking and since Sally's death, I haven't had the stomach to keep going," Jackson said.

"So, what you're telling us is you won't produce the piece voluntarily?" Barnes said.

"I really don't know where it is. I know I didn't unpack it and I'm sure if Sally found it in a box she was unpacking, she would've said something. She hated guns," Jackson said.

Appleton turned to the evidence team and said, "Why don't you guys start in the garage with the boxes and we'll look through the house. Mr. Jackson, I need to ask you to stay with us while we're searching the house."

An hour and one-half passed with nothing to show for all the efforts. "I don't understand why you haven't found it," Jackson said. "I know it's here and I want you to find it, because it'll prove I didn't kill anyone."

He was sitting in the family room where Barnes was going through the books on the shelves and the ones still in boxes. He stopped and went over to Jackson and sat on the sofa with him.

"Look. Why don't you make this easy on yourself? I can understand where you're coming from. If some drunk killed my wife and walked out of the court a free man, I would think about doing it, you know. You probably didn't mean to shoot him. You were mad and wanted to scare him and things got out of hand."

"What are you talking about?" Jackson asked. "I didn't do anything. First my wife gets killed and now I have to defend myself."

"Detectives. You better come out here," one of the evidence officer called from the garage.

Barnes and Appleton brought Jackson with them to the garage. The officer was holding a plastic bag containing a .25 caliber Smith & Wesson semi-automatic pistol.

"See, I told you it was here," Jackson said.

"Where did you find it?" Barnes asked.

"It was wedged up behind the water heater," the officer said pointing to the corner of the garage.

Barnes put a fresh set of latex gloves on and took the pistol out of the evidence bag and checked the chamber.

"It's loaded with one in the pipe," he said and very carefully took out the clip and dropped it in the evidence bag. He then ejected the live round from the chamber and put it in the bag also. He held the barrel up to his nose and sniffed.

"Has it been fired?" Appleton asked.

"Maybe," Barnes said.

"Mr. Jackson, can you explain why the gun was hidden behind the water heater?" Barnes asked.

"No. I didn't put it there. Why would I do that? I've nothing to hide," Jackson sputtered.

"Can you think of any reason your wife would've hidden it there?" Appleton asked. "Maybe she didn't want you to have it."

"No. That's not right. She hated guns and would never even touch one," Jackson said.

"I think we should continue this conversation downtown," Barnes said.

"Are you putting me under arrest?" he asked.

"Not at this time, but we do need to talk more," Barnes said.

"What about my house?" Jackson asked.

"The evidence unit will secure your house when they are finished. Let's go," Barnes said.

Appleton told the evidence unit to check Jackson's clothing and shoes carefully for blood spatters and see if they could find any hats.

Jackson sat quietly in the back seat of the detectives' car on the way to the station. The two detectives knew from years of experience that sometimes silence is a powerful motivator in getting a suspect to talk. Most people can't stand prolonged periods of silence. Unlike the cops on television and in the movies, slapping suspects around was generally frowned on.

Besides these two detectives knew that given enough time and talk, most suspects will tip their hand. People confess to crimes that were not even under investigation. Most of these folks were not hardened criminals, but rather criminals of opportunity or passion. They hadn't thought out their crime in great detail or were not smart enough to see the obvious flaws in their denials.

Jackson was something else. On one hand, he looked to be fairly transparent. A young guy whose wife had been killed under tragic circumstances – snatched away when he least expected it. His anger at the victim was real and justifiable. But, was he a killer? On the other hand, maybe he had acted on his hatred, but not in an emotional, explosive manner. Rather he was one of the few "non-professional" criminals that go through the system and are smart enough to cover their tracks to the extent that a conviction is difficult, if not impossible without some luck.

Appleton and Barnes had spent several hours during the day and while they were waiting for Jackson to come home debating these two points. This was one of their investigative tools and it served them well. The detectives had solved more than one murder using this technique and uncovering possibilities that may not have presented themselves independently.

The two detectives were still uncertain which way it could go until the pistol was found hidden behind the water heater at Jackson's house. While it was true that the most obvious suspect was not always the criminal, it was true most of the time. It was just a matter of finding out where they made mistakes. And they all made mistakes sooner or later. The hidden pistol was Jackson's mistake. In the interrogation room, Jackson remained adamant in his innocence and as the interview wore on became more sullen and less responsive.

Andrew Schapiro, an assistant DA, watched the interview process from behind the two-way mirror. After an hour, Barnes came out to talk.

"Well, what do you think?" he asked Schapiro.

"Why did you drag me down here in the middle of the night? You don't have anything but circumstantial evidence at best," Schapiro said.

"What do you mean? We've got motive, opportunity, and means," Barnes said.

"You've got nothing to physically put him at the scene of the crime and the ballistic test on the gun was inconclusive," the assistant DA said.

"He can't prove he was at home. He could have left anytime. And what about the hidden gun? The lab said it had been fired recently and wiped clean of prints. Doesn't that count for something?" Barnes said.

"It counts for zip and you've been doing this long enough to know better. Mr. Jackson doesn't have to prove he was at home. We have to prove he was at the crime scene. The dead wife could have put the gun there. And how do you know there aren't 15 other people with a motive to kill Mr. Bonnelli?" Schapiro said.

"We gotta feeling about this guy," Barnes said.

"Well, I can't take your feeling to court. Find a witness or some evidence to put him at the scene and it's a different ball game. If you can't do that right now, cut him loose," Schapiro said.

Barnes returned to the interrogation room and rolled his eyes at his partner with a slight shake of his head. "Mr. Jackson, that'll be all for right now, but please stay in town in case we need to talk some more. There'll be a patrol car waiting downstairs to take you home."

Jackson left without a word.

"What do you think?" Barnes asked as he and his partner watched Jackson leave.

"We either have the wrong guy or this is one is going to be tough to crack. What next?" Appleton said.

"Next is a good night's sleep. Tomorrow, I think we better start over and see if we can find anyone else with a motive to murder Mr. Bonnelli," Barnes said.

"Yeah, I guess you're right. But I gotta tell you that I think the murderer just walked out of here. I mean, think about it. What would you do if one moment your wife was alive and you were young and in love and the next moment, your life changes forever? Everything you dreamed about – a family, a future – was taken from you. Just like that. No chance to say goodbye; no chance to stop it; nothing you could ever do to make things right. And to make things worse, the bastard who did it walks out of the courtroom a free man. What would you do to the man who caused you that much pain?" Appleton asked.

"I'd blow his fucking brains out," Barnes said.

Chapter 10 – Wednesday/Thursday – Jim & Vic

'Can things get any worse?'

Jim wondered as the police car pulled up in front of his house. Fortunately, it was late and maybe most of the neighbors did not see his return, although at this point he couldn't imagine being any more humiliated.

His house was a disaster. Drawers were open and the contents rifled. Moving boxes were emptied out in the middle of the floor and his garage looked like a bomb had gone off. All he could think of was how much Sally would hate this. The thought of strangers pawing through their belongings would've made her scream.

The first message on his voice mail answered the question about things getting any worse. It was from Ross Schwartz, vice president of marketing, and Jim's boss. His message was to the point:

"See me first thing in the morning."

Jim wished someone would pull the railroad spike out of his forehead. Migraine headaches had been a part of his life for several years, but they never failed to surprise him with the intensity of the pain.

He had left his medicine at home when the police took him away and the migraine built the whole time he was with them. The stronger it grew, the more withdrawn he became. The police probably thought he was "clamming up" like some hood on television.

The truth was his migraines took over his life when they went untreated. He had medicine that would abort them, but when it wasn't available for some reason, the pain grew from merely annoying to excruciating in just a few hours. Light bothered his eyes, but worst of all, he just couldn't think right. Simple cognitive functions became unfamiliar. He did know enough to not attempt anything complicated while under a migraine's thumb.

He found his briefcase amid the rubble and retrieved one of the "magic" pills that would remove the spike and took it with a glass of water. It would take about 40 minutes or so for the pain to subside. He went into the family room and cleared some of the mess off the sofa and lay down.

When he got off the sofa about an hour later, he could think. So much had happened that day it was hard to know where to start analyzing.

An unexpected visit by the two cops first thing in the morning got things started. Yet even after their pointed questions, he remained detached from the events unfolding around him. He knew he was innocent and innocent men don't go to jail.

However, the search warrant and discovery of the pistol really unsettled him. Obviously, having a bunch of cops crawling through your house looking, literally, for the smoking gun was unnerving. But, even to that point Jim felt this misunderstanding would be cleared up quickly.

The discovery of the pistol behind the water heater and the questioning downtown pushed this experience from the humiliating to the threatening very quickly. Even now, Jim was trying to think if he knew any criminal lawyers. He had never used a lawyer for anything in the past and had no idea where to begin beyond the Yellow Pages.

But the thing that was really making him crazy was the gun. How could it have gotten there? There seemed to be only one obvious answer, but it was so unthinkable he resisted even considering it. Sally could not, would not have put it there. It was impossible. She hated guns so much that she had made Jim promise that it would be under lock and key, as if it could somehow get out of its vinyl case and hurt her.

The phone rang and he almost threw up it startled him so much. The caller ID showed the call was blocked, meaning whoever was calling entered a code to prevent their number from showing up on the ID.

"Yes," Jim said into the phone.

"Jim. It's Vic. I wondered if you needed some company?" Vic said.

"How did you know I would be awake?" Jim asked.

"Because I'm parked in front of your house and can see you moving around behind the curtains," Vic said.

"You are?" Jim said and hurried to the window to look out.

"What are you doing here?" Jim asked.

"I know what happened today, at least the major parts, and I thought about you coming home to that house alone and with no one to talk to. I guessed you probably wouldn't have called anyone this late at night," Vic said.

"How do you know . . . Yeah, come on in," Jim said.

Jim checked his watch as he walked to the front door. It was 1:22 am.

He made some coffee and cleared a space at the breakfast bar in the kitchen.

"I'm no lawyer, but don't you think you need one?" Vic asked.

"I suppose I do, but I honestly don't know any or where to even start. How did you know what was going on today?" Jim asked.

"As they say in the newspaper business, 'I've got my sources,'" Vic said.

"I got to tell you that I'm not in a mood for games. My butt is on the line here. The police think I may have killed a guy and my boss, Mr. Pole-Up-His-Ass Schwartz, is probably going to fire me," Jim said.

"Sorry," Vic said. "I actually was doing some work for the police department and saw them bring you in this evening."

"The nightmare started this morning when those two characters out of a bad detective movie showed up at my office," Jim said. "They accused me of killing Bonnelli. He's the drunk who killed my wife. Well, they didn't come right out and say I killed him, but that's what it's all about. Even after they questioned me this morning, I didn't think I was a serious suspect. I mean, I know I'm innocent and innocent men don't go to jail.

"I'm sure the whole office was buzzing behind my back. Before my wife was killed, nobody at work would have believed I could kill. They would have stuck with me, for the most part. But, you know, ever since Sally died, it's like people don't know me anymore. They're nice enough, but it's just not the same. I'll bet there is more than a few of them who are thinking, 'I can understand how crazy with rage he must be. How his wife's death drove him to do this horrible thing.'"

"Maybe they're reacting that way because you're not the same," Vic suggested. "People who haven't experienced the sudden violent loss of a loved one just don't get it. They want you to be the same as you were – like you could get over it if you only tried harder. But, believe me, you will never be the same person you were before. The sooner you accept that fact, the sooner you can begin to discover who you have become. A lot of us find that we can't keep our old jobs and old friends. They knew us one way and we aren't that way anymore. We may even be resentful that their lives seem to go on as before, as if the loss meant nothing to them. That's not fair, but it's the truth just the same."

"Is that why you still go to the grief support groups – because the people there understand in a way others can't?" Jim asked.

"Yeah, I guess so. Like I said earlier, part of my healing is helping others in the same boat. Maybe the person I've become is a social worker," Vic said. "But enough of this touchy-feely stuff. What can I do to help you stay out of jail?"

"I need to tell you that I mentioned your name to the police," Jim said.

"Oh. What exactly did you say?" Vic asked.

"Nothing much. I told them I spent the night at home working and they wanted to know if I could supply any witnesses that could place me here at the time of the murder. I told them you were the only person I talked to that night."

"I see. What was their reaction?" Vic asked.

"When I told them we talked around 8:00 pm or so, they didn't pursue the matter because there was plenty of time after that for me to get to Bonnelli's house," Jim said.

"Did you tell them my last name?" Vic asked.

"No. I didn't and I couldn't have if I'd wanted to, because I don't know your last name, although you seem to know a lot about me," Jim said.

"I'm sorry if it appears that I am 'spying' on you or something. I don't have any real secrets. I learned most everything I know about you from the group sessions, observations, and a little work on my computer," Vic said.

"For example, you were surprised when we first met in the parking lot after the group session that I knew you worked for Aargon Insurance. That was easy. You said in the session that you worked for an insurance company and when I approached you in the lot that night, I saw you company's parking sticker on the windshield. I'm sorry if I played a game with you about guessing where you worked. It's just one of my personality quirks."

"I guess right now that all doesn't seem very important," Jim said. "I've so many things racing through my mind I can't concentrate on anything."

"You probably need some sleep. I'll be going," Vic said.

"I couldn't sleep now if I tried," Jim said. "How could this happen to me? Is it never going to end?"

"What did the police want to know? Maybe it would be helpful to go over their questions," Vic said.

"They wanted to know why I killed Bonnelli. Actually, they know or think they know why I killed him. The truth is I thought a lot about killing him," Jim said.

"But, you didn't, right?" Vic asked.

"No, of course not. I can talk a pretty good game, but when it comes down to it, I'm not a violent man. I didn't enjoy playing sports when I was a kid. As close as I want to come to violence is watching football from my sofa. The thought of actually killing a person makes me sick at my stomach. As far as the police go, I don't understand why they questioned me for a couple of hours, then let me go," Jim said. "They found the gun, which I have no idea how it got there and I've no way to verify my alibi of being home all evening."

"My guess is the gun could not be tied to the murder. They probably checked it for prints and took a sample bullet to see if it matched the one that killed what's his name. If the gun didn't match or they couldn't tell one way or the other, then they have no physical evidence tying you to the shooting. As far as your alibi, it is their responsibility to place you at or near the shooting. They don't have any hard evidence you did it. You had a motive, but they have to link you through some evidence to the shooting," Vic said.

"I hope you're right," Jim said. "It all seems so clear on television. Even the plots that twist and turn – you can usually figure those out before the show is over. But when you're right in the middle of it, nothing seems black and white anymore. Take the gun for example. How in the world did it get hidden back behind the water heater?" Jim asked.

"Well, as Sherlock Holmes used to say: 'When you eliminate the probable, whatever is left, no matter how improbable, must be the truth,' or something like that. The answer is your late wife must have put it back there," Vic said.

"I know that's how it looks, but you didn't know my wife. I can't imagine her even touching a gun much less loading it," Jim said.

"What do you mean loading it?" Vic asked.

"I never kept the gun loaded. I bought the thing after there had been some robberies around my apartment complex. I think the guys in the gun shop thought I was some kinda of pansy for buying such a small gun. I took it to a firing range once. Then I put it away unloaded. The gun was in a vinyl case and the clip and some bullets were loose in the original box. I doubt if I cleaned it before packing it away and I know I didn't wipe my prints off. Why would I? There's no way Sally would've loaded the clip and put it in the gun. You might as well ask her to kiss a rattlesnake. That's how frightened she was of guns," Jim said.

"I haven't touched or even seen that gun since Sally and I were married. I always meant to get rid of it, but never did. That's another part of the mystery. The cops seemed to think it had been fired recently, certainly more recently than 18 months ago. I just can't figure out what is going on. Can all of this be coincidental?" Jim wondered. "Oh, my God! Somebody is trying to frame me. Someone wants the cops to think I killed Bonnelli. I'm being setup," Jim said.

"Whoa. Don't you think you've been watching too much television? Who would possibly want to frame you? Do you have those kind of enemies?" Vic asked.

"No. Not at all. I don't have any enemies as far as I know. There may be some envious people at work, but I'm about as innocuous as they come. If this were high school, I'd be voted most likely to never do anything to piss anyone off," Jim said.

"So, why would someone want to frame you? That doesn't make any sense," Vic said.

"What if this isn't about me? What if whoever killed him just wanted to divert attention to someone else?" Jim asked.

"Could be, I suppose, but isn't that still a stretch? I mean that really sounds like a bad episode of *Law and Order*. There's got to be another answer," Vic said.

"I don't know what to think anymore. The most logical explanation is that my wife did something so out of character for her that I didn't know her at all," Jim said. "And that's almost as scary as facing the police questions again."

"How well did you know her?" Vic asked. "I'm sorry. That was a very personal question and I didn't mean to suggest anything."

"It's all right. At this point, I'm questioning everything myself," Jim said.

"We knew each other about three years before we married and dated each other exclusively for about a year. She was in marketing also, but was self-employed and worked for several clients, all in the women's clothing business. That's how we met. We were both at a gathering sponsored by the local marketing association. We ended up at the same table for dinner and thought the whole event was a waste of time. We snuck out after dinner before the speech and went for a drink. We dated off an on for a while, then lost touch. We were both traveling a lot and never seemed to find time when we were both in town," he said.

"Then, about a year before we married, we bumped into each other one weekend and it was like magic. We enjoyed being together before, but this time it was like nothing I had ever known before. We were inseparable. I couldn't think about anything but her and she said she felt the same way. It was not just a sexual attraction. I felt like she was a part of me that had been missing and I hadn't even known it was missing. I felt like I could do anything, but all I really wanted to do was be with her for the rest of my life. When she died I felt like I was going to die too. Actually, it was worse than that. I felt like I was condemned to live so that every minute of every day would remind me that something was gone that can never be recovered. What great sin did I commit that this should be my punishment? Or maybe God was just ticked off and thought it would be great fun to set me up just to watch me fall. Either way, I'm doomed to a life of putting one foot in front of the other. And, if those cops have their way, that will be right to prison," Jim said.

"Sounds like a powerful motivation to kill the man who did this to you," Vic said.

"Yeah, I'm sure it is and if I thought it would bring Sally back or even make me feel just like getting out of bed in the morning I would have gladly killed him with my bare hands. But what's the use? Nothing would change by killing him," Jim said.

"Well, at least he couldn't hurt anyone else," Vic said.

"That's what the judicial system is for," Jim said.

"And they've done such a good job so far, haven't they," Vic said.

"Are you suggesting a vigilante action is what we need to rid society of bad guys?" Jim asked.

"All I'm saying is the judicial system had its chance with Mr. Bonnelli and it failed like it often does. But in the end, true justice was served," Vic said.

Chapter 11 – Wednesday – Shannon & Ling

"Hi. It's me," Ling said.

"Oh. Hi. What's up?" Shannon asked.

"I suppose I could tell you that I was thinking about you and just wanted to hear your voice," Ling said.

"But," Shannon said.

"Well, that's true, but unfortunately this is business. I think I've found something interesting about that shooting victim in the park a couple of days ago," she said. "I happened to overhear another assistant ME here talking about an autopsy of another shooting victim. The guy was shot once in the back of the head with a small caliber gun."

"Really? What else do you know?" Shannon asked.

"That's about it. The autopsy on this guy looked a lot like your park victim. I thought there might be a connection," Ling said.

"Say if that doctor thing doesn't work out, you may have a career in the criminal justice system," Shannon said. "A single gun shot to the back of the head is not all that unusual, but it is close enough to be worth another look. Do you know who the cops are on the case?"

"Detectives Appleton and Barnes," Ling said. "I've worked with them before. They are good cops, I guess, but definitely from the old school. They both still wear overcoats and I heard some other cops laughing that these two still carried revolvers instead of the semi-automatics all the other detectives carry."

"Yeah, I know them too. They work out of the 35th Precinct. I've only bumped into them a couple of times. They solve cases, but haven't had an original idea in the past 15 years, including the notion of female cops," Shannon said. "Maybe I'll run over there and touch base with them. Thanks for the tip."

"How about some lunch later?" Ling asked. "I'm sorry, maybe I'm being too pushy?"

"No, not at all. But I've got a pretty full day and will be on the other side of town at lunch following up on my victim," Shannon said.

"Okay. Sure I understand," Ling said.

"But, if I don't get hung up, maybe we can grab some supper?" Shannon said.

"Oh. That would be great. Will you call me?" Ling asked.

"Sure. Talk to you later," Shannon said and hung up.

'Damn. Why did I do that?' Shannon asked herself. She had made up her mind to put the brakes on this relationship or at least take some control. She dodged lunch successfully, but then put herself right back in the fire for no reason with that dinner invitation.

Was she a lesbian or bi-sexual? She surprised herself by how unimportant the answer to that question was and wondered if her lack of reaction was, in fact, the answer. She had never had a homosexual relationship, but had always been closer to her girl friends than any male lover. She thought that was probably just a girl thing.

She hadn't been kidding when she told Ling that most men considered her a lesbian already. She had not met many men that weren't put off by her size and take charge attitude. Most men didn't really know what to do with a woman who is strong physically and mentally. They often dealt with it by dismissing her as a dyke that way they didn't have to explain to their buddies why they hadn't nailed her.

She couldn't deny the fact that Ling was attractive. The young doctor was almost the physical opposite of herself – small and fine featured. Her Asian skin was clear, smooth, and the color of Shannon's coffee and milk. When the old drunk confronted them in the parking lot that first night, protecting Ling was automatic and it wasn't a police officer's protection. Shannon knew she would have severely damaged the old man if he had touched Ling. The thing that set her off was the immediate fear she sensed from Ling when the man confronted them. No woman should have to feel like that on her way to breakfast or any other time.

She knew that fear. She had felt it herself despite being over six feet tall, athletic, and carrying a large pistol. She could only imagine what Ling must feel – what most other women must feel. Maybe it was too much to ask men to understand how vulnerable women felt and how that powerlessness was reinforced by society. How many times had she heard a male family member say after a woman was murdered or raped at night, 'she should have known better than to go out at that time of night,' like it was the victim's fault.

But, for now, she needed to drop her bid for the Nobel Peace Prize and get back to finding the murderer of a young black man. Nobody in the office seemed to think this was anything more than another gang-related hit, despite the fact that the victim didn't come close to any gang profile, other than being a young, black male.

It was a long shot, but Shannon thought she should check in the Barnes and Appleton on their case. It wouldn't be hard to get information from them, but they always found a way to push her buttons. It was some sort of stupid male ritual that required them to prove their superiority to younger cops, especially female cops. Although it was irritating in its inefficiency, Shannon was smart enough to use it to her advantage.

The 35th Precinct was across town. The homicide detectives there caught a better class of murderers because of the wealthy neighborhoods in their area. Rubbing elbows with the town's wealthy hadn't done anything for the wardrobes of Barnes and Appleton – they still dressed like they did 15 years ago when they got their shields.

The two were expecting Shannon because she called first to make sure they were in, which just gave them time to rehearse their stupid jokes.

"Well, Lenny. Look who's here? It's Dirty Harriett," Appleton said loud enough for the whole squad room to hear.

"Great. She can help us with all these cases us poor dumb flat foots can't handle," Barnes said.

"Hi guys. I see you've been practicing your snappy one-liners," Shannon said.

"Hey. We're 90s kinda guys. You know, sensitive," Barnes said.

"Gee, didn't anyone tell you yet? The 90s are long gone. Real men have gone from being sensitive to submissive," Shannon said. "So submit."

"That's the best offer I've had all year," Appleton said.

"That's the only offer you've had all year," Barnes replied.

"Well, are you guys going to help me out or are we going to do stand up comedy all day?" Shannon asked. She knew a request for help was just the right way to get what she wanted.

"Okay, little girl. You said you had a case with the same MO as one of ours. So what's the story?" Appleton said.

"I understand your victim, a Mr. Bonnelli, had a hole in the back of his head from a small caliber round," she said referring to her notes. "I got one just like that from Monday."

"Could be something," Appleton said. "But aren't you in the low-rent district? Our guy was way up town."

"Okay. We'll show you ours and you show us yours," Barnes said tossing a file across the table to her with a big smile on his face.

"I'll bet you've been waiting a long time to say that," Shannon said with a smile.

"Yeah, but a lot of good it'll do me," Barnes said.

She handed her file to Appleton and began looking over their case. The autopsy report was very similar to her case – single shot to the back of the head from a small caliber round and not at close range.

"Hey," Appleton said after briefly scanning her file. "What are you wasting our time for with this case?"

"What's wrong," Shannon asked.

"I'll tell you what's wrong. Your victim was a young, black male shot late at night in Baker's Park, a known gang hangout," Appleton said. His partner rolled his eyes and shook his head.

"Other than they were both shot in the head, what do a gang banger and one of the most successful real estate developers in town have in common?" Appleton asked.

"First off, the kid wasn't a gang banger. He was a college student and worked in a bank," Shannon said. "And they were both murdered the same way. Isn't is possible there is some connection?"

"Yeah. Maybe Mr. Bonnelli was really a closet gangbanger and tried to muscle in on your guy's turf," Barnes said.

"My victim worked at First United Bank. Maybe Bonnelli had an account there and something fishy was going on?" Shannon asked.

"Yeah. Right," Barnes said.

"You don't think it's worth a look?" Shannon asked.

"No. I don't," Appleton said. "But, we're going to pull Bonnelli's financial records anyhow and if something pops up that could tie your boy to our case, we'll let you know."

"Oh. Gee. Thanks," Shannon gushed and walked out the door.

'What a couple of jerk offs,' she thought.

Her next stop was the bank where Washington had worked. She had been there once the day after the murder, but his supervisor out on vacation. She had called the supervisor, a Ms. Ellroy, and made an appointment to come by.

Ms. Ellroy was well organized and had Washington's file on top of her desk when an assistant showed Shannon in to her office.

"Abraham was such a great kid. I just can't believe he's dead," Ellroy said. "He was smart, ambitious, and a quick learner. To top it off, he was a really nice young man."

"I know this is difficult, but I'm trying to find out why someone wanted to kill him," Shannon said.

"The paper made it sound gang related, although I'll never believe he was mixed up with a gang," Ms. Ellroy said.

"I believe you're right. I don't think it was gang related unless he just happened to be in the wrong place at the wrong time and got caught in a cross fire," Shannon said. "But there has been little gang activity in that park for some months. The cops on that beat say it has been very quiet. The gang task force in looking into that possibility, but even they say it is unlikely that gangs are responsible.

"Can you tell me something about what Mr. Washington did at the bank?" Shannon asked.

"You don't suspect a connection to the bank do you?" Ms. Ellroy asked.

"I'm just looking at all the possibilities. I'm hoping someone here can shed some light on why this young man died," Shannon said. "Can you tell me exactly what he did at the bank?"

"Abraham was in a management training program that lasts two years. During this time he is rotated through just about every department in the bank for some hands-on training. At the end of the program, he would have been recruited by one of the departments. The program is also an opportunity for department managers to identify high-potential individuals," Ellroy said.

"My investigation showed that he was still in college. Is it unusual for someone without a degree to be in a management program?" Shannon asked.

"Unusual, but not unheard of," Ms. Ellroy said. "If I can be candid with you and off the record, we have a difficult time recruiting qualified minority employees. Banks don't pay much until you get into the management ranks. This was a way we could get Abraham locked into our system. I was afraid if we waited until he graduated in the spring that some other company that could pay more would recruit him."

"So you obviously thought highly of him," Shannon said. "Can you tell me where he has worked in the bank and where he was working at the time of his death?"

"Here is his training schedule it begins 14 months ago and lists each department where he worked and the supervisor he reported to," Ms. Ellroy said. "His last assignment was in the safe deposit area."

"Is that considered a high-security job?" Shannon asked.

"Of course, and we did a thorough background check on Abraham before he even joined the management training program. You will find all the details in the folder," Ms. Ellroy said. "But, I'll stake my job on it that you will not connect him to any wrong doing either here or in his private life. He was a fine young man. Besides, there are security cameras everywhere in that area monitored by real people, not just making recordings. You couldn't get away with anything down there."

"Would you mind if I walked down there and looked around?" Shannon asked.

"Well, no, but I'll accompany you. We're a very old bank, trusted by our customers. I would appreciate it if you could be as unobtrusive as possible – without compromising your job, of course," Ms. Ellroy said.

Shannon started to ask Ms. Ellroy if she should change into something more appropriate, but decided against it. The woman had been very forth coming and well organized; no need in ticking her off.

The safe deposit vault was indeed highly secured. There were cameras everywhere and other safeguards. It didn't seem likely that Washington was involved in something illegal here.

Back at her desk, Shannon read through the materials the bank lady had given her. Washington was an ideal employee and, from all she could tell, well liked by everyone he worked with at the bank.

The background report was done by a private security company run by retired cops and respected in the department. It showed Washington was pretty much what he appeared to be. His only living family was an aunt in California. Shannon recognized the name as the person she called to tell of the young man's death. The aunt had taken it hard. As soon as the case closed, the aunt arranged to have the body sent to California.

Her investigation was going nowhere. When she interviewed staff and students that knew Washington, none of them could come up with a reason someone wanted him dead. No jealous boyfriends, no drugs, no cheating, nothing.

As much as she hated to admit it, Barnes and Appleton were probably right. The two cases were not related, which left her with no motive and no witnesses.

Shannon was beginning to think the young man's death was a random act of violence. If that were true, it would make the case difficult, if not impossible to solve. Unless someone came forward with information, she may never know who killed Abraham Washington.

There was another possibility that Shannon hadn't considered so far. Young Mr. Washington might be a victim of a serial killer. Shannon barely considered it a possibility for several reasons. First, serial killers are not as common as people might think. Plenty of cops never work on a serial killer case. Secondly, there was none of ghoulish ritual associated with a serial killer's work. Nothing about this case stood out in any way that was meaningful. Normally, a serial killer wants to sign his work with some kind of mark.

Mutilation and sexual disfigurement were common trademarks of serial killers.

This case had none of those trademarks. It didn't even come across as a hate crime. People who killed in hate crimes were usually filled with rage. They often tortured their victims or humiliated them in some way. Mr. Washington wasn't gay, as far as Shannon could tell and if he was murdered because he was black, there were no indications.

The young man's past was clean. He was not into drugs, or gangs or any type of destructive behavior that Shannon could see. He was just an average citizen that happened to be more ambitious than most.

If she could find a motive, the one most obvious answer was that he was killed by a professional – someone who had one objective and that was to kill the victim as quickly and quietly as possible, then fade away with no witnesses.

Whatever the circumstances, Shannon knew she would solve this case. The answer would be obvious when she had gathered enough information. That's what detective work was really all about. Keep gathering information until two pieces that may not individually seem important fit together in a way to give you a different perspective on the problem.

She listed possible motives and the probability of each on a sheet of paper – a trick her partner had taught her. It was not magic and the answer didn't usually jump off the page, but it could help direct your efforts at the most probably targets.

1. Robbery – Although the money was missing from his wallet, Shannon doubted Washington was robbed. More likely the money was taken as a diversion. Still, it could not be completely ruled out.

2. Lovers' quarrel – Nobody reported any suggestion that he had a steady girlfriend or even dated much. Between a full time job and a full college schedule, it would be hard to find time for much of a social life. Shannon felt she knew the young man well enough now to be fairly sure that a lovers' quarrel or triangle wasn't much of a possible

3. Accident – Maybe the victim walked into a gang incident and caught a stray bullet. Again possible, but not probable. They had

conducted a thorough search of the park and found no evidence of a shooting – no shells were found and no one reported any noise. Besides, gang bangers liked big guns – 9 mm or bigger – and usually went for semi-automatics. Their idea of shooting someone was to empty a clip in their direction and hope one bullet hit. The small caliber of the weapon, probably a .22 or .25 caliber, was inconsistent with the gang image.

4. Professional hit – The method of execution was consistent with a professional job – small caliber gun, maybe with some silencing device, and a single shot to the back of the head. A pro would normally have gotten closer to make sure he only needed one shot, but if the killer had used a rifle, then the shot could have come from a short distance, but far enough away to not leave powder burns. The problem with this possible solution was why Washington? He didn't seem to have any enemies or be mixed up in any activity that would attract a professional killer. The bank was doing its own investigation of Washington to make sure nothing was going on, but Shannon didn't think that was likely.

5. Serial killer – Shannon resisted giving this possibility much consideration. She had never worked on a serial murder case and didn't know any cops who had. However, it did solve one puzzling question: motive. Serial killers were, by definition, crazy, so their motives were something personal that only became apparent when several killing were put together and some pattern emerged that linked the victims. At least, that's what she had learned at an FBI-sponsored workshop she attended a few years ago. Sometimes the pattern was so twisted by the killer's psychosis that it took a long time to discover. A young, attractive black man may have been the type to set off a serial killer.

Shannon looked at her list and thought that she must be missing something – some piece that would make sense, even in a crazy way, of what happened. Absent that, she fell back on what her years of experience and training told her to do. She decided to go back to the park about the same time the victim left the college to walk home. She would re-canvass the students and anyone who might be on the street or in the park at that time of night. She would also talk to the girl again to see if she remembered anything. Police work like so many other jobs was basically putting one foot in front of the other until you got somewhere that things began to make sense.

And, even though she thought it was a waste of time, she put in a request through information services for any other murders that fit this description in the past five years. If, on the very odd chance, there were a serial killer out there maybe a pattern would emerge. The same search might point to a professional that killed this way.

She wished her partner were here. Koslowski had a way of cutting to the heart of a problem. He had five more years of experience in homicide and had been her original partner when she joined the unit. Once he got past the need to protect her, they had been a good team. He was a solid man with a stable marriage and three kids. Shannon had been to their house on many occasions and the kids called her "aunt Shannon." His wife, Mary Ruth, was a no nonsense woman with no obvious insecurity about her husband partnered with a single woman. Although she and Shannon didn't really have a lot in common, they had a kind of "big sister – little sister" relationship even though Shannon was a good 10 inches taller.

Mary Ruth was a strong, self-reliant woman who would have been appalled to be labeled a "feminist." Nevertheless, Shannon admired her emotional strength and sense of purpose. They talked on several occasions about Shannon's relationships or lack there of. Shannon realized that she wanted to talk to Mary Ruth as much as she did her husband. This whole thing with Ling was unexpected, frightening, and exciting all at the same time.

Too many times is the past few days, Shannon, who prided herself of being focused, found herself somewhere else. A place that she didn't remember existing before Ling. Now, it was hard for Shannon to get her out of her mind. Ling's dark eyes seemed to look right inside of her. Every time she looked at Shannon with that very slight smile, it was as if there was some energy flowing between them. Shannon felt a warmth, both physically and emotionally, that was at once wonderful and disturbing.

Shannon hadn't thought too much about the possible physical aspects of this relationship and when she did it almost made her laugh at her naiveté. However, Shannon wanted to take things slowly. No matter how this turned out, she liked Ling and didn't want to destroy a burgeoning friendship. Maybe that would be impossible, but at some point, she was going to have to make a decision and if they had not become physical, that decision might be easier. Once they became lovers, things would get real complicated. Shannon wanted to keep her options open as long as possible. Mary Ruth would say, as she had so pointedly in the past, that Shannon was just like a man – unwilling to commit to a relationship, then confused about why it didn't last.

Shannon dialed Ling's number after looking around the squad room to make sure no one was close enough to over-hear her conversation.

"Dr. Ya speaking."

"What are you wearing?" Shannon asked.

"What did you say? Who is … Shannon?"

"Sorry. I couldn't resist," Shannon said.

"Okay. What's this all about?" Ling laughed.

"Are you still free for dinner?" Shannon asked. "How about I pick you up at your office in two and a half hours or so?"

"That sounds great. I should be clear by then, but I forgot I'm on call again tonight. I hope that doesn't screw up our evening."

"You're talking to a cop. I know all about evenings being screwed up. Now, I still need to know what you're wearing," Shannon said.

"I'm wearing a pants outfit. Do I need to change into something nicer?"

"No, pants are perfect. I'll see you about 6:30," Shannon said and hung up.

Shannon had enough time to get back to her apartment, change clothes, and get her motorcycle cleaned up before heading back to pick up Ling. She had looked for a long time to find an apartment in the near downtown area with a garage. It was expensive, but she wasn't willing to part with the cycle that her father rode for years before he died. They had not been close for many years, but Shannon wanted to hold on to one of the few things they shared. Her father had taught her to ride just before he and Shannon's mother divorced. Shannon had another motorcycle; one more suited for a young woman her dad thought, which she rode for years, but never again with her dad. When he left her the Harley in his will, she sold her other bike and taught herself to handle a "man's bike."

She was strong enough to muscle the big bike around and was an accomplished rider. The only time her partner had ever told her she looked sexy was when she showed up at his house one afternoon for hamburgers in the backyard wearing her black leather pants and jacket and her long blond hair pulled back in a pony tail. She never wore the leathers back to his house again.

It was a cool evening, but Shannon decided to go with jeans and her leather jacket rather than the full outfit. She cleaned up the bike and tied down an extra leather coat she had on the seat behind her. She wasn't planning to go very far from Ling's office for the first ride. Besides, Ling's pants would be no match for the cool night air on the back of a motorcycle for very long.

Shannon was strangely excited as she rode back into the downtown area. The wind felt good on her face and the bike vibrated between her legs. Although she was not sexually aroused at the thought of being with Ling, she was excited with anticipation at Ling's surprise when she saw the bike.

When she got to the ME's office, Shannon parked her bike in an official vehicle only slot. She got off the bike and started in, then thought better of it. She dialed Ling's number from her cell phone and told her she was doubled parked out front and would Ling mind coming down?

Shannon sat on her bike and waited. Her parking place was just to the left of the entrance to the building. Ling would see her almost immediately when she came out.

The look on Ling's face when she walked out the door was worth any inconvenience making the arrangements had entailed. Ling's mouth dropped open and her dark eyes opened wide with surprise. Her right hand flew up to her mouth as if to stop a scream from escaping.

Shannon stood up and stepped away from the bike so Ling could get a good look at the Harley.

"What is this?" Ling asked.

"I told you I would take you for a ride, didn't I?" Shannon said.

"I didn't think you … I mean I …" Ling sputtered. "It's so big."

A small look of panic passed over Ling's face. "I've never been this close to one before."

Shannon threw her right leg over the bike and pulled it upright and kicked the kickstand back. "You haven't changed your mind have you?"

"Oh. No, not at all. I … you just caught me off guard," Ling said.

Shannon kicked the bike to life and Ling covered her ears at the roar. The sound seemed to physically push her back slightly.

"You'll get used to the noise," Shannon said and handed Ling the spare leather jacket. "You'll be more comfortable with this on."

Ling put on the coat and almost disappeared. Shannon laughed and Ling did too. Shannon held out her hand to help Ling on. The young doctor was almost too small to get on the bike. Shannon showed her the foot peg and Ling stepped on it with her left foot and swung up on to the bike. Shannon made sure both feet were on the pegs.

"Keep your feet on the pegs and hold on to me," Shannon said over her shoulder. "We don't have far to go."

Ling reached around Shannon's middle and leaned against her back. Shannon took Ling's hands and put them under her coat to protect them from the cold, at least that's what she told herself. Even through her leather jacket, Shannon could imagine she felt Ling's breasts against her back and Ling's hands were half way between her waist to her breasts. All Ling had to do was move her hands up a few inches.

Shannon shook her head slightly to get focused on getting them where they were going without eating someone's bumper. She hit the throttle and the big bike accelerated sharply. Ling's grip tightened around her and it felt good.

Shannon took them to a diner on the edge of downtown near an industrial district about 30 minutes from the ME's office this time of night.

When they arrived, Shannon backed the bike into a space where other motorcycles were parked. She reached around and helped Ling off the bike, then leaned the Harley over on its kickstand and got off herself.

"Wow," Ling said. "That was nothing like I imagined it would be."

"I hope it was okay?" Shannon said.

"I just need to catch my breath," Ling said. "You were magnificent. I was scared, but not frightened. Do you know what I mean? It's like going to a horror movie and you're scared, but you know it's going to be all right and you're safe. That's how I felt. Thank you so much," Ling said and threw her arms around Shannon, then pulled back self-consciously.

The diner looked like it hadn't changed since the day it opened in the 50s – alternately black and white linoleum square tiles; lots of chrome on the table and chair legs; and best of all, a jukebox in one corner. A closer look revealed that most of the diner was new. The owner was riding the "everything old is new again" trend in restaurants. The diner was a popular hangout for bikers that were CPAs and other professionals during the day.

They found a booth in a corner and slid in. Shannon reached behind her back, then took off her jacket and put it beside her.

"You're carrying a gun, aren't you?" Ling asked. "I thought I felt it when we were on the bike."

"Sorry. Department regulations. Even when we aren't on duty, we're on duty," Shannon said. "I guess I kinda of forget that it can be disturbing to civilians."

"I think it's sexy," Ling said.

"Really? I assumed that someone who regularly had to cut up people killed with these things would find them offensive," Shannon said.

"Have you ever, you know, shot anyone?" Ling asked.

"No. Thank God. I've pulled my weapon several times, actually quite a few times when making arrests, but I've never fired it in the line of duty and I hope I never have to," Shannon said.

They talked over cheeseburgers, French fries, and milk shakes about everything it seemed to Shannon. It was almost like they couldn't get to know each other fast enough. Somehow, when she was with Ling the questions and doubts about this relationship seem far away and unimportant. Shannon prided herself on her concentration on the job, but it was nothing like she felt now. If there were other people in the diner, she wasn't aware of them and the jukebox must have been broken, because later she couldn't remember a song that played.

"How did you come to be a doctor?" Shannon asked over coffee.

"That's a long story I'm sure you don't want to hear," Ling said.

"I want to know everything about you," Shannon said.

Ling stared at her for a moment and her eyes became moist. "I'm sorry," she said as she regained control.

"You know something? You don't have to be sorry for anything with me," Shannon said.

Another tear rolled down Ling's cheek. "You don't have any idea what a gift that is," Ling said.

"Tell me," Shannon said.

"My parents came to the U.S. from China right after World War II as children of refugees. The two families both were settled in San Francisco. When they were in their late teens, they married. Neither spoke English, but they worked two jobs each and saved their money. After a couple of years, they bought a small dry cleaning business with an apartment over it near China Town. They continued to work hard even after they owned the business and building free and clear. I was an only child and they poured everything into me. I was smart and inherited their work ethic. My parents thought doctors were gods and that's what they wanted for me. I was smart enough to get a scholarship to any state college in California, but that wasn't good enough for me. My parents sent me to Northwestern. I got some scholarship money, but private college is very expensive," Ling said.

"I was admitted to medical school at the University of Chicago, where I graduated with honors. My parents were in heaven. They were a little confused about my choice of pathology as a career path; I think they thought I would be a brain surgeon or something. But I was a doctor and that made all their sacrifices worthwhile. Then, I ruined their lives," Ling said.

"You told them you were a lesbian," Shannon said.

"They couldn't handle that and they will barely speak to me now. I haven't talked to them in many weeks," Ling said.

"That must have been tough – to disappoint your parents, I mean," Shannon said.

"Oh, no. I just blurted it out one morning over breakfast like I was asking for a cup of tea. Miss sophisticated, big city girl just rips out the hearts of her parents. All my gay friends used to brag about how "out" they were and if you weren't out you were a coward and denying who you are. That sounded really cool when we were together, but dumping it on two old people who barely understand English much less the notion of anyone being gay was a different experience. I just took everything they worked for their whole lives and threw it back in their faces," Ling said. I love being a doctor, which is a good thing because it is the only thing I've going for me," Ling said.

"No it's not," Shannon said and reached across the table and took her hand.

They starred at each other for a moment, before Ling said, "Your turn."

"Oh, well. My story is not as inspiring as you and being a cop is a long way from being a doctor," Shannon said.

"Don't put me on that pedestal. I've a talent for learning – that's it. I'm sorry; I guess my life story sounded like bragging. School is all I've ever been good at, so I've never thought it was that special," Ling said. "I know you're a good cop. I've asked around."

"You've been investigating me?" Shannon said. "Okay. I grew up in your typical American home with a stay-at-home mother and hard-working dad. I've a sister who lives in Arizona. We talk, but we're not really close. I was an athlete in high school and got a scholarship to college," Shannon said.

"In basketball?" Ling asked.

"No, in ping pong. Of course, in basketball. I could dunk with both hands. But, I didn't take it," Shannon said.

"Why not?" Ling asked.

"Because I also got a scholarship in music, which was my real love," Shannon said.

"You're a musician?" Ling said.

"Don't sound shocked. Yes, I'm or was a musician," Shannon said. "I got a good music scholarship to a state university. My mother was excited, but my dad didn't understand why I wouldn't pursue basketball. He assumed I would be an all-American and get a great coaching job somewhere. I tried to do both for a while, but a violinist can't afford to get her hands banged up, which happens about every day in basketball."

"I love the violin," Ling said. "Do you still play?"

"No, I gave it up in my junior year. My parents divorced and it just took everything out of me. I was really mad at my dad. I thought he was the most selfish man in the whole world. My mom was devastated and I guess I took her side. I didn't speak to my dad for quite a few years. When my mom died of breast cancer, I told him I didn't want him at the funeral. About six months after my mom's death, I started thinking about reconciling with my dad. He had moved to California and remarried. I meant to write him a letter or give him a call, but I never seemed to get around to it. I had to finish college, so I went into the criminal justice degree program and graduated two years later. I joined the force and worked patrol of several years. When the chance came, I took the entrance exam and to my surprise was accepted into the detective program and, as they say the rest is history," Shannon said.

"Is your dad still in California and did you ever contact him?" Ling asked.

"No, I never got around to contacting him. Two years ago, he dropped dead of a heart attack. I met his wife for the first time at the funeral. I was sure she would hate me, but she was very gracious. After the funeral we went back to their house. There were a lot of his friends there and some of our relatives. His wife, her name is Jane, took me aside and said she had something to show me. We went out to the garage and there under a tarp was the motorcycle. She told me that she knew my dad wanted me to have it. She said that he had told her how he taught me to ride when I was in high school and how he had bought me my own motorcycle, although a lot smaller and tamer than his Harley. She said that it had been his dream for the two of us to take a long motorcycle trip when I got out of college. I guess he hadn't counted on me cutting him off," Shannon said.

They sat there in silence for a while. The jukebox was playing Elvis singing *"Are You Lonesome Tonight?"* Shannon and Ling looked into each other's eyes and began to giggle.

"Wow. That was right out of a grade B movie, wasn't it?" Shannon said. "The script probably said:

Poignant moment.

Cue music.

Makeup, where are the false tears?"

"Hey, I liked those old tear jerkers," Ling said.

Shannon didn't want to break the moment, but it was getting late and the diner was closing.

Shannon mounted the bike after giving Ling the leather coat. Ling hopped on the back like she had done it a hundred times. Shannon fired up the Harley and began pulling away. She felt Ling pressing against her back and her hands around her waist.

As Shannon was easing out of the parking lot, Ling's right hand slipped under her sweatshirt. Shannon felt her hand on her bare stomach and as it slid up. She felt herself tense. Ling's small hand covered Shannon's large, bare breast.

Shannon felt a surge of energy through her whole body. She was paralyzed with excitement. She stalled the bike and managed to put her foot down in time to keep them from falling over.

She sat there for a few seconds or hours. When the bike stopped, Ling's touch became tentative. Now she quickly withdrew her hand and leaned back away from Shannon.

Shannon's head cleared slightly. She twisted around and looked at Ling. Ling had pulled back and her head was bowed. Shannon gently took Ling's chin in her hand and slowly raised her head. Ling would not meet her gaze. Shannon could sense an 'I'm sorry' about to spill out.

"If you do that while I'm trying to drive, I'll kill us both," she said.

She quickly kissed Ling on the mouth. Ling opened her eyes in surprise.

"Hold on," Shannon said.

She fired up the Harley and roared out of the parking lot and down the street.

Chapter 12 – Thursday – Jim & Sam

As Jim parked his car the next morning, he wondered how he was going to get through the day. Two hours of sleep and two pots of coffee is not the recommended breakfast of champions.

Last night his emotions were completely out of control one minute and completely numb the next. Like most men, Jim prided himself on being in control most of the time, but last night he was sure he had lost his mind. It was like being in a boxing ring blind-folded with ten opponents – no matter which way he turned, he got hit.

He couldn't calm down. Every time he thought he could relax, a wave of panic swept over him – it felt like his heart was floating in his chest and it was hard to breathe. He couldn't stop moving or peeing.

Then, just as quickly, he went numb. It was like all of his emotions just died – as if all sensory information that might affect an emotion was blocked.

At one point, he began to wonder if maybe he didn't kill Bonnelli after all. He was alone that night and the police did find the gun. Maybe he just blocked it out.

Right now, all he knew for sure was that every part of his body hurt, his emotions were raw as fresh ground beef and he had to face his boss, the most annoying person in his life. Getting through that meeting without blowing up will be a real accomplishment, Jim thought, especially since Schwartz was probably going to fire him anyway.

His friend Bill in Graphics was from Texas and he would come in on Monday after one of his wild weekends and pronounce: 'I feel like I was shot at and missed and shit at and hit.'

Jim never quite understood until this morning what Bill meant by that. He wished he could call Bill and tell him he finally understood what the crazy Texan meant, but Bill, like so many of his other so-called friends didn't seem to know how to act around him. Invitations to after-work beer and darts stopped after Sally's death and never really resumed along with most other social invitations.

He put on his most confident smile and strode resolutely into the building – all of which crumbled when his ID card failed to open the security gate and the red light flashed. He swiped the card again, but it still didn't work. There was a line forming behind him. A security guard was walking toward him.

Just then, an arm reached around him, took the card out of his hand, and turned it around. He swiped the card again and the gate opened.

He looked back to thank his savior with a snappy one-liner about a tough night only to look into the eyes of Samantha, his secretary. For a brief moment, he desperately wanted to hug her or, more specifically, he wanted her to hug him. And, for just the blink of an eye, Jim thought he saw something in her eyes – a warmness that he could easily sink into right now and tell the world to go to hell.

He quickly righted himself the best he could emotionally, but not completely. He had always been a little more open with Samantha than was prudent in most 'boss-secretary' relationships. Samantha had never betrayed a confidence and never indicated she considered the relationship anything more than it was.

When Jim had made Assistant V.P., he 'inherited' Samantha because secretaries were assigned to positions, not persons. Everyone rolled their eyes when her name came up, because she was supposed to be a real bear to work with.

Jim quickly discovered that Samantha was a very intelligent, dedicated worker capable of a great deal, but never given the chance. Previous supervisors had been either condescending or were threatened by her abilities.

Jim began giving Samantha more responsibility and she took it and wanted more. The whole marketing department was amazed at how Jim had "tamed" Samantha, which he resented and quickly pointed out that the only thing he did was recognize a good employee and let her do her job.

Samantha was about Jim's age and attractive, but not "flashy." She worked her way up from an entry level job out of high school and along the way got a college degree in psychology by going to class a night. Jim offered to get her into a management-training track, but she refused.

When Jim and Sally married, Samantha was the only person from work who came to the wedding even though others were invited. She was genuinely happy for Jim and seemed to hit it off with Sally right away.

The horrible days after Sally's death are like a fog in Jim's memory with one exception and that was Samantha. She was there almost immediately it seemed. She brought casseroles. She helped Jim make the funeral arrangements. She cleaned the house and made dinner.

When Jim's sister finally showed up from out of town the day of the funeral and started giving Samantha orders, Jim took her into another room and told her Samantha was a friend, not a servant.

He remembered all of this, but the thing that really stuck in his memory and his heart was that Samantha was the only person who did not look him in the eyes and ask, "Are you alright?"

She didn't ask, "what can I do to help?" or "call me if you need anything?" She took charge and did those things that obviously needed doing and most of it was on her own time.

"Thanks," he mumbled, as they walked into the building. "I guess everyone in the company knows what's happening to me."

"Yeah, pretty much," she said.

Samantha was honest even when it hurt.

"You have a meeting with Schwartz at 9:00," she said. "I'm sure you would rather have a root canal without pain killer, but I couldn't arrange the swap."

Jim smiled despite the pain. "You're fired," he said.

They reached the office and Jim looked at the mail Samantha had arranged on his desk. He shuffled through the mail twice without any idea of what he had just looked at. The truth was since Sally's death Samantha had kept things going pretty much by herself.

"Samantha, could you come in please?"

Samantha sat in a chair across from Jim with her pad.

"Sam, there is a good chance I'm going to be fired at this meeting," he said. He rarely called her Sam – it seemed too affectionate for the office, but he knew she liked it.

"You don't know that for sure," she said. "They might just want you to get counseling or something."

"No, I think after the police searched my house and all but charged me with murder, I can pretty much kiss my career goodbye," he said. "Besides, you and I know my work has been less than inspired since Sally died and anything good that has come out of this office has been your idea, not mine."

"I never meant to undermine your…" she said.

"No, no, that's not what I meant," he said. "I'm very proud of everything you have done and you deserve a lot more credit than you've received. I just don't want you to feel like you have to go down with a sinking ship. I'll do everything I can to make sure none of my stink rubs off on you. The one coherent thing I've done in the recent past is to place a detailed written evaluation of your performance in your personnel file complete with documentation of projects completed, goals accomplished, the whole works. Hopefully, it will serve as a solid recommendation to keep your career on track."

"I don't know what to say," Samantha said. "No one every did anything like that for me. But, you aren't down yet and I'm not giving up on you and you shouldn't give up either."

"I don't know," he said. "The police found a gun I own hidden behind the water heater in the garage. They said it had been fired recently and matched the type of gun that killed Bonnelli. I've no idea how it got there. I couldn't provide an alibi for the night he died. I don't remember what I was doing, except that I was home alone. They almost have me convinced that I killed him. God knows I hated him enough. Maybe I did and just blocked it out."

"I'll never believe that," Samantha said. "I'll never believe you could kill someone, no matter how much you hated him."

"Before Sally died, I couldn't agree with you more. I couldn't imagine circumstances in which I would kill another human," he said. "But I'm not that person anymore. I changed and I'm not sure who this new person is. You're the only person I knew before Sally died I can still talk to. Everyone else either walks around me like I'm made of crystal and one wrong word will shatter me or they are mad because they want everything back the way it used to be.

"I met this guy at the grief support group I went to and he said that when you suffered a horrible loss like I did – and he did too – that you change. You're not the same person you were before the loss. Your old friends and even some of your family don't know you anymore. They're uncomfortable around you – afraid to have a good time and that makes them angry. They want you to be the way you were so they can be the way they were, but that's just not going to happen. He says most of us end up changing jobs and maybe even careers, dropping old relationships because they remind us too much of what we have lost," he said. "Does any of this make sense to you?"

"Yes, it does to a certain extent," Samantha said. "However, I think it sells the human soul's capacity for healing a little short."

"What do you mean by that," he said.

"I should probably keep my big mouth shut," she said.

"No, I want to know what you think. It's important to me," he said.

"I've no right to talk to you about healing after what you've gone through. I couldn't begin to understand the pain you must feel," she said.

"Well, at least tell me if you think I've changed since Sally died and why is it that you're the only person in my life that still seems to think I'm Jim Jackson," he said.

"I suppose we can get bogged down in semantics, but I don't believe you have changed at a fundamental level. If you had broken a leg and were in a cast up to your hip, you would have 'changed.' You couldn't climb stairs or swim or play golf and I imagine sex would be challenging. But, if the doctor set the leg correctly and you allowed it to heal and did physical therapy, at some point the leg would be back to some semblance of normal. You could then climb stairs and play golf and whatever," she said. "You suffered a severe emotional fracture, one that may never heal as completely as a broken leg, but it will get better with time and therapy. Which is a long answer to say, yes you have changed, but I believe you're still Jim Jackson, a man of intelligence, honor, and courage," she said. "And, you're not a murderer."

Jim starred at her for a moment and realized his eyes were filling with tears. Rather than turn away with some fake cough or phony throat clearing sound, Jim took out his handkerchief and wiped his eyes, then handed it to Samantha for her eyes were quite teary also.

"It's almost 9:00. I guess I better go," he said.

Chapter 13 – Thursday – Shannon & Jimmy

"Hey, O'Brien, you got a message from that chink ME about that spook that got wasted in the park the other night," Jimmy hollered as she walked into the squad room.

Jimmy was a 20-something civilian employee of the department who answered non-emergency phones, got coffee, made copies, and was a flaming asshole. He had some kind of strong family political connections to get this job, probably because he wasn't smart enough to get it on his own.

As Shannon walked through the squad room toward the locker room in the back, she discretely motioned Jimmy to follow her. The locker room was not built with the idea that there would ever be female police officers, so it was an informal unisex arrangement with men on the left and women on the right and a small shared exercise area in the middle.

Jimmy followed her into the locker room and his eyes lit up as she turned into the women's side. He was stupid enough and vain enough to believe that she had something in mind for him. She did.

Shannon looked around the women's locker room to make sure it was empty. Jimmy was almost drooling. When she turned toward him, he stepped to her and to his surprise, she grabbed his crotch and squeezed. He started to scream, but she put her other hand over his mouth and slammed him back against the lockers.

"If you ever use words like that in my presence again, I'll pull these two little peanuts you call testicles off and stuff them down your throat. Do you understand me?" she said. "Do you?"

Jimmy had both hands on Shannon's trying to break her grip to no avail. The harder he struggled, the tighter she squeezed. He nodded in agreement and she let go.

He slid to the floor, doubled over in pain and gasping for air.

"I'll have your badge for this you Amazon bitch," he said. "My family has connections with the police commissioner. Nobody does this to me a gets away with it."

"That's where you're wrong again, Jimbo," Shannon said. "You aren't going to say anything or I'll be forced to charge you with the attempted sexual assault of a police officer."

"What are you talking about? You lured me in here – that's entrapment. You attacked me," he said.

"I don't know what you're talking about," Shannon said. "Remember the security cameras they put in a couple of months ago? When the investigators review the tapes, they will see you following me into the women's locker room. Where, I'll testify, you attacked me and I was forced to defend myself."

"But, you motioned for me to follow you – that's entrapment," Jimmy said.

"Unfortunately, Jimmy my notepad might have been positioned so that it blocked the security camera's view of my other hand. The tape may not be able to verify your account. So, it'll be your word against mine. Mine, and every other female cop and employee in this squad who has been harassed by you at some point. Besides, Jimmy you know what happens to people who make trouble for police officers. Now get your scrawny ass out of my sight and if I even get a hint that you're thinking about some kind of pay back, I'll make this little incident look like a tea party with your grandmother. The word is out on you Jimmy. Don't make any mistakes or there will be some very angry cops looking for you," Shannon said.

Jimmy got to his feet and stood up as straight as he could. He glanced out the door to see if he could leave the women's locker room unnoticed and turned and gave Shannon the 'bird' and left.

"That's not nice, Jimmy," she said as he left.

Extortion, assault, and entrapment – three felonies and she hadn't even broken a sweat. Shannon didn't feel good about what she had done to Jimmy, well that was not exactly true. She actually felt pretty good about banging the little worm around. He was a parasite, a racist, a pervert, and God knows what else. What bothered her was that it didn't bother her.

She knew what set her off. It was the comment about 'that chink ME' that really got to her. She couldn't lose control every time some jerk made some slur or looked at Ling funny.

She hung up her coat in her locker and went to her desk to call Ling after looking through her other messages. Most were routine, but there was one from Appleton, which mildly surprised her. Ling's message said she had some 'interesting news on the Washington case.' Shannon wondered if this was a ploy to see her again.

Their last contact was at the diner when they had talked and shared their stories like they were life-long friends. Then as they were leaving on Shannon's motorcycle, Ling's small, delicate hand slipping under Shannon's sweatshirt and covering her bare breast. The electricity that shot through her body was incredible – she could still feel it.

Shannon had surprised herself as much as she surprised Ling by turning around and kissing her full on the mouth. It seemed so natural that Shannon never thought about it until the next day.

As they roared off on Shannon's bike, they were both charged with sexual energy and anticipation, but unsure of the other. As they rode, Shannon panicked with indecision and uncertainty. Should she go to her place or Ling's or where? And what would they do when they got there? Had Ling's beeper not gone off, Shannon might have driven around all night unsure of what next.

The beeper cleared everything up for both of them, at least for that moment. Shannon had no idea what Ling was thinking. But the way Ling's arms were wrapped low on her hips as they roared through the streets made Shannon think Ling wasn't ready for the evening to end until the beeper threw cold water on their emotions.

Shannon had not talked to her since last night and felt a little awkward calling now, even though this was business.

"Hey, it's me," she said when Ling answered.

"Oh, hi stranger," Ling said.

"Ouch. Listen. I'm sorry. I've been…I guess I wasn't sure what to say," she said.

"Just don't say it was a one-shot deal that won't happen again," Ling said. "Please don't say that."

"Look. I don't know what it was, but I'm sure it wasn't that. I'm not looking to back out of anything or claim temporary insanity and since we weren't drinking, I can't say I was drunk. I just never considered this type of relationship and I'm trying to get my mind around it," Shannon said.

"Forget your mind," Ling said. "What do your emotions say?"

"I'm not sure I can always trust my emotions," Shannon said. "But right now they are more alive than I can remember in a long time. I'm not going anywhere anytime soon."

"Well, that's a start," Ling said.

"So, let's get back to police work, before I beat someone else up today because of you," Shannon said.

"What!" Ling said.

"Never mind. I'll tell you later. What did you find out that was so interesting about the Washington case or were you just trying to come up with an excuse to hustle me?" Shannon said.

"You're a naughty girl," Ling said. "I'm glad I called your buddies, Laurel and Hardy with the same information."

"So that explains the call from Appleton," Shannon said. "Listen, if you keep sharing information with those guys no more rides on my motorcycle, got it?"

"You are domineering, aren't you? I discovered something interesting that links Washington case and the case your two friends are working. Based on some further ballistics examinations, it's highly likely they are related," she said.

"How do you figure that," Shannon said. "There's no weapon from my case and you said the bullet fragments were too small for matching."

"I was looking at some of the fragments under the microscope and noticed some abnormalities. I'm not an expert in ballistics, so I packed them off to the FBI lab, and they confirmed that the bullets were tampered with to make them even more explosive than normal hollow points.

"On a hunch, I sent Twiddle Dumb and Twiddle Dee's fragments off and the feds say they were doctored in the same way," Ling said.

"Wow. Way to go. That's what we call a break in the case. No wonder Appleton called. All of a sudden we got a new ball game," Shannon said.

"There's more," Ling said. "I went back ten years. There have been eight other unsolved murders involving single shots to the back of the head with small caliber weapons like these two. I've an order to pull bullet fragments for all the cases so we can ship them to the FBI."

"Are you saying this may be the work of a serial killer?" Shannon asked.

"That's your department," Ling said. "But it seems worth checking out."

"You're right on about that," Shannon said. "Let me know as soon as you get any results back. And good work, girl."

Shannon had never worked a serial killer case and the thought was exciting, although this was case was nowhere near that stage yet. She needed to calm down before she called Appleton. If he got wind of her excitement, there would be no end to the jokes.

When Shannon finally got Appleton on the phone, he was less than excited about looking for a connection between the Bonnelli case and the Washington murder.

"Yeah, I know, but we think we got our shooter," Appleton said. "We have a reasonably strong case against the husband of the woman Bonnelli killed in a car crash. He had motive, opportunity, and a gun of the right caliber. We just can't put him at the scene."

"Doesn't the possibility of a serial killer seem worth pursuing?" Shannon asked.

"Listen kid, when you've been doing this as long as we have you find out that most so-called serial killer cases are not that at all," Appleton said. "Young detectives want to make everything complicated and look for the hardest answer. I'm here to tell you, it is almost always the easiest, most obvious that's the correct answer."

"But, we can't ignore the evidence of the fragments can we?" Shannon said, thinking 'you condescending bastard.'

"I would if I could," said Appleton. "But my captain has already gotten a call from the police commissioner about a 'break' the in Bonnelli case. So, I have to waste my time chasing this rabbit. Say, you wouldn't know where that leak came from would you"

"It didn't come from me, you arrogant jerk. We're on the same team, remember?" Shannon said.

"All right, don't bite my head off. Let's just get our cases solved and get everybody off our backs," Appleton said. "If you're free, my partner and I can be in your shop in an hour with our files on the Bonnelli case. Maybe we can go over both cases again and see if we missed something."

"That sounds like a plan. I'll have us a room to work in and I'll even spring for some coffee and donuts," Shannon said.

"See you in an hour and we'll bring the eats," Appleton said.

Well, this is going down in the books as one of her more unusual days and she was only 90 minutes into her shift. She secured one of the workrooms and assembled her file on the Washington case while waiting for Appleton and his partner Barnes to show up.

No matter how many times she ran through the facts, nothing about the shooting or Washington's life pointed to a direction she should follow in solving the case. The new information that the bullets that killed Washington and Bonnelli were both doctored in the same way had seemed very important 20 minutes ago, but not sitting alone in the workroom with all the other evidence pointing nowhere, she began to think that Appleton was right.

Speak of the devil, she thought as Appleton walked in with a box full of files and evidence. He was followed by Barnes carrying a couple of paper bags from the deli down the street.

"We got some of low-fat bagels, but weren't sure what flavor you might like, and low-fat, flavored cream cheese, of course," Barnes said.

"Of course," Shannon said with some surprise.

"And double lattes with skim milk all around. Here's some bottled water and that ought to hold us for awhile," Barnes said.

"I'm speechless," Shannon said.

"What did you expect? And what was that crack about coffee and donuts? Do you have any idea how much fat is in one of those donuts? I could bust you for attempted assault on my arteries," Appleton said.

"I'm sorry, this is just not what I expected," Shannon said.

"Hey, what can I say? We're 90's kinda guys," Barnes said.

"Lenny, the 90s have been over for many years now," Shannon said.

"We're moving as fast as we can," Barnes said.

"Okay, now that we've got the pleasantries out of the way, let's solve some murders and earn us all some brownie points," Appleton said. "Why don't we go over our case against this guy Jackson, who we like in the Bonnelli shooting?"

Shannon let Appleton and Barnes talk for the next 20 minutes as they built their case against Jackson. Despite their appearance, she had to admit these guys were thorough – they didn't miss much and followed up on all the leads. Their case against Jackson was compelling, but circumstantial, by their own admission.

She took the floor next and went over the Washington case, which was much less complete, because there was no suspect, no motive, no weapon, and no clues.

"Bruce, you said over the phone that the answer was almost always the easiest and most obvious," Shannon said.

"Look, I was just mouthing off," Appleton said.

"Yeah, you were, but you were also right," Shannon said. "Even though I don't have the years on the job like you guys, I know the killer is almost always someone with a reason, whether it's a pissed off lover or a bad drug deal or a gangbanger or whatever, there is always a reason someone kills someone else. The reason may seem really stupid to civilized people, but the reason is there.

"That's why you focused on Jackson. He had a great motive to kill Bonnelli. If he's not the killer, there are probably ten other people in this town Bonnelli has screwed over that could be suspects too. But, this kid Washington. He's squeaky clean. There's not a spot on him anywhere or if there is, it is so well hidden, I can't find it. And we've got a rich, drunk of a real estate developer who likes to throw his political weight around and beat DWI raps and manslaughter charges. The only thing they appear to have in common is they were both killed with a bullet doctored to be more lethal and self-destructive than normal. Where does that leave us?" Shannon said.

"Let's put it on the board," Barnes said walking up to a white board that covered one long wall of the workroom.

"Possibility One," he wrote. "Bonnelli and Washington were connected in a way we haven't discovered that's material to their deaths at the hand of a single killer."

"Possibility Two. The killers of Bonnelli and Washington are different individuals with different motives, but were supplied the same or similar weapon and or ammo.

"Possibility Three. Bonnelli and Washington were not connected in any way except in the mind of a serial killer who saw some kind of pattern we have yet to see.

"Possibility Four. Bonnelli and Washington weren't connected in any way. Both were victims of a previously unknown hit man with a signature execution style.

"Can you think of any more?" Barnes asked.

"Let's start with these," Shannon said as she studied the scenarios.

"Okay. Let's come back to the first one in a minute, but I think number two has some problems. I already talked to the ATF about doctoring the bullets and they were familiar with the technique, but unaware of anyone using it in this part of the world and no one in the gang unit has heard of it either. I think if someone was out there selling this stuff, we would have heard about it by now," Barnes said.

"Possibility Three, a serial killer. Even serial killers have motives, although they're not obvious. But they often have a pattern. Maybe if some of the other unsolved murders seem to fall into this same MO we can start to construct a pattern," Barnes said.

"If this starts to look like a serial killer case, we'll need to bring in a lot more help," Shannon said.

"Better than that," Appleton said. "We turn the whole thing over to the major case unit and forget it."

"Possibility Four. This is the work of a previously unknown hit man – or woman," Barnes said. "In which case, we are right back where we started with individual cases that can only help each other if we can find the person who hired the shooter."

"I can see the wife or one of his business associates or even this Jackson guy hiring someone to whack Bonnelli, but I still don't know why anyone would want this kid Washington dead," Shannon said.

"Let's get back to the first possibility, which seems the most likely to me. Maybe the connection isn't between Bonnelli and Washington, but between the killer, Bonnelli, and Washington," Shannon said.

"As you pointed out in our first meeting, these two didn't exactly run in the same social circles," she said. "Could it be that Washington heard or saw something he wasn't supposed to?"

"Why didn't he say something to somebody? Your notes said his boss at the bank reported nothing out of the ordinary and had nothing but good things to say about the kid," Barnes said. "Maybe he was the inside guy on something."

"No way," Shannon said. "Not this kid. My guess is if he heard or saw something, he didn't know what it was and had no idea he was in danger."

"Well, that's the most plausible theory yet for explaining how the two murders could be linked, but there's one problem," Appleton said. "It pretty much eliminates our shooter unless we can tie him to Washington somehow."

"On the other hand, if we can tie him to Washington and he doesn't have any alibi for that murder that may be enough to put the guy away," Barnes said.

"Okay. Let's set some priorities and get moving," Appleton said. "See if this sounds right to everyone."

"Possibility One is that there was a connection between Bonnelli and Washington that we haven't discovered which would explain both of their deaths. This seems the most promising area to pursue.

"Possibility Two is that someone is selling doctored ammo gets us nowhere towards solving the crime, besides the ATF is already looking into this.

"Possibility Three is that we're dealing with a serial killer who does see a connection between Bonnelli and Washington that we can't. We'll see what turns up on the other murders and bring in more help if it looks like this is what we are facing.

"Possibility Four is that there is a hit person on the loose. This complicates our case and confuses O'Brien's case even more," Appleton said. "Does that about sum it up?"

"Yeah. So we need to focus on Possibility One, forget Two, and put Three and Four on hold until we get more information," Shannon said.

"The Jackson guy is our suspect, so we'll see if there is a tie to the Washington kid," Appleton said. "Would you like to be in on this?"

"Yeah. If I can swing it. My captain isn't wild about spending a lot of time on other officer's cases," she said.

"We know all about that," Barnes said, as they begin to pack up their evidence.

Chapter 14 – Thursday – Jim, Vic, & Shannon

'Now, what am I supposed to do?' Jim thought as drove home from work in the middle of the morning.

It was a familiar question he asked himself almost every day in one form or another since Sally's death. It was a practical question. He really wasn't particularly interested in the greater meaning of events or the philosophical nuances others might find significant. Right now, he just wanted to know what he was supposed to do.

The meeting with his boss this morning had gone about as expected, although Schwartz didn't fire him. Instead, Schwartz put him on long-term disability leave at 80% pay for six months, which included counseling. At the end of six months, a medical evaluation would determine whether he was emotionally fit to return to work. Of course, if the police have their way, he'll be in jail charged with murder long before six months are up.

Jim had to admit Schwartz's solution was more humane than he expected and, in all fairness, he wasn't anywhere near pulling his weight on the job. Still, here he was without the one thing left in his life that provided any structure at all.

When he opened the front door and saw the shambles left by the police executing their search warrant – and some of the shambles that were there before they arrived – he couldn't help but smile at the metaphor for his life. This annoying habit of spotting metaphors, especially contrived, melodramatic ones, was a "professional curse" according to Jim. Sally had called it a "pain in the butt." It was one of many of the running jokes between them.

Cleaning up the house sounded like the last thing he wanted to do, but at least it was a temporary answer to the question of 'now what am I supposed to do?' Unfortunately, when he was able to come up with some kind of answer, the 'other question' invariably popped into his head: 'what's the point?'

Part of his disability leave – it felt more like probation, but he was all right with that – was getting some professional counseling in addition to the grief support group he was attending. The company contracted with the counseling center that provided the grief support group to distance themselves from employees' medical and psychological problems. Under the conditions of the long-term disability agreement Jim had signed that morning, he agreed to see a counselor for a minimum of twice a week for eight weeks. His first session was this afternoon.

He was not opposed to seeing a psychologist and felt no stigma about counseling. It was clear that he needed help if he was to get past these persistent feelings that his emotions were somehow coming unhinged or out of control. Despite what Samantha said, he felt a growing sense in his heart that he was very capable of murdering Bonnelli.

His memory of the night Bonnelli died was so blurred that he wondered if the concerns he expressed to Samantha about blocking out something horrible were true. Before Sally died, he would have laughed at the notion that an otherwise sane man could leave his house, drive across town, kill another person, come back home, and not remember doing any of it the next day.

Now, he wasn't so sure. Most of the time, his mind felt like it was either covered with crawling ants or stiff like a frozen margarita. One minute he couldn't turn off the thoughts and feelings and the next he couldn't feel anything. If a shrink could help him get some control over his emotions, he was all for that.

The doorbell rang and he realized he'd been wandering aimlessly through the house for ten minutes or so and still hadn't taken off his overcoat. He went to the front door and there was Vic.

"Oh," Jim said. "You seem to know whenever I'm home."

"Where you about to leave?" Vic asked, nodding to the briefcase in Jim's hand.

"No. No, I just got here a minute ago. Please come in. I'm sorry if that sounded rude. I could use some company right now," he said. "The place is even messier than before, thanks to the police."

"No problem," Vic said.

"How about some coffee? I was just about to put a pot on," Jim said.

"Sounds great," Vic said.

Jim took Vic's coat and put it with his own in the hall closet and they went into the kitchen.

"I guess you're wondering why I'm here in the middle of the morning," Jim said. "When I got back from the police station last night, there was a message on my voice mail from my boss that he wanted to see me this morning. How's that for bad news traveling fast? I was sure he was going to fire me, but Samantha wasn't convinced and, as it turned out, she was right. They put me on long-term disability for six months. I've got six months to get straightened out to keep my job, assuming, of course, the police don't have me locked away by then."

"Samantha has a lot of faith in you, doesn't she?" Vic asked.

"Yeah, she does – always has. I think in many ways she's been the best friend I ever had. She was like a rock when Sally died. I don't mean unfeeling, but someone who helped me do things without being asked. Plenty of people offered to help, but it was a passive kind of help – dependent on me to give them something to do. Not Samantha. She jumped right in and organized things, made a lot of small decisions for me, anticipated needs, she was great," Jim said.

"But, there's more to it than that," Vic said.

"Yeah. She and I hit it off almost immediately. A lot of people at work wrote her off as hard to work with and stubborn, but it was like I saw a completely different person. I don't really think of myself as particularly insightful – I tend to take people at face value and that gets me into to trouble sometimes. But Sam is the real thing. She is what you see. There's no pretense, no illusion, no games, and I think that's what bothered some of the people at work," Jim said.

"Do you have a romantic interest in her?" Vic asked.

"What? Oh, no. It's not like that and besides there could never be anyone after Sally," Jim said.

"Don't feel like you've just betrayed your dead wife's memory for even considering the possibility," Vic said. "Maybe not now, but at some point in the future you may be ready for another relationship and Samantha seems like a wonderful choice."

"How do you even know who Samantha is?" Jim said. "I just realized I've been talking about her as if you knew her, but I never told you who she was."

"She's your secretary, right?" Vic said. "It's really not magic or spying, but just an educated guess. You're not the type to have a lover and you probably don't discuss personally sensitive information with peers. So it was a good guess that Samantha was your secretary."

"That's amazing and a little scary," Jim said.

"You don't have any close family ties, do you?" Vic asked.

"No. There's just my sister and me and we're not close. Our parents have been dead for some years and whatever other relatives there are have all drifted out of the picture," Jim said.

"What about Sally? Did she have any family?" Vic said.

"Her mother is still alive, but in failing health. Sally's death almost killed her. I send her a card periodically, but I never hear from her. I think she blames me for Sally's death," Jim said. "I don't think there are any other close living relatives – none showed up at the funeral. You know, every time we talk, I do all the talking, and I don't know anymore about you than the day I met you. Yet, you seem to know more about me each time we meet," Jim said. "Should I be concerned about this?"

"I'm sorry. I told you I don't have any spy tricks or motives. It just helps me understand your situation better if I know some details," Vic said.

Just then, the doorbell rang.

"Where you expecting someone else," he said.

"I wasn't even expecting you," Jim said as he started for the front door.

When he opened the door, Jim saw one of the most striking women he had ever seen in his life. She was well over six feet with long blonde hair and an athletic build that was powerful, but sexy at the same time.

"Mr. Jackson?" Shannon said as she flashed her badge. "I'm Detective O'Brien. May I have a few minutes of your time?"

"Yes, of course," Jim said, slightly embarrassed that he had been staring.

He stepped aside as Shannon came into the foyer. As she was coming in, Vic, who had retrieved his coat, was on his way out.

"Sorry, I must run," he said and brushed past Shannon and out the door.

"Did I interrupt something?" she said.

"Well, not really," Jim said. "Vic just shows up unannounced and asks a lot of questions."

"Vic?" Shannon said. "Isn't that the name you gave the officers as the person you talked to on the night Bonnelli was killed?"

"Yes. That's right. I assume you're here about that case or am I being accused of some other crime?" Jim said.

"No, no other crimes that I know of. I'm just following up on some loose ends. Say, I'd really like to talk to that fellow Vic. Do you have his last name?" she said.

"No, I don't and I don't have a phone number or anything else and it is starting to spook me a little," Jim said.

"Why's that?" Shannon asked.

"He knows a lot about me, that's why," Jim said. "We're in the same grief support group. I've only gone twice and he already knows details about my life that weren't discussed at the group and that no one in the group knows."

"Maybe he's some kinda of sicko who gets off on other folk's pain?" Shannon said.

"I thought about that, but I don't think so," Jim said. "At first, I thought he was a counselor because he seem so interested in the details of my life, but that's not the case – I checked. The people that run the center where the support group meets all know him. Apparently, he's like a volunteer member of the staff. According to Judy, she's the facilitator of my group, Vic lost his wife and kids and came to the group for support and never left. He told me that one way he deals with his grief was to help others through their grief," Jim said.

"You don't sound convinced," Shannon said.

"Well, it's like I said, he seems to know a lot about me that I've never told him, but that's not all," Jim said. "He just shows up at the weirdest times."

"Like this morning?" Shannon asked.

"Yeah. Like this morning. How did he know I would be home? I mean he was here not 15 minutes after I got home. No one knew I would be home this morning except a few key executives at work and they're so afraid of lawsuits they wouldn't tell anyone," Jim said. "By the way, how did you know I would be at home?"

"Mr. Jackson, you're a suspect in a murder. We keep tabs on suspects," Shannon said.

"You mean I'm being followed," he said.

"No, not exactly," she said. "It's just that we want to know where you are so an officer checks on you periodically. If we thought you were a significant flight risk, we would have a tighter leash on you."

"You still didn't answer my question," he said. "Did you follow me from work?"

"No, sir. To be honest, I wasn't even going to talk to you today, but a unit reported your car was in the driveway and I wasn't far away on another matter, so I thought I'd drop by to see what was going on," she said.

"Well, thank you for that," Jim said.

"So, what are you doing here in the middle of the morning?" Shannon said.

"Would you like a cup of coffee," Jim asked, gesturing towards the kitchen. "I made a pot for my previous guest, but he seemed to have other plans."

"That sounds great. After you," Shannon said as they walked back to the kitchen.

Jim stopped. "Oh, I get it. You don't want to have your back to me. Is that it?"

"Something like that," Shannon said.

"Do I look like I could hurt you?" he asked.

"Two years ago a detective in our squad was interviewing a grandmother about the shooting death of her grandson. She asked him to get something off the mantle. When he turned his back, she pulled a .38 from her knitting bag and shot him," Shannon said. "He now has just one kidney and walks funny."

"Why don't you follow me," Jim said.

"Good idea," Shannon said.

"Hey, what's he doing in my backyard?" Jim said.

"That's officer Morton. He's my backup today. My regular partner is on vacation, so when I go interview suspects, I often pickup a uniformed officer as a backup. By the way, the detective that walks funny, that's the other rule that he broke. He went alone to the interview," she said.

"Well, would it break a rule if he came in for a cup of coffee too?" Jim asked.

"No, not at all," she said and motioned Morton to come in through the patio door.

Morton stuck his head in and said, "You need something?"

"Mr. Jackson wondered if you would like a cup of coffee," she said.

"Yeah. Thanks that would be great," Morton said as he took a cup. "But if it's okay with you O'Brien, I'll drink it outside here on the patio."

"Sure. No problem," she said.

"What's that about," Jim asked after the policeman left.

"Oh, nothing much. Just a little jealousy I guess. He took the detective exam twice and failed both times and he resents babysitting me," she said. "But enough of our dirty laundry, let's get back to you.

"Why are you here in the middle of the morning on a work day?" she asked.

"I'm not sure I should be answering any more questions without an attorney present," he said.

"That is certainly your right, Mr. Jackson," she said. "And you were read your rights before about not having to answer questions without an attorney present and they still apply to this session."

"Yes, I remember all of that and I wish I had more confidence in our judicial system," he said.

"What do you mean by that?" she asked.

"It seems like every time you pick up a paper these days some poor soul is released from prison or taken off death row because new

DNA evidence has cleared him of a crime he didn't commit. In the meantime, celebrity criminals or corporate big shots get off with murder or massive rip-offs because they have the money for high-priced lawyers. I would think as a cop you would see this every day. People you know are guilty, but you can't touch because of some legal technicality or other crap. Then to top it off, you can't catch a quarter of the violent criminals out there because you're under staffed and out gunned," Jim said.

"So, you're saying that the system doesn't work," she said.

"I'm sure it works some of the time, but it sure didn't work for Sally," Jim said, a little surprised at the tone of his voice. "She got no justice through the system."

"But Sally got justice, didn't she?" Shannon said.

"Yes, she did," Jim said. "And, that's all I really want to say. If you have anymore questions, you'll have to wait until my lawyer is present."

"Okay. Thanks for the coffee," Shannon said.

Jim was glad when the detective was gone. He liked her almost immediately, but the way things were going he couldn't trust anyone except Samantha and maybe Vic. They seemed to be the only people in his life right now that cared anything about him and he wasn't too sure about Vic. Vic's endless curiosity and intimate knowledge of his life made him a little nervous. Jim never really enjoyed being the center of attention. He didn't particularly enjoy his birthday parties because of all the attention. That was one of the reasons the support group was so hard – all that attention focused on him. It was the same with Vic at times. That much attention made him uncomfortable.

As if on cue, the phone rang. Jim knew it was Vic.

"Hello Vic," he said.

"How did you know it was me," Vic said.

"Just a lucky guess," Jim said.

"Did everything go alright? What did that cop want?" Vic asked.

"Why don't you come over and we'll talk about it," Jim said.

"Sorry, I can't right now. I've an appointment in a few minutes," Vic said.

"Okay. Some other time then," Jim said making sure he sounded like he was about to hang up, betting Vic had one more question.

"Wait. Before you go. Did you by any chance mention my name?" Vic said.

'There it is,' thought Jim, 'how did I know that was coming.'

"Well, actually I did. When you rushed out, she wanted to know who you were. When I mentioned your name, she recalled it from the report I gave the other cops as the person I talked to on the night Bonnelli was shot. She said she would like to talk to you and did I have your last name or address and, of course, I don't, which is kinda of strange, don't you think?" Jim said.

"What do you mean," Vic said.

"Well, I've been sharing some fairly intimate details about my life and you've apparently discovered others on your own and you've been to my house several times, but I still don't know you last name or where you live. Some people, including the cop, might call that strange," Jim said.

"Listen, there's nothing strange at all. I've got to run, but I'll call soon and we can sort this whole thing out," Vic said.

Jim wasn't so sure.

Chapter 15 – Thursday – Shannon

Shannon stopped at a McDonald's to use the restroom and get a large coffee to go. She was only about a mile from the lake, so she drove to a park on the lake to make some notes about her conversation with Jackson and collect her thoughts before she relayed the information to Appleton and Barnes.

Jackson didn't impress her as a killer, but she had learned over the years that while gut instinct is important, it also can blind you to reality.

However, she was sure her gut was right about telling her this guy Vic was involved in this somehow and she needed to follow up on him.

Jackson's anti-judicial system comments could indicate a willingness to take matters into his own hands, however it's a reach from complaining about the system to declaring yourself judge, jury, and executioner.

She also wrote down a physical description of Vic: mid 50s; graying hair, receding hairline, 5'10" 180 lbs., didn't get eye color, wearing dark grey overcoat. Shannon noted several cars parked on the street when she arrived at Jackson's house, but none in front of his house. She asked Morton when they left if he saw anyone leaving when he arrived about a minute behind Shannon and he said no.

She phoned her report into Appleton and Barnes and they agreed that she should check out this Vic character. They were due in court all day on another case.

Shannon wondered at the change in attitude. Just a week ago if she had interviewed one of their suspects without their permission (which they wouldn't have given) they would have ripped her head off and then really gotten nasty. They must be under a lot of pressure to get this case solved.

Her next stop was the counseling center to see if she could get any information on Vic from the staff. The center was located in a church in the near downtown area. She had an appointment at 2:00 with the center's director, which meant she had about an hour before beginning the trip downtown.

As she watched the small waves break on the lake's shore, her thoughts turned to Ling. She could think of about a hundred reasons the relationship was a bad idea, not the least of which was Shannon's uncertainty about a sexual relationship with another woman.

Intellectually, she was open to accepting people the way they are and if they choose people of the same sex as partners, so what.

Emotionally, it is quite a different thing to accept yourself as "one of those" kind of people, which made Shannon suspect her intellectually openness wasn't as open as she proclaimed it to be. Did she secretly feel lesbians were inferior or less than heterosexuals?

Shannon had to endure years of snide remarks and odd looks ever since she topped six feet in the 9th grade. Her athletic build and ability attracted all sorts of comments and assumptions. Now she was beginning to wonder if some of those were true.

Thank God, her father was dead. If he were alive and got a hint that she was a lesbian, it would devastate him. Of course, I did a pretty good job of that, when I dropped sports and took up music as a major, Shannon thought. Why did I have to be so stubborn? I could've figured out a way to mend my relationship with dad.

I could've sold him on music, thought Shannon, but how could I've sold Ling, a 5'4" Chinese doctor as my lover? Maybe there are some things you shouldn't expect your dad to accept. Besides, I don't even know what I feel for her. Her hand on my breast, my mouth on hers, set me on fire, but I was really afraid. What does that mean? An unaccustomed tear rolled down her left cheek.

Shannon tried to imagine a long-term relationship with Ling. The thought of the small, warm, coffee-and-cream, body next to her every night was enough to make Shannon squirm in her seat with anticipation. Waking up every morning with someone next to you; someone who loves you; someone who wants to be with you; someone who doesn't want you to be anyone else but you; she thought it sounded too good to be true.

Of course, there was the whole issue of how she would handle it at work. Most of the guys thought she was a lesbian already, so it probably wouldn't be a big deal if she and Ling didn't flaunt the relationship in public. The city was big enough they could be a couple without having worry about bumping in to people they work with every day.

Still, Ling was looking for someone strong to hold on to and Shannon wasn't so sure she wanted to be the strong one all the time. It was the role she had to play as a homicide detective, it was a role she had to play as an athlete and the role her father expected of her.

Be the leader – take charge – take the shot. It was a role she took naturally, yet there were times when she would just like to rest for a while and let someone else take the lead or be strong. This was the point that finally drove a wedge between her and her father. It was a point he would never concede and the only way she could win was to drop out of basketball altogether.

Could Ling understand this? Shannon tried to imagine the tiny Ling comforting her and, although the physical picture might be a little amusing, the emotional one felt very good.

As usual, Shannon was projecting a relationship much farther along than it was and making assumptions about the other person. What if Ling didn't want that type of relationship? What if Ling was only interested in sex? What if ...? She had a bad habit of beginning and ending relationships before they ever had a chance.

The drive into the city cleared her head and got her focused on the case. She hoped the director of the counseling center could shed some light on this Vic character. He may be a dead-end, but this case could use a break and breaks tend to come when you follow leads no matter how weak.

The Lutheran church was on the northern end of the downtown area, where the neighborhoods were transitioning from commercial into residential. The old, large structure was home for a primary school as well as the counseling center and the playground was a blur of blue slacks and skirts with white shirts in constant motion.

She hadn't been in church since her mother died when she was a junior in college. Her mother was a cold, aloof woman who took no interest in Shannon's sports and only mildly interested in her music. She worked in real estate and was gone most of the time showing houses or whatever real estate agents do. Shannon suspected her mother was having an affair, but later decided that was a way for an angry young girl to explain her mom's lack of interest in her.

Signs at the front of the church directed her around to a side entrance to the counseling center. The basement decor of the church was "1950s institutional." The walls were concrete blocks painted a pale green and the floor was linoleum.

However, once inside the counseling center offices, Shannon immediately noticed that through tasteful wall hangings and art, plus area rugs, the center lost the institutional feel almost immediately. The reception area was furnished with easy chairs, a sofa, and a coffee table. Over in a corner, was an area with toys and children's books.

The center director, Dr. Cynthia McGuire, saw Shannon right away.

"How can I help you, detective?" Dr. McGuire said. "With the understanding, of course the patient information is confidential."

"Of course, doctor," Shannon said. "Just for my report, what kind of doctor are you?"

"I have a Ph.D. in psychology," said Dr. McGuire.

"Thank you, doctor," said Shannon. "Can you tell me about your grief support group?"

"Well, in general terms our grief support groups help people who are going through a grieving process. Some of the groups help those who have lost a spouse while others help those who have lost a child. We also have support groups for terminally ill cancer patients," Dr. McGuire said.

"I'm more interested in the one you didn't mention, doctor," Shannon said. "The one for people who have lost loved ones in sudden and violent circumstances."

"I also didn't mention the support group for HIV positive people, detective. What's your point?" Dr. McGuire said.

"My point is that one of the participants in the support group for people who have lost loved ones is a prime suspect in the murder of the man who killed his wife and unborn child. That's my point, doctor and I think you knew that before I got here," Shannon said.

"You know I can't talk about specific patients," Dr. McGuire said.

"Really? I'm not so sure. Is Mr. Jackson actually receiving counseling here?" Shannon said.

"I can't comment on that," Dr. McGuire said.

"See, I think if all that is happening is he is sitting around with a bunch of other people who are not counselors and they're just talking to one another – that's not therapy and there is no patient-doctor relationship to violate," Shannon said.

"I would like to talk to the leader of this group, please. Can I have this person's name?" she said.

"I disagree about the confidentiality, but the lawyers can settle that. I anticipated you would want to talk to the group leader, so I have her standing by," he said.

"Send Judy in, please," he said into the intercom.

Judy was a slightly plump woman in her late 40s with short hair and wearing a tailored suit. She carried a file folder.

"Judy, this is Detective O'Brien. She is interested in your grief support group. I've told her we do not discuss patient information, but she wants to talk to all the same," Dr. McGuire said.

"Detective, this Judy Frankel. You should know and I say this again in front of Judy, that all of our group leaders are thoroughly trained in their legal responsibilities. If someone in their group suggests they are about to commit a crime or have committed a violent crime, our counselors are obligated to report it," Dr. McGuire said.

"Okay, Judy, thanks for coming in. What can you tell me about Jim Jackson that doesn't violate a relationship that I personally don't think exists," Shannon said.

"Detective, you want to know if Mr. Jackson has given me any clue that he committed a murder or is capable of committing a murder. My answer about him would be the same about most everyone else that has gone through my support groups: you're asking the wrong person. We provide comfort and a place for people to go and know they are with others who feel the same way they do. We are not asking probing questions by pushing people or challenging them – that's what therapy is all about," she said.

"But, he has expressed anger, hasn't he," Shannon said.

"He has expressed a normal range of emotions for a man in his circumstances," Judy said. "Speaking in general, I believe it is the people who do not express that range of emotions that you need to watch very carefully. Would you agree, Dr. McGuire?"

"Absolutely, Judy. Again, not speaking about any patient in particular, but when someone exhibits the standards stages of grief – the depression, the anger, the other stages – that is a patient we can help. The patient that shows none of these stages or gets stuck in one stage, such as anger, that is the patient who needs intensive help," Dr. McGuire said.

"Have you seen many such patients?" Shannon said.

"Many, no. Some, for sure. They can even fool you sometimes by pretending to go through the stages if they are clever enough," Dr. McGuire said.

"What happens to these people if they don't get help," Shannon asked.

"Some we never know about. Others unfortunately, become self-destructive and kill themselves quickly with suicide or slowly with drugs and alcohol," Dr. McGuire said.

"What about murder – a revenge killing?" Shannon asked.

"I suppose it's possible, but this is really out of my area of expertise. You need to find a psychiatrist that is a specialist in this area," Dr. McGuire said.

"So, you're basically saying, you don't have a clue as to whether one of your patients is capable of murder and all you do is sit around talking about how you feel. Is that pretty much it?" Shannon said.

"Tell me, detective, how many suspects have you identified by a sign around their neck that said 'I did it?' How many murderers have you questioned, then let go because they had a perfectly believable story?" Dr. McGuire said.

"Okay. I get your point. There's another person I would like to ask you about and I don't think he's a patient, so maybe we won't stumble of the same obstacles," Shannon said. "What can you tell me about a man who apparently serves in a volunteer capacity here by the name of Vic."

Shannon was looking at Dr. McGuire, but Judy was in her peripheral vision and it was her reaction that interested Shannon the most. Her hunch was right. Judy may be a great counselor, but she would have gone broke at the poker table. As soon as she heard Vic's name, she flinched – not much, but enough to call her bluff in any two-bit poker game in town.

"Who," Dr. McGuire said.

"Listen, doctor," she said, "I'm trying real hard to be nice, but I have to tell you how I feel right now and that's like you're jerking me around. Obstruction of an officer in the investigation of a murder is enough for me to get on my cell phone to this assistant district attorney who is waiting in his office for my call. He has a search warrant ready for a judge's signature. In two hours, I can have a dozen cops and evidence people tearing this place apart. Even if we don't find anything, it will take a week to put everything back together and, in the meantime what are your patients going to think when they turn on the evening news tonight and see the cops swarming all over this place? There, I feel better already."

"You can't be serious?" Dr. McGuire said. "This is outrageous. I'll call my lawyer and see what he has to say."

"Fine. Be sure he understands you're also facing criminal charges for obstructing an officer," Shannon said as she pulled out her handcuffs.

Dr. McGuire's face went white and she sank back into her chair.

"Okay. Okay. Judy, tell him about Vic," Dr. McGuire said.

"Dr. McGuire, I'm not very comfortable talking about Vic. I still consider him a patient," Judy said.

"For God's sake, Judy, he's been hanging around for years. No one is a patient for that long," Dr. McGuire said.

"Well, I actually 'inherited' Vic. He was here when I started with the center six years ago. He's always been with the grief support groups for people who have lost loved ones under sudden and violent circumstances. My predecessor told me that he volunteered to keep coming when men were in the group. He does have a good way of helping men open up and he has never come with any agenda that I could detect," Judy said.

"I'm sure he's a great guy," Shannon said. "I would love to talk to him because he may be able to help in this investigation in a very minor way. Can you give me his last name and an address or phone number?"

"I don't know his last name," Judy said. "And that's the truth. I never asked and he never volunteered. He just shows up when a new group starts. I guess I assumed he was all right since he was here before me."

"What about it, Dr. McGuire," Shannon said.

"Cathy, please locate the file on Vic, the gentleman who attends all the grief support groups that Judy leads and bring it in please," Dr. McGuire said into the intercom.

"Thank you," Shannon said.

After a few moments, there was a light knocking on the door and Cathy, the office manager, walked in carrying several folders. She walked around behind Dr. McGuire's desk, put the folders in front of the doctor, and whispered in her ear.

Dr. McGuire flipped through the three folders quickly and handed them back to Cathy and there was more agitated whispering back and forth.

"Something wrong, doctor?" Shannon said.

"This is most irregular," Dr. McGuire said. "We keep a cross index of patients by first name, so we can find a file if all we know is the first name. The index references a file number and that's all. We have four patients in the index named Vic, but only three files. She bought me those files and I can assure you none of those three is the man you're interested in. The fourth file was empty. She looked on our computer system and the file number doesn't exist in our database, but it has to exist because that's how the index is created. It's all so confusing."

Shannon believed her. It was too screwy for her to make up on the spot and she wasn't any better poker player that Judy. Even though it looked like the doctor was telling the truth, Shannon didn't want to let her off the hook just yet.

"A missing file that just happens to be the one I'm looking for – gee, what a coincidence. You know, I've the DA's number on my speed dial," Shannon said as she pulled out her cell phone.

"No, you must believe me," Dr. McGuire said. "I've no idea how this happened."

"You have a man you don't know involved in your counseling center for years and you can't find a file on him. You don't know his name, his phone number, anything," Shannon said. "Doctor, this doesn't seem like a prudent way to run a practice that is supposed to be helping people a particularly vulnerable times in their lives."

"Detective, do you think Vic is involved in the murder you suspect Mr. Jackson committed?" Dr. McGuire asked.

"My turn to be closed mouthed doctor," Shannon said. "However this turns out, I think you might want to review your security procedures and precautions. You might also want to make that call to your lawyer and check your potential liability. Doctor, I deal in worse case scenarios. It's time for you to tell me everything you know about Vic. If this missing file is a simple clerical error and Vic is not involved, I'll see to it that none of your information makes its way into the case file. But, I got to tell you, my experience tells me too many coincidences aren't coincidences," Shannon said.

"I can't believe Vic is involved in anything illegal," Judy said. "He has been in a several of my groups and has always been helpful and compassionate with the participants. He relates to the men and they relate to him."

"What's his story," Shannon said.

"Quite tragic," Judy said. "Some ten years ago, he was out of town on business and the furnace went out. His wife got a message to him and he gave her the name of someone to call to come look at it. Apparently, the man came that afternoon, looked at the furnace, and told Vic's wife he would be back the next day with the part to fix it. That night he broke into the house raped and killed her and killed the two children ages three and five."

"Did they catch the guy?" Shannon asked.

"According to Vic, the man was an old Army acquaintance that had looked Vic up and told him he was in the furnace repair business. What he didn't tell Vic was that he had just been released from a mental institution for the criminally insane for murdering someone else," Judy said. He never really stood trial – they just sent him back with no chance of release this time," Judy said.

"So Vic sent this maniac over to his house where his wife and two kids where slaughtered. Wow, I can't imagine the guilt and anger Vic is carrying around," Shannon said.

"He certainly admits to the anger, although I've never heard him talk about guilt, now that you mention it. He says he channels his anger into something productive like helping other men through this process. He says you can't really get rid of the anger, but you can redirect it to accomplish something positive," Judy said.

"Do you buy that?" Shannon asked.

"Sometimes, people use clinical terms in a context that is not quite correct, but close. This is where you get the popular phrase "psychobabble." Words thrown around by people who make them sound correct, but really lack any clinical foundation," Judy said.

"I think both Dr. McGuire and most of the other counselors here would agree that we see many patients who are able to get beyond their anger. They may redirect energy, but they move beyond anger," she said. "I always assumed that this is what Vic was really talking about even if he didn't have all the phrases exactly right."

"Earlier, doctor, didn't you say that a patient stuck in one stage of the grieving process – anger, for example – should be watched very carefully?" Shannon said.

"You have excellent recall detective," said Dr. McGuire. "It seems we may have been missing some cues right here in our own house."

"If Vic is involved, does that mean that Jim, Mr. Jackson, is cleared?" Judy asked.

"First of all, let's not jump to any conclusions about Vic," Shannon said. "Everything we know or don't know about him could have a simple explanation. So, no it doesn't change anything. You folks are in a profession that counts on building trust and confidence. I'm in a profession that doesn't trust anyone until I'm satisfied of their innocence."

"I thought everyone was innocent until proven guilty," Dr. McGuire said.

"That's in court," Shannon said. "Out here in the field, when we are tracking down a killer we have to assume everyone is a potential suspect and start eliminating them one by one. I think it would be prudent for you to not discuss this conversation with anyone either in this clinic or at home. Doing so could jeopardize an on-going investigation. If either of you happen to come into contact with Mr. Jackson or Vic, please do not mention this conversation or my asking questions about them. Alerting them will only hamper my work and, if they are innocent, could cause unnecessary emotional strain."

Shannon left the counseling center and headed for the police garage to return in the car still turning over what she learned from the doctor and Judy. She stopped to pickup some dry cleaning at a laundry not far from the garage.

"Hey, your card's no good," the clerk said.

"What, did you say," Shannon said to the over-weight, greasy-haired teenage boy behind the counter.

"You heard me. Your card's bogus," he said. "It's been rejected. In fact, I'm going to confiscate it."

"The hell, you are," she said. "There's nothing wrong with that card. I don't even have a balance on it."

"That's not what the machine says, bitch," the clerk said.

"Oh, really," Shannon said. She reached into her purse, got a $20 bill, and put it on the counter.

"You owe me some change and my credit card," she said.

"Here's your change, but I'm keeping the credit card," he said.

She took her change, put it in her purse, and pulled back her jacket to reveal the 9mm pistol in the holster under her left arm.

"What did you say?" she said.

"Here's your credit card," he said.

"Have a great day," she said. "And, by the way, if you ever call me bitch again I'm going to break your legs."

As soon as she got in her car, her cell phone rang. "O'Brien," she answered.

"Pesky credit cards. Just when you think you can count on them they dry dock," a male voice said.

"Who is this?" she asked.

The caller hung up.

When she got to the squad room, she was officially off-duty but so mad that she wasn't about to let this drop.

She called her credit card company and after being on hold for 30 minutes finally got to a human. She explained what happened.

"Mary" her customer service representative said that in fact the card was reported stolen and the account closed.

"But I didn't report it stolen," she said.

"Yes, you did," Mary said. "You had all the proper account identification numbers including your social security number and you knew the correct answer to the secret question only the account owner would know."

"Secret question," Shannon said.

"Yes, when a person opens an account they supply a secret question and answer only they would know. That way, we can identify them in situations like this," Mary said.

"But that is impossible. It's my card and I didn't report it stolen," Shannon said.

"I'm sorry," Mary said. "I really can't discuss this with you."

"Listen, I'm a homicide detective and I think someone is trying to intimidate me off a case," Shannon said. "Now I need some information about how this card was reported stolen.

"Lady, do you have any idea how many times a day I hear that one," Mary said. "Have a nice day."

The line went dead. Shannon was ready to shoot someone; fortunately for that weasel Jimmy, he had gone home.

The next call she made was to Ken Connelly an Assistant District Attorney who had the hots for her at one time. That was water under the bridge, but he would do her a favor. She knew he would be at the office late, he always was.

"Ken," she said. "It's Shannon. I need a favor."

"What can I do for my favorite homicide detective," he said.

"My credit card..."

"Oh, come on, Shannon. You know I can't fix things like that," Connelly said. "You want to get us both busted."

"No. No. It's not what you think. This is actually tied to an ongoing investigation," she said.

"I'm listening, but this better be good," he said.

She quickly summarized the case and then told him what just happened at the dry cleaners and the call that she interpreted as a threat.

"Okay. What do you want me to do?" he said.

"Could you light a fire under the chief of security at the credit card company? I would like to see if they can pinpoint when and where the call canceling the card came from," she said.

"Yeah, that's not a problem. They're very cooperative most of the time. I'll have some one call you directly," Connelly said.

"Are you going to bring me something to prosecute on this soon," he asked.

"I hope so," Shannon said. "But what started out as a pretty simple case is becoming more complicated every day."

"Let me know if you need anything else, okay?" Connelly said. "It was nice hearing your voice again."

"Yeah. Thanks," Shannon said.

Her next call was to a "friend" at her cell phone company. This "friend" enjoyed an adventurous lifestyle and had asked Shannon on more than one occasion to help her out of a compromising situation. Nothing too bad, but enough to earn Shannon favors when she needed them.

Shannon's friend could tell her who phoned her with the cryptic message about her credit card. Unfortunately, the information wasn't very helpful. The call came from a prepaid, disposable cellphone and no way to trace the owner. However, the friend was able to tell Shannon that the caller was less than a block away, meaning the caller was following Shannon.

Her phone rang and it was the chief of security for the credit card company. 'Damn, Ken must have really used a big match,' she thought.

The man introduced himself as Roger Allister and asked Shannon for all of her personal identification information from her account.

She told him what had happened and wanted to know if he could trace how the card was canceled.

"We record those calls for security purposes, detective," Allister said. "But it will take several hours at least to retrieve that specific conversation. Why don't you call me tomorrow morning? We should have it for you by then."

"Thank you for your cooperation," she said. "I'll do that. One final question. How hard would it be for someone to do what they did to my account?"

"I can't answer that directly without compromising our new security procedures, but just let me say no one has been able to do it," Allister said. "Until now."

Shannon sat at her desk for a few more minutes replaying the events of the day and trying to make some sense of the turns this case was taking. She needed some help and clarity in more ways than one. She picked up the phone one more time.

"Could I come over for a little while? I've had an interesting day and I'd like to see you," she said.

Chapter 16 – Thursday – Jim & Sam

Jim had just parked his car when he saw Detective O'Brien come out of the counseling center. 'Damn, what's she doing here?' he thought, but he knew the answer to his own question.

She didn't see him and he stayed in his car until she was gone. He was stuck with indecision. Should he go in and keep his appointment? Was he walking into a trap? If he skipped the appointment, would that make him look guilty? Dr. McGuire would report his absence to the company and that would probably be the excuse they needed to fire him.

He started to call Samantha, but decided that the police might be monitoring his cell phone or the company could be keeping tabs on her calls at work. Probably paranoia, but better safe than sorry.

He would have to trust Dr. McGuire. She was a psychologist after all and anything he said in a counseling session should be privileged information, at least that's what they said on the TV cop shows.

A light rain was blurring the street scene through his windshield as he sat in his car. Another melodramatic, but appropriate metaphor for how he viewed his life. He was probably one piece of evidence away from a murder charge and he still had not contacted a lawyer. The best he could do was quote TV shows. Most of his life had just happened – it wasn't the result of any particular plan or of any goal that he achieved – it just happened and he just happened to be in the way when it did.

Professionally, he was better off than he had a right to be, at least that's the way he felt. He could not point to strategic career decisions that got him the promotions. His work was good, but not brilliant. Everyone would agree that he was "above average" in just about all areas of assessment, but in a competitive corporate environment, that was hardly a ringing endorsement.

He was not a political animal either. Most of the nuances of inter-offices politics escaped him and he found the endless discussions about maneuvering among the executives boring and more appropriate for high school halls than corporate conference rooms.

Although he had privileges in the executive dining room, he often ate with his staff in the employee cafeteria. During one of his evaluations, Schwartz criticized him for not spending more time in the executive dining room, networking with his peers and superiors. The truth was, Jim felt more at ease with his staff in the employee cafeteria than sitting at the formal place settings in the executive dining room discussing the stock market or golf or exotic vacation spots.

Undoubtedly, Dr. McGuire would want him to talk a lot about that, Jim thought. In some ways, he always felt like he was just slightly out of synch with the rest of the world and especially his peers. They all seem to know exactly what they wanted out of life and had specific plans to achieve their goals. He envied their focus and the success that came with that commitment. His early achievements matched theirs, but he could already see they were slowly pulling away and he seemed to be decelerating.

When he married Sally, it energized him in a way he had never known before, yet he still had no real passion for his work. That was what separated him from the real stars – a passion for his work that was simply not there.

'How did I end up with this much of my life invested in a career I've no real passion for,' Jim wondered. It occurred to him that this might be the first time he had ever examined his life so critically. He never thought of himself as a "passive" individual, but clearly he had drifted into his present situation without much thought if this was the way he wanted to live his life.

'I guess I should save some of this introspection for Dr. McGuire,' Jim thought as he got out of the car and headed for the counseling center. Thanks to the light rain, the late afternoon appointment, and short Fall days it was growing dark as he crossed the parking lot.

"Jim, over here."

Jim started at the voice coming from the shadows near the building's rear entrance, which was closed except on Sundays.

"Who's there?" he called.

"It's me," Vic said, stepping out of the shadows long enough for Jim to get a look at his face.

"What are you doing here?" Jim said.

"Waiting for you," Vic said. "Be careful what you say in there. The cops have been here questioning Dr. McGuire and Judy."

"How do you know that," Jim asked.

"Never mind. Will you listen and quit asking so damn many questions? The cops are contending that the grief support group is not privileged and anything that is discussed can be used against you," Vic said.

"So what," Jim said. "I've never said anything that could hurt me, because I've never done anything wrong. They can get anybody in the group they want to testify."

"Are you really that naïve or are you just stupid?" Vic said.

Jim felt his face get red. It was like his father had just caught him masturbating.

"You have no idea what the testimony of those sobbing biddies will do to a jury. They will convict you with their sympathy – 'Oh, I'm sure Mr. Jackson didn't mean to do it, he just loved her so.'"

"So, what do I do?" Jim asked.

"Just be careful what you say," Vic said. "The police may have intimidated them into setting you up."

"Dr. McGuire wouldn't do that," Jim said.

"Maybe not," Vic said. "But she might be reporting back to the police any information that would be helpful in their investigation. They might be able to bully her into that. For your own sake, be careful."

"Okay, thanks," Jim said and started back around the building toward the counseling center entrance.

"And Jim," Vic said.

"Yes, Vic," Jim said.

"For both our sakes, please keep me out of it."

"Sure thing, Vic," Jim said.

He took a few more steps, then looked back over his shoulder, but Vic had disappeared, although Jim wasn't sure how he could have vanished so quickly since there was nothing be open parking lot behind the building.

By the time Jim got to the Counseling Center offices, he was nervous and angry with Vic for his obvious attempt to cover his own ass. Jim, who often found himself more concerned with the well being of others at the expense of his own, was slowly beginning to realize that this time the stakes were too high for him to just let things ride.

Dr. McGuire was pleasant, but guarded in her greeting – she was no poker player. Several degrees in psychology didn't prepare her for this situation, Jim thought and she doesn't know that I know what's going on.

As they were walking back to Dr. McGuire's office, Judy came out of her office and almost bumped into Jim. There was a "deer in the headlights" look on her face that transitioned into the phoniest smile Jim had ever seen. She mumbled hello and dashed off down the hall.

Dr. McGuire's office furnishings included a "conversation area" of three comfortable over-stuffed chairs around a small coffee table. She sat in one and motioned toward another for Jim, but he didn't sit down immediately.

"Jim, as you know, the company has asked me to meet with you for a period to help you get your emotional bearings back. I'm pretty sure we can do this if you're willing to work with me and trust the process," Dr. McGuire said.

"Is this session being taped?" Jim asked.

"What did you say?" Dr. McGuire asked.

"Are you tape recording this session?" Jim repeated.

"No, of course not. Whatever gave you that idea?" Dr. McGuire said.

"Then let's cut the bullshit. Okay?" Jim said. "I know the police were here this afternoon so don't try and trick me into saying anything."

"Jim, I assure you that I would never try to trick you into anything and I would never tell the police anything," Dr. McGuire said.

"But you did tell them something about me this afternoon," Jim said. "I know the detective that was here. She wouldn't leave without something about me. Well, I'm innocent. I didn't kill anybody. But everything seems to be pointing in my directions and I've a feeling you and Judy didn't help my case any today."

"Jim, I swear we didn't tell her anything specific about you – that information is confidential and it will take more that her bullying to get us to talk. Although there is not really much we could say since you have only been here twice," Dr. McGuire said. "Besides, she really wasn't all that interested in you. She had more questions about your friend Vic."

"Why is it that every time I turn around, there's Vic?" Jim said. "When Detective O'Brien dropped by my house this morning, Vic was there. As soon as she arrived, Vic left in a hurry. She was real interested in finding out more about him, so I wasn't surprised to see her here when I arrived this afternoon. What did you tell her about Vic?" he asked.

"I can only tell you what he has shared in the grief support group – anything else would violate his privacy," she said.

"Isn't the support group private also," he said.

"Normally it would be but since he attends your group, this is information he will share in the course of normal group meetings," she said.

Jim thought that sounded like a rationalization for breaking a confidence and wondered how many other rationalization hoops Dr. McGuire had jumped through while talking to that detective. Even though Vic's warning was clearly self-serving, Jim could see now that he was right in his distrust of Dr. McGuire and Judy.

Still, Jim was curious about Vic who knew so much about him.

"Okay. What's his story," Jim said.

Jim listened to Dr. McGuire's account of the death of Vic's wife and children in silence. He felt tightness in his chest. That was not the story Vic told him, but he decided to play along.

"That's horrible. What a terrible burden – to go through life knowing your wife opened the door to your house to that animal because you told her he was all right. She trusted you and you let an animal in the house that killed your whole family," Jim said.

"Yes, it is, but I think he has come very far in dealing with his grief, don't you?" Dr. McGuire said.

"I guess, that's really your department and quite frankly I'm having a little problem focusing on the concerns of others right now," Jim said.

"Perfectly understandable," Dr. McGuire said. "How are things going with you?"

"Before we dive into my cesspool of a life, I've a few more questions about Vic," Jim said. "Like, what's his last name, for example?"

"I'm sorry, but that's information I can't share," Dr. McGuire said. "And I didn't share it with the police officer either."

"This is just a guess, you understand, but I bet you don't play much poker, do you doctor?" Jim said.

"I beg your pardon? I'm not sure how that has any bearing…"

"I'm not a great poker player, but I've played enough nickel-dime to know when someone is bluffing," Jim said.

"What in the world are you talking about," Dr. McGuire said.

"Every time you say something that strains the truth, you move your lower jaw back and forth slightly just before you speak," Jim said.

"I do not and I resent the implication that I'm bluffing as you call it," Dr. McGuire said.

"Whatever you say, doctor, but I still believe you're not being completely open with me," Jim said.

"I'm being as open as I ethically can be under the circumstances. If that is not good enough, then I'm sorry, but I'm bound by a code of ethics to keep certain information confidential," Dr. McGuire said. "I don't think we are going to accomplish anything productive today given the negative start to this session, so why don't we conclude and start over with our next session on a more positive note?"

"Fine with me," Jim said.

As he was leaving the center, he met Judy again, this time in front of the reception desk. Instead of a frightened look, she had a pleasant smile and extended her hand.

"How are you doing, Jim?" she asked.

"As well as can be expected, I suppose," he said.

When he took her hand, there was a piece of paper in it. He quickly put it in his pocket.

"Group meets Monday, will you be there?" she asked.

"Wouldn't miss it," he said as he walked out the door.

The rain had stopped but a light fog remained. It was dark now and the parking lot lights were on casting spotlight like beams through the fog onto the few cars below. He half expected Vic to step out of the shadows, but no one approached him on his way to his car, which about three spots away from one of the light poles.

Once in his car, he locked the doors and took the note from Judy out of his pocket. The parking light on the nearby pole was bright enough to read by. She wrote the note on the back of one of those preprinted telephone message notes that come in pads. It read:

"More going on here than you know. Be careful."

As he re-read the note, the light went out and almost simultaneously there was a loud crashing sound to his right and the sound of objects hitting his car. He reached in his glove compartment and grabbed a flashlight.

The flashlight revealed glass fragments on the hood of his car. He got out and walked around to the right side of the car. Larger pieces of thick glass covered the ground. He looked up and the flashlight beam could barely cut through the light fog, but he could see that glass fixture over the parking light was gone.

His cell phone rang.

"A shot across your bow."

"Who is this?" he said, but the other person hung up.

Then is hit him. Someone had shot out the light as a warning.

He just stood there – his feet nailed to the ground and his knees felt like they were going to melt. He had a strong urge to piss and almost did in his pants.

When he could move, he was wobbly and put one hand on his car hood for support. A sharp pain shot up his arm, but he just kept moving toward the driver's side. He finally got in the car and locked the doors again. Only then did he notice that he had an ugly cut on the palm of his left hand. He got his handkerchief and wrapped it around his hand.

It took him three attempts, but he finally got Samantha's home phone number on this cell phone's directory and called her.

"Samantha, it's me," Jim said. "I'm sorry for calling you at home, but I didn't know…you're the only person I trust in this world right now and I need to talk."

"Oh no. What's happened? Are you all right?" she said.

"I'd rather not talk about it over the phone. Would you mind, I mean could I come over to your place, if you're not too busy, just for a minute?" he said.

"Of course," she said. "I'll be expecting you."

Samantha lived in a duplex in an older neighborhood about 30 minutes from the church. Jim and Sally had eaten there once before they were married and once after. Samantha did not have a date on either occasion. They had Samantha over several times along with other people from work for hamburgers or pizza and board games. She always came alone.

Jim knew that until a few years ago she was taking care of a younger sister with Down Syndrome. The sister died of complications following surgery for ovarian cancer. Samantha was the sister's primary caregiver for the past 15 years. Her father was dead and her mother was in a nursing home following a stroke that left her severely incapacitated. Jim guessed there hadn't been much time in Samantha's life for anything but taking care of other people and here he was, asking her to take care of him once again.

When she opened the door, she saw his bloody left hand wrapped in the handkerchief and rushed him into the bathroom where she gently unwrapped the makeshift bandage.

"That's a deep cut, Mr. Jackson," she said. "We should go to the emergency room. See, it's still bleeding."

"Maybe in a little while, don't you have a bandage or something temporary so we can talk for a little and I can rest for a minute. I'm so tired I don't think I can stand up much longer," he said.

She was one step ahead of him and already had a roll of gauze out and some gauze pads. After cleaning the wound with some warm water and drying it the best she could, she packed the pads into his palm and wrapped the roll of gauze around his hand several times, finishing off with some adhesive tape to hold it in place.

"There, that'll hold it for awhile," she said. "Come on into to the living room and sit down. Do you want some wine or coffee or something to eat?"

He sat on the sofa and it felt like the most comfortable sofa he had ever sat on in his life. His left hand was throbbing, but he found that if he rested in on the sofa arm, which was about "heart high" it didn't hurt so much.

"A glass of wine would be great if it is not too much trouble," he said. He leaned his head against the high back of the old-fashioned sofa and thought he would just close his eyes for a minute.

He woke, not with a start, but with a slow clearing of a fog and realized he was leaning against Samantha. He pulled away quickly.

"I'm so sorry. I didn't mean to…I must've fallen asleep," he said.

"It's alright, Mr. Jackson," she said. "You were exhausted and you did fall asleep. You began to tip over and I was afraid it would wake you, so I sat down next to you."

"Thank you," he said. "This has been another in a string of very bad days in my life, but it always seems that I can count on you when everyone and every thing else in my life fails me."

"Are you hungry? I've some bread, cold cuts, sausage, and cheese on the table. We can have a bite to eat and you can tell me about your day if you're up to it," she said.

Jim realized he was starving and the simple meal sounded like a feast to him. Between bites, he recounted the day from the time he left her in the morning until he left the counseling center. She listened without interruption, but with her full attention to every word.

"Before I go any further, I'm curious if you know anyone named Vic?" Jim asked. "And I mean outside the company."

"No, I don't," she said. "Why do you ask?"

"Well, you've heard his name come up and he knew who you were when I mentioned your name," Jim said. "I'm just trying to figure out where this guy gets all his information."

"And you think he's getting in from me?" Samantha said.

"Oh, no. I didn't mean it that way at all," Jim said. "You're the only person in the world I can trust. It's just that this guy seems to have ways of finding out things just by being around people. It's all very weird."

"No, it's no weird at all Jim, I mean Mr. Jackson," she said.

"Sam. Don't you think it's about time to drop the Mr. Jackson?" he said.

"Yes, I suppose it is. Okay. This Vic guy seems to know stuff about you without being told. Where can a person find that type of personal information?" she said.

"Of course," Jim said and smacked himself on the forehead with his left hand. "Ouch. Of course, he even told me he was a computer geek who worked on databases and he has worked on the company's system.

"Sam, do you think you could snoop around our vendor list and see if you can find a computer consultant named Vic? I sure would like to know more about him," Jim said.

"That shouldn't be a problem," she said. "But you haven't told me how you hurt your hand."

"That's the scary part of the day. Judy, the grief support facilitator, met me on the way out and palmed me a note. I was reading the note in my car, which was parked under one of those parking lot lights on a tall pole when it went dark and there was this sound of breaking glass.

"When I got out to see what happened, I could see with my flashlight that the glass cover of the parking light fixture was gone and on the ground shattered. As I was standing there, my cell phone rang and this voice says, 'A shot across the bow' and hangs up. That's when I realized the light had been shot out," Jim said. "I cut my hand when I put it on the hood of my car to steady myself and there was a piece of glass there."

"Oh, my God. Someone shot at you," she said.

"No, not really. It was just a warning," Jim said.

"How do you know that," she said.

"That's what the phone message meant," he said. "In a naval conflict one ship might fire a shot across another ship's bow or front as a warning for them to stop.

"It was still very frightening," he said and began to shake at the thought. "Whoever fired that shot could've killed me just as easily as they shot out that light fixture."

"Come sit on the sofa," Samantha said. This time she sat on her legs and very close to him. She put her right arm around his shoulder and pulled him close to her. They stayed like that for a very long time.

Jim had almost forgotten what a human touch felt like. He realized how much he missed the simple feel of Sally's hand on his arm or her leg next to his when they sat next to each other. Like so many other simple pleasures, he had taken this one for granted when she was alive. It was not a sexual pleasure although in certain times and places it certainly was, but most of the time it was an intimate pleasure – another way of connecting to a person.

Strangely, he didn't feel guilty here with Sam. He was aware of her arm around him and the gentle pressure pulling him into her body. It felt very good in the same intimate way he felt with Sally. He could smell her gentle, clean scent and feel her breath on his neck. He realized his wounded hand was resting in her lap and he could feel his shoulder between her breasts.

"I should probably go," he said. "But, I'm not sure I can drive."

"You're not going anywhere. You can spend the night here," she said.

"Sam, I…" he said.

"I've a second bedroom with its own bath," she said. "You'll be comfortable there and we can see what we should do in the morning."

She got up and went into the second bedroom. A moment later, she came out and helped him to his feet.

"There are towels, soap, anything you need," she said. "If you get to feeling bad in the night, there in a button on the night stand. Push that and I'll come see what you need."

"Thank you, Sam and good night." He leaned over and kissed her on the cheek.

Chapter 17 – Thursday – Shannon & Ling

Ling's apartment building was in a neighborhood that bordered a small park near the lake. It was a high-rise and her apartment was on the 15th floor overlooking the park and lake.

Ling opened the door to her apartment with a warm smile that instantly made Shannon feel at ease.

"Welcome to my home," Ling said.

"Thank you for having me on such short notice," Shannon said. "It is really an imposition on my part, but I really needed to be with you right now."

"Rough day?"

"Not so much rough as disturbing. I think we may be mucking around in something much bigger than any of us realize."

"Were you planning to stay for awhile," Ling said with a smile glancing at the large sports bag Shannon was carrying.

"Oh, no. Sorry. I've been going for 14 hours straight and I feel like I've most of the city's grime on me. I've got some clean gym clothes in here and I was kinda wondering if it would be okay if I took a quick shower."

"Of course, it would," Ling said. "Follow me."

Ling led her back to the bedroom and got out a fresh set of towels.

"There's shampoo, soap, use anything you want," she said. "How about I fix us something to eat while you get cleaned up?"

"That'd be great, thanks."

Ling shut the bedroom door on her way out.

Not only was Ling Shannon's physical opposite, she was also her neatness opposite. Everything was in its place and not a speck of dust anywhere. Ling decorated the apartment with contemporary furniture and art, but Shannon noticed there were no Chinese or Asian pieces anywhere.

Shannon stood under the shower for ten minutes or more letting the steaming hot water wash away some of the tension that had built up during the day. Some of that tension was in anticipation of this evening, which she alternately was going to do, then not.

When she dried off and came out of the bathroom, there was a glass of wine on the dresser waiting for her. Although she wasn't a knowledgeable wine drinker, this red wine was wonderful.

She dressed in nylon parachute pants, a light top, and some light slip-on shoes she used in kickboxing. She stuffed her day clothes into the sports bag and left her pistol and shield on top of the pile.

When she walked back into the living area, Ling was busy in the kitchen, so Shannon walked over to the patio doors to take in the night view. It was spectacular – the city lights lining the curving lakeshore and stretching inland as far as she could see from this vantage point.

"Beautiful," Ling said.

"Yes, it is," Shannon said.

"I was talking about you."

"Oh, please. No makeup, dressed for the gym. And look at you. You're perfect."

They both started laughing.

"Okay. Let's both agree that we're beautiful. Now can we eat?" Ling said.

"Works for me," Shannon said.

Dinner was a salad and a chicken Alfredo dish that Shannon thought was wonderful. She ate two helpings of everything.

"How did you have time to make this while I was taking a shower?"

"I just happened to have everything and it goes together pretty easy," Ling said. "Let's go into the living room and you can tell me what's going on."

Shannon ran through the day summarizing what had happened at each step and ending with the credit card incident.

"So you think the call was a warning," Ling said.

"No doubt about that," Shannon said. "And whoever is trying to warn me off was following me fairly closely, which reminds me."

She got up from the sofa, went to Ling's front door, and engaged the deadbolt lock.

"Is there another entrance to the apartment?" she asked.

"No, just this one," Ling said. "What's going on? This apartment building is very secure. It has the latest electronic monitoring and control entrance devices, at least that's what they tell the tenants."

"I guess I'm just a little nervous that someone could get that close to me without me knowing it. And now, I'm thinking I made a big mistake coming here tonight," Shannon said.

"I'm sorry you feel that way."

"No, that's not what I mean," Shannon said. "I think I may have put you in danger by coming here tonight."

"I don't think someone screwing around with your credit card sounds too threatening to me."

"You don't understand," Shannon said. "There's something going on that I'm not seeing and that frightens me. I started out investigating a simple, although puzzling, murder case, but every day it gets more complicated and involves more people. That's the opposite of how a simple murder case ought to evolve. Besides, I didn't come here tonight just to talk shop. I could've done that tomorrow morning."

"I was hoping there was more to your visit than just a consultation," Ling said. "And I'm really glad to see you, but do you notice anything different about this time we're together."

"Yeah, I do," Shannon, said. "But I wasn't sure if it was just me or not. I'm excited to be here and I've thought about you all day, but I didn't want to rip your clothes off the minute I saw you. I'm not saying the sexual attraction is gone, because it's not, but some of my tension is gone."

"I guess I feel the same way. It's been so long since I've had a relationship I wanted to grow and nurture, I almost forgot how," Ling said. "Although, when I came into the bedroom to leave the glass of wine and I heard you in the shower, it was all I could to do to stop myself from joining you."

"Wow, that got the heart pumping," Shannon said. "Let's put that on the 'things to do list.'"

Ling's leather sofa faced a long wall that included the patio door on the right, and fireplace with a built-in TV above it in the center, and a glass wall to the left.

Ling got up, lit the gas fireplace with a remote control, and dimmed the lights so they could see the city lights stretching out below. She took a remote control off the coffee table in front of the sofa and pointed toward a sound system in the built in bookcases on the right wall. The gentle, stirring music of Itzhak Perlman filled the room.

"Why did you pick him?" Shannon asked.

"I thought you might like it since you have something in common."

"On my best day, I had nothing in common with him," Shannon said. "I was expecting Billy Bob and the Tub Thumpers or something."

"Do you want me to turn it off?"

"What I want you to do is come here and sit very close to me," Shannon said.

Before Ling took a step there was a knock on the door and the sound of someone turning the door handle.

Shannon bolted to her feet.

"Were you expecting someone?" she whispered.

Ling shook her head. Shannon walked over turned up the lights and walked quickly into the bedroom. When she came out, she was wearing her shield around her neck on a chain and had her pistol in her hand.

She went to the door with Ling and signaled her to see who it was.

"It's just this jerk who lives down the hall. I made the mistake of going out with him once and now he won't leave me alone," Ling said. She opened the door a crack.

"Barry, will you go away. I'm busy."

"Oh, come on down," Barry said. "I've got some friends over and we're having some drinks."

Barry was big, loud, and drunk. Shannon could smell his cologne through the door. He was probably one of those fashion causalities that read about a new cologne in a men's magazine and figured if a dash was good, a handful was better.

"Barry, I've told you before to leave me alone. Now, I've got company," Ling said and tried to close the door.

"I don't see nobody," he said with his size 12 shoe stuck preventing her from closing the door. "Come on over and have a drink, don't be such a stuck up bitch."

There was that word again. Shannon put her gun down. Shannon motioned Ling to back up. Barry took that as an invitation to come in, but instead, Shannon stepped in front of him. He was about two inches shorter than she was and wearing shorts and a Hawaiian print shirt unbuttoned. A thick mat of hair covered his beer gut and was overlapping the collar of his shirt.

"My friend asked you to leave, now I'm telling you to leave or I'll bust your drunk ass for trespassing," Shannon said.

"Well, what have we here," Barry said. He turned and yelled down the hall to an open door. "Hey boys, come look at this. It's the jolly green giant."

Two men came out of the apartment laughing. They stopped laughing when they saw Shannon's badge.

"Hey, Barry, she's a cop. You don't want to be doing this man," one of the said.

"Oh, yeah she's pretty tough hiding behind that badge," Barry said. "But, she still sits down to pee."

"Is that what's bothering you," Shannon said. "Well, I can fix that. Step out into the hall. I'll tell you what. I'll take off my badge and I'll make you a wager. I bet I can give you two black eyes and before you land a punch," she said. "If I win, you leave my friend alone for good. If you win, we'll both come down to your place for drinks. Deal."

"No charges for hitting a cop," Barry said.

"I'm not a cop right now," Shannon said.

"And all I got to do his hit you once?" he said.

"That's right," she said.

The hall was about ten feet wide, which wasn't much maneuvering room, but enough for what she had in mind.

Barry looked back at his friends and laughed.

"Okay, let's get it on," he said and rushed her, which is exactly what she thought he would do.

Before he took a full step, her right foot arched out and caught him square in the face, breaking his nose. He dropped his arms and she hit him in each eye with a left and right jab so fast he had no time to react. He sank to his knees and finally got his arms up to protect his face.

"Too late, Barry, you lose," she said. She took his wallet and got his drivers license. She motioned for Ling brought her a paper and pen and she copied down the number and other information.

"Barry, I'm not going to press charges against you – that was our deal, but if you ever bother my friend again I'll have ever cop in this town on your case. You step across the line and I'll come down on you like a ton of bricks," Shannon said.

"Hey, boys, you what to give your buddy a hand. I don't think he can walk so well just yet," she said. "Put some ice on that face, it's a mess."

She went back into the apartment as Barry's buddies helped him back to his apartment. Ling was staring out the patio door at the night sky.

"I don't think he'll be bothering you anymore," Shannon said.

Ling didn't say anything or turn around.

"Are you all right?" Shannon said.

"No, I'm not all right. I really appreciate your wanting to look after me, but I'm not completely helpless just because I'm small," she said. "And I wish you would find another way to solve problems besides beating some jerk's face in."

Shannon felt like Ling had kicked her in the gut.

"But I thought he was bothering you and …"

"He was bothering me, but don't you think I can take care of my own problems? I'm a grown woman and a medical doctor and I can handle jerks like Barry in my sleep," Ling said. "When you step in with that macho shit, it makes me feel like you have no respect for me as a woman just because I'm not athletic. I don't want to be kept like some delicate flower on a pedestal."

Ling turned her back to Shannon and looked back at the lake.

"Oh, this is just freaking great," Shannon said. "What do you want from me? What you see is what you get doc. I'm like that jerk said, 'the jolly green giant.' Except I'm not jolly. I'm mad as hell most of the time. I'm just a big, dumb, blonde cop. Sorry if I don't have all the sensitivity you need, but there you are. All I know how to do is hurt people. Get in my way and I'll kick your teeth in. Try to get close to me and I'll disappoint you ever time. I'm real good at both. Do yourself a favor and forget about me. I'm no good for you or anyone else," she said.

Shannon went into the bedroom and pulled on a sweatshirt, grabbed her sports bag and returned to the living room. Ling was standing by the sofa with tears running down her cheeks.

"I don't want you to go," she said.

"You don't know what you want," Shannon said. "If you did, you wouldn't want me. I'm damaged merchandise. You can do better – a lot better."

Shannon started toward the door. "Where's my gun?"

Ling pick it up off the coffee table, but in a backwards manner so that the gun was upside down and the barrel was pointing towards her.

Shannon quickly put her large hand over Ling's, and twisted the gun so the barrel was pointing away from Ling.

"I should've given you a lesson in gun safety," Shannon said.

"Shannon, what are you afraid of," Ling asked.

"I'm not afraid of anything," Shannon said. "Except the one thing I want most of all and every time I manage to screw it up."

"This time will be different," Ling said.

"No it won't. You don't think it was just a coincidence that your buddy is the second jerk in as many days I've banged up in your name do you?" Shannon said.

"The second? Who was the first?" Ling asked.

"There's this prick who works in the squad room. His family has connections, which is the only way he got the job. Everybody hates him. Anyway, he made a racial slur about you, so I took him into the locker room and bounced him around a little. Nothing like your friend down the hall, but out of line just the same. I zeroed in on the thing that's going to drive you away and two poor smucks are licking their wounds. I'll keep beating up men who look at you crooked or say the wrong thing until you can't stand me anymore, which sounds like it shouldn't be too long now," Shannon said. "So I'm going to save you the trouble and make my exit now before I really hurt someone."

"You have really hurt someone – me," Ling said.

"I rest my case," Shannon said. "Like I said, I'm just a big, dumb blonde thug, who will disappoint anyone who tries to get close to me. You're better off without me."

Shannon started towards the door when a small book thrown by Ling hit her in the back.

"Ouch, what the…" she said and turned around.

Ling was in her face almost immediately.

"How dare you? Who do you think you are? You don't walk out on me until I say you can walk out," Ling said, her finger poking Shannon in the chest to emphasize every point.

"I don't care if you are the Jolly Green Giant, you don't decide what I feel – you got that? I'm madly in love with you and you aren't going to push me away because you have issues to deal with or whatever. That's not good enough sister."

Ling was backing Shannon up until she was pinned against the door unable to move.

"But…" Shannon started.

"Shut up," Ling said. "I'm not through with you. I'm sick and tired of this 'big, dumb blonde' crap. Okay? You're not dumb and you know it. I'll bet you dumb yourself down around the guys at work so they don't look stupid – don't you? You know the answer ten minutes before they do. It was that way in college too, wasn't it? I was lucky. Asians were supposed to be smart. It must have been hard for you, but that's no excuse for you to buy into the crap, especially now. So, if you really don't care for me, then you can go and that'll be the end of it. But if you have feelings for me like I think and hope you do you're not getting out of this apartment unless you give me one of those karate chops or whatever it was you did to ole Barry," Ling said and stepped back.

Shannon sank to her knees and cried tears that had been waiting for many years. Ling was there in an instant – holding her, running her fingers through her hair, and wiping away the unrestrained flow of tears.

"Why are you doing this to me?" Shannon asked. "I'll hurt you – you know that."

"Is it me you're worried about," Ling said. "Or are you protecting yourself?"

"Everyone I've ever loved has abandoned me and you will too," Shannon said.

"There you go again. Telling me what I'll do before I even know what I'll do," Ling said. "Don't you see that you're setting up the relationship for failure?"

"Sure I do. I'm not dumb, remember," Shannon said.

"Yes, I remember, but I know these decisions have little to do with intellect and much to do with emotional scars. Everyone you loved abandoned you – at least in your heart they did and now you're afraid that anyone you love will also abandon you. It actually makes sense," Ling said.

"I'm so afraid of you," Shannon said.

"Well, that'll be a first for me," Ling said. "I'm usually the one in the relationship who is terrified most of the time."

"You seem so strong," Shannon said. "I want to hold on and never let go, but I'm afraid."

"I'm not going to tell you to not be afraid," Ling said. "I'm afraid too. That's my nasty little secret. I'm as afraid of rejection as you are of abandonment. If you look me in the eye and tell me you have no feelings for me, I'll not eat for a week and then be really depressed."

Shannon almost laughed.

"Sorry, I'm sure you didn't mean that as a joke," she said.

"No, but it did come out kinda of goofy," Ling said. "Can I assume that since you haven't walked out the door that you do have feelings for me?"

"Oh, yes," Shannon said. "Yes you can."

"Can I offer an idea of how we might move forward?" Ling said. "Why don't we say we are going to explore our relationship one day at a time and not try to anticipate the future. We'll also pledge to one another that if we are feeling insecure about something the other has done or said or not done or not said we'll ask before jumping to conclusions. Are you willing to do that? Will you trust me one day at a time?"

Shannon, still on her knees, looked up into Ling's eyes and held her gaze for a moment. She wiped her eyes with the sleeve of her sweatshirt and pulled it off along with the top underneath. She slid her hands into the tops of Ling's pants along with her panties and pulled them to the floor.

Ling pulled off her top and stood before Shannon completely naked. Shannon picked up Ling like a groom carrying a bride and slowly walked back to the bedroom.

Chapter 18 – Thursday – Shannon, Jim, Sam, & Ling

"Hey. Wake up. Shannon. Wake up."

"What? What is it," she said.

"It's your cell phone," Ling said.

"What time is it? Oh, crap. 6:10. Okay. Where did I put it?" she said. "O'Brien."

"Detective O'Brien?"

"Yes. Who is this?"

"Sorry if I woke you up, but you said to call if I wanted to talk and I think I need to talk now."

"Okay, but who is this?"

"Oh, sorry. This is Jim Jackson."

Shannon sat up in bed. "Mr. Jackson. I'm glad you called. What did you want to talk about?"

"Is that your murder suspect?" Ling whispered.

Shannon nodded.

"I'd rather not talk about it in detail over the phone, but I believe someone shot at me last night," Jim said.

"You believe you were shot at," she said. "Where are you calling from?"

"Mercy General Emergency Room," Jim said.

"Were you hit?" Shannon said.

"No, I cut my hand on some glass when it happened. I don't think they were actually trying to shoot me. I think this was a warning shot," Jim said.

"Why do you say that?" she said.

"Because they shot out a light fixture in the parking lot of the counseling center that I was parked under. That's how I cut my hand," he said.

"Do you believe you're in danger now?" she said.

"No, I don't think so, but I don't know," he said.

"Okay. You stay there. I'm sending a uniformed officer to stay with you until I arrive. Until that officer arrives, hospital security will send someone. Don't leave no matter what until I come for you. I'll be there in about 45 minutes. Okay. Do you understand?" she said.

"Someone took a shot or at least a warning shot at Mr. Jackson last night," Shannon said as she closed her cell phone.

"I guess that means you have to go," Ling said.

Shannon looked at Ling curled up in the rumpled sheets and smiled. "Last night was better than I ever dreamed it could be."

Ling's face lit up as she stretched her arms and legs.

"How can you eat like you do and have almost no body fat," Shannon asked in mock wonder.

"I wish I could take credit for it, but it's all in the genes," Ling said. "Do you want something to eat before you go?"

"Do you have a glass of juice?" Shannon said as she got dressed. "I've just got time to run home, change clothes and get to the hospital."

While Ling was getting the juice, Shannon called the hospital security office and had them send someone to stay with Jackson. Next, she called the watch commander and asked for a uniform to stay at the hospital until she got there. Finally, she called the evidence unit and asked them to get to the counseling center parking lot and see what they could find.

She drank the juice in one gulp, but paused to give Ling a long and lingering kiss. "Thank you for one day," she said.

Shannon was thankful she had taken a police car the night before, because she used the lights to get to and from her apartment to the hospital in a hurry, which was strictly against regulations.

The emergency room at Mercy General Hospital was busy even at 7:00 in the morning. Mercy was a trauma center for the northern part of town and did a brisk business just about any hour of the day or night. In addition to major traumas, they treated a number of minor cases like Jim's and people with the flu or other ailments who had no doctor.

The waiting area was crowded, so the hospital security officer had put Jim and Samantha in an examining room at the end of the corridor that ran the length of the ER. On the other end was the unloading area where ambulances brought in patients. Lining the corridor were various examining rooms and five major trauma rooms where attendants brought the most seriously injured.

"Here she comes," the police officer said who was guarding the curtained entrance to the room.

Jim leaned out and saw Shannon coming down the long corridor and felt like Sam was right in insisting he call her. She carried more authority than most men and he needed someone to trust who could help him.

"Are you all right Mr. Jackson?" she asked.

"Yes. Ten stitches and a tetanus shot and I'm good to go," he said.

"Who's your friend?" she asked.

"This is Samantha Weatherby," Jim said. "She brought me to the hospital and convinced me I needed to trust you."

Shannon turned her attention to the uniformed officer. "Everything okay here?" she said.

"Quiet as a mouse," he said. "I haven't left his side, even went to the john with him."

"Great," Shannon said. "Thanks for taking this seriously."

"Do you want me to hang around or can I clear?" he said.

"Go ahead and clear. I'll be sure your sergeant hears some good things about your…"

Something splattered in Shannon's face and she felt a sharp pain on the right side of her face that made her recoil. The cop crumbled to the ground. It took a second, before she realized she had been shot. She pulled her pistol and tackled both Jim and Samantha, knocking them both to the ground. She grabbed the policeman's radio off his belt.

"Command. Command. Officer down. Officer down. Mercy General Emergency Room. Mercy General Emergency Room. Shots fired. Shots fired."

The emergency room was in chaos. People were screaming and running.

Shannon was shouting for them to get down. A couple of doctors and nurses were working on the cop. Shannon pushed Jim and Samantha into a corner and was protecting them with her body while looking for a shooter.

One of the doctors crawled over to her and she pushed him away. "You help him."

"There's nothing we can do for him," the doctor said. "Let me look at your face, you've been shot."

"Not now, the shooter may still be here."

"Okay. Just hold this on the wound." He handed her a gauze pad.

In a matter of minutes, the place was swarming with cops.

Jim and Samantha were hurried off to a private suite the hospital kept for V.I.P. patients who wanted to stay out of the public eye and had the means to pay for it. Three officers guarded the door.

Shannon was bleeding but wouldn't stop for attention. The cops did a sweep of the neighborhood and a room-by-room search of the hospital. Two blocks away officers found a set of hospital scrubs in a dumpster.

Finally, her captain ordered her to get her wound attended to or he would personally put her in cuffs. They took her into one of the trauma rooms for the examination.

While they were working on her, she heard Ling's voice. She was just outside looking at the officer's body. Shannon wanted her to do the examination because she was familiar with the other cases. She hadn't talked to Ling directly.

"Where can I find Detective O'Brien?" she asked one of the uniformed officers.

"She's being treated in that room over there," he said.

"What do you mean she being treated?" she asked.

"She was shot," he said.

Ling flew through the door of the examination room.

"You can't come in here," a nurse said.

"Get out of my way. I'm a doctor. Shannon, my God."

"I'm glad you're here. It's not as bad as it looks. I took a fragment in the face, but the good news is the doctor here is just about to get it out. So bag it for evidence."

"Doctor, do you mind if I've a look," Ling asked.

"No, here's your fragment," he said, putting it in the evidence bag Ling was holding open.

She stretched to look at the wound on Shannon's face, which ran from just under her right eye for about two inches. Another one-half inch higher and she would have lost an eye or worse.

Ling's eyes filled with tears, which she quickly wiped away hoping the others in the room didn't see.

"Why didn't you tell me?"

"There just wasn't time. I'm sorry. I really need you to be strong and help us figure out what's going on or there will be more deaths," Shannon said. "Have you looked at the body?"

"First look it seems just like the others and this fragment fits the pattern. I'll know more when I get him downtown, but I think you can safely work on the assumption that whoever is doing this has struck again."

"Call me as soon as you know anything that might help us."

"I need to sew you up now officer," the doctor said.

"I can't believe this is happening to us," Jim said. "It's like a bad dream that just gets worse every day. I can't believe I saw someone die right in front of me and maybe that poor young man died because of me."

"You can't blame yourself for the actions of a maniac," Sam said. "And the only way to make this stop is to figure out who is behind all of this and stop them."

"I wonder if the police still think I'm involved after all of this," Jim said. "I'm sorry I've dragged you into this mess. When they let us go, you should put some distance between you and this mess and get on with your life."

"Why don't you let me decide what's important in my life," she said.

"Well, I didn't mean anything by it. I just thought you might not want to be associated with the kind of baggage I'm carrying these days," he said.

"Did in ever occur to you in all the years we've been together that I …"

There was a knock on the door and Shannon stuck her head in. "Sorry to bother you folks, but we need to talk."

She opened the door wider and walked in followed by Detectives Appleton and Barnes. Jim felt a big knot in his stomach.

"What are they doing here?" he said. "I didn't agree to talk to them."

"I know, Mr. Jackson, but obviously the events of the last few hours plus some things that have happened over the last 24 hours have changed this case dramatically. Something is not right and we've got to get to the bottom soon or I'm afraid that we're going to have more incidents like the one downstairs," Shannon said.

She motioned for everyone to sit around a small dining room table.

"Look kid," Appleton said. "We're just doing our job. It was nothing personal. You probably don't see it that way, but believe me 9 times out of 10 when we have the amount of evidence pointing at someone like we had on you – we have a murderer. My partner and I've been doing this for a long time and we don't put innocent people in jail. We've had cases like yours before where a person looked real guilty, but they weren't. But those we can count on one hand. Despite our ugly faces, we're the good guys. On more than one occasion, we've gone to the DA after a suspect we arrested has been indicted and said 'we got the wrong dude.'"

"Okay, enough of this Robin Hood crap. Bottom line is we got to find out what's going on and stop it before someone else dies. And we think you can help," Barnes said.

"Does that mean you don't think I'm the killer?" Jim said.

"Let's just say you're nowhere near the top of the list anymore," Appleton said. "We never let anyone off the hook completely until we get the actual bad guy behind bars."

"Before we go on, can you tell us what happened downstairs," Sam said.

"Sure," Shannon said. "The shooter was in the ER behind one of the curtains. The shooter drew the curtain so that he or she had a clear shot at the officer, but blocked my view so I didn't see anything. He or she was dressed in hospital gear so as not to draw attention. The shooter used a pillow to muffle the sound of the pistol – we found it behind a curtain with powder burns."

"Was he or she aiming at me or you," Jim asked.

"No, I don't believe so. The shooter hit the officer – his name was Cory Wayne, he'd been on the force four years and was going to be married next month – the shot hit him just at the base of the skull. He was dead before he hit the floor," she said. "A fragment of the bullet hit me in the face."

"How do you know the shot wasn't meant for me or you," Jim said.

"Because, and this must stay in this room, this is exactly how Bonnelli and a young black man died. They were both shot in the same place – the back of the skull. We believe there may be other unsolved murders with the same pattern – a shot to the base of the skull," Shannon said.

"I know of another," Jim said.

"You what…" Appleton said.

"I know of another murder where the victim was shot once in the back of the head. The victim was a petty thief who had killed a store owner in cold blood," he said.

The three cops exchanged glances.

"Mr. Jackson, that's incredible information. Would you mind telling me where you learned of this crime," Shannon said.

Jim related Carolyn's story from the grief support group about the man who killed her father being found dead months later in an alley.

"When did this happen," Barnes asked.

"I believe she said it was two years ago," Jim said. "That's all I know and, before you even ask, I don't know her last name."

"Okay. I want a time out," Appleton said. "Things are moving way too fast for this old flatfoot. We've got more new information on the table than we can digest and my partner and I don't even have all the old information."

"You're right," Shannon said. "We need to regroup. This case is out of control and I get the feeling the murderer is playing with us. Besides my face hurts like hell."

"First of all we've got to get these two to a safe place. Lenny, can you arrange protective services in the safe suite downtown?"

"Sure, I'm on it," he said and walked off to talk on his cell phone.

"I'm not sure we need…"

"Mr. Jackson, a police officer was killed not three feet from you today. Whoever did this will have no hesitancy to kill you when and where he wants. You and Ms. Weatherby are at risk. You can go into protective custody voluntarily or I can hold you as a material witness, involuntarily. Your choice."

"Jim, trust her," Sam said.

"I'm sorry, we'll go," he said.

"Thank you. And we'll want to talk some more. Real soon," Shannon said.

"The safe place is all arranged. There will be a protection unit here in 15 minutes to take them to their homes to pickup clothes and stuff, then take them to the safe place," Barnes said.

"Great. Thanks for getting that going so quickly."

"Those guys cut a lot of red tape when a cop goes down," Barnes said.

"No offense, but you look like hell," Appleton said. "You need to get off your feet."

"For once, I'm not going to argue with you. The painkillers are wearing off and my face feels like someone shot me. Why don't we meet at my shop at 3:00 and I can bring you up-to-date on what I know and then we can go visit this couple around 4:00, if that's okay with everyone," she said.

"We'll stay with these two until the protection unit arrives, why don't you go home and sleep for a couple of hours?" Appleton said.

"Thanks, I'll do that."

Jim found the protective services unit thorough and very professional although he wondered what good bulletproof vests would do them if the killer shot them in the back of the head.

The officers took them down a service elevator to a back entrance where a van with heavily tinted windows waited. It took them to pick up clothes and toiletries.

The safe place was an older hotel in the near downtown area where the police kept a large apartment for witnesses and others they wanted out of view. It had two bedrooms, a kitchen, dining area, and living room.

The police picked this particular hotel and this particular apartment for a reason. Due to an odd placement in the city's geography, there were no taller buildings on the apartment's side of the hotel, which meant no snipers could get a shot into the apartment from a nearby taller building.

Once Jim and Samantha settled into their rooms, they wandered out into the living area and were surprised to see an officer sitting in one of the easy chairs reading a magazine.

"Sorry," he said. "Someone will be here 24/7, but we'll try not to bother you – it's just the rules."

"No problem," Jim said. "What do we do about food?"

"Oh, that's the best part," the officer said. "Just call room service and order anything you want. It's on the city."

Shannon went downstairs to make sure the evidence unit and all the other personnel were on task. Her captain told her the shooting team would want her report ASAP, but he could hold them off for 12 hours. She gave him a quick update on the case and what their plan was. He agreed to call Appleton and Barnes' captain and clear the way for them.

She walked to her car and had to put her hand on the trunk to keep from falling, she felt so weak. An arm reached around her waist, although not all the way.

"Let me help you into the car," Ling said.

"What are you doing here," Shannon said. "I thought you would be downtown working on the officer."

"It'll be at least three hours before I can get him on a table, but I'm pretty sure I'm not going to find anything we don't already know," she said. "Right now, you need me more."

Ling helped her into the passenger side of the car.

"What are you doing now, I've got to get home."

"Roll up your sleeve."

Ling produced a syringe and an alcohol swab. Shannon recoiled.

"What are you doing? What is that?"

"A little something for the pain. Are you allergic to any drugs?"

"No, but I've got to drive home and I've meetings this afternoon. I can't be 'under the influence' for either."

"I'm driving you home and this will wear off by your meetings, so quit complaining and roll up your sleeve or are you afraid of a little shot?" Ling said.

"I'm not wild about needles. Ouch."

"You big baby. Put on your seat belt and quit whining."

"Say, that's pretty good stuff. I feel better already."

"Try not to drool. It's not very sexy. I'll have you home soon."

Shannon woke up in her bed with no memory of how she got there. Her face was sore, but she felt rested and relaxed. She could hear Ling singing to herself in the living room/kitchen area. It must be some country and western song, because it about a lonesome woman and a wayward man. Ling's voice was pleasant and Shannon enjoyed the idea that she was in her apartment, until she realized what a disaster it must be compared Ling's.

She got out of bed and noticed she was completely naked. After using the bathroom and washing her face around the bandage, she put on a robe and went into the living room.

"How long have I been out?"

"Oh, you're up. About three hours. Are you hungry? I've got some soup on the stove and the makings of a sandwich ready to go."

"That sounds great. What was in that needle? I haven't felt this rested in a long time. Sorry about the mess, I…"

Shannon stopped short. Her living room looked immaculate. The kitchen was spotless and she could see all of her laundry was done and neatly folded waiting to be put away.

"You did all of this in three hours? It would have taken me all day."

"I'm an over-achiever, remember. Sit down, I want to change your dressing."

"Yes ma'am."

"Don't be a smart ass. You may have a scar. Didn't they have a plastic surgeon available to fix this?" Ling asked.

"Yeah, but she couldn't come down for another hour and I couldn't wait. Besides, a scar will make me look even meaner, don't you think?"

Ling applied the new dressing.

"You scarred the shit out of me," she said.

"I'm sorry," Shannon said. "I know I should have told you myself, but things were just happening too fast and I had a dead cop and these two other ..."

Her voice trailed off and tears rolled down her cheeks. Ling held Shannon's head to her chest.

"That cop was just 24 years old. He was going to get married next month to his high school sweetheart. I was standing right next to him and I couldn't do anything to help him. His name was Cory and he never knew what hit him. One second he was alive and the next he's dead. His fiancée is Cheryl. They put a deposit on a little house near his parents.

"What must this be like for her? Her wedding is all she's dreamed about through high school and in an instant her whole life completely changes. His dad was a cop that took me in when I was a rookie. He was about the only one of the old timers that gave female cops the time of day. He retired five years ago with a bad back and was so proud his son was a cop too. He would come by to shoot the breeze and fill me in on the boy. I made it my business to meet Cory and request him for special assignments when I could.

"I was really pleased to see him at the hospital this morning. I knew he would do a good job; he had his dad's work ethic,"

Shannon said. "I have go see his dad and tell him I couldn't save his son."

"I guess I need to eat something and get going," she said. "I need a shower too."

"You can't get that wound wet," Ling said. "Come over to the kitchen sink and I'll shampoo your hair here and you can take a bath."

"You're a remarkable woman," Shannon said. "Have I told you that today?"

"You can't tell me that too often."

Shannon and Ling drove to the home of the dead cop's father so Shannon could pay her respects.

"Why don't I wait in the car," Ling said. "They don't know me and this is not the time to meet strangers."

"I won't be too long," Shannon said and started up the walk to the front door, but stopped about half way and looked around. She walked back to the car and opened the passenger door.

"I think you should come in," she said.

"Why? What's wrong?" Ling said.

"I don't know, but I'll feel better if you're inside, please," she said.

There were relatives and friends gathered inside. The meeting between Shannon and her former mentor was very tearful and painful. Ling felt very awkward and wished Shannon had left her in the car. Shannon finally said she had to leave and the old cop understood.

When they returned to the car, Shannon walked around to the driver's side, unlocked the door and, as she was sliding in, hit the 'unlock' button to let Ling in the passenger side. As Ling slid in, she let out a gasp.

"What's wrong," Shannon said.

"Look," Ling said.

On the inside of the windshield in front of where Ling was sitting was one of those stick-on decals that are suppose to look like a bullet hole in your windshield. It was placed exactly where her head would be.

Chapter 19 – Thursday – Vic & Russell

"Are you out of your fucking mind!" Vic screamed into the phone. "You've put the whole operation at risk with this unauthorized action."

"Calm down. I made a clean exit. They can't trace this back to me," Russell said.

"Maybe, but killing a cop puts every other cop on high alert. One false step, one miscue and we'll be compromised," Vic said. "And, to make it worse, the two people we need to snatch are now in police protective custody. We could've grabbed them any time we wanted with low risk, but now I have to come up with a plan in a hurry. I hate operations that aren't carefully planned; there's just too much that can go wrong."

"I'll take care of it," Russell said.

"No you won't. Don't do anything until I contact you with a plan. Your actions have seriously threatened my plans. And, by the way, what was the purpose of firing a warning shot at Jackson? This is just the kind of lone wolf bullshit that got you eased out of your previous position. Yes, I know all about your past and where you learned both skill sets. I also suspect you've been continuing your dual career since then. We know they're being held at the safe suite in the hotel the police use for protective custody. Station yourself within two blocks of the hotel in case I need you. When my plan is in place, I'll let you know and what your role will be. Until then, stay low and don't kill anyone else," Vic said.

Acquiring Russell as an asset was a lucky stroke four years ago. A call from a contact alerted him to Russell's availability. The contact was with a private company that provided "special services" for the U.S. The contact spoke highly of Russell's qualifications as a "closer." Vic and the contact spoke in a code to avoid any entanglements should someone else be listening. Some sales professionals use the term "closer" to describe someone with the ability to make the sale or close the deal. Vic understood the term to mean assassin. He arranged for Russell to join the grief support group as a place they could make contact.

Russell showed up for his first meeting with a story about how his wife and children were killed. It didn't take Vic five minutes to realize the story was bogus. There was coldness in his eyes that belied any phony sorrow he projected. Vic made sure Russell didn't go back to the support group again.

Russell was a well-trained assassin and was use to following orders and plans. An asset like that would be valuable. The double jackpot was Vic's discovery that Russell was not only a killer, but also had considerable hacking skills.

However, Russell came with some baggage that frightened Vic a little and very few people frightened Vic. That baggage was now a threat to what he had worked so hard to achieve.

Five years ago, after a long career in "government service," Vic's information business was just getting off the ground. He specialized in corporate intelligence – gathering information on companies and selling it to rivals or investors. By combing public records, interviewing former employees, and searching online records he was able to connect the dots for his clients. He was making a modest living, but was weary of how slowly the business was growing. So he began cutting a few corners to get information that was not available to the public.

At first, it was some simple hacking into corporate databases and digging through emails and internal reports. That produced some spectacular results with only a modest effort. Later, Vic escalated his 'black ops' and the business really took off.

He set Russell up in business as a database consultant and referred some of his clients. Russell did good work and at prices that Vic knew would assure repeat business and referrals. While most of the work Russell did was legitimate, his real mission was to make it possible for Vic to slip into the company's network. This gave Vic access to even more sensitive information. Russell set up the entry so that Vic could come and go as he pleased with no obvious record that he had been there.

Vic kept Russell and that side of the business separate – they rarely met in person and Russell never came into the office. He only contacted Russell using pre-paid phones, which were swapped out every two weeks, more frequently during sensitive operations, with different drop points each time.

He escalated Russell's involvement from hacking to extortion. Vic's 'volunteering' at the grief group yielded several lucrative contacts. A woman who lost her father to a gunman during a robbery of their store was more than happy to provide Vic with some key inside information and a job for Russell at her company. She knew who killed her father, but they never went to prison.

One phone call to Russell and the gunman was dead 48 hours later. The woman got her justice and the assurance that the animal would never hurt anyone again.

Other contacts through the grief support group required some "persuasion" in the form of a threat from Russell. Vic stayed out of the picture on these operations so his cover would not be blown. Russell threatened the person with harm or, more often, threatened someone they loved. This was a very effective strategy. Many people will do something when a love one is threatened that they may refuse to do if threatened directly.

Show a woman a video of her sister and nieces and nephews shot through a telescopic sight of a rifle and you can usually get what you want. Send a man a photo of his mother sleeping peacefully in her bed at the nursing home with a large knife held under her chin and he will do whatever you want.

Russell had a signature way of killing that made Vic nervous. A single shot to the back of the head was all he needed. Among Russell's talent were incredibly steady hands. While working for his previous employer, he would regularly win bets using this ability. Russell would aim a pistol at a target and have someone put a full shot glass on his hand. He could fire the pistol and not spill a drop from the shot glass. His weapon of choice was a small caliber, single shot pistol.

Vic worried that too many deaths in this manner would alert the police and lead to a deeper investigation. Vic wanted the pressure of getting caught to stay below a comfortable level. If they tagged these deaths as the work of a serial killer it would bring too much attention. He could control Russell most of the time. However, Russell had a bad habit of killing for the apparent fun of it. In other cases he improvised, which turned out well most of the time. Still, Vic didn't like Russell's unpredictability. He would have to terminate Russell soon to avoid a threat to his operation.

Vic was very careful, but he knew it was only a matter of time before Russell's hacks were discovered. His five-year plan was to amass enough to retire and live the rest of his life in quiet luxury. Two and a half years into the plan, he hired Sally Markowitz as a sales associate.

Hiring Sally was one of his better decisions. He needed another front person and she was smart, tech-savvy, and very attractive – a combination that opened many doors for Sally. She was just the type to represent the company. His investment in her paid off handsomely. Sally brought in new business that doubled the size of the company in a year. Vic kept her in the dark about how he acquired so much sensitive information. He knew she wouldn't stay with something illegal. He did insist that her connection with the company remain confidential, which he rationalized to her with the admonition that their business was confidential information and it was better if everything was kept on a very low profile. New business leads came from referrals, which she followed up on.

However, she began to ask questions and was becoming suspicious. How did he acquire so much information so quickly? He slowly revealed some hints and shared enough with her that over time, she became a co-conspirator, at least in a legal sense. She would have a hard time convincing a court that she was completely innocent. She married this Jackson character and that took her mind off the business for a while. That didn't last long and it was clear she was becoming more of a liability than an asset. Vic survived by knowing when to cut loses. He was about to turn Russell loose on her when she hijacked a large sum of money along with account names, numbers, and passwords for a cluster of offshore banks where he stashed his profits. She threatened to give all of his money to charities unless he left her alone. She promised to return control of the overseas accounts back to him when she felt safe.

That she hacked him was particularly embarrassing and Vic decided that when he found a way to get his money and information back, he would do her himself. His first mistake had been not terminating her when she first started asking questions. His second mistake was bringing that drunk Bonnelli into the business. Bonnelli was well connected and opened a lot of doors, but he learned too much and wanted bigger piece of the action. Worst of all, he took it upon himself to deal with Sally. Her death could have been the end of Vic's whole operation. A call to Russell had ended the Bonnelli problem.

Vic could still view his offshore balances, but Sally had changed the account settings, so he couldn't get to his money to make withdrawals or transfers. For days after her death, he checked the accounts and no money was missing. After several weeks, he concluded that she had not told her husband about the accounts and had probably not told him she no longer worked in fashion marketing. He had no doubt that Sally hid the information and his money. Fortunately, she didn't leave a notice with her lawyer or someone else to release the information upon her death – a mistake on her part.

He kept a close eye on Jackson for months and was able through a contact in the HR department at Aargon Insurance to get him referred to the grief support group. Vic saw no unusual change in Jackson's behavior that would suggest he had found the money or information. As he suspected, the police began asking Jackson questions about Bonnelli's death, since he was a natural suspect. This put pressure on Jackson, which Vic used to get closer to him. By observing him at work – Russell had planted a camera in his office – Vic concluded that he could use his secretary for leverage. Jackson was a straight arrow, but it was clear he was close to Samantha, his secretary.

If Jackson didn't know about the money and information, he probably knew where Sally hid it even if she never told him. It was somewhat of a long shot, but it was the best chance he had to find his money. Although he and Russell were good hackers, getting into these offshore banks was out of their league. He could bring in other assets that might be able to do it, but that presented a huge risk. What would stop the hacker from simply transferring the money to his own account if he did get into the systems? Even if the hacker gave control of the accounts back to Vic there was the possibility the hacker would want a bigger share. Vic had no problem giving Russell the green light, but the hacker would have put in some protections to prevent that. It would be real messy and Vic didn't like messy. Still, this was the fallback plan if all else failed.

Vic had a plan and a contingency plan for getting his money and information by using Jackson's secretary for leverage. He didn't have a contingency that covered Russell killing a cop and the two targets put in protective custody. But, he was the veteran of many 'black ops' actions and the one rule that never changed was flow with the situation, not against it. Plans were important, but sometimes it was impossible to think of every possible situation.

Now thanks to Russell's impulsive action, he had to come up with a new plan quickly, before that nosey Amazon cop and her ME friend figure out some connection between him and Jackson or Jackson and Russell. Either way, they are getting closer to causing him a lot of trouble. He had to move quickly, while the two were still together in protective custody.

How can I get them out of that hotel suite without the police knowing? Then he got the break he needed. A program on his computer alerted him that Jackson was online. It is unlikely the police would be looking over his shoulder, so maybe he could get a private message to Jackson.

But, first he needed a diversion. It was not his first choice, but it was the only choice that could work immediately.

He phoned Russell.

"I've got a job for you."

Chapter 20 – Thursday – Jim, Sam, & Vic

Email follows you everywhere, which is a mixed blessing at times.

"Mind if I check my email," Jim asked the officer in the living room.

After a stern lecture about being sure to not tell anyone where he was, Jim was able to access the hotel's Wi-Fi network.

Jim and Sam were waiting for Detective O'Brien and the others to continue the questioning. He was already getting stir crazy and they had been there less than four hours. His mood lightened when he saw the hotel had wired the suite with a broadband connection to the Internet.

He wasn't a big game player, but the Internet would connect them to the outside world in a more interactive way than television. But, after only 15 minutes of browsing news sites, he was bored and returned to his email in-box, which had about 30 new messages.

"I'm going to step out in the hall and check with the officer out here for a moment. I'll be right back," the officer said.

Most of the messages were spam for home mortgage refinancing, penis enlargement, DVD rentals, and such. However, one new message arrived while he was deleting the others. When he saw it was from Vic, he got a very peculiar feeling, somewhere between fear and excitement.

The text of the message simply said:

"You and Samantha have to get out of there right now."

"Sam, come look at this," he said.

Sam read the message over his shoulder. "I don't like the sound of that at all. How does he know where we are? This is very scary. Where is that officer?"

"He said he was just stepping out into the hall. I'll get him," Jim said.

Jim started to open the door, then thought better of it and opened it very slowly and only a crack. He only needed a crack to see one of the officers lying in a pool of blood in the hall. He slammed the door and locked it. He pulled the easy chair over in front of the door and backed away.

"Sam, we've got to get out of here."

"Oh, my God. Jim, are they…"

"Come on. Let's get out of here."

"But how are we going to get out."

"The fire escape. It's our only chance."

"Why don't we call Detective O'Brien? She'll come for us," Sam said.

"We'll likely be dead by the time she gets here. Sam, we may have minutes at the most. We can't wait. Whoever this killer is they can know everything the cops know, which means they may be a cop. Who do we trust now?"

Jim went into his bedroom where he knew the fire escape was outside his window. What he didn't count on was that the cops had installed bulletproof glass in a solid metal window that was locked into the frame. He couldn't open the window no matter how hard he tried.

"There has to be a key somewhere nearby. Look around for it," he said.

Jim was frantically tearing through the room pulling out drawers and looking for a key. Meanwhile, Sam went to the window looked at it for a minute and pulled over a chair. She climbed on to the chair and retrieved the key from the top of the metal frame.

Jim opened the window and they climbed out and began the 15-floor descent.

Shannon and Ling were both shaken by the bullet hole decal that someone had placed in the car. Shannon was also nervous about the two civilians in the safe suite downtown. She decided to check on them before she went to the office.

As she approached the hotel, she called the suite number on her cell phone and got no answer. She got her radio and tuned it to the frequency used by the protection unit and tried to raise them, but got no response. She got on her command frequency and asked for "officer in trouble" backup. In two minutes, there were ten squad cars at the hotel.

"Okay. I need all of the hotel exits covered. I need three officers with me to the 15th floor. I need one officer with Dr. Ya at all times. She is a potential target, is that understood? Okay, let's go," Shannon said.

When they got to the 14th floor, two of the officers got off and went up the stairs to the 15th floor. Shannon's worse fears were realized when they secured the 15th floor. Two dead cops outside the safe suite. She tried the door, but it was locked. She got the key from one of the dead officers, but the door was still resisting. She could see there was a chair blocking the way.

"We're going in. Remember there are two civilians in there, a man and a woman, so make sure anybody you shoot has a weapon in their hand," she said.

She took several steps back and charged through the door pushing the chair back and rolling across the floor. The officers swept the apartment.

"Detective, in here. Someone made it out on the fire escape."

"Damn. They're out there on the run by themselves or prisoners."

"Detective, here's something else."

"Son of bitch," she screamed.

Shannon read the e-mail from Vic and wondered what it meant. Was it truly a warning or a trap? How did he know where they were? How did he know something bad was going to happen?

"Get Dr. Ya up here now," she yelled into the radio.

Just then Appleton and Barnes rushed through the door.

"Holy shit," Appleton said. "What have we got ourselves into?"

"I'll tell you what we got – we got three dead cops in one fucking day," Barnes said. "We've got a maniac cop killer running loose. This has got to be the most screwed up investigation in the department's history and we're all going to lose our shields over this. And it's all your fault little girl."

"My fault? How do you figure that you old fool? If we left it up to you, we'd still be wondering who killed Bonnelli and never connect anything together. And if you ever call me little girl again, I'll kick your butt so hard your breath'll smell like shit for a week," she said.

"Ease up partner. We're on the same team here, but I do have to agree with him on the cop killer angle," Appleton said. "Something set this bastard off and now he's declared open season on cops."

"I'm not so sure," Shannon said. "Something else is going on and we're just not seeing it. Jackson has some information that'll help us and he probably doesn't even know it – like knowing about that other murder – and now he's disappeared. I've got an 'all points' out on those two. I believe they are in grave danger. Jackson may have been right to run. It may have saved their lives, but for how long? How long can he and his friend hide from this shooter who knows more than we do?"

Ling walked into the suite, removing latex gloves.

"My crew is on the way, but here's the preliminary. Both were shot within 5 minutes or less of each other. The officer sitting outside got it in the back of the head like the others, but the other officer took it right between the eyes. My guess is the shooter was either surprised by the second cop or couldn't get into position for his favorite shot," she said.

"No offense doc, but you keep referring to the shooter as a 'he.' That sounds like a conclusion I would jump to, but do you have any basis for that or are you just going with the odds," Appleton said.

"Well, as you know detective, the odds are in my favor, but in this case, I've some evidence that it was most likely a man, not conclusive by any means," she said.

"This ought to be good," Appleton said.

"The officer that came out of the door was shot just above his eye brow line. He is approximately 6 feet 4 inches tall. The wound is reasonably straight in. Unless, Detective O'Brien fired the shot, and I know she didn't, the odds are it was fired by a person approximately 6 feet tall," Ling said. "The average woman is going to be 6 to 8 inches under that height."

Shannon's cell phone rang.

"Yes, I know a Dr. McGuire. Give her this number."

"That's the psychologist at the counseling center where Jackson went for his grief counseling. She's been trying to reach me back at the squad room and the desk sergeant says she sounds desperate," she said. Her phone rang again.

"O'Brien. Yes, Dr. McGuire, how can I help you?

"When is the last time you talked to her?

"And nobody has heard from her today? Okay. Give me her address and phone number and I'll see what I can do." Dr. McGuire, there's something you can do for me. If you hear from Jim Jackson, please tell him to call me. He is in a great deal of danger. I can tell you he is no longer a suspect, so you don't need to worry about disloyalty, but I'm afraid for his life. I can protect him, but he must call me. Will you do that please? Thank you," Shannon said.

Shannon went to the hotel phone, called dispatch and gave them Judy's name and address. "Send two cars code 3 to this location to investigate a possible homicide. If there is no answer at the door, break it down on my authority, there may be a murder victim or someone seriously hurt. Report to me on my cell phone as soon as you know anything," she said.

"What was that all about?" Appleton said.

"Judy, the grief counselor that worked with Jackson didn't show for work this morning, which has never happened and she's not answering the phone. Dr. McGuire got concerned and called me. Jackson told me Judy slipped him a note as he was leaving the center last night, but I never got a look at the note. If my guess is right, Judy is dead. Whoever this nut case is he somehow ties back to that counseling center, which brings me back to that Vic character," Shannon said.

She showed them the email from Vic on Jim's computer. Shannon quickly told Appleton, Barnes, and Ling what Jim had told her about Vic being a computer whiz and how he seemed to know so much. She described the scene at the counseling center where Vic's computer file mysteriously disappeared and how her credit card got screwed up and the warning message she got.

She also told them about Jim's belief that someone had fired a warning shot at him in the counseling center parking lot.

Shannon motioned one of the uniformed officers over and asked him to check with the evidence unit to see if they found anything at the counseling center parking lot.

She also told them that she thought the cop killed in the hospital was a warning, since the killer could have shot her or Jackson just as easily. She also related the bullet hole decal inside the windshield of her car.

"And those are just the high points," she said. "We haven't even stopped to consider forensic evidence."

"Detective," the uniformed officer said. "The evidence unit found a bullet hole in the cover of a parking light fixture at the counseling center, but no fragments. The janitor had already cleaned up the glass and the dumpster was empty."

"Thanks for checking on that for me," Shannon said.

"So Jackson was right, there was a warning shot," she said. "That makes three warnings for sure and four if you count the death of the cop at the hospital."

"Okay, but why didn't the killer just come in here and finish off Jackson and his friend after killing the two cops?" Barnes asked.

"And how do the murders of Bonnelli and that kid Washington figure into this? Bonnelli was connected to Jackson who was connected to the counseling center, but we still haven't connected Washington to anything or anyone but the killer," Appleton said.

"But all three cops were connected to Jackson," Shannon said. "All the deaths so far connect to Jackson in some way, except for Washington. Jackson may have some information or the killer thinks Jackson has information that is somehow important to the killer. Jackson may not even know he has the information or he truly may not have the information."

"What kind of information would Jackson have that someone would literally kill for," Barnes asked.

"I've no idea," Shannon said.

"And what about Washington," Barnes said. "We can't find any connection to Jackson."

"Washington may be an innocent victim who accidentally learned something or saw something that the killer viewed as a loose string, that had to be eliminated," Ling said. "Sorry, I should leave the police work to you guys."

"Not at all doc. If you hadn't been on the ball, we wouldn't be this far along. You're a member of this team so if you have a thought, let's hear it," Appleton said.

"This makes a lot of sense, but it doesn't get us much closer to nailing this guy," Barnes said. "You still don't have a clue who the shooter is or what his motive is or where he might strike next do you?"

Shannon's cell phone rang.

"O'Brien."

"Shit."

"We'll be right there."

"The responding units at the grief counselor's house got no answer. The cops who went around back saw her slumped over the breakfast table – one shot in the back of the head," she said.

"Why don't you let us handle this? You got a police commissioner downstairs who is about to shit a brick with your name on it and a real mess to clean up. I think the main thing we need to do is find those two civilians as soon as we can," Appleton said. "And, for the second time today, you look like hell."

"You're going to hurt my feelings if you keep talking like that. Here's the address. Maybe it would be a good idea to get a guard on Dr. McGuire. I'll deal with the brass and coordinate the search for Jackson and his friend," she said.

After Barnes and Appleton left, the suite was empty except for Ling and Shannon, the evidence unit was still taking pictures and looking for fingerprints or other evidence in the hall. Ling's crew was waiting for the transport vehicle, which was tied up in a monumental traffic jam.

Shannon sat down in one of the large easy chairs. Ling sat across from her.

"He's right. You do look like hell. Let me get you a cup of coffee," she said.

She came back with coffee and a glass of water and some pills.

"Here, take these," she said. "They'll help the pain and won't slow you down."

"Thanks. You know, I feel like I've lived a whole life in these past few days. It seems like years ago we were walking down that path in the park in the middle of the night and you tried to hustle me," Shannon said.

"I what?" Ling said. "You're just a flirt and you know it. Bouncing those boobs around at me and then taking me for a ride on that over-sized vibrator you call a motorcycle."

"I never had a chance and you know it," she said.

"I've been curious about something though," Ling said. "You said you had never considered a gay lifestyle, but based on our time together, I'd say you're pretty comfortable with it. Is that how you feel?"

"I've always had a pretty open mind about lifestyles, but I could never express anything but the traditional concepts while I lived at home or my father would have died. I grew up with lots of jokes about being a lesbian because of my size. Am I comfortable with it? I have to say the sex is better than anything I've ever imagined. Although, I was concerned before that somehow I was going to hurt you. Do I love being with you? Yes, I cherish every minute we've had when it's just the two of us and we can be together and not be cop and doc. I still need to take this whole thing one little step at a time. I'm sorry if that sounds like I'm hiding from commitment, but I made a promise to you and to myself that I would be honest about how I felt. There's something I want you to do for me. I want you to go visit your parents for a week or so."

"You want me to do what? No way," Ling said.

"Look. Things are likely to get worse before they get better. I just thought you would be…"

"There you go with that macho shit, again. Man, that makes me mad. Who do you think you are that you can just send me off like that?"

"I just don't want anything to happen to you and I can't keep an eye on you all the time."

"And if you aren't watching me, I'm going to get in trouble. Poor little me. Whatever will I do without big, strong Shannon? Well, you can take that idea and shove it."

Ling left the room and slammed the door behind her.

'Oh, great,' Shannon thought. 'Now I've really done it. She's pissed. Appleton and Barnes are pissed. What else could go wrong?'

The door to the suite opened and Police Commissioner Frank Howell walked in followed by Police Captain John Gonzalez.

"O'Brien, I'll get right to the point. You know it's department policy to take wounded officers off the street until they are fully recovered and have passed a psychological exam. So, as of right now you're on medical suspension for ten days. Go home," Captain Gonzalez said.

"Captain, you can't do this to me right in the middle of an investigation. I'm the only one who has a chance of pulling this together. You can't really call this a wound – it's barely a scratch. There are two civilians out there who trusted me and they may be the next victims. Captain, you got to let me stay on the job – they won't trust anyone else," she said.

"Sorry. This comes from the very top. I need your gun and your badge," Captain Gonzalez said.

Shannon put her gun and badge on the table and walked out the door and past Ling in the hall without pausing.

"What's wrong?" Ling said.

Chapter 21 – Thursday – Jim, Sam, & Vic

"Don't look down," Jim said. "Just keep moving."

The climb down 15 floors on the fire escape was taking longer than he anticipated or maybe it just seemed that way when he expected someone to begin shooting at them any minute.

Sam was frightened, but she kept moving. He had gone first, so when she did look down she could see him. Fortunately, they were both in blue jeans and sneakers, so their outdoor exit was not uncomfortable with the jackets they grabbed on the way out.

They ended up in a dark alley between the hotel and a smaller building. Jim looked around, unsure what to do next.

"We need to get away from here, but we can't go to either of our homes," he said.

"Let's find a train station," Sam said. "I've an aunt on the southeast side of town. She'll put us up."

"The police will be watching the trains," Jim said. "And we can't walk, it's too far. We need some transportation that won't attract attention."

"Why don't we just call the police?"

"Not until I figure out what's going on. They were supposed to protect us, now three of them are dead. What if the killer is one of them? How do we know who to trust?" Jim said.

"I trust Detective O'Brien."

"I do too, but I don't think she can control what's going on. When I think we're safe, I'll call her. Something very strange is happening and I think somehow I'm at the center of it. That killer at the hospital could've shot me, but he didn't and why didn't the killer just come in and do us after killing the cops at the hotel? It's almost like I'm being kept alive for a reason, but why? Maybe the killer thinks I know something. At any rate, we've got to move now. Let's go."

They started moving down the alley past rows of dumpsters. There was a dim light over a door ahead on the right, so Jim moved to the left side of the alley.

"Jim, over here," said a voice from behind a dumpster.

Jim and Sam both jumped at the voice, but Jim recognized it almost instantly as Vic's. For a moment, he hesitated.

"Come on, I've got some transportation to get you out of here," Vic said. "We've got to hurry though. I don't know how long before you're discovered missing."

Jim and Sam ducked behind the dumpster where Vic was standing.

"This way," he said.

He led them back the way they came, past the fire escape and down the alley. Parked next to some boxes and trash was a dark colored mini van.

"Hop in and let's get out of here," he said.

The van had tinted windows and Jim noticed that the interior lights did not come on when the doors opened. Jim and Sam sat together on the second seat. Vic took off as soon as the door was closed. He didn't turn on the headlights until he reached the main street. In a matter of minutes, they were on a northbound freeway speeding out of the downtown area.

"Where are we going?" Jim asked.

"Some place safe," Vic said.

"That's what the police told us about the last place," Sam said.

"Unfortunately, the police mean well, but they are under staffed and their technology is about ten years behind most video games. Relax, if you can, we have about an hour's drive. If you're hungry, I can stop for something although there's plenty of food where we're going," Vic said.

Sam had a firm grip on Jim's hand and the freeway lights provided just enough light for him to see the fear in her eyes.

"By the way Samantha, I'm Vic. We haven't been properly introduced, but I feel like I know you already. I apologize for this awkward meeting, but when we get to our destination we'll have a chance to get better acquainted."

Sam's grip on Jim's hand tightened.

"Why are you doing this?" Jim asked.

"You're in trouble – I'm just trying to help," Vic said.

"There's more to it than that, isn't there?"

"Yes, there is and I'll be glad to tell you all about it when we get to our destination. It's a little complicated," Vic said.

"Okay. How did you know where we were and how did you know we were in danger?" Jim asked.

"That's an easier answer. I saw what happened at the hospital on television this morning and I was working on the police computer system when I spotted a hacker in the system. I couldn't stop him before he accessed some secure systems. I scanned for your Internet email account and saw you were online, so I sent you the warning. I got in my van and drove over to the alley – it's only about two blocks from the police computer center," Vic said.

Sam squeezed Jim's hand twice. He looked down at her hand and she took her index finger and wrote 'no' on the back of his hand.

"Well, that was lucky for us," Sam said. "Could we make a restroom stop? We left the hotel in a hurry."

"We're almost there. Maybe another 30 minutes or so. Can you make it that long?" Vic said.

"Actually, I think I could use a break too," Jim said. "I think the adrenaline is wearing off."

"There's an exit in about two miles."

"Thanks," Jim said.

Sam was sitting next to the door and Jim next to her. Jim put his right arm around her and nuzzled her neck. He could see Vic glancing back at them through the rear view mirror.

"Please forgive me for what I am about to do, but it is necessary to pass my cell phone to you in a way he doesn't see," Jim whispered in her ear. "He won't let us wear our coats into the rest stop or he will search them. I need to put the phone where he won't look. Please forgive me and don't jump."

Jim palmed his small cell phone in his left hand and slipped it under Sam's jacket. To Vic, it appeared he was groping her breast. He was trying to slide the phone in between the buttons on her shirt and into her bra, but his hand was too large. Sam reached up and unbuttoned her shirt. Jim looked her in the eyes and gently put the phone into her bra feeling her warm, soft breast in the process. He removed his hand, but Sam put it back over the outside of the bra to maintain the illusion while she adjusted the phone to the side of the bra so it would not be noticeable.

She looked at him and he kissed her gently on the lips as the van slowed and exited the freeway. Vic pulled into a convenience store and parked away from the lighted parking area. When Jim tried to open his door he found it was locked and there was no way to unlock it.

Vic opened the sliding side door and looked at them and smiled.

"I'm embarrassed to ask this, because what I'm about to ask you is going to seem paranoid or weird or something, but I need to know if either of you has a cell phone, because if you do, I need to have it before you go in the store," Vic said.

"Why for God's sake?" Jim said.

"I've kept the place we're going safe by taking some extraordinary measures over time and this is one. I have to ask you to trust me for a little while more, even if it appears that I don't trust you. Please remember, I just possibly saved your lives," Vic said.

"Why do you need such a secret safe place?" Sam asked.

"That's an excellent question that will be answered when we get there. Once you hear the answer, what I'm asking now won't seem so strange. So, please take off your coats and leave them in the van and let me take a look to make sure you don't have a phone in your pockets. Thank you."

Jim and Sam took off their coats and got out of the van. They turned around while Vic looked them over. He patted Jim's back pocket to confirm the bulge was a billfold. Sam's pants had no back pockets and were so fitted that there was no way a cell phone could hide undetected in the front pockets. Her shirt had no pockets.

Vic went through their coats checking the pockets and patting down the rest of the coats.

"Here," he said handing them back to Jim and Sam. "I'm sorry about that. I hope when I've had a chance to explain everything you'll understand and forgive this intrusion. Let's go."

The three went into the store and Sam headed for the women's room. Jim hesitated counting on Vic to stick with him.

"My stomach is a knot. I'm going to see if they have something to calm my nerves," Jim said.

Vic followed him down the aisle, but kept glancing back to the women's room.

Sam locked the door behind her and retrieved the phone from her bra. It was very uncomfortable wedged next to her breast, but she couldn't avoid a small smile remembering how it got there.

She powered it up and noticed that the power indicator was at its lowest point and the signal strength was at the minimum. She climbed up on the toilet next to a small window hoping to improve the signal strength and pressed 'redial,' which should be Det. O'Brien's cell phone number.

The phone rang once…twice…'come on, answer' she thought.

"O'Brien."

"Thank God."

"Who is this?"

"It's Sam. Vic has us. We're in a store at Exit 143 northbound on I-94. He's taking us to a secret place about 30 minutes north of here. We're playing along, but I think he means us harm. Battery's low."

"Hello, Hello. I can't hear you. Speak up. Speak…"

The phone went dead.

Sam looked at the dead phone in dismay. How much, if any of her message got through and what good would it do. She had to think of a way to leave a message for the detective and quick. The restroom had a dispenser of feminine hygiene products and some toiletries. She put fifty cents in the machine and selected some hand lotion in a small pouch. She opened the pouch and spelled out 'O'Brien go north' on the mirror – counting on the appearance of the restroom suggesting that is wasn't cleaned very often. She flushed the toilet, ran some water, tore off a paper towel, and came out of the restroom to find Vic right in front of the door.

"Everything okay?" he asked.

"That's a rather personal question, isn't it," Sam snapped and walked passed him.

"I'd like a soft drink, how about you?" she said to Jim.

"Yeah, that might help my stomach. What about you Vic?"

"No thanks, I'm good, but I'd like to get back on the road."

They were back on the interstate headed north. Sam was trying to note exits and anything else she might use to provide directions if she got the chance. After about 15 minutes they exited and began a series of turns down increasingly rural unmarked roads. Soon, it was impossible for her to keep track of which way they were headed or how far they had come since leaving the interstate.

They came to a gate that looked like any typical farmer's gate of the area. Vic pushed what looked like a garage door opener and the gate swung open. He drove through and continued for another one-half mile, Sam guessed.

The van stopped and Vic opened the door. It was pitch black and overcast. Vic led them without a flashlight straight-ahead and then around a small mound. On the other side of the mound was a door. Vic used a small flashlight to illuminate a keypad, punched in a code, and opened the door. Once all three of them were inside and the door closed, he turned on a light switch.

The lights temporarily blinded Jim and Sam. When their eyes adjusted to the light, they saw a large room that looked more like a bunker than a home, even though it was furnished with a kitchen and what might pass for a living area. The whole structure was clearly under ground. There were no windows and the door was the only visible way in or out. The room appeared to be about 20 feet wide by 30 feet deep. At the rear of the room, were two doors, which Vic explained led to a bathroom and bedroom respectively. There were also bunk beds along one wall of the room – enough to sleep six.

"Make yourself comfortable," Vic said. "How about some food? I'm in the mood for an omelet, myself. I don't like to brag, but my omelets are world class. What do you say?"

"Sounds great," Jim said.

"Why don't you two get settled in the bedroom while I get supper going?"

Jim and Sam made their way back to the bedroom, which was small and sparsely furnished. The double bed was firm and the linens appeared clean.

Sam started to speak, but Jim put his finger to his lips and motioned her to come closer. He held her close and whispered in her ear.

"This room might be bugged, be careful what you say. We should play along until we figure out what's going on. Did you get through to O'Brien?"

"Yes and no. The cell phone battery died, so I don't know how much she heard, but I left her a message in the restroom."

"Good thinking. You know, I kind of like talking to you like this."

"Me too, but if this room is bugged, we better have a regular conversation soon or it will arouse suspicion."

Chapter 22 – Thursday – Ling & Shannon

"Shannon. Shannon. Open the door. It's me. Come on. Open the door," Ling said, banging on the door.

"Will you knock it off or I'll bust you for disturbing the peace," Shannon said as she opened the door. "What are you doing here?"

"I heard what happened, I'm so sorry."

"No you're not. Nobody's sorry. 'She got what she deserved.' That's the line downtown. No one believes this medical suspension crap. They want me off the case and are afraid if they outright take me off, the feminists will howl and I'll sue their ass for discrimination. Just when the pressure is on I can't make the shot and three cops are dead, three civilians are dead and two other civilians are missing and presumed dead. And it's all my fault. My career as a cop is finished and once again I've proven to my father what screw-up I am."

Tears were streaming down her face as she turned away from Ling and walked back into her apartment. Ling followed her in and closed the door.

Shannon stopped at her couch with her back to Ling still sobbing. She was wearing an old set of sweats and her hair was a mess. There was an empty pint of chocolate ice cream on the kitchen table and a half eaten package of Oreo cookies beside it.

"Hey, you blubbering bitch look at me when I talk to you," Ling yelled.

Shannon's head popped up and she slowly started turning around, but not fast enough to see one hundred and eight pounds of Ling come flying through the air and tackle her as she was in half turn.

Caught off balance, Shannon with Ling on top of her went over the couch and rolled off the other side. Some how Shannon repressed her natural instinct to counter attack and Ling ended up pinning her to the floor.

"What the hell is wrong with you, woman? Are you going to let them get away with this? Come on, where's the woman I love?" Ling asked.

Shannon looked up at Ling, who had two fists full of her sweatshirt and was straddling her middle yelling like a wild coach. She began to laugh.

Ling tried to look even meaner and that made Shannon laugh even more. Soon Ling couldn't contain herself and she was laughing too. In a moment, they were both very nearly in need of oxygen.

"I would give my pension for a video of you tackling me and the two of us going over the couch," Shannon said when she found some breath.

When they had regained their composure, Shannon pulled Ling close and kissed her long and hard.

"What was that for? I thought you might hate me for all the mean things I've said to you today," Shannon said.

"That was for reminding me that I don't have to live anybody's life but my own. I'm going to take a quick shower and then see what I can do about this mess. Will you still be here when I get out?" Shannon asked.

"You bet," Ling said.

Shannon's cell phone rang.

"O'Brien...who is this?"

"Hello, Hello. I can't hear you. Speak up. Speak up."

"What was that all about," Ling asked.

"I don't know," Shannon said. "Really poor connection – sounded like they said 'Sam,' but it sounded like a woman. Something about I-94 and exit 143 north. I couldn't make out the rest. I guess they'll call back if it was important. Be out in a minute."

While Shannon was showering, Ling cleaned up the ice cream and cookie's mess, but something about the garbled phone call troubled her. Then it hit her. She rushed into the bedroom as Shannon was just coming out of the bathroom completely naked.

"Are you going to tackle me again? This could be fun," Shannon said.

"No, no, at least not right now. That call, something you said about the name 'Sam,' but the voice sounded female, right? Jim Jackson's friend was named Samantha," Ling said.

"Oh, my God. You're right and I think I may have heard him call her Sam once."

Shannon grabbed her contact book off the dresser and called her friend at the cell phone company.

"I got a call on my cell phone about 10 minutes ago from 555-945-7834. I need to know who has that number and most important I need to know exactly where that call was made. And before you give me grief about how hard it is, two people may die if I don't get that information in the next 10 minutes. Call me back on my cell phone. Thanks," she said.

Shannon finished getting dressed in blue jeans and a long-sleeve denim top. She went into her closet and reached up on the top shelf behind some shoeboxes and retrieved a pistol in a shoulder holster. She took the pistol out, checked the clip, cocked the 9mm semi-automatic to put a live round in the pipe, and strapped on the holster under her left arm.

"You might want to leave now," Shannon said.

Ling looked devastated.

"When I walk out that door, I'm committing a felony by carrying a concealed weapon. Without my badge, I'm just a citizen and citizens can't carry 9mm weapons. If you hang around with me, you can be charged as an accessory, which will probably mean you'll lose not only your job, but your license to practice medicine. This goes way beyond me wanting to protect you. I'm strictly outside the law on this and I can't protect you from that," Shannon said.

"Why don't you turn the information over to the police and let them follow up on the lead?"

"Because nobody will believe me in the first place. In the second place, those two civilians trusted me to protect them and I've an obligation to fulfill," Shannon said.

"I won't let you do this alone. You need my help, even if you're too proud to ask for it."

"You're right on both counts – another reason I love you. Let's head out. I know we need to be at or near exit 143 on I94 heading north. I hope my friend comes through with the information we need before we get there," Shannon said.

Half way to exit 143, Shannon's contact at the cell phone company confirmed the phone belonged to Jackson, but could not pinpoint where the call originated more precisely than the intersection.

It was approaching midnight when they took exit 143. All that was open at that hour was a convenience store.

"We may be lucky," Shannon said. "This looks like a place they might stop if this Sam faked a bathroom break or they needed gas. Let me do the talking."

"Yes sir." Ling saluted.

"All right, all right. I get the message. But I may have to bluff my way through this since I don't have a badge and I'm adding another felony – impersonating an officer – to the list."

The clerk behind the counter was a greasy-haired kid who looked like he could care less about anything. There were no other customers in the store.

"I'm Detective O'Brien from Homicide and this is my partner Detective Ya. We're looking for two men and a woman who may have come in here at 10:45 tonight. Do you remember seeing them?"

"A lot of people come in here. I don't remember them all."

"This is important. Will you try to remember, please?" Shannon said.

"Look lady, I'm kinda busy right now. Okay. So, either buy something or get lost."

Shannon felt herself losing control, but held back when she noticed a security camera over the counter.

"Does that camera record to tape?" Shannon said.

"Yeah, it's in the back."

"I want to see the play back for 10:30 on," Shannon said.

"No way."

"What do you mean 'no way'?" Shannon asked.

"First, I ain't seen no badge and second, only the manager can authorize someone looking at the tape."

Ling pulled out her ME's badge and shoved it in his face.

"Here's a badge you little shit. Now get your scrawny butt off that stool and show us that tape. Two people's lives are in danger and if anything happens to them because you're giving us the run around, I'm going to see you get charged as an accessory to murder," she said.

"Murder? You're crazy. Okay, it's back here."

"I need to talk to you about this macho shit," Shannon whispered to Ling as they followed the clerk to the back room.

The grainy security tape in fact showed Jim, Sam, and Vic in the store. The sweep of the camera showed Sam coming out of the women's restroom at one point. They bought some soft drinks and left.

Shannon went back to the women's restroom and found Sam's message about going north and Jim's cell phone with the dead battery. Shannon and Ling sat in her car outside the convenience store wondering what to do next.

"Did you notice anything odd about Sam's behavior in the store," Shannon said.

"What do you mean?"

"She seemed to take a long time to decide what kind of soft drink she wanted – at least it seemed that way to me. Don't most people drink the same thing most of the time? She fumbled around in the case for longer than I expected."

They jumped out of the car and raced back into the store.

"Not you two again."

"Shut up," Ling said.

Shannon began looking at the case where Sam was fumbling around for some clue as to what she was doing.

"I don't see anything," she said.

"I do. Sometimes being short has its advantages," Ling said. "Look on the bottom of the shelve. There are numbers and letters written in the frost."

"My God. It's a license plate. She's given us the license plate of that bastard's car," Shannon said.

Chapter 23 – Thursday – Vic, Jim, & Sam

"Come and get it," Vic shouted from the kitchen.

Jim and Sam could smell the omelets from the bedroom and they smelled delicious. Whatever else Vic was, he had a talent in the kitchen.

They sat down to heaping plates of omelets made with fresh tomatoes, mushrooms, peppers, olives, and cheese. There was coffee and orange juice. An oven timer rang and Vic came back with croissants and butter.

They ate in silence, a testament to how hungry Jim and Sam were after a terrifying day that wasn't over yet.

"Wow. That was quite a spread. How did you manage it all by yourself?" Sam said.

"It's just a matter of organization. If you organize your work, you can accomplish great things. Don't you agree Jim?"

"Yes, I do. Fortunately, Sam was always there to organize things for me at work and Sally at home. I'm afraid my personal organizational skills aren't very strong."

"I can see how Sam – you don't mind if I call you Sam, do you? – would be a great help at work. She's a remarkable person. Taking care of her sister all these years while managing a career and finishing a college degree is quite an accomplishment," Vic said.

"How do you know all of those things about me? Jim said you knew a lot about him also," Sam said.

"Information is my business. It's the commodity I buy and sell, so I make it a point to know everything I can about the people around me," Vic said.

"But Jim told me you were in computers, something about databases."

"Yes, well that's true, but there's a little more to my enterprise than that. Let me clear the dishes and I'll give you that explanation I promised."

"I'll help," Sam said.

"No, I wouldn't hear of it. You're my guests. Please refill your coffee cups if you want more and make yourselves comfortable in the easy chairs. I'll join you momentarily."

Sam and Jim watched as he efficiently cleared the tabled and loaded a dishwasher under the counter in the kitchen. In less than ten minutes, the kitchen was spotless and Vic was joining them. There were four overstuffed chairs arranged around a circular coffee table.

"The story I'm about to tell you may seem fantastic and I'll omit some details for reasons that will become obvious. Jim, I'm afraid part of this story is going to be very difficult for you to hear. I'm glad you have Sam here for support," Vic said.

"What do you mean by that?" Jim asked.

"Let me get to it in proper order so it makes some sense, please."

"Before you begin, I've a question," Sam said. "If we want to leave right now, this minute, would you stop us?"

"I'm afraid so, although I hope you will hear me out before considering yourselves my prisoners," Vic said.

"What's to stop the two of us from just overpowering you," she said.

"This first of all," he said and pulled back the light denim shirt he was wearing over a turtle neck shirt, revealing a pistol in a holster under his left arm.

"And, secondly I'm an ex-Navy Seal and still in good enough shape to kill both of you without raising a sweat, so please let's not talk about these unpleasant topics anymore. There are more than enough unpleasant topics in my story already. If you don't cause me any trouble, I do not intend to harm you. When our business is completed, you will be free to go. May I begin now?

"I'm a spy – no, not the CIA or James Bond type of spy. I deal in corporate secrets. Pending mergers and acquisitions, patents, anything that is valuable to a competitor, including information on key executives," Vic said.

"Industrial espionage," Jim said.

"That's a somewhat outdated term for it, but yes, that's what my associates and I do. We buy and sell information. In the legitimate world, we are known as information brokers, but my enterprise has cut a few corners along the way – there's more money in getting answers quicker. Due to an unfortunate set of circumstances, my organization must dissolve. To do this, we need to liquidate our assets," Vic said. "Jim, I'm coming to a part that's going to be difficult for you to believe, but your lovely late wife, Sally, was a part of my organization."

"What are you saying?" Jim said. "That my wife was a criminal? That's insane. What are you trying to pull here?"

"Please, I know it is difficult to hear, but it is the truth. In her defense, she was recruited into what she thought was a legitimate business intelligence company. The further she got into it, the more trouble she had with the ethics of some of our operations. When she discovered some of our 'black ops' she wanted out, but it was too late by then. She was already in so deep that if we were caught she would've had a hard time pleading innocent. She stayed with us for another two years and became the money person for several major operations. Then the clever girl figured out a way to get out. She took a large sum of money – several million dollars actually – along with some offshore bank account information. Her deal was that if we left her alone she would release the money to us over a period of time. If we bothered her, she had a mechanism in place to empty the offshore accounts over to a charity and we would never see a penny."

"I don't believe any of this," Jim said.

"I don't either," Sam said.

"Unfortunately, you have to believe it, because your lives may depend on it."

"I thought you said we were in no danger from you," Sam said.

"If you cooperate. I'm a patient man, but time is running out and we don't know what Sally left behind. Besides, other members of my organization aren't as patient or as civilized as I am. And that brings me to another part of the story that's going to be hard for you to hear Jim. Very hard to hear. Sally's death wasn't an accident. She was murdered," Vic said.

Jim felt the blood rush out of his head and he put his head between his legs to avoid passing out. Sam put her arm around his shoulder.

"What are you saying? Sally was murdered? By you?" Jim asked.

"No. No. Not me, please believe that. That's the last thing I wanted. She was no good to me dead. Without her, I couldn't get to the money. I had no reason to kill her," Vic said.

"That means it was Bonnelli, wasn't it?" Jim said.

"Yes, that drunken fool. He financed some of our operations, but I was never comfortable with him because of his drinking. He got tired of Sally's game and took matters into his own hands, the idiot. Now we don't know whether the money is gone or what. She changed all the passwords on the offshore accounts, so I can't access them other than to look at balances" Vic said.

"Who killed Bonnelli then?" Jim asked.

"That's another story that intersects this one with some disastrous results. That same person is responsible for all the other recent deaths and many others. He is out of control, which is why I got you out of that hotel suite."

"So let me see if I got this straight. My wife was some kind of industrial spy, who double-crossed you so she could lead a normal life, but Bonnelli killed her and now you don't know what's happened to your money. Is that about right?" Jim said.

"Yes."

"So, what are Sam and I doing here?" Jim asked.

"You're going to help me find my money and retrieve it."

"And why would I do that after you killed my wife?" Jim asked.

"Because if you don't, I'm going to kill Sam."

Vic said it in such a matter of fact manner that Jim had no doubt that he meant exactly what he said, yet it was almost unbelievable at the same instant that someone would sit not three feet from him and threaten to kill Sam.

"Why don't you two get some rest and we'll get started first thing in the morning on figuring out how to retrieve my money. If you look in the closet, you'll find some clean clothes and toiletries. They'll fit, because they're yours. You've got 20 minutes to attend to your toilet needs and then I'm locking the bedroom door. Please don't be foolish and try anything in the night – it'll just irritate me," Vic said.

Jim and Sam went into the bedroom and found two suitcases of their clothing in the closet along with toothbrushes, shampoo, and other toiletries.

While Sam was away, he found himself crying and wondering how he could be married to a woman he didn't even know. Was he so dazzled by the idea that an attractive woman would marry him that he was blind to obvious signs that something was not right? It would be typical of him to not see the obvious. He pulled himself together before Sam came back and took his turn in the bathroom.

When he came back, Sam was wearing sweats, instead of the clothes she had on when he left.

"I didn't want to sleep in my clothes," she said.

"I've some sweats, too. I'll change."

When he came out to the bathroom, Vic was headed toward the bedroom.

"Time for bed," he said and closed and locked the door behind Jim.

Jim and Sam looked at each other for a moment. There was only one bed and no other place for any one to sleep.

"Why don't you get under the covers and I'll sleep on top of the covers," Jim said.

"Why don't you sleep under the covers with me. We are both fully dressed, after all," Sam said.

Jim was nervous about getting too close to Sam, but it was impossible not to touch one another.

"I can't imagine what it must of felt like to hear him say those things about Sally," she said. "How horrible for you on top of everything else."

"I keep thinking it's going to end, but it just seems to get worse. And now, I've really gotten you in a serious mess. I'm so sorry. I don't know how, but I promise I'll get us out of this. One thing that I've come to realize this past week is how passive I've been about life, pretty much taking what comes my way. Up until eight months ago, what came my way was all right, but when Sally died things began to unravel and I realize that I've little or no control over my life because I had little or no control in getting where I am now. I want to believe Sally truly loved me and that she did want out of this life Vic described. But I also believe I would be real easy to fool if it suited her purposes. When we get out of this, I'm going to look at things differently and see if the real Jim Jackson is still in here somewhere."

Sam moved closer to Jim and rolled over on her side facing him. Her face was very close to his. Her breath was sweet. He could feel her body against the full length of his body and it felt very good. Her hand was on his chest.

"I've always known the real Jim Jackson. He's in there and he's his own man. I'm afraid, but not terrified. I have faith in you and I've always had faith in you. We'll figure this out together."

"Sam, you've been better to me than any man deserves. I wish I could tell you right this moment that I love you and maybe I do, but so much has happened, so fast I'm just not sure what…"

Sam put her first two fingers on Jim's mouth.

"You don't have to say anything or make any commitment. I'm don't expect you to and would not trust one if you made it now anyway. The emotional wounds you have suffered are deep and will take a long time to heal. I'm offering you my love and expect nothing in return, although I know you have affection for me. When you come out the other side of this emotional hell, I'll be there if you want me to be there. If you want a completely clean start, I'll understand and that's the way it'll end."

Jim leaned over and kissed her gently on the lips. She sat up and in one smooth motion took off her sweatshirt revealing her bare breasts in the dim light. She reached down and peeled off her bottoms. Jim could make out her surprisingly muscular naked body in the light. She sat him up and pulled off his top and he kicked off his bottoms. Her skin next to his was like electricity coursing through his body. In addition to the sexual attraction, the intimate feel of another human's skin was a pleasure he had almost forgotten.

Chapter 24 – Thursday – Ling, Shannon, & Jimmy

Shannon and Ling went back to her car in the convenience store parking lot with the license plate number that Sam had left for them.

"What do we do now," Ling said. "You have go to the police with this information – it's the only way to find out who owns that car."

"No, not necessarily. There may be another way, but it means making a deal with the devil," Shannon said.

"What are you talking about?"

"Remember that prick I told you about that I bounced around because he said something nasty about you? He may be the only one who can help us. He's on the graveyard shift, thanks to me."

Shannon dialed the internal line for her squad room that only detectives use to call in for information.

"Jimmy."

"Well, if it isn't Miss Suspended Ass herself. You aren't supposed to be using this line."

"Jimmy, listen to me very carefully. I'm offering you a chance to make a life-changing decision here. So pay attention."

"Or what? You'll bust my balls again?"

"Nope. Just listen. I need you to run a license plate for me and then I need you to find out everything you can on the owner and I mean everything, but in particular if he owns or rents in property north of town near I94. He is holding two civilians and their lives are in danger."

"O'Brien, you know I can't do that and I won't do that for you."

"Listen Jimmy. Here's the deal. Help me with this information and I may be able to save these two people. This guy or one of his gang is also responsible for killing three cops today. If you help me bring him in, you'll be a hero. Let me tell you Jimmy, the guy that helps collar a cop killer gets cut a lot of slack in the department. So here's your life-changing decision. You can hang up and go on being a little prick for the rest of your life getting beat up by worse than me or you can decide that you're going to be a man and do the right thing for a change. What's it going to be Jimmy?"

The line was silent for a moment.

"What's the number?"

"I knew you had it in you Jimmy. I knew when it counted you would be a man. Okay, the tag is 342Z56A. Please work as quickly as possible and don't tell anyone what you're doing – they'll bog you down in paperwork and these two will be dead before you get the forms filled out. Call me on my cell phone as soon as you have anything. Thanks."

Three minutes later, Shannon cell phone rang and Jimmy gave her the name of Victor Hugo and an address on the near northside.

"Let's go checkout his apartment," Shannon said. "Jimmy says it will be awhile before he can get access to property records."

"Don't we need a search warrant or something," Ling said.

"Yeah, or something."

The apartment building had an electronic entry system, which Shannon stared at for a moment, then walked out to the front and found a paving brick used in the landscaping. She took the brick and smashed the keypad several times until it came loose.

She began crossing the wires until there was an audible click and the door was unlocked. Ling was staring at her wide-eyed.

"Make a note to add breaking and entering to our crime list," Shannon said as they got on the elevator.

Fortunately, Vic's apartment was secured with just a deadbolt lock, which Shannon easily picked using a couple of tools hidden in the holster. She drew her gun and motioned Ling to stay back. She pushed open the door and went through the apartment before calling Ling.

The apartment was completely empty – no furniture, no clothing, nothing. Shannon shut the door and turned on all the lights. There were marks in the carpet where furniture had recently been placed, but other than that there was no indication anyone had ever lived here. The place was spotless. No dust on the cabinets or counters and the refrigerator look brand new inside and out.

"He hasn't been gone long," Shannon said "There's no dust anywhere and my guess is there's not a fingerprint in the whole place. He's on the move and this thing is coming to a head very soon. On the chance he missed something, let's look everywhere."

Jimmy called again to say that the property database was offline for at least two hours and he would check when it was available. Shannon thought it odd that the database went down when Jimmy began his search.

"Jimmy, you're a computer whiz, right?"

"Yeah, I guess so. Why?"

"Can you make it look like the inquiry about Victor Hugo is coming from a different computer in a different location?"

"Sure, but why would I want to do that. It just slows things up."

"There may be someone trying to stop you from getting information on him and this person might resort to violence. For your own protection, it might be safer to throw this guy off your trail, but remember he's a genius so don't try any cheap tricks, he'll see through those."

"Don't worry. By the time he figures out what's going on, it'll be too late," Jimmy said.

"Okay. Just keep safe."

"We might as well go back to my place and wait. Maybe Sam or Jim will find a way to contact me," Shannon said.

Back at Shannon's place, they stretched out on the bed, but neither had sex on their minds. They both drifted off to sleep almost immediately.

Ling awoke from a wonderful dream filled with beautiful music. As she became more fully conscious, she realized the music wasn't a dream, but was coming from the living room and Shannon was not in the bed.

Ling slipped out of bed and went over to the door to the living room. Shannon had turned on the gas fireplace and was standing in front of it playing her violin with a music stand to one side.

Ling didn't recognize the piece, but it was soaring and moody at the same time. She sat down on the floor with her back against the wall and listened for five minutes until Shannon stopped playing.

"Bravo, bravo," Ling said.

"Spoken like a country music fan, but thank you anyway. That was actually terrible, but it felt good to play. I'm afraid kick boxing has not been good to my fingering."

"Then you should give up kick boxing."

"I'm a better kick boxer than a violinist."

"Why is it so important that you be the best at everything you do?"

"I get pleasure in being the best. It's what drives me to excel."

"I understand that, believe me. I've that same drive academically, but I also enjoy doing things that give me pleasure just because they give me pleasure, not because I can excel at them. You joke about my country music, but I like other music too. I took piano from age six through college and can still play fairly well. I would love to play if I had a piano, but with all my lessons and practice, I couldn't approach what I just heard you do. You have a gift."

"I'm sorry. I had no idea you were a musician. I would love to hear you play. There is so much we still don't know about each other. When this is over, let's take some time off and just spend it getting to know each other. No guns, no dead bodies – just two girls who want to have some fun," Shannon said.

"Yes!"

Chapter 25 – Friday – Jim, Sam, & Vic

Jim felt the bed move as he slowly woke up. There was the smell of fresh coffee and shampoo in the air. His body was relaxed for the first time in many months. This is how he remembered waking up on weekends when Sally was alive. No alarm clocks – just a slow climb out of sleep. Sally was more of a 'jump out of bed and get going' type, but she respected his routine and left him alone.

He didn't want to open his eyes because he knew as soon as he did he'd have to deal with the reality of the past several days and what Vic had told him last night.

"You'd better get up. He wants to get started soon."

Sam was sitting on the side of the bed towel drying her hair. There was a cup of coffee on the nightstand. He raised himself up to a sitting position and looked at her. It there was anything good to come out of this horrible mess it was a new awareness of Sam. She had always been there for him at work and was the rock he clung to when Sally died. How had he not noticed her for more than his secretary and friend?

"Last night was so…"

"Yes, it was, wasn't it," she smiled.

"It was that and more, but that's not what I was going to say. I felt more loved last night than I can ever remember. Thank you."

She lowered her head and her eyes were moist.

"Can we get going, you two," Vic shouted from the other room.

"I'll keep him busy, while you shower," Sam said and gave him a quick kiss.

Breakfast was much less elaborate than the night before nor was Vic the jovial host. Jim found Sam had some fruit, cold cereal, and toast on the table. Vic was busy at a desk studying some papers and didn't even acknowledge Jim's presence.

Even before Jim and Sam finished this simple meal Vic was up pacing around, clearly irritated that they were taking too long. Finally, he could take the waiting no longer.

"Okay it's 7:30. We've got to get going. I hope you had some time to think about what I told you last night and accept it as the truth, because your friend Sam's life depends on your full and unqualified cooperation," Vic said.

"I believe you will do what you say and that's enough to buy my cooperation. You don't have to keep threatening me and Sam."

"Oh, but I do. You see Jim, that's how I run my business. That's the secret of my success. I can share it now because very soon, thanks to you, I'll be in a country with no extradition treaty and protected by a government that makes a handsome sum off the books taking care of individuals who wish to lead lives of quiet luxury. Originally, we did the same things my competitors did to gain information – interviewed ex-employees, gather intelligence at trade shows, and some more sophisticated, but legal data mining techniques. The trouble is those tools are very slow and terribly unreliable. Then a most remarkable thing happened. My wife was killed in a car-jacking. Terrible thing. Despite all my training, I was totally unprepared for losing my wife this way. Long story short. I ended up in the same grief support group where I met you Jim."

"Hold on. That's not the story you told the Dr. McGuire and Judy at the Center. You told them you were out of town on business and the furnace went out at home. You called some guy you knew from the military. He went to your house raped and killed your wife and killed your children," Jim said.

"That story isn't true, but it got me into the grief support group. I don't share personal information. I met another man at the group. He became a partner in my business. I steered him out of the Center after only one meeting. They never heard his story, but I did. A man with a similar military background, but much more 'black ops' than mine. A frightening man actually in many ways and I don't frighten easily. In addition to a particular skill the military found very useful, this fellow was an absolute genius at breaking into computer systems – the modern term is hacker. He learned some from the government, but went way beyond what they could teach him," Vic said.

"Unfortunately, this man is always on the verge of completely losing control. He has no social skills at all and I must keep him away from customers at all costs. In fact, I keep my contact with him to a minimum and do most of it by phone if possible. I also met several people in the group who I discovered covertly were in positions to provide very valuable information to me. It didn't take much to figure out how to manipulate them. One was so full of hate at the person who killed her father in a robbery she was willing to trade access to information at her employer for the sure justice I could offer."

"So you killed the man who killed her father in exchange for the information," Jim said.

"Well, I personally didn't kill the man, but you have the general idea. Of course, others were not so willing and this is where I developed the technique I took beyond the support group and used quite effectively to build an organization worth many millions of dollars. I learned that you must correctly judge your target and how much and what kind of pressure they can take. Too much pressure and they'll crack and run to the police or start acting so erratic that they blow the whole operation. On the other hand, too little pressure and you don't get the depth of results that produces the real profits. For instance, I could've simply gotten you alone and told you the story of your wife and demanded you find the money or I would kill you. My guess is you would've headed straight to the police the first chance you got," Vic said.

"On the other hand, with Sam's life at stake – and you know it's no bluff – you will do anything I ask rather than take a chance of harming her. It's that simple. I go to the vice president of information services at XYZ company and tell him I need access to his company's database and if I don't get it, his wife's sister – the one with three young children – is going to die. To prove I mean business, I show him a video clip on my iPhone of her getting the kids into her mini-van in front of her house. The video is taken through the telescopic sight of rifle and she is in the cross hairs."

"That's the most disgusting thing I've ever heard," Sam said.

"Oh, I've done much worse, much worse," Vic said.

"Like I said before, I believe you," Jim said. "What do you want me to do? I'll do whatever you want, but you must understand I know nothing about any money or secret accounts or anything."

"Yes, I do believe you Jim. If I didn't, I would be torturing you about now to get the information out of you. I know your wife would not have passed this information along to you for your own protection. You're looking for bank account numbers and passwords.

It could be in a safe deposit box or some kind of safe. She may have kept the cash hidden somewhere. I know it is not at your house because we've already searched it and so have the police. Somewhere in her possessions is a clue as to where the money is and how to get it. We had virtually no contact with her several months after she married you, so you're in a better position than anyone to figure out what happen to the money," Vic said.

"What if the money's gone? What if she gave it away like you say she threatened to do?" Jim said.

"Bring me proof and you're off the hook, but I'm betting the money is still around somewhere. Sally was holding on to it as an insurance policy so it makes sense that she still had it at the time of her death."

"Exactly how much money should I be looking for," Jim said.

"$2,000,000 in $100 bills all neatly wrapped in banker's bands – you know how tidy Sally was. It will fit in a suitcase or backpack. Okay, you have all the information I can give you. The rest is up to you."

"I don't know if I can do this by myself. Can I get someone to help me if I need it?" Jim said.

"Like that Amazon cop?" Vic said. "Do you think I'm stupid or something? If you're confronted by the police or anyone and they ask about Sam, tell them you sent her out of town for her own safety and you aren't going to tell them where. The cops suspended your friend for blowing the investigation, so she's not going to be much help. Don't tell anyone what you're doing or why or Sam suffers the consequences. Here's the bottom line, as you corporate types like to say: in 24 hours I'll have my money or Sam is dead. It's that simple and if you run off to the police, I'll know about it within ten minutes and she'll be dead in 11 and I'll be gone in 12. So, don't insult my intelligence with some chicken-shit scheme to involve the police. I think I've already demonstrated how ineffective they are at protecting people. Remember, I'll be watching your every move while you're away."

"You two have 10 minutes to say you goodbyes while I get ready. Then I'm going to blindfold Jim and drive him into town.

Sam you will stay here and I suggest you stay in the bedroom until I get back," Vic said.

Vic gestured toward the bunk beds on the far side of the room and Jim and Sam saw a man sitting on the bottom bunk with his back resting against the wall and his feet drawn up on the bed. He was so far back it was impossible to see his face. Had he been there all this time?

"Three guesses and the first two don't count who that gentleman is," Vic said with a smile.

"You can't leave her alone with him," Jim said.

"She'll be perfectly safe, but like I said please stay in the bedroom until I come back. Now say your goodbyes while I confer with my associate."

Jim and Sam went back to the bedroom and shut the door. They held each other tightly.

"Jim, I don't think we can trust him to keep his word. I believe he means to kill us, no matter what he said."

"I'm afraid you're right. He wouldn't leave a couple of loose ends like us around and since he has no problem killing cops or anyone else who gets in his way, we're no big deal. I've got to find that money to buy us some time to figure a way out of this. The money is the only thing keeping us alive, so I've got to find it, but I don't have a clue about where to begin looking," Jim said.

"Jim, no matter what happens I want you to know that I love you and have loved you for a long time. I believe in you and trust that if there is a way out of this you will find it," Sam said.

"I promise that I'll get us out of this and when it is over I want to spend a great deal of time trying to understand why someone as wonderful as you could love someone like me. I hope you will spend it with me."

"Okay, love birds. Time's up," Vic said.

They kissed and Jim quickly left the bedroom and shut the door behind him.

When he came out, Vic was wearing a security guard's uniform shirt.

"What's that about," Jim said.

"I'll tell you on the way to town."

"I want some way to contact you, to know that Sam is still alive while I'm searching for the money," Jim said.

"Of course, anything you want. You little shit. Don't you dare start making demands to me or I'll kill the both of you right now," Vic said.

"I don't think so. If you were going to do that, we'd both be dead a long time ago. I've no desire to challenge you. I'm playing your game, but I need to know she is still alive while I'm searching or I've no motivation to keep looking. Besides, how am I going to contact you when I find the money? I doubt you're in the phone book."

"Very funny. I'm going to give you a cell phone – it's one of those pre-paid disposable types with a few modifications. You can only receive calls – you can't make them. I'll check in every three hours. Don't get any ideas about tracing the call. My computer friend has devised a way to reroute the call so it will take at least six minutes for tracing software to work and I won't let the conversation go that long. Now, unless there is something else I can do for you, let's get going. The clock begins right now – my money or in 24 hours Sam dies," Vic said.

Chapter 26 – Friday – Jimmy, Shannon, & Ling

"O'Brien, I'm hitting nothing but dead-ends," Jimmy said.

"Is he blocking your access to the files?"

"No, that's not it. He's just covered everything up with dummy corporations and partnerships. There are dozens of them. It's just taking a long time to chase down all these leads."

"Okay. Keep trying. We've got to figure out where he's holding those two before he kills them."

"I did come across one name that sounded familiar: Bonnelli. Isn't he connected with this case somehow?"

"Bonnelli and Victor Hugo. Yes, he's connected. And that ties Vic to Jim Jackson in a different way than we knew before. How did his name come up?" Shannon asked.

"If you cut out all the intervening companies and partnerships on both sides, Bonnelli apparently sold some property to Victor and financed the purchase himself."

"That's it. That's the property we want. Can you find out where that piece of property is located?"

"How do you know that's the one we're looking for?"

"I just feel it in my gut. This guy Vic would not want to leave any paper trail if he could avoid it. You've discovered how hard he worked at covering his tracks, but you can't buy property without creating some paper. However, if you buy it from an associate and that associate does the financing, then you've significantly cut down the amount of paper with your name on it that is in the public domain. Can you find that property?" Shannon asked.

"Yeah, but it may take awhile if I do it by the book."

"And if you don't do it by the book…"

"It could take forever to look through the public records, so I'm going to hack into Bonnelli's personal financial files on his corporate computer and see if I can find any property listed as sold in the area you're searching, but you didn't hear that from me."

"Hear what? Call me if you find out anything from that thing I didn't hear about."

"Did I hear you say Bonnelli?" Ling asked. She had put some sandwiches and chips on the coffee table in front of the sofa and they were eating when Jimmy called.

"Yeah. Jimmy found his name in Vic's records, which means they had a connection before Bonnelli killed Jim's wife, which could mean that was no accident. If that's the case, then Jim has something they want or he would be dead already," Shannon said.

"Doesn't that imply that Jim's wife, Bonnelli, and Vic had some kind of relationship? A lover's triangle perhaps?"

"You're right about the relationship, but I don't think it was a lover's triangle. This guy Vic is too cold for that and Bonnelli was no prize catch. Maybe a business arrangement gone bad. So Bonnelli kills Jim's wife – what was her name…Sally – and Vic kills Bonnelli leaving Vic the surviving partner. But Sally had something Vic wanted – money, incriminating evidence, whatever – and he thinks Jim has it or knows where to find it so he buddies up to Jim at the grief support group to find out as much as he can and then kidnaps Jim and Sam to force the information out of him. Now what?"

"Why doesn't Jim just bring the information to the police," Ling said. "Why didn't he do that when this started?"

"I don't know. Maybe he doesn't know he has the information or where it is. Maybe he didn't know about the relationship with Vic and Bonnelli. Either he is an exceptional liar – and that's certainly a possibility – or he is completely clueless about his wife's business partners. He seemed to have no idea who Vic or Bonnelli was beyond what he had observed. Right now, I'd say it's even money either way. He could be playing the innocent victim and using the police to protect him from his former business partners or he is what he appears to be: an average citizen who took his wife on face value and never suspected she led a double life."

"Wow. How would you like to wake up one day and find out that a person you loved was someone totally different than you thought they were," Ling said.

"Yeah. Kinda like your parents and my dad," Shannon said.

Ling turned away and began to sob.

"I'm sorry. That wasn't kind."

"No, you're right. I think about it all the time. How horrible is must have been for my parents. All their years of hard work and sacrifice only to have me come rub the one thing they could not understand in their face. I could have kept my mouth shut and lived with their questions about boyfriends and grandchildren, but no, I was more concerned about my sophisticated friends than my parents. The truth is my so-called sophisticated friends are self-centered, shallow, and desperately lonely people with no real roots to ground them. They look perfect on the outside, but like a painted shell are hollow inside," Ling said.

"Do you ever wish you were…you know, heterosexual?"

"I used to. I tried to be for a long time, but it just didn't work. I was miserable. Yes, life would be easier and I wouldn't have this problem with my parents, but it is not who I am. When I stopped fighting myself, my life became a lot saner. I don't advertise the fact that I'm a lesbian, but I don't hide it either. There is still a lot of discrimination and I hear the jokes and snide remarks. People don't know what to do with you. This is a 'family' oriented society and it is hard for a lot of people to understand that homosexuals can have families too – they just may not look like the typical American family. What about you? Are you sorry I lured you into this world of mine?" Ling said.

"I came with both eyes open, believe me. I don't know where I am on the sexual continuum. You're the first female lover I've ever had, although I've been attracted to different women for a long time. My relations with men have, for the most part, been superficial and unsatisfying, both physically and emotionally. I've never felt closer to anyone than I feel to you, but I don't have much faith in my emotions – they've let me down so many times before. I want to be in love with you and I want you to be in love with me, but I'm not sure anything I'm feeling right now is real, given what has happened the last several days. Does that make any sense at all?" Shannon said.

"Yes, it makes perfect sense. I would give anything to make this all go away so we could just take off for some island in the Caribbean and spend about six months getting to know each other without this pressure," Ling said.

"That sounds great. If you've got a magic wand, now would be a good time to wave it."

"Sexual continuum. That's not bad for a cop."

"Hey, I went to college. I may not have as many degrees as you have, but did learn a few things."

"Sorry. That sounded patronizing and I didn't mean it that way. It's just that when you're around other cops your vocabulary and sentence structure seem to drop down a couple of notches."

"It's hard enough being a female cop without everyone knowing you're the smartest one in the room too. I don't hide my ideas, but I try to put them into words that make me sound like 'one of the guys' so they will go down easier. It's a stupid game, but one I've played for a long time," Shannon said.

"I had just the opposite problem. Because I'm Asian, everyone assumed I was smart and I would get good grades. Well, I am smart, but not that smart. I studied my butt off to get the top grades everyone assumed I was going to get anyway. When I graduated at the top of my class, it was like 'well so what.'"

Chapter 27 – Friday – Vic & Jim

Vic led Jim out of the house and into the van blindfolded. They drove for what seemed like a long time, at first bouncing over twisting, bumpy country roads in need of maintenance. Without any visual clues, Jim had to hold on with both hands to keep from being thrown off the second seat of the mini-van.

Jim judged that they finally left the country roads and merged on the interstate –- their speed increased and the bumps smoothed out. Jim did not attempt to peek out from behind his blindfold. He was sure Vic was watching and there was no point anyway since he had no idea where they entered the interstate.

"You can remove your blindfold now."

Jim recognized the northern suburbs as they drove south into the city.

"Where are we headed?"

"To your house."

"Won't the police be watching my house?"

"No. They think someone kidnapped or murdered you so they don't expect you to be coming home. There is one person though we do have to fool – your neighbor across the street."

"Yes, Mrs. Greene. She watches everything that goes on in the neighborhood. How are you going to get by her?"

"Oh, we already have, several times. Look in the sack on the floor and you'll find a shirt like mine. Put it on and the hat and sunglasses. Put your stuff in the sack. Your keys are also in the sack. When we searched your housed, we came as the Action Security Company hired by you to look after the place. The first thing I did was introduce myself to Mrs. Greene. When we get to your house, you go directly to the front door and go in. Don't look back at me. I'm going to her house and tell her that we'll have someone in the house and she shouldn't worry if she sees a person moving around in the house. I'll come back with more instructions," Vic said.

Jim felt foolish in the "rent-a-cop" shirt and cap, but followed Vic's instructions exactly. His house was an even bigger mess then he remembered. How was he going to find something that he didn't know existed in this mess?

He made a small opening in the curtains and looked at the van in front of the house. It had a magnetic sign on the passenger-side door that read: Action Security Company. Presumably, there was another on the driver's door. Vic didn't leave anything to chance.

"Your busy-body neighbor is a fountain of information. The cops were here again late yesterday searching the place. God knows what they were looking for," Vic said.

"I could've told you that. This place is a mess – an even bigger mess than before."

"That's actually good news. It means that they probably won't be back anytime soon. It also means that it is unlikely the money is on site, so you're most likely looking for a clue to its whereabouts. It could be anything such as a safe deposit box key, something like that. Here's the cell phone. Keep it on you at all times. I want to be able to reach you instantly if I need to. I may call more often than three hours, but no less frequently than three hours. If you need anything, be prepared to tell me quickly because our conversations will be short. There is a rental car in your garage with the keys in the ignition. When you find the money, I'll arrange a place to make the exchange and you can meet us there. Any questions?"

"I'll want to talk to Sam."

"I may let you hear her voice to know that she is alive, but don't push me."

Vic's cell phone rang and he stepped away to answer the call. Jim could not hear what he said to the caller but the conversation didn't last more than 30 seconds.

"Okay. There's a change of plans. You now have 12 hours to deliver the money," Vic said.

"12 hours. That's not fair – you said…"

"The money or Sam dies at 9:05 p.m."

Chapter 28 – Friday – Shannon & Ling

Shannon hated waiting almost more than anything else – it was such a waste of time. However, she'd learned that patience could yield significant rewards in homicide investigations. Under the watchful eye of her partner, she had developed a sense of when to move and when to wait.

Now was the time to wait. Charging off with only partial information would only drive Vic underground or worse out of town and probably result in the deaths of Jim and Sam. Jimmy found three pieces of property in Bonnelli's corporate files that fit the profile of where Vic may be holding the two civilians.

She had gone over every step of this case from the beginning to see if there was something she was missing and concluded she was missing a lot. If Ling hadn't tied the deaths of the young black man and Bonnelli together, this case probably would have stalled and never gotten this far.

Even with that, she could only see a very small part of the picture and that was what got three cops and several civilians killed. There was a monster at work here and she had to stop him. She knew he would be long gone before the cops caught on to what he was doing.

Jimmy dropped off the maps, but was too embarrassed to come in with Ling in the apartment. Shannon stepped out in the hall with him and told him to be careful. She suggested he not go back to his apartment for a couple of days or until this all blew over. She gave him a prepaid phone, which was one of several she bought on her way back home from the convenience store.

"Keep this with you, but don't use it unless I call you," she told him. "If you need to contact me, send a text.

All three properties were in the right geographic area and Bonnelli had sold all three in the past five years.

"I'm going to check them out," Shannon said.

"Let's go," Ling said.

"No, I want you to stay here this time."

"Why?"

"If those two civilians managed to escape, I want them to have a safe house to go to. I need you here in case they contact me. I'll send them here and you can watch them until I get back."

"What a load of crap."

"Come on. I don't want to argue about this."

"Then be honest with me and cut the bull," Ling said.

"You're right. I may have to do some cross-country scouting of this property and that can be pretty rough country. I know you're not a fragile little woman, but with all due respect, you can't keep up with me and I can't be worried about you and do what I need to do too."

"Thank you. I'm tougher than you give me credit for, but you're right I probably can't keep up with you. Anyhow, this is not the time to test my endurance. I'll stay and next time just tell me the truth, okay?"

"Deal. I'll call you when I get there. Answer my phone if it rings," Shannon said.

She left her apartment and headed north on the interstate, wondering when she was going to quit lying to Ling. Fortunately, Ling couldn't read topographic maps or she would've seen her lie immediately. The terrain around the three properties was gently rolling at the worst. There was nothing Ling couldn't handle.

Shannon didn't want her along because there was a good chance she would not be able to take Vic without a fight and she didn't want Ling to see what she may have to do. She was not a vigilante and didn't believe in taking the law into your own hands, but this was different. This maniac killed at least six people this week alone and God knows how many before now.

He knew what the police were going to do before the police knew and the minute he got a whiff of them closing in on him, he would kill the hostages, vanish, and they would never catch him. If she could take him alive with no risk to the hostages or herself, she would, but if the only way to ensure their safety was to take him out without warning, she was prepared to do that.

Either way, this was the end of the line for her as a cop. She wasn't sure what was next, but if she survived this and didn't go to jail, she planned to take some time off with Ling and just decompress. Maybe it was time to just say 'Dad, you're going to have to accept me for what I am or not at all, because I can't keep playing this game.'

However, all this introspection would have to wait until she got past Vic. She almost hoped it would come down to hand-to-hand combat, but doubted he would leave his fate to chance. He undoubtedly knew a lot about her, as he knew about Jim and the others. Unless she was able to surprise him, he would shoot first and ask questions later, as they say in the movies. Plus, she had no idea if he used any other hired guns.

Besides, it would be around noon when she got to the area and a real bad time to go poking around. Her plan was to locate the three properties and see if she could narrow it down to the right one by observation from a safe distance. A house on the property with kids would probably not be the one Vic was using. She wasn't sure what she would do if she could not find the right piece this way, but one step at a time.

Jimmy had brought over a detailed road map of the area that was fairly current, although parts of the area were showing signs of rapid growth. She found the first piece of property a few miles off the interstate. It was easy to eliminate because it was a field of corn stalks cut close to the ground. She parked on the side of the road plotting her course to the next site when her cell phone rang.

"O'Brien."

"I just captured half of your fleet."

"What did you say? Who is this?"

The phone went dead.

'What the hell did that mean,' she wondered. 'Oh, my God.'

She dialed her home number and it rang until the voice mail picked it up. She hung up and dialed Ling's cell phone. It also rang until her voice mail picked up. Shannon slammed the car into gear and roared back toward the interstate – her heart racing faster than the car.

The return trip took about half as long and fortunately, no one died along the way. Shannon got off the elevator on her floor and looked around, but didn't see anything unusual. She took her key in one hand and her pistol in the other and slowly checked her door. It was unlocked – a bad sign.

She slowly turned the knob and pushed the door open with her free hand. She moved into the room in a crouching position sweeping from right to left with her gun until she was satisfied the room and kitchen were clear. She made her way to the bedroom and did the same thing. The apartment was empty.

Ling's purse was on the coffee table and there was something cooking in the oven. There was no sign of a struggle, but Ling's coat was gone from the rack beside the door. Ling hadn't gone willingly, but she hadn't put up a fight, so whoever did it probably used a gun to intimidate her.

"Son of bitch," Shannon screamed and kicked a hole in the wall. "Someone is going to die for this."

Chapter 29 – Friday – Jim

Jim watched as Vic drove away in the van. A wave of panic swept over him. How was he going to find the money in 12 hours? But, that wasn't the real problem. Whether he found the money or not, Sam was going to die and he would too unless he could find a way to get her free and get to the police.

That didn't even seem like a workable idea. Vic wasn't bragging when he said the police couldn't protect them. They could run, but given Vic's amazing access to information he would find them eventually and kill them. How was he going to do any of this alone? Some how he had to get some help and the only person he could trust was Shannon O'Brien. He didn't believe she was responsible for the cops' deaths and, besides, Sam trusted her, which was a ringing endorsement.

He was sure Vic had planted video cameras in his house based on the admonitions that 'I'll be watching you.' It was actually not hard to spot the cameras and this puzzled Jim at first. Cameras covered the front door, the patio door, and the garage door. There were, what appeared to be alarms on all of the windows. Essentially, Jim could not leave the house without tripping the alarms or being spotted by Vic.

Then it dawned on Jim. Vic had told the old lady across the street that he was with a security company when he first visited the house. This was after the police searched the house, top to bottom. It was unlikely they would return for another search, so he could quickly set up his cameras and alarms and didn't worry about them being discovered.

Jim quickly looked through the rest of the house, but found no microphones or other cameras. He knew the cellphone Vic gave him was monitoring his movements, but since the phone was in his pocket, it was a good bet it did not have a camera operating all the time – just the microphone.

Vic may have other gang members watching the house, but they couldn't stay in one spot too long without arousing suspicion. He guessed Vic was relying on the gun to Sam's head as the main deterrent.

If he was going to involve O'Brien, he would have to figure out a way to communicate with her that didn't involve using the telephone or email, since he was sure that would be monitored. He had her card with her work and home phone numbers on it and it took about a minute of looking through the 'S. O'Brien' listings in the phone book to match her number to the right listing and get an address.

Now, how could he get a message to her without arousing Vic's suspicion? Phone's out; email's out; messenger service's out; what's left? Who delivers things? He couldn't call a delivery service that would tip off Vic that something was up. He walked into the kitchen, realizing that he was hungry. Then it hit him…

'I could get the pizza guy to deliver it,' he thought. Why not? Order something delivered here and then get the delivery person to take a message to O'Brien – make it so worth their while they won't ask questions or hesitate. The trick will be the handoff and making sure that it's done with no talk, so Vic is not alerted.

It was a little after 10 a.m. That gave him a couple of hours to compose his message to O'Brien and figure out how he was going to do the handoff so Vic didn't get suspicious and the delivery person didn't freak out. He sat down at the desk in the family room where Sally used to pay bills and began writing a detailed description of everything Vic told them and what the current situation was with Sam.

As he was writing, the cell phone rang.

"What," he said. "It hasn't been three hours."

"What are you doing?"

"What do you mean?"

"You heard me? Are you looking for my money?"

Jim realized Vic was concerned that he couldn't hear any movement around the house.

"I'm going through some papers and I'll make more progress if you'll let me get back to work. I want this done even more than you."

The phone went dead. It felt good to be aggressive with Vic, but he had to be very careful – the man had no boundaries about killing another human. However, the call raised an important issue: even if he was successful in getting a message to O'Brien, how was she going to communicate back to him? Vic would get suspicious with another delivery. Part of his note to O'Brien was a warning about the cameras, alarms, and the microphone he was carrying. She would have to figure out how to communicate with him in a way that didn't tip off Vic.

His next task was to figure out how to block the camera on the front door so he could pass the letter to the delivery person. The camera was in the corner of the foyer attached to some molding and secured with what appeared to be two-sided tape. Jim glanced at it infrequently so as not to tip off Vic. One the thing he did notice was there were no wires coming out of the camera.

Finally, there was some luck going for him instead of against him. The camera was positioned such that if you opened the door only part way and put your body against the door, the camera could not see your front or the person at the door. If Jim put the note to the delivery person and the letter to O'Brien inside his shirt the camera would not see him pass them off to the delivery person.

Jim felt it could work without Vic becoming alarmed. Of course, the whole scheme depended on the delivery person, who would undoubtedly be a teenager, keeping their mouth shut during the handoff. Even if the handoff went well, Jim's life and the lives of several others depended on that teenager actually delivering the letter to O'Brien. Not the best odds for success, but it was all he had.

In the meantime, he had to think about finding the money. It might be possible to bluff Vic without the money, but he would feel better if he actually had the money. First things first. He finished the letter to O'Brien being careful to emphasize that she should not call or come by because Vic had cameras and alarms. The house may also be under surveillance by one of Vic's henchmen. He still did not have a clue about how she should communicate with him, but put that problem on her.

It was 11:00. He would call the deli in the strip mall near his house and have them deliver a sandwich around 12:45, hoping it would be the last lunch delivery. Until then, he would look for the money and make enough noise to keep Vic happy.

Vic said the police had searched the place and he had too, so there didn't seem to be much point in going through everything again. Two million dollars was not easily overlooked. Unless, he thought, you didn't know where to look. He walked from room to room looking for someplace Sally might hide the money. Knowing her, it would be hidden in plain sight, but in a manner that Jim alone could find it. Even after all Vic had said about Sally, Jim felt certain her love for him was genuine and that she would want him to find the money. He slowly walked through the house looking for something that he would know was special, but others would overlook. It would be special to her or to him or to both of them.

He walked into the bedroom and looked around. He sat on the antique cedar chest at the end of the bed. This had been Sally's pride and joy. In fact, she insisted that he rent a van and move it from her apartment to the house rather than let the movers take it along with everything else. Jim and his friend Bill from work almost broke their backs getting the thing into and out of the van and into the house. Jim didn't know much about antiques, but the chest did not strike him as particularly valuable. In fact, it was very plain with almost no decoration.

He opened the heavy top and saw that the contents had been pawed through, probably several times. Sally kept several expensive sweaters and skirts in addition to some antique quilts and other needlecraft.

A lift-out tray sat across half of the opening. Sally kept some of her grandmother's jewelry, old photographs of relatives, and some mementos from college and high school.

Jim had never seen her open the chest, which was curious given how concerned she was that it arrive at the house safely. He removed the tray, put it on the bed, and looked through the clothing as he pulled it out of the chest. Clearly, there was no $2 million hiding here, but he wondered if she put some clue to its location in the chest. There was no lining, just the cedar paneling for the natural pest protection it afforded.

He had one hand on the bottom of the chest feeling for any imperfection when the cell phone fell out of his chest pocket and on to the floor. He bent over, with his left hand still in the chest to retrieve the cell phone from the floor with his right hand when he noticed something odd. His right hand was much lower than his left hand – lower than the few inches the chest sat off the floor. He stiffened both arms and his left shoulder was definitely much higher than is should be given that the chest was on legs only an inch or so off the floor. If the legs on the chest were about an inch and the floor of the chest and structural pieces added another inch, then his left hand should only be two inches higher than his right hand resting on the floor. However, it was clear that his left hand in the chest was much higher than two inches off the floor – more like four or five inches.

This could only mean one thing: the chest may have a false bottom. Jim's heart began to race, but he forced himself to slow down. He had to do this in a way that the sounds would not give away what he was doing.

He looked around the outside of the chest for any clue that might indicate where the secret compartment might be, but couldn't find any. Next, he tilted the chest up with some difficulty – even empty it was very heavy – to see if there was any clue to the compartment underneath, but he found none.

He sat down on the bed and thought for a moment. Surely, there wouldn't be an obvious way to access the compartment. Someone went to a great deal of trouble and expense to make this cedar chest a safe hiding place, so the access point wouldn't be easy to find.

On the other hand, the purpose of the chest was to never draw suspicion. Once the chest is suspect, an axe would thwart any clever scheme to keep the compartment concealed. Therefore, the access would be designed so that someone with no knowledge of the compartment couldn't accidentally stumble upon it, but once its purpose is known there's not much point in trying to foil an axe or chain saw.

Jim looked at the chest resting on its left end with four legs pointing to the right. He began to examine the underside more closely and, in doing so noticed that the front right leg was slightly twisted out of alignment. He gave it a turn, but realized that he had turned it the wrong way and loosened it more rather than tighten it.

That gave him an idea and he kept turning it counter clockwise. The leg was on a threaded stainless steel shank with some four plus inches sticking out of the wooden leg, which surprised him. It surprised him because it was stainless steel, which you wouldn't expect to find on an antique, and because it was very long. He unscrewed the other three after going to the garage (while avoiding the camera pointed at the door) and getting a pipe wrench because they were in tight. In the process, he did some real damage to the legs themselves.

With all four legs off he could see a gap just inside the ornate molding that surrounded the bottom of the chest. He took a small screwdriver and worked it gently into the gap and the bottom of the chest fell away. It was a solid piece of wood about one-half inch thick and it fit like a glove.

Behind the piece of wood was a grey metal box that filled the hole completely. In each corner of the box, were holes for the screws from the legs. Jim moved the piece of wood out of the way and lowered the box to the floor. It was very heavy. He was startled by how heavy it was, especially since it was only about two inches deep by 28 inches wide by 52 inches long.

After wrestling it to the floor, he looked at the box and concluded it must be fireproof to account for the weight. The latch to open the box was simple – there was no lock or any security device.

He opened the heavy lid and, even though he was sure the money would be there, the sight of $2 million in $100 bills took his breath away. He went over to the closet and rattled some hangars and slammed some drawers just to let off some excitement and to let Vic know he was still working.

When he came back to the box, he noticed there was an envelope taped to the inside of the lid and it was addressed to him in Sally's handwriting.

He almost fainted – it was like a message from the grave.

The note began:

'Dearest Jim: If you have found this letter, it is probably because I am dead. I am so sorry you have to find out about my past this way, but I only wanted to protect you and this was the best way I knew how. Please know that I love you and that no matter what I've done in the past, you're the best thing that has ever happened to me…'

The letter went on to recount in great detail her involvement with Vic and his business intelligence company. It was very much like Vic described it. She began to question some of the ethics of the organization, but stayed on until it was too late. If Vic were arrested, she would go to jail too.

She used Vic's own technique on him to win her freedom. She "kidnapped" $2 million in cash of his money and threatened to give it away if he didn't leave her alone. Sally included in the letter a separate list of offshore accounts and passwords, Swiss accounts, and other holdings of Vic's organization. The totals were almost two years old, but were still more than $15 million. She had changed all the passwords so that Vic no longer controlled this money, but could see the balances.

Her plan was to tell Vic he had to leave the country and never come back. Only when he was out of the country, would she release this money to him. She implied to Vic that all of this information, but not the cash, was in the hands of someone who would turn it over to the police if anything happened to her. Sally's letter urged Jim to give the information and cash to the district attorney if anything happened to her.

Jim had to read the letter three times he was so overcome with emotion. With tears streaming down his face, it was all he could do to keep from sobbing uncontrollably.

Based on the rough timeline Jim constructed, Vic must have been trying to figure out if she was bluffing or not when Bonnelli killed Sally. As long as she held the money and the account information, she felt Vic would leave her alone. She hadn't counted on Bonnelli acting alone.

Chapter 30 – Friday – Vic

Vic didn't like the way this was playing out. His professional career was based on well-planned operations where risks were known and accounted for in the mission. Sure, there was always the chance that things would go badly in any operation, especially those that had made him so rich in the last five years. But, he usually had three different ways to react to unexpected changes.

Thanks to that idiot Bonnelli, who took matters into his own hands, he didn't have time to figure out if Sally was bluffing or if she had followed through and put the evidence in someone's else's hands. Since there had been no changes in the accounts and the police weren't looking for him specifically, he had to assume that she still possessed the money and bank account information. Sally's clown of a husband had no idea what she was doing or her connection to his operation.

He had no one to blame but himself for her hacking his accounts. He trusted her too much and trust will bite you in the ass sooner or later. She was tech savvy, but no hacker. She used some simple tools off the Internet to capture the account information. She also knew where he stashed the cash. It all was so embarrassingly easy for her.

She knew he checked the accounts first thing every morning when he got to the office. He used a secure network of his own creation, so anyone snooping his online activity would have a hard time learning anything. He never used a public network for anything but legitimate work activity.

He knew when it happened. On a Tuesday some three months before her death, Sally was in the office before him, which was unusual. After he logged into the secure network, she brought him a cup of coffee – something she never had done before. That raised a minor red flag with him, but he assumed she was leading up to asking for something.

Suddenly, it felt like someone had kicked him in the gut. He rushed to the bathroom barely in time to avoid shitting his pants. The pain was intense and he thought he might die right there on the crapper – an inglorious end for an old soldier. After about 20 minutes, the pain subsided and he went back to his office. On the door was a sticky note from Sally saying she was off to meet a client. He reviewed the accounts online and satisfied himself that all was in order.

Only later, did he realize that she had drugged his coffee and while he was emptying his gut, she had installed a simple keystroke reader. Using another simple hacking tool, the keystroke reader transmitted the information to her computer, which was still on her desk using the Bluetooth connection. Two hours after it was installed the whole hacking package was erased.

After Sally made her demands, he easily found artifacts of the hack. It was all he could do to restrain himself from killing her. However, he hadn't survived this long by letting his emotions get the better of him. He played along with her demands until he could figure out a plan.

Thanks to that drunken pig Bonnelli, the situation became much more complicated and risky. He was prepared to flee at a moment's notice if he got any hint the police knew about his operation. Fortunately, he was so entrenched in the police "secure" network that he would know if they had any idea of his activities. It was almost disgusting how the police systems leaked information.

That took some of the immediate pressure off, however he still needed to retrieve his cash and bank information. Since no one had come forward with the information, he had to assume that Sally's threat was hollow. He had watched the husband closely for months following Sally's death for any signs he had the money and information. The widower's life was as boring as ever.

He saw three possibilities:

1. Jackson was much smarter than he looked and had the money and information. Conclusion: Not likely.

2. Sally gave the money and information to someone else. Conclusion: Not likely. He had recreated her digital life from the time she hacked his system until she died and could find nothing to suggest she had passed the money and information. Sally had no close friends and little contact with her mother, who was a drunk like Bonnelli. She couldn't keep a secret if her life depended on it. Still, he had an associate break into her house and go over it completely. Nothing was found.

3. Sally had left the money and information or a clue to its location with Jackson and he was too dense to even know it. Conclusion: Highly likely. Jackson was not the sharpest tool in the shed and Sally's death had pretty much fucked up what few brains he had. Vic watched him closely, including bugging his office at work with a camera and microphone and monitoring everything Jackson did digitally. After observing him for months, Vic got Jackson connected with the counseling center by manipulating his boss with false emails from the Human Resources Department. Vic used his "volunteer" position to observe Jackson firsthand.

When he was convinced he was right about Jackson, it would be simple to go through the house and find his money and information or the clue to where Sally hid it. Thanks to his surveillance, he knew Jackson was close to only one person in the world: Samantha his secretary. Vic was an excellent reader of people and it was obvious to him that the secretary was in love with Jackson – God knows why.

Jackson was so consumed with grief he couldn't see how she felt. Still, she would make a good lever to prevent Jackson from running to the police. The plan was to get close to Jackson through the grief support group and gain his trust. When Vic was certain Jackson was harmless, he would "invite" him to find the money and information. Using a threat to the secretary as leverage against him, Vic was sure Jackson would cooperate. If that didn't work, he would kidnap both of them and hold the secretary while Jackson looked for clues to the money and information. If that didn't work, he would kill both of them and leave town for a couple of months while things cooled down. He would make it look like a murder-suicide.

But, that maniac Russell complicated matters by killing that black boy in the park for no apparent reason. That made it possible to connect the murders of the boy and Bonnelli. Russell swore the police would never match the bullets, but the FBI said there was enough similarity in the fragments to suggest a common weapon, thanks to that assistant ME who seemed too smart for her own good.

He knew Jackson would be a suspect in the Bonnelli murder and planted his gun behind the water heater so the police would find it. This would put more pressure on Jackson and make a murder-suicide seems more plausible if he needed to end it that way.

Russell destroyed those plans with more of his lone-wolf bullshit. The warning shot he fired in the parking lot at the counseling center was stupid and, again, unnecessary. It only resulted in Jackson calling O'Brien for help from the emergency room. Shooting the cop guarding Jackson and the secretary, with O'Brien right there meant every other cop in town was gunning for the killer and looking for clues. With Jackson and Samantha in protective custody, Vic had to act quickly and dramatically if he ever had a chance to get his property. Russell was handy for this, adding two more murdered cops to his wanted poster. Vic would kill him as soon as he had his money and information.

As Vic watched the monitors of Jackson's house, he wondered how he ended up in this mess. It was a sad testament to his previous career as the "pointy end of the stick" that kept America's enemy at bay. How many missions? How many enemies eliminated? How many plans to do us harm foiled? Now, he found himself precariously close to jail and at the mercy of the idiot Jackson and the homicidal maniac Russell. Still, he could save this if Jackson found the money and information. It would be a simple matter of cutting off all the loose ends. Let Russell bloody his hands with the murders of Jackson, Samantha and that ME doctor. Throw in O'Brien if necessary and then eliminate Russell.

With any luck, he would be out of the country with his money and access to the foreign accounts in eight hours or less. Jackson had to find the property first, so he had to live long enough to finish that task. And, if he didn't, just tie off the loose ends and leave town with enough evidence to pin all the murders on Russell. The danger was getting too greedy about recovering his property. Greed made men do stupid things – look at the stock market. Vic was not stupid and he hoped finding his money and the account information would justify the risks he was taking.

Chapter 31 – Friday – Jim

Jim checked his watch. It was not time to order the sandwich and, more importantly, the mail hadn't come yet.

He rushed into the family room and sat down at the desk. He found the phone book and addressed an envelope to the District Attorney. He wrote a short note explaining that the person responsible for the deaths of the policemen this week was a master extortionist and here was the proof. He made copies of the documents with his multi-purpose printer, including Sally's letter. He put his note and the copies in an envelope and added two stamps.

His mailbox was by the front door, but Vic would see him open the door and the mailman would probably come before the delivery guy showed up. He would have to put it in the mailbox when the delivery guy came and hope Vic did not find it later.

He went out into the garage and dug around until he found a brand new backpack he bought for a camping trip that never happened. It was huge, and something he never considered was how he was going to carry it very far when it was full. He was about to find out.

He filled it with $2 million and it wasn't very heavy at all. He decided that putting the legs back on the cedar chest was not a good idea given how badly they looked, so he slid the empty box back under the chest and sat in on the floor with no legs. It didn't look exactly right, but if you didn't know it was suppose to have legs, it might not stand out.

It was time to make the call for the sandwich. The guy at the deli told him it would be there in about 20 minutes. As soon as he hung up the phone, the cell phone rang.

"Yes."

"What do you think you're doing?"

"I'm hungry. What did it sound like? In case you didn't notice the last time you searched the place, there's nothing to eat here."

"How is the search for my money going?" Vic said.

"I want to talk to Sam."

"Report first."

"Well, between you and the cops everything is pretty screwed up. I can't find anything. Nothing is where I left it and the boxes I would've wanted to look through first are all over the place."

"What difference does that make?"

"I want to talk to Sam."

"Jim, is that you. Are you okay? I'm …"

"There, you heard her voice. She's still alive and no one has touched her. Now answer my question."

"You know how organized Sally was. If she left a clue – and I'm sure she did – it will be in a very logical place for me to find."

"Why you?"

"Because she would've anticipated that this exact scenario could happen. She would want me to have the money, so the clue would be something that would be logical to me."

"Like what?"

"Look, I don't have time to play games with you. By my watch, I've got less than nine hours until the deadline."

The phone went dead. He had a mental image of Vic boiling mad and it made him smile for a minute. At the end of the day, Vic would kill him unless he could contact O'Brien and they could figure out a way to rescue Sam and save themselves.

He got ready for the delivery and rehearsed how he would execute the handoff without alerting Vic or spooking the delivery person. He made some notes out of letter size paper and a large marker. The delivery guy had to be able to read them instantly and grasp the instructions.

He walked around the house, too nervous to sit and concerned that inactivity would alert Vic. So he walked through rooms occasionally opening and closing a closet or drawer. Jim heard a car door slam. He rushed to a living room window and saw the delivery person coming up the walk with his order. Fortunately, the person making the delivery was a young man in his late teens – just right, Jim thought.

Jim answered the door after the young man rang the bell. He wanted to make sure Vic heard the doorbell. The instructions he printed and the envelope to O'Brien were tucked into his shirt. Since

Vic would only see his back as he opened the door, the bulge would not be noticed.

"Good afternoon. I got your sandwich, chips, and soda. That'll be $11.25."

"Great. Can I write a check?"

"Sure. Make it out to Mid Town Deli."

Instead of writing a check, Jim handed the young man the first note and put his finger to his lips to indicate he should be quiet. The note said:

'Don't Say a Word

My Wife is in the Kitchen

Want to Make $100?'

The young man had a suspicious look on his face and Jim showed him the second note. It said:

'All You Have to Do

Is Deliver This Letter

To My Friend.

$50 Now and $50

When You Deliver

Okay?'

He handed the young man the envelope addressed to Shannon O'Brien with a $50 bill paper-clipped to the top. The young man stared at the envelope for a second, then a knowing look spread over his face followed by a sly smile and a wink. He took the envelope and put his finger to his lips.

Jim reached in his shirt pocket and pulled out a check made out to Mid Town Deli for $15.

"Here you go."

"Thanks. Thanks a lot."

Fortunately, the mailbox was to his right just outside the door. He put the envelope addressed to the DA in the mailbox and closed the door.

The young man tucked the envelope under his arm after putting the $50 in his pocket. He got in his car and left, rap music blaring so loud, Jim could hear it inside the house. Jim breathed a sigh of relief and hoped that the young man was trustworthy and greedy enough to want the other $50 and that he would do it right away and not six hours from now. Several people might live or die depending on what the young man did or did not do in the next few hours.

Chapter 32 – Friday – Shannon

Shannon wanted an assault rifle – the fully automatic kind. She knew where to get one; it was just a matter of picking up the phone and making a call. But, she also knew that was exactly the wrong thing to do. There is nothing she would like more than to find Vic's place and walk in with an assault rifle in full automatic, but with three hostages, even the stupid cops on television wouldn't do that.

She still hadn't pieced together how they got in or how they even found her place, but as smart as Vic seemed to be, nothing was impossible. They could've followed her or Ling or even Jimmy. She should never have left Ling alone. Once again, her stubborn insistence on doing things by herself had resulted in disaster. The more she tried to prove herself to her father the worse things became.

Maybe the brass was right to pull her off the case. Was this overwhelming need to prove herself clouding her judgment? Was she responsible for letting this case get out of control because she refused to acknowledge her weaknesses?

'Okay,' she said aloud. 'Enough self-pity. You have to think this thing through. Why would they snatch Ling?'

The obvious answer was to keep her off Vic's trail, but how did he know what she was doing? Once again, he was two steps ahead of her. Somehow, he discovered what Jimmy was doing and concluded that I wasn't off the case just because the brass said I was. He always knows more than I do – so how do I reverse that? I can't beat him at his game, so I've got to make him play my game, but how?

Just then the intercom buzzer from the lobby sounded.

"Yes," she said.

"Mid-Town Deli. I've a delivery for you," said the voice from the lobby.

"You have the wrong apartment. I didn't order anything," she said.

"This is a special delivery from your friend, Mr. Jackson," the voice said.

"What … from who?"

"Mr. Jackson."

Shannon pushed the button that let the delivery person in through the security door.

Her mind raced. Was this a trick or had Jim managed to get a message to her? Better not take a chance, she thought.

She cracked the front door and watched for the elevator doors to open. As the doors began to open, she closed her door, but kept the knob turned so the latch did not catch. She had her pistol in one hand and the other on the doorknob.

As soon as the deliveryman knocked on the door, she jerked the door open and grabbed him by the arm and pulled him into the apartment. She pushed him against the wall and put the barrel of the pistol against his neck.

"Oh, God. Please don't hurt me," the young man cried.

"Quiet. Let's see that package. Turn around and put your hands on the wall," Shannon ordered.

Shannon opened the envelope. Clipped to the front of the several hand written pages was a $50 bill and a sticky note from Jim telling her the young man knew nothing and to give him the money.

"You can lower your hands and turn around. I'm sorry about that. It's just that I've had some trouble lately with people coming to my door pretending to be something they're not. I hope you understand. The gun's not even loaded. Here's your money," Shannon said.

"Thanks," the young man said.

"Oh, do yourself a favor," Shannon said. "Forget this ever happened."

The young man looked even more frightened and walked as fast to the elevator as his dignity would let him.

Shannon read through Jim's notes about everything (almost) that had happened since he and Sam left the hotel. He described the hideout in detail and recalled landmarks.

Oh great, she thought now I've two hostage situations. Ling and Sam are probably together in one place and Jackson is being held a virtual prisoner at his house. I might be able to save one group, but not both. I have to assume Vic has help, so a real person may guard both. Knowing the precision with which Vic had played his plan, she was sure he had every contingency covered. If something went wrong, he would probably signal his accomplices and everyone one would die – no witnesses – and the team would disappear.

Even if Jackson found the money or a clue to where it was, they were all going to die. This monster kills without a second thought, so there is no way any of them live.

Based on Jackson's timeline in the note and when Ling was probably abducted, it was a safe bet that Vic was not working alone. It seems likely that an accomplice kidnapped Ling. But, did that mean Sam was left alone wherever she was being held or was there a third person on the team? Or, maybe Sam was already dead.

Jackson was right; we can't trust any form of electronic communication. Vic and his team are monitoring our email, phone calls and may be bugging her apartment.

How do I get the ball back in my court, she thought. I'm tired of playing defense – it's time to take the game to him, she thought, but how? How was she going to outwit someone who was two steps, at least, ahead of her all of the time?

Chapter 33 – Friday – Shannon & Jimmy

Shannon paced around the apartment, acutely aware of the clock on the wall which was just ticking past 2:30 p.m. – less than seven hours left before the hostages died, one way or the other. As she walked past the music stand, she picked up the bow to her violin in her right hand and unconsciously tapped the palm of her left hand with it.

She picked up her violin and played an opening to one of her favorite violin concertos, hoping it would help clear her mind. She knew the piece by heart, even after all these years, it felt like she had never stopped playing. A few measures into the piece and she could hear that, even though she remembered the notes, she was not executing very well – her former violin teacher would be appalled. 'You're not sawing logs; you're playing a beautiful instrument that requires a gentle touch and finesse,' her teacher would chide.

All of a sudden some mental fog cleared and she began to look at the problem in a totally different manner. "Of course," she said out loud, and then caught herself remembering her apartment could be bugged. 'I've been playing basketball and getting my butt kicked, when I should be playing the violin,' she said to herself. 'I'm not going to solve this by kicking in a door with guns blazing like some cowboy. I need a way to turn the tables on Vic and his gang, so they're playing defense, even when they may believe they are playing offense.'

She found the pre-paid phone that could connect her to Jimmy and went into the bathroom. She turned on the shower and called Jimmy. He answered on the fourth ring.

"Holy shit, O'Brien. What have you got me into? Three cops dead and a couple of civilians."

"It's worse than that and it's going to get even worse if you can't help me," O'Brien said. "Meet me at the coffee place on North Lincoln. Do you know where it is? Be there in 15 minutes."

"Okay. I guess I'm in this deep," he said.

"Oh, one other thing, don't bring anything electronic except the phone you're talking on," she said and hung up.

She changed into her leathers and tucked her gun into her pants behind her back. She left her personal cell phone on the table and hoped her motorcycle didn't have a tracking device on it.

Jimmy was already at the coffee shop when she arrived. She moved to a booth at the back of the shop that put them out of sight from the street and made sure no one was sitting close by.

She brought him up-to-date as quickly as she could. The problem was getting a message to Jackson who was being held a virtual hostage in the house. The phone he was carrying had a microphone that could pick up surrounding sounds. Cameras monitored the doors and the windows had alarms.

If Jackson tried to leave or contact anyone, Vic would kill Samantha and Ling. She needed a way to get around Vic's technology so she could get a message to Jackson.

Jimmy thought for a minute. "We have to assume that the cameras and alarms are connected to a Wi-Fi network, probably through Jackson's router," Jimmy said. "There may be a way I can give you a few minutes, but not much more. Will that be enough?"

"It's more than I have now, so we'll work with that," she said. "How are you going to get passed his technology?"

"I'm not sure I should tell you. What I need to do is probably a federal offense or worse," Jimmy said.

"Look, I committed about six felonies before lunch, so don't worry about that. When this all comes unraveled, I'll forget to mention your involvement. So, what's the plan?"

"I can't attack his cameras and alarms without him knowing it, so I plan to crash the ISP."

"The what?"

"The Internet Service Provider for that area. When that goes down, Vic will lose his cameras and alarms," Jimmy said.

"What about the cell phone Jackson is carrying?" she asked.

"This wacko is going to scream bloody murder when he loses his cameras and alarms. If he lost the cell phone too, he will know something is up. I'm hoping when he discovers the whole network is down, that he will view it as an incident with the ISP. It is not uncommon for networks to go down briefly. And that's the problem.

It will take the ISP a few minutes to bring the system back up and I won't be able to stop them. That's the window you will have."

"That sounds like something I can work with. Now I've to figure out how to contact him during your blackout without alerting Vic," she said.

"O'Brien, before you agree to this, there is something you should consider. When the ISP goes down, it goes down for everyone. I don't know who or what is relying on their network connection. We could cause some major economic damage or, God forbid, put someone's life at risk with this scheme," Jimmy said.

She was touched that he thought of collateral damage. Maybe there was a real human under there after all. She didn't know his story – maybe no one ever trusted him before.

"Look Jimmy, I hear what you're saying, but I'm 100% sure this guy will kill three people tonight. We may be able to save them and we'll just have to hope we do more good than harm. I promise you I'll never reveal your involvement, so tell me how much time you need."

"I'll get things set up. When you give me the word, it will take about three minutes to execute. After that, I'm estimating you will have three to five minutes to do whatever it is you plan to do. I can warn you about 15 seconds before the network comes back up and the cameras and alarms are connected again," Jimmy said.

"What do you think Vic will do when things go black?" she asked.

"If I were him, I would demand to see Jackson's router and cable modem. I assume the phone has a camera. I would have Jackson point the camera at the router and modem. When he sees they are down, he will check to see if the ISP has a problem or if Jackson has messed with the hardware," Jimmy said.

"So, that will mean Jackson will not be in the garage during that time. If I can find a way to get a message or something into the garage during that timeout, maybe I can communicate with Jackson and figure out a way to end this with only one death," she said.

"One death?"

"No way that bastard Vic comes out of this alive. He's killed three cops and I don't even know how many civilians. He may have killed or hurt someone close to me"

"I didn't hear that," Jimmy said. "And, I'm sorry I've been such a prick, since coming to work at the station. That's not how I used to be."

"A couple of days ago, I would have called you a liar, but you've really come through when it counted and gone beyond what I had any right to ask. If I come out of this alive, if the three civilians come out of this alive, it will be in part because of your help. As far as I'm concerned, our relationship started when you agreed to run that license plate for me. A man did that and he was there when I needed his help."

"Thanks," Jimmy said with a voice that almost cracked with emotion.

"Well, let's not get too cozy. If I survive, I'll be off the force and probably in a prison cell somewhere. If they don't track you down, you can bake me a cake with a file in it or something."

"Prison would be preferable to my cooking," Jimmy laughed.

"Get set up and I'll let you know when to push the button."

Chapter 34 – Friday – Russell, Sam, & Ling

Shortly after Jim and Vic left, the man in the shadows knocked on the bedroom door. Sam didn't open the door, but there was no lock on the inside and nothing to prevent him from coming in.

"What do you want?" she asked.

"I've to run an errand. Before I leave, I'm going to lock you in the bedroom. I'll be gone about two or three hours. Do you need to pee or anything before I lock you in?" the man asked.

"No, I'm good," she said.

"Please don't try anything stupid, like trying to escape. It's quite impossible. Besides, Vic will be monitoring the cameras in this place. If you should manage to get out of the bedroom, you will not get past the front door. If you try this, you might just piss Vic off enough to kill your boyfriend. Are we clear?"

"Yes," Sam answered.

She heard the lock on the door engage and a moment later heard the door to the outside close. She was alone; at least she thought she was. The idea that Vic might have a camera in this room was disgusting. She had nothing else to do, so she began a methodical search of the room for a camera, including climbing on a chair to examine the light fixture. She found no camera or microphone.

She remembered the butter knife she took when Vic first brought them here. The end was rounded like most butter knifes and there was no edge on the blade. Still, if she could shape the point, it might serve as a weapon. The walls were concrete block so she began "grinding" the point of the knife by rubbing it vigorously on the wall.

After about an hour and a half, Sam was beginning to wish she had taken him up on the bathroom offer. The knife had a point of sorts and her arms were tired from rubbing it on the wall. She slipped it up the sleeve of her blouse and it felt like it would stay. The sleeve had three buttons on the cuff and fit snuggly against her arm. The knife was held fairly well by the buttons.

She had nothing to read and there was nothing to do but lie on the bed and think. It was clear to her, as it was to Jim, they were going to die before the day was over. She hoped to see him one more time before they did. She was surprisingly calm about the idea of dying in a few hours.

Her sister had passed on and no longer needed her help. Her mother was in a nursing home and barely knew her when she came to visit. Her mother would be cared for until the end. Sam's only regret was not telling Jim how much she loved him before they both died. When he became engaged to Sally, it was like a knife in her heart. She kept her feelings to herself. Sally was good for Jim and that made her happy. She would never do anything to jeopardize that relationship, so she kept quiet. Sally was wonderful and Sam liked her instantly. They did not socialize much, but when they did Sally was gracious and kind. Sam was sure Sally knew how she felt about Jim, but never said a thing.

When Sally was killed, she rushed to help Jim with no thought about what this meant for any future she might have with him. There was a lot to be done and Jim was in no condition to cover all the bases. He seemed genuinely grateful for all her help. But, Sally's death wounded him deeply. He was struggling just to get through the days. Sam was able to take up some of the slack so the department kept running.

Taking care of details and people were Sam's strong suites. She had spent so many years looking after her sister and her mother, that thoughts of a life apart from them were few. Following her sister's death, which she took very hard, she began thinking about how she wanted to spend the rest of her years. She hoped that some cosmic force would find a way she could live to show Jim her love and hoped he could some day return that love. She had no illusions that their time together last night was a commitment on Jim's part, but it had been wonderful.

If her bladder hadn't been so full, Sam could have drifted off to sleep. As she almost dozed off, she heard the outside door open and voices. Her guard had returned, apparently with someone in tow. That someone was not happy.

"Take your hands off me, you pervert," a female voice screamed.

"Look, I'm trying to take your restraints off for God's sake, so hold still. I'm using a very sharp knife and if you make me slip, I could cut your hand off," the guard said.

The captive seemed to calm down.

"Where am I? Do you know who I'm connected to? She will cut your tongue out and shove it up your ass for what you did to me," the voice shouted.

"Now, now. Let's not be making idle threats. We all need to get along and there is no sense in making it unpleasant," the guard said.

"What do you mean we? Is there someone else here besides you and me?"

"Come on over here and meet your new roommate. She may not have the same, how shall I say, orientation as your Amazon friend, but I believe you will find her pleasant company. You both should know that any attempt to escape will result in your Mr. Jackson's death and yours too."

Sam heard a key turn a lock and the door opened. There was Dr. Ya from the Medical Examiner's office. She saw Sam and rushed into the room and hugged her.

"Are you okay," Ling asked.

"Yes, I'm okay, but I'm worried about Jim, Mr. Jackson Dr. Ya."

"Please, it's Ling. We, detective O'Brien and I, got your message and began tracking you, but that thug kidnapped me and Shannon probably came back to find me, but it was too late," Ling said.

"My friends call me Sam and I wish you would too," Sam said.

They spent the next 15 minutes getting caught up with what happened after they saw each other in the hotel under police protection. Sam told her Vic was looking for some money and information that Sally had taken. He was convinced it was in Jim's house or Sally had left a clue about where to find it. Although she didn't know the details, Sam thought Vic was somehow monitoring Jim's activities. He told Jim not to try to escape or contact the police or he would kill her, Sam said.

"What is going to happen to us?" Sam asked.

"I honestly don't know. If Shannon can't find us, I don't see us coming out of this alive. Sorry, if that's too blunt," Ling said.

"No, it's not. Jim and I came to the same conclusion. We'll need a miracle to survive this whether Jim finds the money or not," Sam said as tears welled up in her eyes.

"Something tells me those tears are more about Mr. Jackson, Jim, than dying," Ling said.

"You're very good," Sam said with a smile through her tears.

"Does he know?" Ling asked.

"We spent the night together here last night. I offered my love with no expectations in return. If we live through this, I hope we can have some 'normal' time together and see where it goes from there. Right now, we are both under too much stress to make commitments," Sam said.

"That sounds familiar," Ling said.

"I thought I caught a spark of something between you two," Sam said smiling. "Since we have some time before we might die, how about some girl talk?"

"Wow, I think you're the first woman who ever talked to me like another woman and not a doctor or a Chinese-American," Ling said. "I can see why you're so important to Mr. Jackson … Jim. And you're okay with Shannon and me as a couple?"

"Sure, why wouldn't I be?" Sam asked.

"You'd be surprised," Ling said. "You first. Tell me about you and Jim and don't leave out any details – especially about last night."

"Stop, you're making me blush."

"Hey, I'm a doctor, remember. I've heard it all," Ling said.

"Oh, so now you're doctor and not a woman," Sam laughed.

"Don't get technical on me. Let's hear it," Ling said with mock seriousness.

With that the two dived deep into their respective relationships.

Chapter 35 – Friday – Jim & Shannon

Shannon parked her motorcycle several blocks from Jackson's house. She wasn't going to sneak up on anyone driving a Harley. Days were shorter and it was getting dark by 5:30. She wanted to have that cover so she could see if anyone was watching the Jackson house. She knew Vic had at least one and maybe more henchmen. One of them could be watching the house.

She slowly moved through backyards and down alleys until she was close enough to see the house. She had small night-vision binoculars and constantly swept the area. This helped her avoid yards with dogs, which might have given away her position. There was an alley behind Jackson's house like others in the area, so if there was a sentry, he could be positioned there if he could find cover.

She saw the perfect spot. It had a good view of Jackson's house, yet was concealed by a garden shed. She assumed there was no dog or the sentry would not be there.

Her observations were correct. There was a man sitting on the ground behind the shed. He looked like he might be asleep. She would have to time this perfectly. She got as close to him as she thought safe. Waiting for it to become darker, her thoughts turned to Ling. If something happened to her, she would never forgive herself. Why was she so afraid of that tiny woman?

Shannon decided she couldn't wait any longer. She sent a text to Jimmy and he began the attack on the ISP. Three minutes passed, four minutes, five minutes – shit, thought Shannon, it's not working. Now what do I do?

Her phone vibrated. It was a text from Jimmy. The ISP was down. She waited, but it was incredibly difficult to remain still. Suddenly, the man's phone buzzed. He answered on about the fourth buzz.

"I was not asleep," the man said. "I dropped my phone and had trouble finding it in the dark."

"No, that's the truth," the man said. "What, no there is no activity at the house. Yes, I'm sure, I'm looking right at it. Nothing is happening."

The man looked at the phone. "Well, goodbye to you too, asshole."

He heard something behind him and turned just in time for Shannon to catch him right on the nose with a kick that sent him down. Before he could get up, she was on top of him and with a punch, knocked him out. She bound his hands behind him with plastic ties used by police when there were not enough handcuffs and did the same to his feet. She took a nasty looking rag she found in the alley and sealed his mouth. Not exactly proper police procedure, but necessary. She grabbed his gun and phone and jumped the fence and raced to Jackson's house.

As Jimmy suspected, Jackson was yelling into the phone that he had no idea what was happening. He walked over to the cable modem and router, which were in the den and pointed the camera at the two pieces of equipment. Shannon could see all of this because she was in Jackson's backyard. She ran to door leading from the garage to the backyard and hoped it wasn't locked.

She didn't know how much time she had before the ISP came back online and the cameras activated. She found the one aimed at the garage door and concluded she could hide in opposite corner of the garage behind some boxes. She wrote a quick note to Jackson on the floor and hoped he would come into the garage soon or this whole thing would blow up. She left a pre-paid cell phone with the note that cautioned no calls, but gave him the number of her pre-paid phone and said to text when he found the phone.

As she was finishing the note, her phone buzzed with a text from Jimmy that everything was about to come on line. She crouched behind some boxes that would hide her from the garage door camera in case it swept the whole garage.

Jimmy texted that the ISP was back up.

Chapter 36 – Friday – Jim & Shannon

Jim was about to go insane, if that was even possible at this point. He had the money and the information Vic wanted, but he had no idea what to do next. If he told Vic without a plan and some help, Sam would die and he would too, no doubt. How was he going to find out if O'Brien was going to help or if she even received his note? Maybe the delivery boy just took has $50 and bought some drugs or something.

Even if O'Brien did get his note, how was she going to contact him without Vic knowing? Surely, someone was watching the house and Vic had the microphone to listen to everything, plus the cameras and alarms. It all seemed so hopeless.

Yet, Jim knew this was not how it was going to end. He would figure out something and not wait for O'Brien or any other help that may or may not be coming.

While he was considering the possibilities, Vic called him and began yelling something about the Internet and cameras. He made Jim go over to the cable modem and router and point the phone's camera at them. After that he calmed down a little.

"Stay where you are. Don't move until I tell you to," Vic said.

Jim asked him what was going on and why was he so upset. Jim knew he had done nothing, but as best as he could figure, something happened to the Internet connection.

While he was waiting for more instructions from Vic, it dawned on him that the cameras and alarms were connected to the Internet and that was how Vic was monitoring his activities. The cameras or the alarms would tell him instantly if someone tried to come or go. But now, Vic was blind.

This was an opportunity, but Jim didn't know what to do with it. He couldn't leave; the cell phone still worked and Vic would hear him move. Even if he could get away, where would he go? He had no idea where Vic was holding Sam and even if he did, she would be dead before he could get there. The main restraint on him was not the phone, the cameras, or the alarms. It was the gun that Vic was holding to Sam's head.

As Vic was making him give a video tour of the house to prove there was nothing going on, Jim heard a faint sound from the garage. That was his next stop, so he began complaining about the time being wasted with this video tour, and Vic relented.

When Vic hung up, Jim carefully opened the door to the garage and looked in. He didn't see anyone or any sign of O'Brien. He was about to go back into the house, because it was getting chilly in the garage when he saw the phone and note on the floor next to the car. His heart began to race – O'Brien had received the note. He walked over to the car and picked up the note and the phone, being careful not to step in the camera's line of sight.

His hands were shaking so badly, he almost dropped the phone. O'Brien was in the garage and the note included the phone number and a warning not to make any phone calls, but to text her when he could do so without alerting Vic.

O'Brien's six-foot-two inch frame didn't easily hide behind a stack of moving boxes. She was on the garage floor with her arms wrapped around her knees. Of course, if Jackson didn't find the other phone and her note, she might be in here for a long time before she could move without tipping Vic.

Just then, the phone vibrated:

"found the phone"

She texted back:

"great thought I was stuck in here forever"

"so what's the plan"

"plan??? got no plan, but will think of something"

"no plan? no hope"

"not true I'll think of something"

Jackson didn't answer right away. O'Brien texted back:

"we just need a way to convince vic you have $$"

"i have the money"

"first good news of the night – ok give me a minute," O'Brien replied.

She would have to react to Vic's instructions to Jackson on where and how to deliver the money. She had an idea the thug she took out in the alley was going to receive additional instructions, which involved killing Jackson and bringing the money to Vic. When Vic discovered he could not contact him, he would become suspicious. She would have to take a chance that he did not send someone else to finish the job.

"ok we're going to start playing offense," she texted back to him.

"what does that mean? he will kill Sam!!"

"you must know that's going to happen unless we do something"

"yes, I know, but it's too painful to consider"

"I understand he has Ling," she texted.

"sorry, I didn't know"

"ok, let's figure out a way to outwit this bastard"

"btw where are you?"

"right behind you," she texted back and stood up.

Jackson turned around and almost fainted at the sight of Shannon standing up behind the boxes. He felt tears coming to his eyes and rushed around the boxes and threw his arms around her. He quickly realized that his head was nearly resting on her breasts and pulled back embarrassed.

She grabbed his face with her hands and pulled him close.

"I'm glad you're alive and were smart enough to get me a message. We now have some hope," she whispered in his ear and kissed him on the cheek.

He put his lips near her ear and asked, "Do you think we can get out of this alive and save Sam and Ling?"

She whispered in his ear, "I've got to believe that or there's no purpose in living, is there?"

"No, there's not. That bastard has caused me more hurt than any man has a right. If I can, I'll kill him myself."

"Understood, but don't go crazy on me. We have to be smarter than he is and beat him at his own game," she whispered.

"How are we going to do that?"

"We're going to give him what he wants," she whispered.

"He'll kill Sam and Ling if we do," Jim said.

Jim's cell phone rang and he jumped. "What now?" he growled into the phone.

"You're not doing anything," Vic snapped.

Shannon mouthed, 'buy us some time.'

Jim nodded.

"Listen, give me 30 minutes and I may have some good news for you … for both of us. I found the clue. I just need some time to make sense of it."

"What clue?" Vic asked.

"Sally left me a note in one of my favorite books. She knew I would open the book sooner or later. The clue is written in a way that only I could figure it out. It alludes to things we did together and places we visited."

"Point the phone's camera at it so I can see," Vic said.

"Once again, you're wasting my time with your paranoid bullshit. I've no reason to lie. I must produce your money and information or tell you where to find it or Sam dies. That's all that matters right now. Call me back in 30 minutes," Jim said and ended the call.

He walked across the garage and placed the phone in a box and came back to where Shannon was waiting.

"I think we can talk quietly now without becoming engaged," he whispered.

Shannon smiled, "That might be hard to explain to two people we know. What instructions did Vic give you if you found the money?"

"He will give me a meeting place and time and I am to take that car, which is not mine, by the way. The car is undoubtedly bugged and has a GPS tracker, so he will know if I try to contact anyone."

"Here's what is likely to happen. He will give a location and time that is far enough away that you will have to go directly there to meet his deadline. I know he is not working alone, but I don't know how many more people he has. I disabled one behind your house, which was how I managed to get in the garage when the Internet went down. He was probably there to watch for interference and to kill you if you found the money or not. I have to assume he has others working for him and they will be at the drop point, probably hidden," Shannon said.

"I need to do some serious texting, so why don't you retrieve your phone and make some noise inside so Vic doesn't spook," she said. "Come back out in 10 minutes or so with the information on Vic's overseas accounts and the money."

Jim put the phone back in his pocket and went inside. He sat at his desk and shuffled papers periodically. He could not imagine how Shannon was going to make this work. They were all going to die and the police would probably pin as many murders on them as possible. Sam trusted Shannon and he did too, but he wondered if that was enough.

It was not 10 minutes yet, but Jim was too nervous to be in the house any longer. He got the backpack full of money and the envelope Sally left him and went back into the garage. Shannon was still hunched over her phone sending a text. He walked across the garage and put the phone in the box.

"Let me see that information on the bank accounts," she said.

"Here it is along with Sally's letter to me. You should read it."

Shannon read Sally's letter and felt tears in her eyes as she imagined how painful for Jim it must have been to read it. As she suspected, Vic had other associates that Sally didn't know about, but suspected.

"I wish we could get this to the police," she said. "If things don't go well for us tonight, it would feel better if someone in authority knew."

"Don't worry about that. I made a copy of everything and mailed in to the District Attorney's office," he said.

"How did you do that with Vic watching you so closely?" she asked.

"I'll tell you all about it some day over a glass of wine," he said.

She looked at him a moment and said, "Your Sam is right to trust you. There's a lot more to you than meets the eye."

She took the account information and began texting again. When she finished, she looked up and said, "Now, we wait."

"We don't have much time to wait," he said.

"I know, but I've reached out for some assistance and I need to know it is on-board before we do anything else," she said.

"And what if your assistance doesn't come through?"

"When you play the violin, you have to trust the instrument. You have to trust it will create the music you're playing. You can't force it; you must trust it and work with it and be patient."

"What the hell are you talking about?" Jim asked.

Chapter 37 – Friday – Ling & Sam

Ling and Sam updated each other on what had happened since the escape from the hotel and capture by Vic. They also exchanged stories about themselves and their love lives for a couple of hours, before the man guarding them knocked on the door.

"Potty break time," he said. "Please don't do anything stupid when I open the door. As you might have guessed, I won't think twice about killing you both if you try anything. You have five minutes each."

"What about something to eat," Ling asked.

"Sorry, but room service is closed for the night," he said.

"Very funny," Sam said.

After they were back in the bedroom, the mood was much more sober. The gunman's words reminded them they were hostages and in grave danger.

"I don't know how this will end, but I'm afraid the odds are against us," Sam said.

"Maybe so, but you don't know Shannon like I do," Ling said. "She won't stop trying to save us and Jim."

"I hope you're right. I know Jim won't let me down if he can help it," Sam said. "I'm afraid this Vic guy and his attack dog out there may be too much for both of them."

"I'm not going down without a fight if I can help it. We need to think of a way we can help Shannon or Jim," Ling said.

"Vic thinks Jim's late wife took some of his money and information about offshore accounts. He expects Jim to find it. If he doesn't find what Vic wants, I suppose there is not much we can do to save ourselves," Sam said. "However, if Jim does find the money, I suppose Vic will arrange some kind of exchange. As far as we know, Shannon doesn't know where Jim is or what he is doing. When she left this morning, she was looking for this hideout. Vic probably kidnapped you to have leverage on Shannon in case she got too close."

"She has a real hot temper when it comes to people messing with me. If she finds this place, her instinct will be to kick in the door shooting," Ling said

"In that case, she might lose. The thug out there will be warned by all of those cameras and Shannon will be walking into a trap. We need some contingency plans based on what might happen," Sam said.

"Okay, let's put down some scenarios and see if we can put together an action plan for each," Sam said. She couldn't find any paper or pen, so she pulled some lipstick out of her purse and wrote 'Scenarios' on the wall with the door the other room.

"Do you normally wear lipstick?" Ling asked.

"I wear it sometimes, but thought Jim might like it if I did," Sam said. She put a '1.' on the wall under the scenarios heading.

"He'll see that," Ling said motioning to the other room.

"Maybe, but he has never come into this room – he's always made us come out. If he sticks to that pattern, he won't see this," Sam said. "What's our first scenario?"

"This is beginning to feel like a conference room brain-storming session," Ling said.

"Sorry, this is just what we do when working on a marketing problem," Sam said. "All of that seemed important at the time, now it seems silly and self-important."

"Not at all," Ling said. "This is just what we need to do. Jim is a lucky guy to have you on his side – literally and figuratively."

"Stop it! You're making me blush," Sam said. "What's our first scenario?"

"Alright, let's get the worst-case scenario out of the way first. Jim doesn't find the money and Shannon doesn't find us. I think we know that we are loose ends and Vic won't let us live," Ling said.

Sam wrote 'Worst case' and under it she wrote 'no Jim, no Shannon' in smaller letters.

She skipped down on the wall and wrote '2. Jim finds cash.' Further down the wall she put a number '3. Shannon finds us.'

Ling said, "I can think of a few more, but they are just variations of these three."

"Good," Sam said. "I don't have an unlimited amount of lipstick here. Keeping the possibilities limited will help us plan better. We'll have to be quick enough to tweak our solutions if we are confronted with some variation of these three. Now, let's profile Vic and his thug out there. Here's my take and it applies to both of them. Vic is very smart and thinks in strategy and tactics. He also has several contingency plans in case events take an unexpected turn. We need strategies that he won't think of."

"How are we going to do that?" Ling asked. "Unless you're retired Special Forces or something like that, he has a big edge. And, he has a technology edge with his cameras and computers. He knows what the police are going to do before they know what they are going to do."

"You're right, we can't beat him at his own game, so we have to change the game," Sam said. "He impressed me as afraid of nothing and I don't think he has much respect for women, being the 'weaker sex' and all. So, how do we change the game to our favor or at least give us a chance?"

"One of us could seduce the guy out there and then when he was 'in flagrante delicto' the other one could get his gun or knock him out or something," Ling said.

She and Sam starred at each other for a moment and then burst out laughing.

"Okay, maybe that's not a workable plan," Ling said. "Neither one of us looks like the type who would throw herself at a monkey like that."

"He's probably too well trained to fall for that trick," Ling said. "However, I think we're on the right track. We need to do something that is so unexpected it throws them off for just an instant. I'm not a violent person and neither are you – I think – so that might catch them by surprise. But, we need some weapons."

"I've got this," Sam said and pulled a butter knife out from the sleeve of her blouse.

Ling looked at it, trying not to chuckle. "Well, it's a start. Where did you get that?"

"The first night we were here I stole it off the table while Vic was clearing the dishes. It's pretty dull, but I was sharpening the point on the concrete block wall before you arrived."

Ling took the knife and could see where Sam had actually managed to create a point of sorts.

"For this to be effective you'll want to stab a fleshy part of the body. If you hit a bone just below the skin's surface, like a rib, that's as far as you will go. It will hurt, but won't slow either one of those gorillas down.

"Let's finish our contingency planning and, then I'll look for something I can use," Ling said.

"I was counting on you being a ninja," Sam chuckled.

"Ha. Ha. Very funny," Ling said.

Sam walked back to the wall and studied the three possible scenarios of how this might end.

"In our worst case scenario, we are on our own and we know that means: we'll both be killed. What, if anything, can we do to counter that?"

"My guess is not much," Ling said. "We don't know if they will kill us here or take us somewhere else. But I'm not going down without a fight. I say, if this is the scenario, we don't let them separate us and we rush them with your knife and whatever weapon I can find. I just had a bad thought. What if this room is bugged and Vic is hearing everything we say?"

"Jim worried about that also. After he and Vic left, I searched for a microphone or camera, but didn't find anything. I'm sure he is clever enough to hide a bugging device that I couldn't find, but I don't think there's one here. Honestly, if there is I doubt Vic is very concerned about us plotting an escape. He's probably busy watching Jim and monitoring the police network to worry about us."

"But what about that guy out there?" Ling asked.

"I doubt he cares either," Sam said. "He knows we can't escape. My guess is his job is to make sure Shannon doesn't get to us and to deliver us to an exchange point if Jim finds the money. Vic will want to make sure he has all of his property before doing anything with us. To do that, we have to stay alive. Let's get back to our planning.

Scenario 2 was Jim finds the money. I think I just outlined what will happen. We'll be taken to an exchange point and, when Vic is satisfied he has what he wants, they will kill us."

"So, what do we do?" Ling asked. "It seems like our options are few and not pleasant."

"You're right. Our goal is to live, but I don't think we can count on all of us living. For this scenario, Vic only needs me alive. You might be killed before we ever get to the exchange. So our goal is helping you escape, counting on Vic wanting me alive for the exchange," Sam said.

"Wait a minute. I'm not sure I like the way this is going. We're in this together and so we need to find a way we all get out alive," Ling said.

"I just don't think that is possible, unless we have some help. I don't want to die and I don't want you to die. I certainly don't want Jim or Shannon to die either. But, I'm afraid if we look for a solution where we all live that will most certainly mean we all die.

"Besides if you escape, you might get us help before Vic kills us all. Those two detectives, Appleton and Barnes, will come if you can reach them in time," Sam said.

"I see your point, but I still don't like it," Ling said. "One way may be for me to jump out of the car. He couldn't chase me down and get you to the exchange at the same time."

"That's good, but dangerous. We know we're somewhere in the country, so you'll have to wait until we're in town where you can get to a phone quickly. I seem to remember Vic locked the doors of the van once we were in. I think it's reasonable to assume the doors on the sides next to the second seat can't be unlocked. So, we'll have to get into the front seat on the passenger side to use the unlock button," Sam said.

"This all seems so hopeless. Every plan we come up with has about a 10% chance for success. Frankly, I don't see anything we do changing the ultimate outcome," Ling said as tears filled her eyes.

Sam went to her and put her arm around her.

"I know, I'm being a big baby," Ling said. "It's so unfair that I finally find someone I may want to spend the rest of my life with and now that life is measured in hours and I won't even be with her when I die."

"I can honestly say I know how you feel, although I've been in love with Jim for several years. When he married Sally, I wanted to die. But she was good for him and that made me happy," Sam said as her eyes filled with tears.

After a minute or so, Ling stood up and wiped the tears from her eyes.

"Okay, enough of this sobbing bullshit. The two people we love need our help and they don't need a couple of sobbing, snotty crybabies."

Sam laughed, "You're right. What is it they say in the movies, 'we've got to kick ass and take names.'"

"That's sounds like Shannon, although I'm not sure it fits Jim," Ling said. "But, I'm sure he is doing everything he possibly can to free you. I doubt he even knows I'm a captive too."

"The only chance we have to make a difference is to do something that distracts this monkey or Vic for a split second and hope that is enough to make the difference somehow," Sam said.

"Let's see if we can find you a weapon. I don't have a watch, but I'm sure it's getting close to the deadline. If one or both of us can stab or poke, Vic or this guy at the right time it might make the difference for one or more of us," Sam said.

"Even if we all die, we die fighting and not like some passive victim."

Chapter 38 – Friday – Jim & Shannon

Shannon thought she had a plan of sorts. It had plenty of opportunities to fail, but at least it was something and they were running out of time. Her grim conclusion was that even if the plan succeeded, it was very possible that more than one of their team will die. She had to protect three civilians and herself from two or more trained assassins. Her plan relied on throwing Vic and his crew off balance by doing something unexpected.

She motioned for Jim to join her behind the boxes to be out of range of the microphone in his cell phone. They squatted on the floor with their faces close together.

"I've got a plan," she said.

"Great news," he said.

"Don't get too far ahead of me. I've a plan, but it has only a small chance for success. There are two trained killers we have to defeat and save ourselves and Sam and Ling. I'm afraid under the best of circumstances, not all of us will live."

"You've got to save Sam – promise me that," Jim said.

"Unfortunately, it doesn't work that way," Shannon said. "If I were Vic, I would kill the only credible threat first, and that's me. If I go down, there's not much to stop him from killing the rest of you. If Vic decides to end this quickly, we may not even get a chance to execute my plan. The one thing I do promise is that if I get the chance, I'll kill Vic tonight and end this. By the way, you can add that to the list of felonies I've committed today."

"What's your plan?" Jim said.

"Like I said earlier, we're going to give him what he wants. I don't think he knows I'm here, but he is very suspicious about the Internet going down and not being able to reach the punk who was watching your house. By the way, if you had told Vic you had the money, that thug's job was to kill you"

"Did you kill him?"

"No. He's just hired muscle, not the other trained killer. He wouldn't have made it out of your house alive. Vic or his partner would have killed him. Vic hasn't survived this long by leaving loose ends that could be traced back to him."

"And we're a bunch of loose ends," Jim said.

"Something like that," Shannon said. "But we're not dead yet, so let's go over my plan.

"In a few minutes, I want you to show Vic the money and give him proof you have the bank information too – I've got a nice little surprise for him. In the meantime, I've reached out to some friends and hope they can help us. However, this is going down very quickly, one way or the other. I'm counting on Vic to send you to a remote exchange point. When we get the location, I'll signal the troops and hope they arrive in time."

Shannon didn't want to get his hopes up, but also didn't want him to give up hope. He had an important role to play and she needed him focused. She use plural pronouns to suggest that multiple friends were on the way, when the only person she could contact or trust was Jimmy and she was not sure how far he was willing to go. He had surprised her by taking down the ISP, but she couldn't count on him showing up at the exchange with a gun. It would do no good to contact the police. Her name was dirt right now and no one on the force would risk their career for her. Kowalski would come, but he was 1,000 miles away on vacation.

"When Vic gives you the location, take the money and the information to the exchange point. When you leave, turn out the garage light before you leave, but don't close the garage door. I'll try to sneak out that way and get to my motorcycle, which is parked a couple of blocks away. I'm counting on him being more interested in you than monitoring the garage door camera. Just be sure to drive down Oak for a couple of blocks so I can follow you, even if that isn't the way you would normally go to the exchange point. Drive the speed limit and don't do anything to draw attention to yourself. Watch for me on a corner along the route and stop. Lower the rear passenger side window and I'll get in the back seat as quietly as possible," Shannon said.

"How will you know which streets I'll take?" Jim asked.

"I'll follow you at a distance and when I see my chance, I'll pass you and park my bike," she said. "Here is what I want you to tell him."

Jim read the hand-written note and almost laughed. "This will really piss him off. But, what if he just decides to kill Sam and Ling and escape?"

"That's always a possibility, but I think he wants the money and those accounts more than anything else right now. I've no doubt if you give him the money and information without some leverage, he will kill us all. That's why we have to use his tactics to have any chance," Shannon said. "If you're okay with this, you better get started. The 30 minutes you asked for are almost up."

"I guess so," Jim said.

"Before you make the call in view of the camera, put this in pants behind your back and make sure you don't turn so he can see your back," she said. She handed him a short-barrel 9mm.

Jim looked at the gun like it was a snake. "I can't take that. I know almost nothing about guns. I'm more likely to shoot myself or you than Vic."

"Here's what I want you to do. If shooting starts, I want you to push this to take it off safety and I want you to aim over Vic's head. Just start shooting until you run out of bullets. This will distract him and he may try to shoot you, so make sure you're behind the car or some other cover. I don't expect you to be 'Dirty Harry' just make a lot of noise and leave the rest to me. However, if I go down and you have a clear shot at Vic – meaning Sam and Ling are nowhere near – aim for him and anyone else who may show up," Shannon said.

"What do you mean 'anyone else'? I thought Vic was working alone," Jim said.

"I did too in the beginning, but now I'm certain he has at least one accomplice and he may be more dangerous than Vic," Shannon said. You'll do great. With any luck, when this is all over the four of us will have a nice dinner, many bottles of wine and reflect on our new lives – assuming I'm not in prison."

Chapter 39 – Friday – Vic

Vic rubbed his shaven head as he watched his monitors tracking the cameras in Jackson's house. Another laptop scanned the police incident database and 911 calls using a neat little program he created a couple of years ago. It flashed and highlighted any activity that contained keywords. This was his early warning system – one of several that helped him stay one step ahead of the cops. He could run it from anywhere he had an Internet connection. Right now, he was on a boat docked at an out of the way boat launch. The speedboat had a sleeping area below and that is where he was set up. His plan was to get the money and information and escape after Russell tied off the loose ends and he tied off Russell. He had a car across the bay and, thanks to a GPS tracker could cross the distance in the dark without running lights.

He seldom let his mind wander while running an operation. That was a good way to experience a nasty surprise. Still, this was a disaster by any measure you want to apply. When you're in the field, things are fluid and you must make quick decisions. Which is why he got out of fieldwork a long time ago. It was much better to run the operation from a command center, where you could see the pieces and plan several moves in advance.

That stupid maniac Russell has put everything in jeopardy. Vic sent him to kill the two cops standing guard over Jackson and his secretary with the hope that Russell would die in a shootout or get caught. Russell wouldn't talk – he had too much training for police interrogators who would follow the rules. They would quickly pin the other murders on him, thanks to his pistol and that would take the pressure off Vic. Russell would not break and, if he did, it would be weeks or months later. Plenty of time for Vic to make his escape.

Vic had a completely different plan for getting his money and information out of Jackson by using his secretary as leverage. Vic planned to snatch the two and make it appear they had run off together. The police would consider that a sign of guilt and begin the hunt. Vic would leave so many false trails, the police would spend weeks chasing rabbits. Meanwhile, the two would be Vic's guests and help him figure out where his money and information was hidden.

Thanks to Russell, that was all scrapped and now he had to come up with a plan on the fly, which made him nervous. There were too many variables and he did not have contingencies for the even the most likely turn of events.

Russell had his uses, but it was clear to Vic that the liabilities out-weighed the benefits. Vic decided to send him on another suicide mission. On his way out this morning with Jackson, he told Russell to go kidnap the cop's girlfriend, so he would have leverage against her. She was the only one who might put all of the pieces together. Vic knew she was at the cop's apartment, because an associate had followed her there. Vic had a handful of local thugs he could call for special jobs. They never saw the whole picture and were assigned a specific job, often not even against the law. He paid them well, so they were always eager for work. None of them ever saw his face.

This was a win-win situation for Vic. If Russell succeeded in kidnaping the doctor, Vic had another hostage. On the other hand, if the cop was there, she would crush Russell and everyone would believe the killer had been caught. The pressure would be off. Either way he won. Somewhat to his surprise, Russell brought the doctor to the hideout before he got back from leaving Jackson at his house to begin the search. Russell still had the police uniform on, which is how he got the doctor to open the door without a question.

The doctor and Sam were locked in the bedroom of his hideout with Russell on guard. He had Russell monitor Jackson and the police network while he went to the boat. He then switched control on the monitoring to his location. This made it easier for him to concentrate on the operation at Jackson's house.

Jackson was either a fool, so smitten by his dead wife he was clueless about what she did or he was a lot smarter than he looked. Either way, Vic knew he had the right leverage, not only on Jackson, but also that Amazon cop. Two hostages would make the handoff – assuming Jackson found his money – a little dicey, but not impossible. Neither Jackson nor the cop would risk the hostages in a shootout. Besides, Russell had eluded the cops at the hotel and was available to clean up the mess. Russell would kill whoever showed up for the handoff and then Vic would kill Russell with the cop's gun, making it look like they killed each other. Off course the hostages would die too, tragic victims caught in a shootout – no loose ends as they say in the movies.

He had been sitting in front of the monitors all day, waiting for Jackson to find the money and information. It was now 5:30 and he was about to think Jackson would not find his property. He had some other money stashed away and it would get him out of the country. But, it was not enough for the retirement in luxury he had been working for and that pissed him off.

He called Russell and told him to bring the hostages to his location – alive. It was time to end this operation. Whether Jackson found the money and account information or not, it would all end in the next couple of hours.

Suddenly, all the cameras in Jackson's house went blank. Vic typed furiously on the keyboard, but there was no connection to the cameras. Something had happened to their Internet connection. He yelled at Jackson, who seemed genuinely puzzled by why Vic was upset. Vic made him go to his router and cable modem and point the phone's camera at them. Their lights were still on, but the modem's lights indicated it wasn't receiving a signal.

Vic was not convinced that Jackson wasn't up to some trick, but couldn't figure out what it was. He connected with some boards he followed and they were reporting the ISP was offline in that part of the town. Some 12,000 customers lost their Internet service. Vic was still suspicious, but didn't see Jackson able to pull that off without some connection to the outside world and he had that covered.

He made Jackson walk through the house where there were no cameras with the phone so he could see if anything looked out of place. Jackson readily obliged, but complained that this was taking time away from his search. Vic reluctantly agreed and called off the search just as Jackson was about to enter the garage. Even with the enhancements, the phone Jackson had would run low on power soon if he kept the camera on.

Another hour went by and suddenly, there was Jackson standing in view of the camera on the front door with an open backpack full of money. Vic couldn't believe his eyes – Jackson actually found it.

"What about the information?" Vic yelled into the phone.

"It's here," Jackson said looking through some papers. "Something called Threadstone account has a balance of roughly $1.3 million. Does that sound familiar?"

"So, you found it. Congratulations your little friend may live after all," Vic said.

"What do you mean 'may live?' I've done what you wanted. I found your money and your bank account information. There was even a letter to me from Sally explaining what was going on and what I should do with the money and information. We have a deal."

"Listen, you little worm. There is no deal and no one is safe until I've got my money and information in my hands. If you try anything funny, your lady friend dies right in front of your eyes. Have you ever seen anyone's throat slashed? Not pretty and I bet you still have nightmares about the way your wife died."

"Fuck you," Jackson shouted.

"No need to get personal. Here's what's going to happen: you and you alone will bring me my money and information. When I'm satisfied that all is in order, I'll release the hostages," Vic said. "If I get a hint of cops, especially that Amazon, I'll kill both hostages without blinking an eye. Understood?"

"Yeah, let's just get this over," Jackson said.

"Meet me at 7:30 o'clock by the old boat launch near 12th Street. Do you know where that is?" Vic asked.

"I know about where it is, but I'll find it and be there."

"Please, no heroics and no cops. I'll know if you have involved the cops and the next time you see your girlfriend, they'll be fishing her out of the bay. Let's keep this simple and we'll all wake up tomorrow with our problems behind us," Vic said.

"Okay we understand one another. I'll see you at the boat launch in about 35 minutes," Vic said.

Chapter 40 – Friday – Jimmy & Shannon

Jimmy was afraid, very afraid. What had O'Brien gotten him into? In the past 24 hours, he had committed crimes that could send him to jail for a long time.

O'Brien and the rest of the cops down at the station had no idea why he was there. Two years ago he dropped out of college because it was boring. He was on his way to a degree in software engineering. But, classes were too slow and many of the subjects, like English and History, had nothing to do with software, programing, or anything practical.

He found a community while in high school of people who shared his love of programing and adrenaline – hackers. His skills coming into to college put him at a mid-level hacker. He knew enough to cause a lot of mischief, but not enough to know when to quit.

He was caught rummaging around a database in a local bank's system. He hadn't stolen anything, but needed to prove to his hacker buddies that he had the chops to pull off a major hack. Getting into the bank's database was easier than he thought it would be.

An experienced hacker would have known it was a trap. Jimmy lacked that experience or maturity and it cost him. He was arrested and would have gone to jail, but his father pulled some strings and got the charges referred to juvenile court, where they were sealed.

Jimmy was glad he didn't have to go to jail, but resented his father and did not want to be seen as a child. The agreement was he would get a job and stay out of trouble or the case would be reopened in adult court. Above all, he was to stay away from hacking and his hacker friends. His father thought association with law enforcement would show him the dangers of flaunting the law. So, Jimmy ended up as a glorified clerk in the precinct office.

Now, thanks to O'Brien, not only was he going to jail, but some cop-killing psycho might be after him too. He had not gone back to his place since her warning, but was running out of couches he could crash on – two, all the people he knew who would even answer his call. He had just about talked himself into going home and telling his father that he needed protection when O'Brien called him on the pre-paid phone she gave him.

What the hell, he thought. He starred at the phone and almost convinced himself the smart thing to do was ignore her call and head home. But, if he ever wanted his father's or anyone else's respect, he was going to have to prove that he could respect himself. Ignoring O'Brien might be the "smart" thing to do, but she was the only person in his life right now that thought he was something more than a smartass little shit.

They met at a coffee shop and she told him what she needed. She also filled him in on the letter she got from Jackson and how he was being held prisoner. Vic and his crew were also holding Samantha and Ling.

It was his idea to crash the ISP. He had hacked their system once before and thought he could knock out the area where she said this guy Jackson was being held in a virtual prison. He also knew the ISP would figure out what happened and fix the problem quickly.

O'Brien sounded really stressed but genuinely thankful for his help.

He needed some place he could launch the hack without having it traced back to him immediately. The library seemed like a good bet, so he made his way there and began preparing the tools he needed to launch the attack. Unfortunately, the library had a 30-minute time limit per user. He could get set up in that time, but couldn't be sure a computer would be available when O'Brien called.

While the person working at the desk had their back turned, he ran a little program that made it appear the computer was broken. The display read, "fatal hardware error," and nothing would clear the message, including attempts to reboot and turning the hard-drive off then back on. The library person taped an "Out of Order" sign to the monitor.

The hack he used allowed him to access the Internet through the computer with his laptop using a Bluetooth connection, even though it appeared broken. Any activity would be traced back to the library's computer and not his laptop.

An hour later O'Brien sent him a text to take down the ISP. He launched his hack, but it didn't work. He made some adjustments and finally got the area to go down. He monitored the ISP's recovery efforts and gave O'Brien a heads-up when it looked like the problem was going to be repaired.

He hoped it had worked and O'Brien had been able to do whatever it was she needed to do. Still he felt there must be more he could do. Just knowing that three people were being held against their will, made him feel responsible for helping solve the problem. O'Brien told him they would all die today if she couldn't do something and right now she had no idea what that would be.

He had done what she asked, but he could do more; he just didn't know what. He didn't want to just sit around and wait for her call. What if her plan didn't work and Vic grabbed her too? He would be the only person who knew that any of this was going on. He could go to the police, but he had no proof and had no idea where Samantha and Dr. Ya were being held. If he tipped the police, he was pretty sure Vic would know almost immediately. Rescuing the hostages was impossible right now unless O'Brien had a plan or could think of one.

The most logical possibility was Jackson finding the money and an exchange of hostages negotiated. O'Brien said that even if they found the money and turned it over to Vic, all of the hostages would be killed. So any chance of freeing the hostages would happen at the exchange. O'Brien was convinced Vic was working with someone and that person was most likely a trained assassin. How was she going to stop two killers, one of which liked to hide and shoot his victims in the back of the head?

If he were going to help her, he would need to be armed. But, he knew nothing about firearms and would probably be more dangerous than helpful. If he didn't shoot himself, he might shoot one of the hostages or O'Brien. Guns were out, but there was an alternative and he had access to it and more.

Chapter 41 – Friday – Russell, Ling, & Sam

Russell didn't mind waiting and didn't mind babysitting two women. He was well-trained enough to know that successful operations depended on the success of each step. He would prefer to be in the action, but knew that time was coming. For right now, he stayed focused on his assignment.

His cell phone vibrated and he saw Vic was calling.

"Bring our two guests to my location in good spirits, please. This deal is about to end and we need to wrap up the details," Vic said.

"Did Jackson find the package?" Russell asked.

"Unclear, but I think it's a good possibility. Either way, we are out of time and need to finish our business and move on to another opportunity," Vic said. "And, don't forget to clean up after yourself."

"Understood," Russell said.

He opened the bedroom door without knocking and his pistol drawn. The two women look startled with a hint of guilt, which meant they were planning something. No matter, they were no match for his training.

"Both of you over here and turn around," Russell said. "Please don't be stupid. My orders are to bring you both alive and my boss gets real grumpy when I don't follow his order."

"Well, we certainly wouldn't want that," Ling said.

Russell grabbed her right wrist and put a handcuff on it.

"Ouch," Ling cried.

He then grabbed Sam's right wrist and spun her around. He put the other handcuff on her right wrist. He then handcuffed their left hands together. This formed a kind of basket weave effect of arms and made it difficult for the women to do anything quickly.

"Does this mean Jim found Vic's property?" Sam said.

"You better hope so," Russell said and pushed them out the door and out the exterior door. He opened the mini-van door and pointed with his gun that they should get in.

That proved challenging with their arms shackled, but with a push from Russell finally made it in.

Russell got in and made a production of buckling his shoulder belt.

"What about us," Ling asked.

"Oh I'm a very safe driver," Russell said. "But, in case you have any stupid ideas about jumping me like I saw written on the wall, think about what will happen to you if we crash. Doctor, I'm sure you've seen what happens to the unrestrained human body in an accident."

He smiled at them and started driving.

After a few minutes they were still on a dirt and gravel road. Russell pulled over and got out his phone. He keyed in some numbers and looked back at the women again and smiled.

Ling and Sam felt a mild jolt like something had bumped into the car. Russell looked in the outside rearview mirror and saw flames where the hideout had been. He continued driving in silence.

Ling leaned over and whispered to Sam, "He didn't put the hoods on us so I guess we aren't coming back here."

"No, I don't think we're coming back," Sam said.

After about 45 minutes, Russell took out his phone and answered another call from Vic.

"I'm not sure, but I think the doctor's tall friend may be interested in our meeting. I don't know if Jackson got a message to her or what, but I think there's a good chance she will show up at my location. It's very important that she not feel unwelcome. I've a special gift for her and she needs to be in good spirits to get it," Vic said. "And Jackson is bringing the package at 7:30."

"Understood. I'll be there before then," Russell responded and put away the phone. He was mildly disappointed because Vic's instructions were clear: the cop must be taken alive. He had hoped to pop her in the back of the head and watch her drop. Still, all of the hostages would die tonight, that much was clear so there was that to look forward to.

He didn't particularly like this job, but Vic provided a framework he that was missing since he left the service. Vic also provided opportunities for him to practice the two things he was very good at: compromising computers and killing. Of course, he sometimes found opportunities for the second skill that had nothing to do with Vic or his projects. Vic was not happy about this because he was afraid a mistake could lead the police back to his business.

Maybe after we clean up this operation, I'll strike out on my own, Russell thought. He wasn't consumed by money like Vic, so he could keep it really simple. Money, however, was a means to an end. So, once all the hostages and that giant cop are dead, why not kill Vic and take the money?

The idea grew on him as he entered the outskirts of town.

Chapter 42 – Friday – Jim & Shannon

Jim stepped into the house and grabbed a leather jacket. He took a deep breath. He went into the garage and threw the backpack full of money and the account information in the front seat of the car. He looked back at the boxes where O'Brien was hiding and turned off the light. The car was a late model sedan, but nothing that would turn any heads.

He pulled out of the driveway and headed toward Oak Street. The phone buzzed. "What now," he almost shouted.

"You're going the wrong way," Vic said.

"You go your way and I'll go mine. I'll be there when I said. As long as you have a gun to Sam's head, you have my undivided attention," Jim shouted. "And there is no need for any more conversation between us, so I'm saying goodbye until we meet at the boat launch."

He threw the phone out the window. It felt good to stand up to Vic, but he hoped he hadn't killed Sam in doing so.

After a few blocks on Oak, Jim turned to the correct route to the boat launch. He didn't see Shannon anywhere and hoped she was following him. He kept looking in the rearview mirror for her motorcycle's single headlight, but saw nothing. If she couldn't follow him, the whole plan, whatever that was, might fail. Suddenly, he saw a single headlight gaining on him fast.

After a block or two, she roared past him and disappeared. He would stay on this street for another 10 blocks, so she must be up ahead somewhere. At a red light, she suddenly appeared out of nowhere and was trying to climb through the rear window on the passenger side. Her large frame wasn't exactly built for this entry. If the situation hadn't been so grim, Jim might have laughed at her wiggling and pulling to get through the window.

Finally, she got through. Jim continued toward the boat launch. After a minute, Shannon leaned over the back seat and whispered in his ear, "One word about this and I'll hurt you bad."

Jim chuckled and motioned for her to put her ear closer, "I got rid of the phone, but I don't know if there is a microphone in here or not."

"Let's assume there is. I'm going to stay low and quiet until we get there."

Something about Shannon gave him hope that they could get out of this alive. She was the first one (besides Sam) to believe in him in a long time. If they got out of this it would be because of her. He hoped that the dinner she promised for the four of them would happen and they could all get to know one another when people weren't dying around them.

However, the closer he got to the boat launch the less certain he was of their fate. How was he supposed to feel knowing that in a matter of minutes he might be dead or, worse in his mind, he might watch another person he loved die? It was almost too much to process.

It was one thing to have "Walter Mitty" type fantasies about being a hero and saving the day. But events of these past several days made it clear that in real life people die and life can change forever in the blink of an eye. His world was nothing like he imagined it would be. He assumed he would grow old with Sally and they would have children and a wonderful life together. That was just as much a fantasy as imagining you're some kind of action hero, instead of a mediocre assistant vice president of marketing at a mediocre insurance company. He had more adventure in the past few days than most people have in a lifetime. That "adventure" had a terrible price. Sally was not the person he thought she was. At least five people were dead in part because they were with him. Right now, he would gladly trade places with just about anyone in the houses he was driving by who were probably watching some stupid "reality" show on television.

However, the gun tucked into the back of his pants was a painful reminder that this was his life and if he wanted it to last passed this evening, he better stay focused on the coming confrontation. He had a role to play and Shannon and the hostages were counting on him doing something that he was not trained for or even emotionally prepared for.

Chapter 43 – Friday – Russell & Vic

Russell pulled up to the boat launch and Vic directed him to park the minivan off to one side. As he left, Vic would detonate a bomb and destroy any forensic evidence in the minivan. The vehicle was registered in Russell's name, thanks to some changes on the title information in the DMV database. Of course, Russell was not aware of the changes, but it would be one more bit of information that would point the investigators towards him.

Russell got Ling and Sam out of the minivan. Vic smiled at Russell's solution to keep them under control. "Secure them to the light pole and then we'll go over our strategy. We don't have much time."

The boat launch wasn't used much because there was almost no parking where people could leave their cars. It was in a park that covered most of the shoreline on the east side of the lake. The new marina had a much better setup for parking and the boat launch was easier to use.

The launch was surrounded on both sides by dense tree cover. The road to the launch was off of the main park road. There was a place for cars to turn around and back down the launch and a short pier where boats could tie up. Vic's large speedboat was tied to this pier. There was an electrical connection that Vic had reconnected for his use. Along the park road, utility poles brought electricity to various parts of the park, but the poles also carried a high-speed Internet cable. Vic submitted a phony work order to the cable company crew who brought the line right up to the light pole next to the pier. This let him handle multiple live video feeds and monitor the police networks.

Russell brought the hostages over to the light pole and unlocked one of the handcuffs. He wrapped the two arms around the pole and locked the cuffs again. The two women were not going anywhere.

"Did you cleanup after you left?" Vic asked.

"Of course, I did," said Russell mildly annoyed every time Vic asked him if he did something as ordered. He was a good soldier and didn't need second-guessing or reminding of his duty.

"Here are the operational details. One way or another this ends tonight. We leave here with the money and accounts if Jackson wasn't lying about bringing them. Like I said earlier, I suspect that Amazon bitch will make an appearance. I want you to stay out of sight and when she shows, disarm her. I don't want her hurt because it must appear she killed herself.

"We'll use her gun to kill all of the hostages and then blow her brains out with her own gun. When the police reach the scene, it will look like she killed everyone and then killed herself. With any luck, they won't be looking for us, at least not initially. This will give us time to be somewhere very far away. If we have the stuff Sally stole, we'll live like kings for the rest of our lives. If not, I've some cash to get us started again. Any questions?" Vic asked.

"What if she starts shooting?" Russell asked. "Can I kill her then?"

"If she starts shooting, kill her and we'll kill the rest. Depending on how it goes down, there may be a way to misdirect the police, but we won't have much time. The most important thing is no one leaves here alive – no witnesses," Vic said.

"Understood," Russell said and slipped into the woods to find a good hiding place. 'No witnesses' sounded like Vic planned to eliminate him too. He decided that Vic could no longer be trusted, even though he never really trusted anyone. Once the cop was down, the others would not be a problem. He would kill Vic the first opportunity he had. After that, he wasn't sure. Vic had a car on the other side of the lake and he could take the boat to it.

Then he would have a clean slate to start over doing what he loved best – killing. With the money, he wouldn't have to worry about a job to pay rent or other boring details. He thought that sounded like a great idea and found himself unexpectedly excited about the possibilities.

He heard Jackson's car go by and saw it stop at the boat launch. He heard Jackson call his girl friend's name and she yelled back something he couldn't understand. But, there was no sign of the cop. The light pole provided plenty of light by the launch, but didn't reach into the trees. The city's lights helped some, but it was hard to make out details. He scanned the trees across the road from his position in case she tried to sneak in that way, but the darkness made seeing much of anything dicey. The leaves were beginning to turn colors, but had not started falling yet. They provided him good cover, but also made it difficult to see others.

He had his sniper's rifle – also liberated from Army supplies – with its night scope and began scanning the area. He had not thought of using it, but if the cop came out shooting, he could drop her without having to get close. If that happened, he just might use the rifle to take out Vic and avoid any possible confrontation.

He heard some more noise from the launch area and, through his scope, saw the cop get out of the back seat where she had been hiding. 'Pretty cheeky,' he thought. He had a clear shot at the back of her head. This was a shot he could do in his sleep – there was no chance he would miss. 'Maybe I just do her now and while Vic is distracted take him out with the second shot' he thought. He could then kill Jackson and the women, take the money and be gone before any police responded. 'No witnesses, remember?' he told Vic in his mind.

He put a shell in the chamber using the bolt-action on the rifle and put his finger on the trigger. He was prepared to fire, when he heard a noise behind him.

Chapter 44 – Friday – Jim, Shannon, & Vic

Jim pulled the car up to the boat launch. He could see the women and Vic gathered at the light pole. Vic was using them as a shield by crouching down behind Sam. His gun was clearly visible and pointed at Ling. Jim began to approach Vic who was about 15 feet away.

"Hold it," Vic shouted. "Business first and then you can have your happy ending. But try anything and they die. Understood?"

"We understand completely," Shannon said as she stepped out of the car from the backseat. "Let's make the exchange and go our separate ways."

"You stupid puke," Vic shouted. "I told you no cops. I should kill them right now."

"You're not going to do that, because I've a better offer," Shannon said. "And, for the record, I'm not 'the police' and you know it. I don't have a badge and I'm unarmed. Before you do anything that will cost you a lot of money, listen to my deal."

"In case, you hadn't noticed, you're in no position to deal. I have all the power. Just give me the money and account information and I may let your girlfriends live."

Vic was confused by this turn of events. He had expected the cop to show up and try to shoot it out with him. Where was Russell? He should be in a good position to capture her, but he hadn't made a move.

"That's where you're wrong," Shannon said. "I do have some power and it's not firepower. We don't want any shooting. There's a way we get what we want and you get what you want and no one has to die. A simple exchange: the money and account information for the hostages."

"What's to keep me from shooting you right now and taking what's mine?" Vic asked.

"Nothing, except you'll forfeit all the money in your secret overseas accounts," Shannon said. "First, a goodwill gesture. Jim, toss him his bag of money, please."

Jim got the backpack out of the car and threw it at Vic's feet.

"Go ahead," Shannon said. "Look inside. We'll raise our hands over our heads while you take a look."

She raised her hands over her head and Jim did the same. Vic studied them for a few seconds, and then slowly reached down for the bag without taking his eyes off the cop. He pulled it up and with his gun hand unzipped the top. He reached in and took a bundle of bills out of the middle and dropped the backpack at his feet. He examined the cash while keeping the cop in sight. It appeared to be real.

"I'm going to lower my hands now," Shannon said. "That was my goodwill gesture with the cash and, it's all there, however much Sally took."

"That would be $2 million dollars," Vic said.

"Count it if you want; we can wait," Shannon said.

"Don't be cute," Vic said. "Where's the account information?"

"Jim, if you please," Shannon said.

Jim tossed Vic the large envelope containing all of the information.

"Tell me again about this power you supposedly have," Vic said. He was dragging this out longer than he wanted hoping Russell would take control of Shannon.

"Take a look online at your Threadstone account. The new password is asshole," Shannon said. "I'm sure you can do that on your smartphone and we'll put our hands up again."

Vic was beginning to suspect what was coming. He had all of the accounts in an encrypted file on his phone, although he seldom used it. It took only a few seconds to connect to the Threadstone account. The balance was $1. He could feel his anger about to get out of control, which was totally against his years of training. Becoming emotional clouded your judgment and led to bad outcomes.

He checked the recent transactions and noted a transfer of $100,000 to a bank account in the U.S. and the rest of the money – more than $1.5 million – was transferred to another of his overseas accounts.

"What is this bullshit," he shouted. "What are the other account passwords?"

"See, this is where we have some power. By the way, the counseling center will want to personally thank you for your generous donation in memory of Judy. You remember her; you killed her." Shannon said. She could see his face becoming flush, which was both encouraging and dangerous.

"Here's how this is going to work. You're going to leave without harming anyone. We're not going to the police tonight, but tomorrow morning the DA will receive a copy of Sally's letter to Jim describing your whole operation, minus the overseas account information. About the same time we'll go to the police and tell them about the kidnappings and murders. That gives you about a 12-hour or more head start. I'm sure a clever guy like you can disappear in much less time than that and you will have a bag of money to help you. In seven days, assuming none of us are bothered by you or any of your ugly friends we'll change all of the account passwords to 'asshole' and you will have full access to your accounts. Six hours after we change the passwords, we'll give the account information to the police. That should give you plenty of time to move the money somewhere else," Shannon said.

"We have an associate who has all of the account information. If he does not see all four of us alive and under no duress tomorrow morning, he will empty your accounts and post a $5 million bounty on your head on the Internet. You probably have a better idea than I do how many mercenaries there are who will kill you for a whole lot less. Since they don't usually play by the rules, I doubt there is any place in the world you can hide where they won't find you," Shannon said.

"How do I know I can trust you?" he said.

"Funny how this trust thing works, isn't it?" Shannon said. "We don't want the money and, even if we did, the authorities will be watching us like a hawk. Jackson is still a prime suspect in a murder and the police brass would love to hang me out to dry. We couldn't touch that money without inviting arrest. The only way out of this for us is to take everything to the police, including the overseas bank accounts. It's not our problem if you empty them out before the police can act."

Vic couldn't believe what he was hearing. This operation was a nightmare of everything going bad that could go bad. He hated fieldwork. He might still salvage this if Russell could disarm the cop. He could then hold all four as hostages and demand their associate change the passwords now. He would quickly move the money out of those accounts and be free to kill the hostages. If they refused, he would kill them one at a time while the others watched until they contacted the associate and had him change the passwords. But, Russell had to disarm the cop. Despite what she said, he knew she had a gun on her somewhere.

"Russell, where the fuck are you?" Vic shouted.

Chapter 45 – Friday – Jimmy

Jimmy wasn't sure what to do, but felt like he should be with O'Brien and the others at the exchange. He was smart enough to know that bringing a gun was a bad idea. He had never fired one before and concluded this would not be a good time to start. Still, he wanted to help if he could. While he was waiting for O'Brien to send him the exchange point, he went downtown to the police station where his job was shuffling paper and making coffee.

When he wasn't being a prick, Jimmy watched and learned. He knew the station was lightly staffed with support people on the weekend. The detectives were in and out on calls and investigations and the uniforms were mostly downstairs. He was invisible to most of the cops, so it wasn't very risky for him to be there on the weekend.

None of the few people in the squad room paid any attention to him as he entered. He sat down at a desk and pretended to be working. His goal, however, was the key to the equipment room, which he knew was in the top right drawer of the desk. The equipment room had all sorts of gear that was not needed in a normal day's work, but could be accessed quickly when needed. It was strictly off limits to him. He was certain he would find something in there to help him.

When he could get in without being seen, he entered the room and shut the door behind him. He turned on the light and hoped no one saw it under the door. The room contained racks of weapons ranging from assault rifles to shotguns to pepper spray and body armor. While it would be cool to show up at the exchange with an assault rifle, he thought better of it. He walked around the large room looking for something that could help him. Handcuffs looked like something that could be helpful, so he took a pair and a key.

At the end of one rack was a shelf with a half dozen Tasers. Jimmy took one down and examined it. The controls were easy to understand and it offered what he was looking for. They were a non-lethal way to incapacitate someone. This model even had a laser sight. The downside was you had to be fairly close to the subject, which meant it was not good idea to shoot it out with someone who had a real gun. Still, it was something.

He carefully exited the equipment room and returned the key. No one was paying any attention to him, so he left without incident. The big risk was the security camera, but he was fairly sure it did not cover the equipment room. More cameras were requested, but the project got zapped in one of the ongoing budget cuts.

As he left the station, he got a text from O'Brien with the exchange location. He knew where this was because he had gone there to drink with his buddies before he attained the legal age. It was not that far from the station.

Knowing this psycho Vic would be there, he parked about a half-mile away and cut cross-country. Even though it was dark, the lights from the city were enough for him to navigate the woods. The terrain around the lake was flat and it was easy walking in daylight. He took it slow to avoid roots and rocks that might trip him. After stumping his toe a couple of times, he was close enough to the old boat launch to see the light pole. He slowed down, because he knew Vic was fond of cameras and other surveillance equipment.

He got as close to the boat launch as he thought safe and found a hiding spot behind the roots of a fallen tree. When the tree fell over, the large roots around the base stayed attached, creating a hiding place about five feet high. He was close enough to the road leading to the launch to see any cars that arrived. There was one more thing he could do to help while he waited. His usual attire of a black sweatshirt with hood and black pants made it difficult to see him when he kept his pale face from view.

He didn't have to wait long. A minivan pulled off the park road and drove down to the boat launch. If he stood up, he had a view through the trees of the light pole and the area in front of the boat launch. As the minivan approached, a man appeared on the short pier next to the launch. Jimmy hadn't noticed it before, but there was a boat tied to the pier.

He assumed the man on the pier was Vic. Another man got out of the minivan after parking it off to the side. Vic and the other man talked for a minute, and the other man went back the minivan and pulled two women out of the back seat. They appeared to be bound together in some manner. Jimmy recognized the smaller woman as O'Brien's friend, Dr. Ya. He assumed the other woman was Jackson's secretary.

The second man took the women to the light pole and secured them. He and Vic then walked off a distance and talked some more. The second man went back the minivan and retrieved a long rifle with a scope and began walking directly towards Jimmy's position.

Suddenly, being here didn't seem like such a good idea. A killer was walking directly towards him carrying a rifle. If he was discovered, the odds of surviving were not good; in fact, there was no way he would survive. This killer could shoot him from 100 yards away. His Taser with a 15 to 30-foot range was no match.

He ducked behind the roots and hoped he wasn't discovered. He also hoped he didn't piss in his pants, which felt like a real possibility at the moment. He could hear the man approaching and hoped the killer couldn't sense his almost uncontrollable fear. Thankfully, the man stopped about 20 feet from his position.

Jimmy decided to stay right here, no matter what happened. Maybe this would be over quickly and the killers would leave without discovering him. He fought the urge to run, knowing the killer would shoot him before he went 10 steps.

As he struggled with his fear, Jimmy heard another car pull up to the launch. This would be Jackson and O'Brien. He heard car doors opening and loud conversation, although he couldn't really make out the words because his heart was pounding so loudly in his ears.

Then he heard the unmistakable sound of the killer with the rifle opening and closing the bolt action on the rifle. He had seen enough action movies to know that meant the killer was preparing to shoot. Jimmy slowly peeked over the tree roots and saw the killer bring the rifle to his shoulder. Beyond him, Jimmy could see the unmistakable silhouette of O'Brien. The rifle must have a night vision scope, because even though the light pole provided some illumination, it was darker where O'Brien and Jackson were standing.

It was immediately clear to Jimmy that the killer was about to shoot O'Brien. Without thinking about his fear, Jimmy took the Taser off safety and turned on the laser sight. The laser put a red dot on the man's back. Jimmy steadied his hand on a tree root and pulled the trigger just as the man began turning his head.

The Taser's two probes, propelled by a gas canister, struck the man in the middle of his back. Despite a light coat, the probes penetrated the man's clothing. Immediately, the man's arms went straight and rigid. The rifle dropped to the ground. The man stood in place for a few seconds and then fell to the ground in a heap.

Jimmy stood and watched him on the ground for a second. Only when Jimmy was convinced the man wasn't getting up did he approach the body. His breathing was so shallow Jimmy thought he might be dead, but then the man began to stir. Jimmy panicked for a second and remembered the handcuffs. He retrieved them from his backpack and rolled the man on his stomach. He pulled his arms behind him and put the handcuffs on. The man began to regain consciousness.

Jimmy searched him and found a wicked looking pistol in a sling sewn inside the man's coat. He took the pistol and put the rifle over one shoulder using the rifle's sling. Jimmy got him to his feet, but it was clear he was still disoriented. Jimmy was afraid if this man got his wits about him, that he could be very dangerous, even handcuffed.

He grabbed the man's arm and pushed him toward the boat launch. O'Brien would know what to do with him and could handle any resistance he put up. But, Jimmy wanted to get away from him as quickly as possible. He had a feeling this was one of the trained killers O'Brien talked about and he was no match for that.

The man could barely walk and stumbled more than once. Jimmy heard shouting from the boat launch and heard Vic screaming for someone named Russell. Jimmy pushed the man, who now appeared to be the Russell person Vic was screaming about, into the clearing.

"Is this who you're looking for?" Jimmy asked.

Chapter 46 – Friday – Jim, Vic, Jimmy, & Shannon

Vic could not believe his ears. The Amazon bitch was using his techniques against him just like Sally had tried. She was going to hold his money hostage in exchange for him leaving them alone – exactly what Sally had tried.

She claimed an associate had all of the information and would empty his accounts if the four did not show up tomorrow unharmed. She also said the associate would put a bounty of $5 million on his head if he harmed them. Unbelievable.

He still saw a way out if that idiot Russell would just do as ordered and disarm the cop. He could then capture her and Jackson and threated to kill the hostages one at a time unless the associate gave him the passwords and he could move his money.

He had to act quickly. His training and experience told him this was a tipping point in the operation and he had to regain control of the situation. He was sure he could take out the cop with one shot, but he couldn't be sure Jackson knew who the associate was. Jackson had somehow managed to contact her, but he was sure it was not done electronically. So, it seemed highly probably that she was the only one who knew for certain who the associate was.

The fact that Russell had failed to disarm her was very troubling. It could only mean one of two things. One, Russell was planning some move that didn't include him. Two, the cop had help in the woods that had neutralized Russell. Either way, he was on his own. He could put a gun to the doctor's head and see if that threat would convince the cop to disarm herself.

There was also that bag of money at his feet. He could shoot the cop and kill the other three. The $2 million would finance a new start somewhere else. But, he would also be a target for either the other cop who captured Russell. And, Russell had his sniper rifle, which meant he could take out everyone from a great distance and not risk a firefight. He could use the women as a shield against another cop, but Russell would kill them all and not break a sweat.

He screamed for Russell, but what he saw coming out of the woods behind and to the right of the cop enraged him. Russell was pushed into the clearing, handcuffed, and clearly disoriented. A young man was behind him with Russell's sniper rifle slung over his shoulder. Vic could not see any other weapon. This was clearly no cop or anyone with any combat or black ops training.

His rage overcame his judgment. In one quick movement, he raised his pistol and put a 9 mm slug in Russell's forehead. His second shot was intended for the young man. He swung the gun around and saw O'Brien bringing her gun from behind her back. He fired twice into her chest and she went down.

Suddenly, Jackson somehow produced a gun and was firing. The bullets were going high, but even a bad shot can accidently fire a true round. He fired at Jackson, but he was well concealed behind the car. He had to wait just a second and Jackson would reveal his position and that would be enough to finish him.

There was a piercing pain in his leg and he stumbled away from the women with a knife sticking out of his thigh. He raised his gun to shoot the secretary, but Jackson began firing again and that kid was holding the rifle like he might try to use it. He fired a couple of more rounds at Jackson to keep him down. In the momentary quiet, he heard the sound of a siren. That could be more cops, he thought and decided to cut his losses. He could kill the women, but that would still leave at least two people alive who could identify him. He hit the secretary across the side of her head with his gun, grabbed the backpack of money, and hobbled to the boat. The wound wasn't deep, so it was only an annoyance it this point.

As he suspected, none of them followed him. The doctor was screaming for Shannon and Jackson was running toward the women. Vic stopped and had a clear shot at Jackson who was not paying any attention. As Vic pulled the trigger, a bullet clipped his side.

The cop had managed to raise herself up on an elbow and fired with her other hand. She collapsed as soon as she fired.

Vic staggered back with pain shooting through his side and leg. He had spent enough time in the field to realize the wound was minor. It was bleeding, but nothing he couldn't control with the first aid kit on the boat. He hobbled the rest of the way to the boat and began untying it from the pier.

Chapter 47 – Friday – Ling, Sam, Jim, & Vic

The ride from the hideout was quiet. Ling and Sam were lost in their own thoughts and the guy driving seldom said anything that was not related to the task at hand. Both women understood that unless Shannon and/or Jim could produce a miracle, they were going to die, possibly at the end of this ride.

Sam noticed they were slowing and appeared to be driving through the park on the southern end of the lake. It was dark, but the road was well lit with streetlights and the lights of downtown. She was thankful the city had protected the park from developers who would love to build on the lake. She was sorry, she had not spent more time here, in fact, she was sorry for many things she had not done and a few she had done.

She and Ling were holding hands. In the sorry column was not having the time to get to know Ling and Shannon. They were a complicated couple, but two strong people in a relationship almost always are. She knew Jim was not strong in the same sense as Ling and Shannon, but she still believed there was much more to him than what appeared on the surface. How would the police tell her mother? Would she understand or would the news confuse her even more? Sam knew her mother was slipping below the surface of awareness and may not even know her if she walked into her mother's nursing home room. She glanced at Ling and saw tears in her eyes also.

Ling was not paying attention to where they were or even noticed that the minivan was slowing down. Her parents did not understand why or how she was a lesbian. How would they understand when the police told them their daughter's body was found handcuffed to another woman on the side of the road? Would they think this was the natural outcome of an unnatural relationship? Shannon, if she is alive, will fly into a rage and Ling hoped this guy and Vic were somewhere nearby when it happened. Killing them was not the answer, but Ling was so angry at losing Shannon and any future they might have had, she didn't care anymore.

There had been no time to find a weapon for her, but Ling was not going to die cowering before this prick or anyone else. She looked at Sam and saw her looking back. She attempted a smile, but it didn't quite work.

Sam leaned her head over and whispered, "If we get a chance, help me maneuver my left hand so I can get the knife out of my right sleeve. With any luck, I'll get to stab this guy and that may buy us some time. Or, it will just really piss him off."

Even if they could manage to get the knife out of her sleeve, Ling knew it would probably not make any difference in the outcome. Still, it would be something.

"Okay, if you get a chance, why don't you castrate this bastard?"

That made Sam smile and chuckle under her breath. They put their heads together and silently let the tears flow.

The minivan pulled off the road and onto another road that ended in a large clearing. Sam could see a light pole and a small pier. Their driver exited, but was out of their view thanks to the heavily tinted side windows. In a moment, the door slid open and their driver pulled them out. They were stiff from the drive and uncomfortable with their arms crisscrossed and handcuffed. He pulled them over to the light pole and uncuffed their left hands and put them around the pole and reattached the handcuffs. Vic was standing off to the side.

Vic and their driver talked some more, before the driver went back to the minivan and got a long rifle out of the back. He then walked into the woods and disappeared.

Vic looked over at them and smiled, "It will all be over in a few minutes, ladies."

"Fuck you, you piece of shit. Shannon is going to tear you into little pieces," Ling screamed.

Vic looked surprised. "Now, now such language. Your girlfriend hasn't a clue about what's going on, so don't look to her for any help. By the time she figures it all out, I'll be thousands of miles away with enough money to live in luxury and safety for the rest of my life."

"If anything happens to us, there is not a rock big enough for you to hide under. She will hunt you down and kill you," Ling said.

Vic just shook his head and was about to go back to the boat when his GPS tracker alerted him that the car Jim was driving was near. He watched the road for a minute and saw the car turn off the main park road and head in his direction. He moved behind the women and put his gun next to Sam's head.

The car stopped, but the lights remained on. Jim got out of the car and called to Sam. He started toward the women, but Vic stopped him and Jim backed up to the open car door. Just then Shannon opened the back door on the driver's side and got out. Ling let out a small scream and Vic put the gun to her head.

Shannon told Vic the terms of the exchange, but neither Sam nor Ling were listening very well. Their eyes were locked on Jim and Shannon. Vic was very angry, that much was clear.

Just then their driver came stumbling out of the woods pushed by a young man neither recognized. Vic's reaction was swift. He shot the driver and fired at the young man who was going down before the second shot was fired. Vic turned his gun on Shannon and fired.

Ling saw the bullets tear into Shannon's clothing and watched her go down. It all seemed to happen in slow motion. Ling lunged for Shannon, but their restraints made that impossible. Meanwhile, Vic was shooting at Jim and, surprisingly, he was shooting back.

Sam pulled on Ling in an attempt to get at the knife in her right sleeve. Ling resisted momentarily, then realized what Sam was doing, and relaxed. Vic was right behind her and the sound of his pistol was deafening. Sam worked the knife out of her sleeve. She turned to see where Vic was and saw his leg was in striking distance. She looked at Ling who gave her all the slack she could in their restraints. Sam took the knife in her right hand and plunged it into Vic's thigh. Surprisingly, the knife went through his pants and into the leg.

Vic screamed in pain, which was the last thing Sam remembered clearly. Vic hit her in the side of her head with his gun and hobbled out of sight. Before she lost consciousness, she thought she heard sirens in the distance.

Ling was screaming for Shannon to get up. Jim began running towards Shannon when something knocked him off his feet. His shoulder felt like someone had poured burning gasoline on it. He put his hand up to his upper chest near his shoulder and could feel the blood. The pain almost made him pass out, but he could hear Ling's voice and that brought him back in focus.

Jim stumbled to Shannon's side and could see a terrifying amount of blood soaking her shirt and left arm. He had no idea what to do, but freeing the doctor seemed to be the most important. Jim ran to the women and saw there was no way to free them. Sam was out cold and Ling was hysterical because she couldn't get to Shannon.

Chapter 48 – Friday – Ling, Sam, Shannon, & Jim

"Get me out of these things," Ling screamed at Jim. She was so focused on Shannon she did not realize that Sam was injured.

"I don't know how," Jim said. He was looking at Sam's head wound, which had stopped bleeding. "Help her."

Ling looked at Sam's head wound and, while it was serious, it was superficial. Sam needed a scan of her head for any bleeding or other internal problems. She examined Jim's wound and had him hold his jacket tightly against it with his other hand

Her focus returned to Shannon. She screamed her name again and was crying.

Just when she thought she would be doomed to watch Shannon die and not be able to do anything about it, the young man who had brought the driver out of the woods appeared.

"I think I can help," he said and produced a handcuffs' key. He unlocked both of the handcuffs and Ling was free. Just then she noticed he was bleeding rather severely from a wound in his side. He almost collapsed, but Ling grabbed him and helped him sit down.

"Jim," she said. "There is nothing you can do for Sam right now, but I need you to hold this tightly against this young man's wound. She had fashioned a compress bandage from the young man's light coat. "I've got to check on Shannon."

Jim took over on the compression bandage. The young man looked like he was going into shock or about to pass out. "Stay with me," Jim said. "By the way, what's your name?"

"What? Oh, It's Jimmy," he said.

"Well, we share something in common, besides being shot," Jim said. "But people call me Jim."

Jimmy had brought the sniper rifle with him and Jim wondered if he should try to stop Vic who had started the boat and was obviously preparing to leave. He decided that would be a mistake. He was in no condition to hold a rifle even if he knew how to use it. Right now he wanted Vic far away from him.

Ling ran to Shannon's side and gasped at the amount of blood. The bullet holes in her shirt indicated Vic had hit her twice, once square in the chest where Shannon's heart is. The other bullet hole was higher up.

Ling ripped her shirt open and was heartened to see Shannon was wearing a bulletproof vest. The vest stopped the first shot, which would have torn through her heart. However, there was blood coming from under the vest. Ling struggled to find and disengage the vest so she could locate the second bullet. As she was struggling, an unmarked police car came from out of nowhere. The two detectives that were working with Shannon came out of the car with guns drawn.

"Shannon been shot and there are three others wounded," Ling said.

"Central, this is Appleton. Officer down, officer down. Shots fired. Old boat launch near 12th Street. Three others wounded. Send a couple of buses and the cavalry, code 3."

His partner Barnes was helping Ling unfasten Shannon's vest. Ling ripped Shannon undershirt and saw a bullet hole spouting blood in her upper left chest. Ling took the undershirt and pressed hard against the wound.

Appleton ran over to where Jim, Jimmy, and Sam were. "How is he?" Appleton asked.

"Stable, I think," Jim said. He had one hand on the compression bandage and the other hand holding his jacket against his wound. Sam was coming around, but still out.

"Okay. Hang on for a little longer. Help is on the way," Appleton said. "Where is the guy who did this?"

Jim motioned with his head toward the pier. "He just took off in a boat."

Appleton picked up the sniper rifle and looked at it lovingly. "Is this was I think it is?"

He walked to the pier and lifted his glasses off his nose and placed them on top of his head. He put the rifle up to his shoulder, made a few adjustments, and began sweeping the lake. The night vision scope made the lake look like it was a green-tinted twilight. It only took a second to spot Vic speeding across the lake. Appleton used one of the tall pillars as a rest. He slowly swung the rifle to his left and squeezed the trigger. The report startled everyone, but Appleton was focused on the lake. In a few seconds, there was a loud explosion and a ball of fire across the lake.

Appleton walked back towards the others. They had all stopped what they were doing and were staring at him. "What?" he said. "He wasn't the only one with special ops training – mine was just a few years farther back."

The air was full of sirens and flashing lights as a half-a-dozen cop cars came screaming into the boat launch clearing. Shortly behind them, three ambulances pulled in to the clearing. The EMTs came running towards Ling and Shannon.

"I'm a doctor. This one first. GSW to the chest. She's lost a lot of blood. The young man up there is next. GSW to the side, probably not lethal, but he has lost a lot of blood too. The other man has a GSW to the shoulder. The woman has a possible concussion and lost consciousness. Alert the hospital to prep the OR and have a trauma surgeon ready to operate. Take her straight to the OR; don't stop for anything. Also have other surgeons ready to look at the two men when you get to the hospital. The woman needs a scan and a neurologist to check her out for brain damage," Ling said.

Appleton and Barnes were securing the crime scene and organizing the cops as they arrived. Appleton sent a couple a cars to the other side of the lake where they could see a fire burning on the shore. "Look for a guy with most of his head gone, if he didn't burn up in the fire."

Jim overheard the conversation while the EMTs were working on his shoulder. "Have them look for a backpack full of money and an envelope with account numbers of overseas bank accounts."

Appleton looked down at him then up at the officers. "Well, you heard the man, get going and call the fire department along the way just in case no one has turned in the alarm yet."

"Am I still on your suspect list?" Jim asked.

"I've a feeling when we sort this out, there won't be a suspect list. I think that guy over there with the bullet in his forehead and the guy in the boat just closed the case for us, except for some details that we'll sort out when everyone is back on their feet."

While Ling and the EMTs were working on Shannon, she opened her eyes and looked around. She tried to get up, but Ling pushed her back down.

"Hold still. You've been shot and we are trying to stabilize you for transport to the hospital," Ling said.

"Are you Okay? Are you safe?" Shannon asked.

"Yes, thanks to you and the others," Ling said.

"What about the others?"

"Jimmy and Jim were both shot, although I don't believe either one has life-threatening injuries. Sam was pistol whipped, but I think she will be all right too," Ling said.

"Jimmy? What was he doing here? And where's Vic?" Shannon said.

"He's not going to bother anyone again," Appleton said as he squatted down on the other side of Shannon.

She turned toward him. "I never thought I would be glad to see your ugly face again."

"I love you, too," Appleton said. "But, we need to get you and the others to the hospital. We can sort out everything later."

Shannon moaned and her eyes began rolling back in her head.

"We're losing her. Pulse is dropping. She's going into cardiac arrest," the EMT shouted.

"Damn you big bozo," Ling shouted and began doing chest compressions.

The EMT hooked up the portable defibrillator. "Clear," he shouted.

Ling pulled back and the EMT fired the defibrillator. "Still no pulse. Again," she said.

The EMT fired again and Shannon's heart began beating.

"We are out of time. Let's get her in the ambulance and to the hospital as fast as possible. I'm riding with you in the back," Ling said.

"Sorry, that's not allowed," the EMT said.

Ling looked up at him and said, "I'm riding in the back. Any questions?"

The EMT noticed she had her hand on Shannon's gun.

"Nope. I think we're good. Let's go," he said.

Appleton followed them to the ambulance and helped get Shannon's stretcher loaded. Ling was about the climb in, but looked past Appleton and the other wounded being attended by EMTs. "Maybe I should stay and help here," she said.

"My turn to pull rank," he said. "There is plenty of help here. She needs you more. I'll make sure the rest are on their way to the hospital as soon as they're ready. Now go."

Ling climbed into the back of the ambulance, but leaned out and gave Appleton a kiss on the cheek. "Thank you."

"Go on, get out of here before you spoil my reputation as a curmudgeon," he said.

Chapter 49 – Friday – Jim & Sam

Jim opened his eyes, but they did not focus immediately. He was in a white room and it was cold. He was shivering. As he became more awake, a pain in his left side and shoulder reminded him of the shooting at the boat launch. He felt someone holding his right hand and slowly turned his head because movement caused stabbing pains in his left shoulder.

Before he could turn his head completely to the right, Sam's face came into view. She looked like an angel, he thought and a smile began to form.

"Hold still," Sam said. "You're in the recovery room of the hospital. You got out of surgery about 30 minutes ago."

"Do me a favor," Jim said.

"Of course, do you want some ice chips or more pain medicine?" Sam asked.

"I want you to kiss me," Jim said.

She leaned down and kissed him gently on the lips, her eyes filling with tears.

"Now I know I'm alive," Jim said. "Your head…are you alright? Have you seen a doctor?" Jim was becoming agitated at the sight of a bandage on Sam's head covering an area over her left ear.

"Yes, I'm fine. A slight concussion and a nasty cut, but otherwise all right," she said.

"The others…Shannon…she was shot. Is she dead?" Jim asked, his anxiety rising.

"Shannon is still in surgery. They are doing everything they can for her. Jimmy is still in surgery, but his wound was not life threatening," Sam said.

"I'll never forgive myself if anything happens to her. I brought her into the mess," Jim's voice trailed off.

His monitor began beeping and a nurse came over. "Your pulse is way up and that's not a good thing, so try to relax. If you can't, I can give you something," she said.

"No, I'll be okay," he said.

"What about Vic?" he asked after the nurse left.

"Vic is dead," Sam said. "They pulled his body out of the lake. The police are pretty sure the guy Jimmy captured was the one killing people with shots to the back of the head. He was working for Vic. It's over. They can't hurt us anymore. Now, no more questions," she said.

"Will you stay with me?" Jim asked.

"Of course I will," Sam said. "That detective friend of yours, Appleton, pulled some strings to allow me to stay with you, since only a next of kin is supposed to have access to your personal health information. He did the same for Ling."

"Appleton, my friend?" Jim asked.

"I said no more questions," Sam said.

Chapter 50 – Friday – Ling & Shannon

The ambulance ride from the boat launch to the hospital had a police escort, but still seemed to take forever. Ling was monitoring Shannon's vital signs, which were not good. Pulse was weak and blood pressure low. Shannon needed surgery to fix whatever damage the bullet did and to stop the internal bleeding.

The ambulance finally got to the hospital. There was a trauma team waiting at the door and they took over from the EMTs. One asked Ling to step aside. "I'm a doctor and this is my patient. I'm not leaving her."

Although it was against policy, Ling's voice made it clear this was not open to debate. "Let's get her to the OR. Is the surgeon ready?" Ling asked.

"Yes, everyone is standing by in the OR," someone answered.

They wheeled Shannon into a large elevator. On the ride up, Shannon opened her eyes. Ling put her face down next to Shannon's. "You're going to be all right," she said. "We're taking you to the OR and you'll be fine."

"Now, don't go lying to me," Shannon said. "I want you to know how much you mean to me in case this goes badly. I love you so much and am so sorry for getting you involved in this mess."

"Shut up, you big gorilla," Ling said softly. "I say you're going to be okay and that's all there is to it." She leaned down and kissed Shannon as she lost consciousness again.

When they got to the OR, Shannon was transferred to another gurney and wheeled into the operating room. Ling stepped aside and went in the surgical prep area and began scrubbing up. A doctor she didn't know, stepped in. "This is not a good idea and you know it, Dr. Ya," he said.

"What do you mean? She's my patient and I want to scrub in," Ling said.

"First she is not your patient and we both know that. While I'm sure your surgical skills in the morgue are first rate, this isn't the morgue. And, you're way too emotionally attached to this patient, which as you know is a no-no in the surgical suite," he said. The best thing you can do for your friend is to go to the waiting room and wait. I've heard what happened and you're going to collapse when the adrenalin wears off. I also heard how you triaged the victims at the shooting. Very impressive and undoubtedly saved your friend's life," he said. "Now, it's my turn. Let me save your friend."

"Thank you," Ling said and went to find the waiting room. On the way, a CNA motioned her aside. "Why don't you change your top? I have some scrubs that look like they will fit you."

Ling looked down and realized she was soaked in blood. She went with the young woman into a locker room and took off her top and cleaned up as much as she could. The scrubs fit, but were a little big, as she knew they would be. "Thanks," Ling said. "At least I don't look like I've been shot now."

She found the waiting room and it was packed with police officers in uniform and others in plain clothes. Appleton and Barnes were there and rushed over to her when she came in.

"Any news? How is she?" Barnes said. The rest of the room became silent and all eyes were on her.

"She's in surgery now. It was touch and go on the way here in the ambulance. I'm not going to lie. She lost a lot of blood and there was still internal bleeding when we got here. I just don't know," Ling said and she broke into sobs.

Barnes put his arms around her and gently directed her to a couch. He sat her down and sat down beside her with his arm around her. She leaned against him crying. Someone brought her a bottle of water and another a handful of tissues. After a few minutes, she regained some composure.

She sat upright and Barnes removed his arm. "Sorry if I got a little familiar there," he stammered.

She looked at him and patted his leg. "Thank you."

Appleton was hovering around her with the look of someone who wanted to do something, but didn't know what.

"We should call Shannon's sister," Ling said.

"That's already been taken care of," Appleton said. "She's on her way, but it will be three or four hours before she can get here. She asked me if I would make sure you are treated like part of Shannon's family."

"She did?" Ling said. "I've never even met her. Shannon must have told her about me, about us." She looked from Appleton to Barnes. "No gabs or snappy one-liners?"

"Let's clear something up right now. Neither of us has a problem with your relationship to O'Brien. That's your business and none of ours. As for the gabs and snappy one-liners, those are all in fun. We knew O'Brien was a top-rate detective before we worked with her. But, we don't hit when someone is down. When she's back on the job, we'll let her have it and she gives as good as she gets. But until then we are – hell, the whole force – is pulling for her."

Ling smiled and felt the tears coming back.

"Is there someone we can call for you?" Barnes asked.

"No, when I know Shannon is all right, I'll call my folks," Ling said. How was she going to do that she wondered? She hadn't spoken to them in weeks and even those conversations were strained. But, she pushed that problem out of her mind. It would have to wait until she knew about Shannon.

After about two hours, which seemed like two days, Ling saw the surgeon come out and wait for her at the end of the hall. She got up to walk towards, but her knees buckled. Appleton caught her. "Can I help you?" he asked.

"I think you better," Ling said and they walked down the hall with Appleton's right arm around her and his left hand holding her left arm for support.

A nurse intercepted them and said, "Sorry, only family members authorized to hear her personal medical information can talk to the surgeon."

"We are family," Ling said. "Now please get out of our way before my father here gets unpleasant with you."

The nurse looked at Ling and looked at Appleton and started to say something, but the look in Appleton's eye convinced her this was not the time to argue.

As they approached, the surgeon smiled. "It went very well, she'll make it," he said.

Ling felt the tears coming again.

"I'll save the medical stuff for later, Dr. Ya, but there was no damage to her lungs or heart. Her major problem, as you know, was the bleeding. I got it stopped, but it took some time," he said. "We put 8 units of blood in her before I got all the problems fixed. By the way, your police friends donated 20 units of blood when we casually asked for donors in the waiting room. Good friends to have. She'll be taken to recovery in about 15 minutes and you can be with her if you want. I'll want her in ICU for at least 24 hours to make sure everything is stable. That's the good news," he said as the smile faded. "The bad news is I'm afraid she may have suffered a stroke during all of this. When she is stable, we'll do a scan and other tests to see for sure."

"Did she suffer brain damage," Ling asked.

"We don't know. One of the reasons for keeping her in ICU is in case a blood clot has moved to her brain. We'll keep a close eye on her until she is stable enough for the tests," he said. "I'm sorry. As soon as we know more, I'll let you know." The surgeon walked by to the OR, but made a call on his phone as he did.

By the time Ling and Appleton were almost back to the waiting area, the CNA who gave her the scrubs top appeared with a wheel chair. "Sit," she said.

"I don't need that," Ling protested.

"Doctor's orders," the young woman said. "You're about to fall over as you stand there, so sit down and let us do our job."

"She's right," Appleton said. "You looked like warmed over death."

"Oh, now we start with the gabs," she said as she sat the wheel chair.

"Payback for that 'father' remark," he said. "I'll go fill in the troops, but just with the good news. We'll worry about the bad news when it is confirmed."

The CNA wheeled her not back to the waiting area, but down another hall to an exam room. "Need help getting up on the table?" she asked.

"No, I'm good," Ling said, but found it was harder than she anticipated. Her legs were rubbery and her arms just couldn't make up the difference. "Maybe a little help."

A nurse came in and took her vitals and a short medical history. Next, came a doctor who did some more physical examinations. "Doctor, I probably don't need to tell you that you're exhausted and dehydrated. You have some bruising on both wrists, but nothing appears broken or sprained. You're in border line shock and need to rest," she said. "I should put you on an IV to get your fluid levels up and admit you overnight for observation. Something tells me that you'll not be a very compliant patient. I'm going to get you a couple of bottles of water and some food. You will eat and drink and rest or I'll admit you to the psych ward and have you restrained. Got it?"

Ling smiled at the doctor's bluff. "Yes, ma'am. Can I go see my friend in Recovery before you force feed me?"

"Ten minutes, and by then your food will be up here. If you're not back on time, I'll send two of your cop buddies to drag you back here in handcuffs."

"Ten minutes, I promise. I've had enough time in handcuffs already," Ling said. "Thanks."

She made her way to Recovery and was shown to Shannon right away. Ling knew she was getting extra privileges, but wasn't sure if it was because she was a doctor or what.

Shannon was connected to an array of monitors and a nurse was hovering over her. "She's doing fine," the nurse said. "But she was heavily sedated during the surgery, so I doubt if she is going to wake up any time soon. She may drift in and out, but probably won't be much aware of her surroundings. By the way, I've got the clock on you. Ten minutes and counting."

"Wow, is everyone in this hospital watching me?" she asked.

"Yes and your friends too."

"Can you tell me about the others?" Ling asked.

"Actually, I can. We've all been cleared to give you any medical information you want about your friends. I'm coordinating the care of all three. Mr. Jackson came through the surgery fine and is in his room. He will have a painful recovery and some rehab on his shoulder, but there should be no lasting damage. The young man everyone calls Jimmy lost a lot of blood, but not as much as your friend here. He's out of surgery and is here in Recovery. The bullet was a through and through, but it missed his vital organs. He'll be sore for a while, but is expected to fully recover. Sam, as everyone calls her, is a remarkable woman. She has been by Mr. Jackson's side ever since he got out of surgery. She has a deep laceration on the side of her head and a slight concussion, but no permanent damage. We may have to restrain her too, if she doesn't eat and rest."

"Thank you," Ling said. "Can I see Jimmy for a minute?"

"Sure," the nurse said. "His mother is with him, but I think she'll be glad to see you."

Jimmy's mother was middle aged and had the 'worried mother' look as she stood by Jimmy's bed talking to him. She was on the other side of the bed and Jimmy didn't see Ling approach.

Ling put on the best smile she could, but before she could say a word of introduction, Jimmy's mother was around the bed and threw her arms around Ling. "Oh, thank you Dr. Ya. Thank you for saving our Jimmy. The doctors here said your fast work probably saved his life."

She began crying in Ling's arms, but quickly regained her composure and released Ling. Jimmy was looking less excited about seeing Ling than his mom was. "How are you feeling, Jimmy?"

"Dr. Ya, I'm so sorry I said nasty things about you. Can you ever forgive me?" Jimmy said with tears rolling down his cheeks.

"Jimmy, if it weren't for your help, all four of us would be dead now and those two maniacs would be free to kill more people. You're my hero, in particular. If you hadn't freed me from those handcuffs, the person I love most in this world would have died right in front of me and I would have watched it happen with no way to help. That is a wonderful gift and I'm in your debt for the rest of my life. And, it more than erases anything that happened in the past."

She leaned down and kissed him on the forehead. "You get some rest and I'll check on you later. I need to go be with Shannon, now. And one more thing, my friends call me Ling."

She stood by Shannon's bed and gently stroked her hair. She couldn't let herself think about what they may find when Shannon woke up and they did the tests for a stroke. Shannon opened her eyes and looked around, although Ling knew she couldn't really see well and wouldn't remember any of this.

"I'll never leave you – no matter what," Ling said. "Please believe that."

"Time's up," the nurse said and pointed towards the entry to the Recovery area. There were Barnes and Appleton with a wheelchair.

"You got to be kidding," she said.

"They don't look like the jolly types," the nurse said. "You better go before they call the SWAT team or something."

Ling laughed and it felt good.

She walked over to Barnes and Appleton, turned around, and put her arms behind her so they could put on the handcuffs.

"Don't tempt us," Appleton said and pushed the wheelchair into the back of her legs and she sat down.

Back in the exam room was a plate full of food and several bottles of water. All of a sudden, Ling was very hungry. Barnes and Appleton stayed in the room with her, but she really didn't mind.

"You want an update or would you rather eat alone," Appleton said.

"No, please tell me what you can and I'll try to hear you over my stuffing my face," Ling said.

Chapter 51 – Friday – Jimmy

Jimmy woke up in Recovery with his mother holding his hand. It was hard to focus and there was a dull pain in his side. "Hi," he said.

His mother squeezed his hand and said, "Your surgery went fine. You're in Recovery, but they are going to take you up to a room soon. Your father is waiting outside – they said only one of us could be in here at a time."

"The others…are they okay?" he asked.

"I don't know, but I believe they just brought in Det. O'Brien from her surgery," his mom said.

"At least she's alive," Jimmy said. "She believed in me when no one else would."

"Jimmy, I know things have not been good in our relationship and I'm sorry," his mother said.

"Most of that is my fault. I acted like a spoiled brat at home and at school," he said. "I want to go back to school and finish my degree, but this time I'm paying for it."

"I'm glad you want to go back to school," his mother said.

As they were talking, Ling walked to his bed from the other side. When Jimmy saw who it was, he became very uncomfortable, but after accepting his apology and the kiss on the forehead, he felt a strong sense of relief.

The nurse came with an orderly to take him to his room. As they were wheeling him to his room, cops lining the hall greeted Jimmy.

"Great job…way to go…you da man."

As they wheeled him into his room, Jimmy noticed this was no ordinary hospital room. It was big and decorated like someone's living room.

"Mom," Jimmy said. "What's this? You didn't have to put me here. We can't afford something like this."

"Jimmy." It was the station commander who had never spoken to him beyond outlining his duties on the first day he started working for the police. "This," pointing to the room with a sweeping motion, "is what we do for heroes and you're a hero. You captured one of the most dangerous killers this city has known and probably prevented the deaths of Det. O'Brien and three civilians. We know this guy killed three police officers and is suspected in the deaths of at least ten civilians. Every cop in town is your best friend. Anything you want, you got. Well, I'll let you get some rest. Thanks again."

Jimmy was dumb-struck. He didn't see himself as a hero. Maybe the commander didn't know about the various felonies he committed. There would have to be a time for the whole truth to come out and he wouldn't be a hero then.

His dad came in and burst into tears. Jimmy had never seen his dad cry; it was disturbing. They had a long talk and got some things into the open that should have been said years ago.

Later they brought up a huge meal for all three of them and he and his dad watched a hockey game of the big-screen TV.

His side hurt, but the pain meds were making it bearable.

During the game, two detectives came in to see him. Jimmy recognized them as Appleton and Barnes. He had seen them working with O'Brien in the squad conference room.

"Sorry to interrupt the game," Appleton said. "But we wanted to come thank you personally. If you hadn't sent me that text last night, I'm afraid today we would've been mourning four more deaths."

"I didn't know if you would come or not," Jimmy said. "Things were pretty tense between you and O'Brien."

"Yeah," Barnes said. "They were, but we never stopped believing she was on the right track. We had no idea this case would come to a climax as quickly as it did. Listen kid, cops are like a family. We may squabble and fight, but when it counts we're there for each other."

"Get some rest," Appleton said. "As some point we'll need to sort this all out for the record, but that can wait. We are convinced Vic and the other guy, Russell, were behind all the killings. We are looking for any others connected with his operation, but think the two responsible are now dead."

"However, there is one thing that can't wait," he said. "Show the others in."

Barnes went to the door and three men came in, one carrying what looked like a laptop bag. "This is Mr. Marcus from Capitol

Bank, Mr. Perkins from the Attorney General's office and Assistant DA Costi. We need that money from the overseas accounts and you apparently are the only one who has access to them. Have you done anything with the money we should know about?"

Jimmy felt very nervous all of a sudden. He had forgotten about the accounts in all the excitement. "I've a confession," he said and that got the attention of everyone in the room. "I did make two transfers out of the Threadstone account. We had to demonstrate to Vic that we really had the codes and weren't trying to bluff.

"I transferred $100,000 to counseling center's bank account and I transferred the remaining balance, except for one dollar, to one of the other accounts. That transfer was over $1.3 million."

The five men standing around his bed looked at each other. "So, you transferred $1.3 million to one of the other accounts. That should show up in the transaction activity of both accounts," Appleton said.

Marcus from the bank nodded his head. "Now, let's get the rest of the money into a safe holding account. Can you give me the passwords for each account?"

"Asshole," Jimmy said and everyone looked startled.

"No, no. You're not an asshole. Asshole is the password for all of the accounts," Jimmy said.

Everyone laughed. Marcus set up his laptop on the tray-table used to feed patients in bed. He had a small sheet of paper with him and read off the balances as he transferred the money. The total was more than $15 million.

"Can you confirm the transfer," Marcus said to Perkins from the Attorney General's office.

Perkins called his office. "Transfer is confirmed."

The men prepared to leave. "What will happen to that money," Jimmy asked.

"We'll return it to the companies that were extortion victims. However, my guess is most of the money will go unclaimed. Companies aren't wild about admitting they were victims in these types of schemes. If we find anyone who paid this gang for information, they may be prosecuted if they knew how it was obtained. The unclaimed balance will eventually go into a fund to help victims of crime," Perkins said.

Appleton and Barnes remained behind. "Let us know if you need anything, kid," Barnes said. "And, you can expect a visit from the Chief of Police and the Mayor later today."

"But, what about the $100,000 I took out of the account," Jimmy said.

"Isn't it great when some anonymous donor forks over a gift of that size," Barnes said.

Appleton leaned over the bed so Jimmy's parents couldn't hear. "At some point, you're going to have to make a formal statement for the record. When you get to this point, you should write: 'I transferred all but one dollar out of the Threadstone account to prove to Vic we had the codes.'

"And that will be the truth," Appleton said.

Chapter 52 – Saturday – Ling & Shannon

As Shannon slowly regained consciousness, the events at the boat launch slowly came back. She didn't remember much before being shot.

The first bullet slammed into her chest, but the bulletproof vest stopped it. It didn't stop it from hurting like hell and pushing her backward. The second shot also hit her in the chest, but the bulletproof vest had slipped out of position because she had not fastened it. The vest was too small and tight when correctly fastened. That left the top part of her chest exposed, which is where the second bullet landed.

She didn't feel the second bullet hit. The shock and pain from the first bullet was all she felt at that instant. The second bullet tore through her chest. She passed out for a few seconds. When she regained some awareness of what was happening around her, she heard gunshots from behind her and shots in front of her. She was able to prop herself up on her elbows despite an incredible pain in her chest. It was getting hard to breathe.

Vic had Jackson pinned down and was waiting for him to stick his head above the car. One short exposure is all Vic would need to kill Jackson. Her gun was still in her hand, but she was having a hard time getting her body to do what she wanted it to do. She saw movement off to her left and Jimmy was propped against a tree and trying to aim the rifle at Vic.

She could not shoot from this position because she could not support her weight with just one elbow on the ground. She would have to aim as she was rolling off this position. Under the best of circumstances, this was a crappy way to get off a shot with any accuracy. And, these were not the best of circumstances. She could feel herself failing fast. If she did not shoot now, she would not be able to shoot at all.

Shannon could hear Ling screaming her name and that enraged her. The thought of Ling bound up like some animal ready for slaughter gave her a shot of adrenalin. She raised her arm and her body began to roll of the other elbow. She fired and clipped Vic just below his rib cage.

It was barely a scratch, but it convinced Vic his best option was to take the cash and run.

As she lay on the ground, she thought she heard sirens. Then things went black.

The next thing she remembered was beeping sounds. It took some effort to focus her eyes, but when she did it was on Ling's face. She would drift in and out of consciousness, but every time she woke up enough to focus, there was Ling.

When she woke up and could stay awake, there was Ling with tears streaming down her face.

"You're alive," Shannon said

Ling could only nod a yes.

"The others?" Shannon asked.

"All alive," Ling said.

Now tears started down Shannon's face. "What about Vic?"

"He and his partner are both dead. It's over," Ling said.

"Where are we?" Shannon asked.

"In the ICU. You had surgery to repair the wound about three hours ago. It's about 6 a.m. You're going to stay here until tonight or tomorrow and then we'll get you into a room," Ling said.

"How bad is it?"

"It was pretty bad. You lost a lot of blood before we could get you to the hospital. In medical terms, you scared the shit out of me," Ling said.

Shannon managed a smile.

"There was no damage to the heart or lungs, just a lot of bleeding. There may be some complications," Ling said.

"What complications?" Shannon asked.

"We won't know for a day or so," Ling said. "Let's not worry about it until we have more information. And, no more questions. You need to rest and give your body a chance to heal," Ling said.

Shannon knew it must be bad for Ling to be evasive like this. But, she decided to let it go for now, she was just too tired.

"One last question and then I think I'll take a nap," Shannon said. "Did I kill Vic?"

"No, Appleton killed him," Ling said.

"Appleton? Where did he come from?" Shannon asked.

"No more questions," Ling said.

Chapter 53 – Sunday – Jim, Sam, Shannon, & Ling

The next time Shannon woke up that she remembered it was in a large room. She was still hooked up to a variety of monitors, but it obviously not the ICU. This time instead of Ling's face, she saw Appleton.

"Oh, crap," Shannon said. "I must be dead."

"Ha, Ha," Appleton said. "I told your partner that I would play nice 'til you're back on your feet. I'm beginning to regret that promise.

"How are you feeling, kid? You had a lot of us worried," Appleton said.

"I feel like I've been shot," Shannon said looking around.

"I sent your partner and your sister downstairs for some food and rest. Neither wanted to leave, but I reminded them I was carrying a gun," Appleton said. "Ling has barely left your side for the past 36 hours and your sister arrived yesterday and has also not left."

"How are they getting along? I told Mary about Ling, but we've never really talked about our relationship," Shannon said, not believing she was saying this to Appleton.

Just then there was laughter outside the door and Ling and her sister came in.

"What do you think," Appleton said. "Okay, officially you two did not take a long enough break, but I'll guess I'll let it go this time."

Ling and her sister looked like they had been friends for life.

"So, I guess you two are getting to know one another," Shannon said.

"It's about time you found someone who would stand up to you," Mary said. "Besides, she saved your life, which means I guess I have to overlook the fact she loves Country music."

The three women laughed. Ling wanted to leave Mary and Shannon, but Mary would not hear of it. "You're family, now."

About 20 minutes later, there was a knock on the door. Sam stuck her head in and asked if Shannon was up for a short visit.

She left and came back in Jim in a wheelchair. His right arm was in a sling. They were introduced to Mary.

"You're hurt," Shannon said.

"Yeah, but not badly. I took one in the shoulder area. They say no permanent damage, but it will take awhile to heal," Jim said. "Look, I want to tell you, all of you how sorry I'm that I got you in this mess. I didn't mean it to end this way."

"First off, this 'mess' is what I do for a living. And second, you certainly saved Sam and Ling by getting that message to me – pure genius. And third, you played a very important role in taking down two of the most vicious killers this city has ever known. None of us would be alive today except for your quick thinking," Shannon said. "I owe you a debt greater than I'll ever be able to repay. And Sam, if you had not put us on to Vic through the clues you left at the convenience store, we might still be in the dark about who he was. By the way, where to you learn to make that prison shiv you stuck in Vic's leg? That was a great distraction, although I can see you paid a price for it."

Sam blushed and looked at Jim, who was smiling up at her. "I didn't know I was getting hooked up with an ex-con."

Sam blushed some more, but had tears in her eyes.

The moment was broken by another knock at the door. Jimmy's mother stuck her head in and said, "Oh my. We'll come back later."

"Nonsense," said Ling. "Please come in."

"Jimmy," Shannon said. "How in God's name did you disarm that guy? He was ex-military, probably special ops, yet you had him trussed up like a Thanksgiving turkey."

Jimmy smiled, "I borrowed a few items from the equipment room at the station, including a Taser with a laser sight. I got to the boat launch before you arrived and hid in the woods. He walked right toward me and then set up with his sniper's rifle. When he worked the bolt action on the rifle, I knew he was going to shoot. So, I aimed the Taser at his back and fired just as he was about to turn around. He went out like a light. It was wicked."

"But, it gets even better," Ling said to Shannon. "You were shot and Jim came to tell me you were bleeding. I was afraid he had hit your heart. But, I was still handcuffed to Sam around that light pole and couldn't get to you. Even thought he was wounded, Jimmy had a key and uncuffed me. If he had not done that, you would be dead right now."

"Before I blacked out, I think I took a shot at Vic," Shannon said. "But, Ling tells me that Appleton killed Vic. Where did he come from and why was he even there?"

"Your shot grazed Vic just below the rib cage – I saw the initial ME report – but it was enough to convince him to stop shooting at Jim and flee. Also, about that time we all heard sirens. Appleton and his partner showed up and called for help. Appleton picked up the sniper's rifle and shot Vic as his boat was crossing the lake."

"Wow. That must have been a hell of a shot," Shannon said.

"You're damn right it was and don't you forget it," Appleton said. He had walked into the room as Ling was completing her part of the story.

"Something tells me, I'm going to be hearing about it for a long time," Shannon said. "But how did you get there in the first place?"

"You can thank you friend Jimmy here for that. He can be a persuasive young man," Appleton said.

"Jimmy? Your orders were to not talk to anyone and, boy am I glad you didn't listen to me again," Shannon said.

"You needed help and seemed to trust these guys, so I told them about the exchange and that I thought you would be out-numbered," Jimmy said.

"What the hell is going on here?" the nurse assigned to Shannon yelled as she walked into her room. "I go grab a bite to eat and come back to a goddamn Tupperware party. You folks need to clear out and let the patient rest. She was shot, you know."

"Let me guess, ex-military?" Appleton said.

"Semper Fi," she said. "Two tours in Iraq and one in Afghanistan."

"Semper Fi," Appleton said. "Desert Storm and other lovely spots."

"Okay, he can stay, but everyone else out," the nurse said.

"Thanks, but some of us have work to do and can't afford to lie around in bed all day," Appleton said. "In a day or two we're going to need formal statements from everyone."

Everyone filed out of Shannon's room, but Ling and Mary remained behind.

"I know, you're staying, but please encourage her to rest. We'll be running some tests later today," the nurse said.

"What tests?" Shannon said.

Ling and Mary exchanged glances. "Just some standard post-op tests," Ling said.

"I thought we weren't going to lie to one another," Shannon said.

"The surgeon thinks you may have had a stroke at some point after you were shot. The tests will confirm that if it happened," Ling said.

"That's probably why my left side feels weak. I can tell it is not the same," Shannon said.

"You don't know that for sure. It could just be an after-effect of the trauma," Ling said.

"I train four or five days a week. I know every muscle in my body and what it can and can't do. Believe me, something is wrong," Shannon said her eyes filling with tears.

Chapter 54 – Tuesday – Jim, Sam, Shannon, & Ling

The Internet, television stations, and newspapers were covered with their pictures and names. They were called heroes: praised for their police work and for civilians who had the courage to take on two vicious killers.

Russell was named as the likely killer who shot his victims in the back of the head. The pistol Jimmy found on him was linked to at least 10 murders. Vic was called the mastermind behind the organization and Sally a victim who was at the wrong place at the wrong time. No mention was made of her letter detailing her involvement.

The participants agreed no one would talk to the press until Shannon was feeling better. All statements were coming from the police department, the district attorney, the mayor, and anyone else who thought they could tie their name to the heroes in some manner. Appleton and Barnes would receive commendations. There were plenty waiting for Shannon when she was ready for them.

But Shannon wasn't ready. Tests confirmed what she already knew: she had suffered a stroke. During her trauma care a small blood clot moved into her brain. Her doctor had noticed a weakness in her left hand immediately following surgery. The left side of her face was also slightly distorted. He gave her a drug to break up the clot in her brain. The unknown was how long ago had she suffered the stroke. The longer a stroke like this went untreated, the more damage it did to the brain. However, there was the risk that the drugs could cause additional bleeding at the trauma site. Fortunately, that did not happen.

Shannon became more and more withdrawn. Mary and Ling worked hard to keep her spirits up, but nothing seemed to help. She had known there was a good chance her police career was over, but she was not prepared to face the world as an invalid.

Her doctor's quick work prevented the stroke from doing major damage. There didn't seem to be any cognitive impairment, although Shannon had trouble remembering much about the confrontation at the boat launch. The doctors attributed this to shock and a mild case of posttraumatic stress syndrome.

Even before she was up on her feet, she had regular visits from physical and occupational therapists who began a series of exercises to help her regain as much function in her left arm and to a lesser extent, her left leg as possible.

Mary had to return to her family and was very concerned about Shannon. She and Ling had several conversations about Shannon's state of mind before she left and talked daily afterwards.

Jim and Jimmy had both been released from the hospital. Jim went home with Sam and slept in the second bedroom. Jimmy began working on the details necessary to return to school, although the police department offered him a very attractive job in data security.

In his formal statement, Jimmy followed Appleton's advice and didn't mention the $100,000 transfer to the counseling center. He also didn't mention his little trick with the ISP or taking equipment from the police locker. He also failed to remember the hacks needed to help Shannon find Vic.

With Shannon out, Appleton and Barnes were the detectives of record. They read his statement without question and put it in the file. Since there would be no trial of Russell and Vic, there was no need for anyone else to see his statement or to question the holes in the information.

Jim also gave his statement, but did not mention Sally's letter. The DA placed Jim's letter to him in the record, but not the copy of Sally's letter. That was returned to Jim.

Jim recounted everything that happened from the moment he met Vic to the shootout at the boat launch. He left out those items and actions that might incriminate his friends or embarrass Sam. Barnes and Appleton read his statement and put it in the file without any questions.

Sam gave her statement beginning with Barnes and Appleton's visit with Jim at work. She factually recounted everything that happened, but failed to mention some of the actions of her friends. She also left out the part about what happened the night with Jim at Vic's hideout.

Appleton and/or Barnes stopped in to see Shannon at least twice every day. They could see her sinking into a depression about her left side.

She was able to walk without help, but partially dragged her left foot when she did. The therapists felt if she kept working with them they could restore much more function.

Her left arm felt useless. She was naturally right-handed, so the left had never been as strong or as quick as the right, but thanks to her rigorous training, it was close.

Now, it felt like lead. She could hold larger items in her left hand, but catching a ball was a real challenge. Her hand would just not open fast enough to make the catch, although that was improving also.

She knew the best she could hope for was to get to a point where she didn't drag her left foot and could hold items in her left hand without dropping them. And, that was great, but it was far short of what Shannon wanted. She knew she would be put on permanent disability by the department. That was the only possible outcome now. She would never be a police officer again. She would never kick box again. She probably couldn't protect Sam if she had to.

What was the point, then? This is hard truth was sapping her energy and will to continue the therapy.

Her chest wound was healing nicely according to the surgeon, but would never completely return to normal. A sharp below to the chest in that area, might undue some of the repair work.

Basically, she felt her life was being reduced to invalid status. She had nothing to contribute anymore. Her future looked like life on a couch in front of the television.

Chapter 55 – Monday – Shannon & Ling

Shannon was scheduled to leave the hospital, but would still need physical therapy and regular visits with the several doctors to check her progress.

She wanted to go back to her apartment and be left alone, but for a while she needed someone – she needed Ling – to help her bath and dress. Shannon felt like everyone pitied her and that made her ill.

Shannon's need to be the best was what her father expected. Even though he had been dead for years, his words pushing her to be the best were hardwired into her head.

Ling tried very hard to help Shannon understand that was all bullshit and that she didn't have to prove anything to anyone. They argued about it regularly.

Jim and Sam came be for visits and that cheered Shannon up some. They were amazing people who came through the hell that Vic created even stronger. They came by the day before she was to be discharged.

Jim's arm was still in a sling, but he seemed to be on the mend. Sam suffered no lasting problems from the cut on her head and concussion.

"You promised us a dinner," Jim said. "I'm holding you to that promise. We'll even bring something."

"Give me a couple of weeks or so to rest and you're on," Shannon said.

"Nonsense, how about this coming Thursday at 7, Shannon's apartment?" Ling said.

Shannon was pissed that Ling had stepped in like that, but the truth was she was reluctant to spend time with Jim and Sam. They would notice her weakness and pity her. And, she couldn't stand that. She argued with Ling all that day about it.

"Why did you do that?" Shannon demanded for the fifth or sixth time the day she was to leave the hospital.

"Because I'm fucking sick of your self pity. Do you think you're the only person with physical limitations? If you do, I'll be glad to take you down to the children's floor and show you kids that have never walked and never will walk. I'll be glad to show you kids who should be outside playing, but instead are taking chemo treatments for cancer. Some of them won't live to their next birthday. I'll be glad to take you to the VA Hospital and let you see the dozens of young people who are missing one to four limbs," Ling said and grabbed her bag and stormed out of the room.

As Ling left the room, she almost ran into a man in hospital scrubs. "Sorry," she said and kept walking.

The man called to her, "Dr. Ya, you'll want to hear this."

She realized she had not seen this doctor before, if he was a doctor. She knew everyone on Shannon's treatment team and he wasn't anyone she recognized. She almost kept going, but decided to see what he had to say in case there were questions about her care and to find out who this man was. Why was he seeing her, there were no orders for another doctor or anyone else for that matter. Shannon's surgeon had already signed the discharge papers. They were just waiting for some more paperwork to clear before she could go home.

She opened the door to Shannon's room and immediately sensed something was wrong. Shannon had this wild look on her face that Ling read as fear bordering on panic.

Suddenly, the man who had already gone into the room pulled her into the room. He clamped his had over her mouth and put a gun to her head. He pushed her towards Shannon's bed, which was several steps away thanks to the large room Shannon was given compliments of the Police Department.

"If either of you makes a sound or signals a nurse, I'll kill you and anyone who walks through that door. Understood?" he said.

"What do you want?" Shannon asked.

"I want justice," the man said.

"Whatever I did, please let her go. She had nothing to do with it," Shannon said.

"It's not you I came for," he said. "It's Dr. Ya. She is all over television as some kind of hero, but they don't know the truth. Do they Dr. Ya?"

"I'll be the first to agree that I'm not a hero," Ling said. "But why are you pointing a gun at me?"

"I told you I want justice and you're going to give it to me," he said. "Three years ago, you ruled my wife's death was suicide. But it wasn't. It was an accident. The life insurance company denied my claim because they had a suicide clause in the policy. Because of that, I lost my business and my house. My children were taken from me and now I've nothing."

As he was talking, Ling set her bag on the bed with Shannon and leaned it over so Shannon could see in. Inside the bag was Shannon's 9mm. Ling's bag had a pull string around the top, which doubled as a carrying strap and a way to close the bag. She slowly opened the top of the bag while partially blocking it from the gunman's view.

"Now, I'm going to get my justice," he said pointing the gun at Shannon. "I'm going to kill her and you will have to live with the realization that your actions killed her."

Ling, who was standing on the left side of the bed, took a step forward partially blocking the gunman's view of her bag on the bed.

"If you feel that strongly about it," she said. "I'll reopen the case and we can have another medical examiner look over my work. Maybe I made a mistake. You know, that sort of thing happens, doesn't it? What do you say? Put the gun down and we'll get another set of eyes to review my work."

While Ling was talking, Shannon reached into her bag and slowly pulled out her gun. She managed to keep it hidden behind Ling. She poked Ling in the back with the gun. Ling threw herself away from the bed. The gunman instinctively followed her motion with his gun.

Shannon had a split second to react and bring to gun up to firing position. The gunman swung toward her and fired. Shannon shot three times and the gunman went down.

Ling got up and ran to Shannon. "Are you shot?" she asked.

"No, not this time," Shannon said.

The door to the room flew open and two police officers came in with guns drawn. One kicked the gun away from the man on the floor. Shannon put her gun down on the bed.

Ling went to the man on the floor. He was bleeding from a wound to the abdomen. She put pressure on that wound and looked to see if he had been hit anywhere else.

One of the police officers said, "You need to step away from him so I can cuff him."

"He's not going anywhere," Ling said. "And, if I don't keep pressure on this wound, he will bleed out."

The other officer was blocking hospital staff from coming in. "Let them in," Ling screamed. "I need a gurney and some compression bandages. GSW to the abdomen – it may have hit the aorta. I've got a lot of blood."

The officer at the door looked over at Shannon for some guidance. "If you know what's good for you, do as she says. While she's working on him, get a team down here to secure the crime scene the best you can and post a guard on Dr. Ya. She was the target of this attack."

Hospital staff poured into the room and took over from Ling. Ling came back to the bed to check on Shannon.

"That was quick thinking, doc," Shannon said with the first genuine smile since the shootout at the boat launch. "You saved my life, again."

Ling tried to smile, but was trembling. "I thought you were shot, again," she said. "And you saved both of our lives."

Appleton and Barnes burst through the door and surveyed the scene. "Holy shit," Appleton said. "We can't leave you alone for a couple of minutes without someone getting shot."

Barnes went to check on the man still being worked on by a doctor and two nurses. Appleton came over to her bed and put out his hand. Shannon handed him the pistol.

He looked at it for a second, put on some gloves and then took out the clip and ejected the round in the chamber and put them all in an evidence bag.

"We've swept a lot of stuff under the rug in this case because there was not going to be a trial. But, kid you're not carrying a badge and this is an illegal weapon. We have a room full of witnesses, so I'm afraid we won't be able to cover this one up. Sorry," he said.

"No problem, just do your job like the good cops I know you are. It will be all right." Shannon said.

Barnes sat with Ling on the sofa and took her statement, while Appleton took Shannon's. After a few minutes, they huddled and compared notes. "Your stories are consistent. We're not going to arrest you now, but it's hard to see how this doesn't end badly." Appleton said.

"We're going to check this guy's story about the autopsy and the death of his wife. The doctor doesn't remember the case, so she's going to look back in the records for her report," Barnes said.

Ling asked if she could leave for a minute to check on the man's condition.

After she was out of the room, Shannon motioned for Appleton and Barnes to come to the bedside.

"I've one more favor," she said. "Can you change the statements so that the gun was in my bag, not Ling's? It was returned to me after it was clear there would be no trial, so it wasn't needed in evidence. I didn't have any place to keep it and I didn't want it here in the hospital. Ling said she would take it to my apartment when she went to get a change of clothes for the trip home today. I'm sure it never occurred to her that she was carrying a concealed weapon. The fault is mine, so lay it all on me. Can you do that for me?"

Appleton sighed. "Sure, kid. There's no sense in the good doctor going down for this too. Look, we'll do the best we can with this, but you know the tough concealed carry law they passed last year carries mandatory jail time. If there's a way we can get it busted down to something else we will, but that decision is with the DA."

"You guys put your careers' on the line for me. I can't tell you how much that means to me," she said.

"You would have done the same for us," Barnes said.

Chapter 56 – Monday – Appleton & Barnes

"Send them in," District Attorney Hal Martin said into his phone. Detectives Appleton and Barnes had requested an urgent meeting. Normally, this was outside operating procedure. They should have gone to an assistant DA first with their case for proper processing. But, the two were solid cops who brought cases with few loose ends. They were methodical and never cracked under questioning by defense attorneys. He owed them a few minutes.

"Thanks for seeing us on short notice," Barnes said.

"What's this all about, detectives?" Martin asked.

The two detectives laid out their case of carrying a concealed weapon against Shannon. It was a clear-cut case against her. The new law was passed to help control gang violence, but it had groups on the left and right angry. Still, the public had been happy with the results. It had put a lot of gangbangers in jail.

"I know what you're going to ask, but my hands are tied here. If I look the other way for a suspended cop, it'll look like the law only applies to those we want to target. That's not the way it works and you know it. I read a copy of the file on the shootout at the boat launch and, frankly, it was very sloppy work – certainly not up to the standards I expect from you. There are enough holes in your work to make Swiss cheese sandwiches. I get that she is a fellow cop and those men were cop killers. Since there doesn't seem to be anyone to prosecute, except possibly the people the city is calling heroes, I won't press the matter, he said.

"But this was a shooting in a hospital and there are several witnesses, including the two officers that responded almost immediately. I can't just pretend like this didn't happen. I know it was self-defense, but that doesn't change the fact that she had an illegal gun. I don't want Detective O'Brien to go to jail, but I don't have a choice in pressing the case and the judge must give jail time, with the minimum of six months, which is what I'll recommend. We can get her out quicker with time off for good behavior but she's going to jail and there's nothing we can do about it," Martin said.

"Yes, there is," said the chief of police as he walked into Martin's office. Appleton and Barnes jumped to their feet. "As you were detectives," Police Chief Jocelyn Stennesberg said.

"This landed on my desk yesterday morning and I signed off on it. It is being routed back to Det. O'Brien's station, but thanks to our antiquated internal mail system hasn't made it back to her captain's desk. Two days ago, her captain requested she be returned to active duty, but confined to administrative tasks. His plan was for her to review cases while she recuperated at home and begin coming in to the station when she was up for it. It was an unusual request, but under the circumstances, seemed like the right thing to do. Because of the special circumstances, he requested I sign off on it. I did that yesterday morning before 8:30 a.m. So, O'Brien was not a private citizen in possession of a concealed weapon, she was on duty. Even officers on administrative duty are required to carry a firearm. Under these new circumstances, the case against O'Brien is voided," Chief Stennesberg said.

DA Martin looked at the form and shook his head. "You're kidding, right? This form was typed on a manual typewriter. It should have been completed using the online system that logs all documents as to time and date of creation."

"The system was down when her captain made the request and, since the city can't be bothered with updating our systems, these things will happen," the police chief said. "In case you have doubts, please call the IT folks and they'll verify the system was down when her captain said it was."

"I should have you all arrested for obstruction of justice. Get the hell out of my office and, if you ever try to pull any bullshit like this again, I'll make sure you all go to jail," the DA said.

The three officers walked out of the building and stopped on the sidewalk.

"Thanks, chief. We won't forget this," Barnes said.

"Yes you will. Never speak to anyone about this – and I mean anyone. It stays between the three of us. Tell O'Brien the case was dropped on a technicality or whatever. This never happened. If I get word that either of you tell anyone else, you will be back in uniform and patrolling the landfill before you can blink an eye. There's one more thing you have to do," the chief said. "O'Brien can never be a cop again. She has to resign today. She'll be put on permanent disability, which means a monthly check, but her police career ends today. Have her resignation on her captain's desk before 5 p.m. today."

"The force and the city need hero cops. Let her go out the hero she is," the chief said and got into a waiting car.

Chapter 57 – Monday – Jim, Sam, Shannon, & Ling

Jim and Sam were arriving at the medical office building next to the hospital when they heard the sirens and saw the police cars race towards the hospital. As they were sitting in the waiting room, the show on the television was interrupted with the bulletin of the 'Hero cop involved in another shooting at the hospital.'

They ran across the skywalk between the office building and the hospital as fast as Jim could manage. A crowd and several police officers blocked the way to the elevator to Shannon's room. One of the cops recognized Jim and Sam and waved them through.

"What happened? Is she all right? What about Ling?" Sam blurted out.

"I don't have many details. All I know is the code for officer-involved shooting went out and we responded," he said. "The other guys have this. I'll walk you up there. We did hear that it was Dr. Ya who was the target. She was in Det. O'Brien's room when it happened. The scene is secure, but until we know for sure what happened, I'm sticking with you two just in case."

"In case of what," Jim asked. The cop didn't respond.

When they got to the floor Shannon's room was on, a police sergeant blocked their way.

"What are these civilians doing here?" he growled, but then he recognized them. "Oh, it's you two. Good idea, bringing them up here. This floor is secured and, until we sort this out, you two should stay close."

"How are Shannon – Det. O'Brien – and Dr. Ya?" Jim asked.

"They are both okay. There are a couple of detectives with them now. Det. O'Brien wounded the shooter and he's on his way to surgery. Apparently, he had a beef with Dr. Ya.

"You two wait over in that lounge area. This officer will stay with you. When the detectives are finished and the evidence unit is done, you can go in."

About 45 minutes later, Appleton and Barnes came out of the room. When they saw Jim and Sam, Appleton rolled his eyes.

"Why is it every time there is gunfire and chaos, the four of you are involved?" he said. "You're all becoming a real pain in the ass."

"What's going on?" Jim said. "I thought Vic and his maniac were out of our lives for good."

"It doesn't look like this was connected to Vic at all," Barnes said. "Keep this to yourself, because this is an active investigation, but it appears like the gunmen was looking for some payback against Ling."

The two detectives highlighted what happened. Neither mentioned the gun Shannon used and the problems it was going to cause. Jim and Sam rushed into Shannon room and found her and Ling crying. Ling was not standing next to the bed, but a few steps away. Soon Sam was crying and Jim was getting teary also. After a round of hugs and kisses, they talked through what happened. Sam noticed a chill and sadness between Ling and Shannon.

"I want to go check on the gunman," Ling said.

"Why don't you walk with her, Jim?" Sam said.

"No need I've my own police escort," Ling said.

Jim looked at Sam and she gave him one of those looks women fire off when men are slow on the uptake.

"Ah, if you don't mind, I'll walk with you. My doctor wants me to get some exercise," he said as they walk out the door.

Sam walked over to Shannon's bed and took her hand. "What's going on with you two?" she said.

Shannon looked at Sam and shook her head. "You missed your calling. You would make a heck of a good detective," she said.

Sam blushed and smiled at the thought. "It's pretty obvious that there is something between you and Ling."

"Yeah, there is something. It's me. I can't seem to do anything right in relationships. But, the big thing now is I'm terrified and I've never felt like this before."

"You don't strike me as ever being afraid," Sam said. "You faced down Vic, when you knew there was a good chance you would be shot."

"Oh, I was afraid then for sure," Shannon said. "But I have training and skills to help me through those times. I've nothing for this."

"What is 'this'?" Sam asked.

Shannon held up her left hand. "This is what terrifies me. I'm recovering some strength, but I'll never be the person I once was. My career as a cop is over. What am I going to do? How can I take care of Ling when I'm a cripple? How do I know she'll only stay with me out of pity?"

Shannon began sobbing. Sam sat with her a moment and let her cry. She grabbed a few tissues and gave them to Shannon. After a few minutes, Sam sat on the edge of the bed, still holding Shannon's hand.

"You're right that I should have been a detective. It seems the main job of a detective is to find the truth of what happened. So, here are some truths. You are Shannon O'Brien today and you're the same person she was before this all started. The essence of who you are hasn't changed. You don't let people see it very often, but it is still there and that is who Ling loves with all her heart. She doesn't love the tough cop you hold up like a shield. She loves you. You have lived your life like a trapeze artist who works without a net. Holding on because you were afraid to let go. If you can't be a cop, there are plenty of things you can do. You're smart and have a tremendous skill set to draw on. You've let your father, your job, and fellow cops define you. It's time for you to realize you're not in this world alone. Ling loves you. Your sister loves you. Jim and I love you. Heck, I even think Appleton and Barnes love you. We are your net and we'll always be there for you."

Shannon was uncharacteristically quiet. She listened and cried some more.

"I know everything you said is true," she said. "But, I'm just so frightened of being alone, without Ling. Yet, everything I do in our relationship is wrong. I lie to her and justify it as protecting her. I'm inappropriately physically aggressive when I sense her threatened. I'm sure I'll drive her away with my stupid big mouth and Jolly Green Giant body."

"You underestimate Ling," Sam said. "She is tougher than she looks. I know it's hard, but if you try, you can drop this protective persona that keeps the real Shannon hidden from harm. Don't try to change all at once, just say to yourself 'just for today, I'm going to let go and let Ling catch me'. Try it one day at a time."

"I'll try, but that doesn't change the fact that I'll never be the physical person I once was," Shannon said.

"That's true, but you will still be able to exercise and keep your body trim and in shape," Sam said. "I've a question for you? Where was Ling standing when you shot the gunman?"

Shannon motioned to the left side of her bed.

"And where was the gunman standing?" Sam asked.

"Over there by the bloodstain on the carpet," Shannon said.

"Of course," Sam said. "Silly me."

She walked over to the bloodstain and faced Shannon. She made her hand into a gun and pointed it at Shannon.

"Shoot me like you shot the gunman this morning," Sam said.

Shannon raised her left hand in the shape of a gun and pointed it at Sam. Just then, Ling and Jim walked in.

"What's going on here?" Jim asked.

"Shannon was showing me how she shot the gunman with the gun in her left hand," Sam said.

Shannon thought for a moment and then looked at her left hand. "Son of bitch! I did shoot him with my left hand. I didn't even think about it being weak."

She started laughing and crying at the same time. Ling burst into tears and so did Sam and Jim. After a minute everyone regained their composure.

"You know, the four of us spend an inordinate amount of time either laughing or crying," Jim said.

Chapter 58 – Monday – Appleton, Barnes, Shannon, & Ling

As Jim and Sam were preparing to leave Shannon's room, Appleton and Barnes came in looking even more grim than usual. Jim assumed this was a follow up to the shooting and started saying goodbye to everyone.

"Stick around a minute," Barnes said. "You all need to hear this."

"There will be no charges filed over the shooting this morning," he said.

"No charges?" Jim said. "Of course there will be no charges. She was protecting the two of them. It was clearly self defense."

"No question about that," Appleton said. "But, that's not the problem."

"Well, what is the problem?" Jim insisted.

"The problem is I had a concealed weapon, Jim. And, that's against the law. I'm suspended and that makes me a citizen just like everyone else. My friends didn't press the issue following the shootout at the boat launch, probably because the only witnesses were the four of us and Jimmy. I expected them to come back with charges against me. Carrying a concealed weapon is a serious crime these days and it carries mandatory jail time. There were too many witnesses to the shooting to sweep it under the rug this time. Besides, it was only one of the many felonies I committed that day," Shannon said.

"Okay. No more talk about other felonies. We don't want to hear it," Barnes said.

"So, it's all good, then," Ling said.

"Not quite," Barnes said. "It comes with a price. Shannon, you need to have your resignation on your captain's desk before 5 pm. The department will put you on permanent disability, but your days as a cop are finished."

"Sorry, kid. You're a hell of a cop and the city is worse off without you, but you know how these things work. We looked the other way on a lot of what you and your buddies did, but it's time to put this whole thing to bed," Appleton said.

"The department will issue a press release saying a lot of 'blah, blah, blah' but that your injuries will prevent you from returning to fulltime active duty," Barnes said.

"Could you find me some paper and a pen?" she asked Ling.

Shannon wrote out her resignation and handed it to Appleton.

"Thanks guys. I probably don't want to know how you managed to keep me out of jail, but I'll never forget it," Shannon said.

"Once a cop, always a cop," Barnes said. "Don't forget us when you're pulling down six figures in some cushy private security job."

Chapter 59 – Tuesday – Jim & Sam

When Jim was discharged from the hospital, Sam insisted he come to her house to recuperate. He didn't argue much. She had already been to his house and picked up clean clothes and toiletries. His wound was painful and he would need physical therapy for some time to regain motion and strength in his shoulder. He could feed and bath himself, however buttons were sometimes challenging, and he still had a bandage that needed changing every day.

While in the hospital, he and Sam had some long conversations about their relationship and where it was going. He was very much in love with her, but was very confused and conflicted about Sally. If he had blindly fallen in love and married a woman who hid so much from him, could he trust his emotions with Sam?

"I've waited a long time for you," Sam said. "I can wait some more, but I hope it's not too long."

They agreed to take some steps back – before that night in the hideout – and spend some time getting to know one another under less emotional stress. Jim agreed to stay in the second bedroom at Sam's house while recuperating. That took off some of the emotional high of sex, but left room for intimacy.

The day they were leaving the hospital, Jim asked Sam when she was going back to work. "Oh, that's not a problem," she said. "They fired me."

"What," Jim shouted. "That's outrageous. They can't do that. I'll call HR and tell them to reinstate you. What grounds do they have for firing you?"

"It seems I forgot to call in and ask your permission to take vacation time while we were being kidnapped," she said.

"I don't think you'll get far in your appeal to HR," Sam said. "I think you've been fired, too. Have you checked your email recently?"

"No, I stopped a few days ago because of all the endorsement ideas and just weird 'fan' mail I was receiving," he said.

"Better have a look," she said and pulled out her laptop.

Jim logged into the Gmail account and scrolled through the numerous requests for appearances and endorsements. There was a message from his boss Ross Schwartz saying his services were being terminated for all the bad publicity he had caused the company. He would get two weeks severance pay and the balance of his vacation time.

The message came while Vic was holding him and Sam captive. There had been speculation in the press that they might be involved in some way. Three policemen were dead and he and Sam were nowhere to be found. While the police insisted they were probably victims, there was just enough room for speculation that they were not.

Days had passed since then and the public knew they were heroes now. However, the company had not contacted them about returning. The old Jim would have taken the news and retreated to lick his wounds. But not now; not after what he had been through. With no formal training and barely able to fire a gun, Jim had shot it out with a dangerous criminal. True, he hadn't hit Vic with his shots, but they were distracting enough that Shannon was able to get off a shot. Between his cover fire, the wound Shannon scored, and Sam's attack with the knife, Vic had made a run for it. Mr. 'pole up his ass' Schwartz was in for some treatment like Vic used so successfully.

He began typing a reply. His face was a little distorted, which told Sam he was really focused on the email.

"What are you going to say," she asked.

"Give me a minute and I'll show you," he said.

When he finished, he turned the laptop around so Sam could read his reply before he sent it. Her eyes opened wider than usual as she read his reply. "You can't be serious?" she said. "He will throw a fit when he reads this. You'll never get your job back."

"I don't want my job back, but they owe us for hanging us out to dry and not having the decency to hear our side of the story," he said. "Besides, it will be fun to think about him turning purple with rage, but unable to do anything about it. When he realizes the only way out of this is to pay us off, he'll be furious, but he'll do it. He can't afford not to."

Here's the reply:

'Your continued support during our terrible ordeal is truly inspiring. I feel the need to express my feelings on the matter at a press conference tomorrow at 4 p.m. (just in time for the evening news). I am sure the company wants the public to know how committed it is to its people, so I invite you to stand with me in front of the TV cameras and explain why you thought it was in the company's best interest to fire me and Samantha while we were being held at gunpoint by a homicidal maniac. The one who killed three police officers and perhaps a dozen civilians. The one who wounded a distinguished police officer, myself, and another man. Please meet me and the press on the courthouse steps at 4 p.m. tomorrow. If that is not a good time for you, please let me know as soon as possible so I can alert the press.'

Jim hit 'send' before Sam could protest. He laughed and gave her a hug. "I've a feeling that you and I are about to begin a great new adventure."

"I'm not sure I want anymore adventures like that one," Sam said, but Jim could see the excitement in her eyes.

Fifteen minutes after Jim sent the email, his cell phone rang. "I wonder who that could be?" he said.

It wasn't Schwartz, but a company lawyer who began the conversation with words like 'blackmail' and 'extortion'. Jim listened for a few seconds, and then interrupted the man.

"I'm not going to say anything that isn't true at the press conference and I've asked for no compensation. So save your theatrics for the courtroom. Thank you for giving me something else to talk about. So, unless you have something civil to say, be sure to catch the news at 5 p.m. tomorrow," Jim said.

"We'll keep you on the payroll with full health benefits for one year. Submit your resignation and it's a done deal," the lawyer said.

"That's for both of us, right?" Jim said.

"Yes, both of you," the lawyer said wearily.

"You have a deal, but you won't get our resignations until a year is up. Thanks for you kind words of support," Jim said and hung up before the lawyer could say anything.

Sam heard the conversation and clamped a hand over her mouth to prevent a laugh. "You were terrific," she said and gave him a big kiss.

"Well, we have a year to figure out what we want to do with the rest of our lives," he said. "How does that sound?"

"I already know how I want to spend the rest of my life," she said.

Chapter 60 – Thursday – Ling, Shannon, Jim, & Sam

The dinner Shannon promised came off on Thursday as Ling promised. It seemed a fitting way to end a terrifying ordeal. Ling invited Jimmy, but he was busy preparing to return to college. Shannon and Ling had relocated to Ling's apartment because it was larger.

Shannon tired easily but she was walking unassisted and, in general, getting in Ling's way. Jim was feeling much better, but his shoulder still hurt and reminded him of the gunshot wound if he did too much. Sam's wound was almost healed, but she would have a scar on the side of her head. She could easily arrange her hair to cover the area where they shaved her head to treat the wound.

After a lot of laughing over dinner, Ling and Sam cleared the dishes. Ling insisted she didn't need any help and Sam insisted she did.

"How are things between you two?" Sam asked.

"We have our good days and not so good days. She is still frightened of letting me fully into her vulnerable side, but we're working on it. That hasn't stopped the sex from being world class, though," Ling said with a laugh.

"So how are you a Jim getting along? Still at arm's length?"

"That is what we promised ourselves. However, we haven't lived up to that promise with 100% compliance," Sam said. "Thank goodness."

"Before we both become really hot and bothered, we better rejoin them," Ling said.

Jim and Shannon were sharing some relationship issues, at least that's what they told Ling and Sam. In truth, Jim was hoping Shannon would teach him how to shoot – not something Sam was fond of pursuing.

"Are you going back to work at the ME's office when you can leave Shannon alone?" Jim asked.

"I could have left her alone several days ago, but I would rather be here," Ling said. "The head ME gave me some time off with pay, but that will run out tomorrow. Honestly, I really don't want to go back. My heart is not in it anymore."

"So, we all have a clean slate to write our future on, so to speak," Jim said. "We're all technically unemployed – or soon will be. There was a time not so long ago, that being unemployed would be a terrifying prospect. Now, I'm excited about what new experiences are in front of me. I've a gift for each of you."

He reached into his inner coat pocket and pulled out four small envelopes with their names on the front. There was one for him too.

Sam's mouth came open in surprise. "You didn't tell me about this," she said.

"Well it wouldn't be a surprise then, would it?" Jim said.

"Before you open them, I want to share some background about what they are and how they came to me. This is going to be tough for me to get through, so bear with me."

Sam took his hand.

"As you know, I found the cash and information Sally hid in her cedar chest. The information contained the account numbers and passwords to Vic's overseas accounts. Sally thought that information would keep her alive until she could convince Vic to flee the country. This was the same strategy Shannon used at the boat launch. Unfortunately for Sally, Vic's partner took matters into his own hands and killed her," he choked up for a moment and continued.

"Shannon got that information to Jimmy and he changed all of the passwords, so he had control of the accounts. Shannon had Jimmy transfer $100,000 to the counseling center and balance to another of Vic's accounts. When it was all over, Jimmy gave the authorities the new passwords and told them about the transfer to the counseling center. They chose to overlook that transfer, but confirmed the balance had gone into one of Vic's other accounts.

"What you and the authorities don't know is Sally set up an overseas account of her own. Information about it was on a note clipped to her letter. I don't know why she did this. Maybe this was her retirement fund or an insurance policy for me. According to her note the money came from legitimate work she did on the side that Vic was not a part of. I'm assuming that's true. With a little help from Jimmy, I was able to access this account. There was more than a quarter of a million dollars in it. Jimmy now has a large down payment on the rest of his college education. And, the rest we converted into prepaid debit cards. Each card has a balance of a little over $50,000," he said as the others tore open the envelopes.

"I divided the money equally, so each of us has our own money. If we want to pool it with our closest friend or friends, we are free to do so. But, I didn't want to presume any pairing off," he said. "As soon as I'm a little stronger and can lose this bandage, I intend to ask Sam if she would take a very long vacation with me. I hope she will say yes."

Sam's eyes filled with tears.

"Tropical island," Ling and Shannon said at almost the same time, which got everyone laughing.

Sam stood up and lifted her wine glass. The rest stood up also and lifted their glasses.

"To Sally," Sam said and the others said, "Sally."

Jim had tears streaming down his face. Shannon put her arms around his and kissed him on the cheek. "She would be proud of you, I know it," she said.

They all settled back down and decided they need another bottle of wine. Jim volunteered to open it, while Shannon and Sam talked excitedly about what they were going to do with the money. Jim brought the new bottle back to the group and jumped right in with what he was thinking about. Ling was looking off with a troubled look on her face.

"What's wrong," Jim said. "There is nothing dirty or illegal about this money, so no guilt trips allowed."

"It's not that," Ling said. "I've been thinking about that guy that Shannon shot in the hospital. What if he was right? What if I missed something and it wasn't suicide? It was not an accident – no one takes that many pills at one time by accident."

"If it wasn't suicide and it wasn't an accident, that means it was murder," Sam said.

"Whoa. Just a minute. Aren't we getting ahead of ourselves? How many autopsies have you blown?" Shannon asked.

"Not that many," Ling said.

"How many as in a number?" Shannon said.

"Well, none that I can actually think of," Ling said.

"So the odds are overwhelmingly against you making a mistake," Shannon said.

"Yes, but it could happen. What I do remember about the case after thinking about it was a woman with a history of substance abuse, financially underwater, and a failing marriage. A prescription for suicide and that's what the body presented. Pathology is a science, but like all science, it is subject to interpretation. The danger for a medical examiner is to see an obvious answer and go no further in the investigation. Did I do that? Did someone hand me a text book suicide and I stopped looking at any other explanation?"

"There was a life insurance policy and the husband was about to lose his business. That sounds like a possible motive. Maybe he somehow fed her all those pills, but wasn't smart enough to stop at a reasonable amount for an accidental overdose. He loaded her up with pills and you interpreted it as suicide, which voided the insurance. Which led him to seek you out for revenge. If you had ruled an accident, he would have the insurance money," Sam said.

"I've got to take another look at that file," Ling said.

"Can I come with you," Sam said

"No, but I'll bring a copy home and we can go over it together. Maybe you'll spot something I missed. And I want Shannon and Jim in on this. We need to get to the bottom of this or a murderer might go free," Ling said.

"The guy is going to stand trial for attempted murder. He's not going anywhere for a long time," Shannon said.

"Don't be sure," Jim said. "I heard on the news today that his lawyer is going to plead temporary insanity. If he can make that work, he might only spend some time in a psychiatric hospital. We all saw a pair of maniacs almost get away with multiple murders, including three cops. If there is a chance this guy killed his wife, he should pay for it," Jim said.

"I've a lot of cred at the station. I'm sure I can get a copy of the police report. Maybe there is something they overlooked. Cops aren't immune to reaching obvious conclusions, too," Shannon said.

"Hold on," Jim said. "This sounds like we may be on to something and I don't mean the whether this guy murdered his wife or not. It sounds like the beginning of a collaboration or a business – a private detective business. I bet there aren't any private detective agencies in this city that have the combination of talent and experience sitting around this table. An ace detective, a medical doctor who is also an experienced medical examiner, a person who can organize the operation and someone skilled in marketing."

Everyone sat in silence for a few seconds and then began talking at the same time. Ideas for names, office space, how to get clients and so on were coming fast and furious.

"Okay, time out," Sam said. "Let's slow down a minute. This sounds very exciting, but we are on an emotional high and coming off a very traumatic experience in which we all almost died. Here's a proposal for the group: why don't we take three months and go on our vacations. When we come back, we'll get together and see if this is still an exciting idea and then decide how to make it happen."

"This is one of the many reasons we need Sam to be a part of this," Ling said. "What she said makes perfect sense."

"That sounds good to me, but I want us to part with a provisional name for the agency," Jim said. "That way we have a label, a name to think about."

"Any ideas?" Shannon asked.

"Actually, I do," Jim said. "As a place to start, why don't we call our idea Blink Investigations?"

"I don't understand. Why 'Blink?'" Ling asked.

"If you think about it, everyone here has had their life changed by significant events in their past. We've just been through an experience where, had things gone another way, we all could have been killed several times over," Jim said.

"Blink is a reminder, at least to me, that we should never take anything or anyone in our lives for granted. It seems like a good mission statement for a detective agency – never take anything for granted," he said.

"Well, as a former police detective, I can say that is spot on," Shannon said.

"It may sound a little hokey, but it opens the way for doing investigations that are not criminal, such as corporate intelligence and so on. Besides, it's just a temporary name. If we decide to make this a go, we can consider some other possible names," Jim said.

The evening stretched into another bottle of wine with ideas and suggestions flying right and left. It was way passed everyone's bedtime and Sam and Jim were in no condition to drive, so they slept on the foldout couch in the living room.

Sam and Jim did not keep their promise to each other that night.

About the author

Ken Little is a veteran writer with 15 traditionally published books.

Blink is his first book of fiction. The story involves mixing some ordinary and extraordinary people in situations where events are out of control. Bodies are piling up and they must make sense of it before they become the next victims.

Ken's books on personal finance and investing target beginning investors and explain complex investing concepts in simple terms.

You can find the books on his Amazon Author's Page (http://amazon.com/author/ken-little).

He lives near the western coast of Lake Michigan and has a day job writing for a major health care organization's website. He and his family enjoy a cabin on five wooded acres most weekends.

Ken lives with his wife and youngest daughter plus Lyra, the cat, and Bailey, a Golden Retriever and trusty writing buddy. Bailey can be found, like his predecessor Andy, curled up near Ken's feet somewhere, protecting him from the zombie apocalypse and squirrels.

www.ingramcontent.com/pod-product-compliance
Lightning Source LLC
Chambersburg PA
CBHW062014170626
46813CB00001B/164